Pippa Wright lives in London and works in book publishing. You can find her on Twitter at: @TroisVerres

THE FOSTER HUSBAND

Kate left her seaside home town of Lyme Regis for the bright lights of London when she was eighteen, and never looked back. She had it all: glamorous career, the lovely town-house, the gorgeous husband. But now she's back: unemployed, separated, and holed up in her dead granny's bungalow. Worse still, she's forced to share the bungalow with Ben, the clueless and domestically challenged fiancé of her bossy sister Prue. Ben is a man in need of simple instruction. And Kate is a woman in need of a project. So, she decides to train Ben, her foster husband, as a selfless pre-wedding gift to her sister. But Kate may still have a few lessons of her own to learn . . .

PIPPA WRIGHT

◆

THE FOSTER HUSBAND

Complete and Unabridged

CHARNWOOD
Leicester

First published in Great Britain in 2013 by
Pan Books
an imprint of
Pan Macmillan
London

First Charnwood Edition
published 2014
by arrangement with
Pan Macmillan
a division of
Macmillan Publishers Limited
London

A catalogue record for this book is available
from the British Library.

ISBN 978–1–4448–1919–9

Published by
F. A. Thorpe (Publishing)
Anstey, Leicestershire

Set by Words & Graphics Ltd.
Anstey, Leicestershire
Printed and bound in Great Britain by
T. J. International Ltd., Padstow, Cornwall

This book is printed on acid-free paper

To Pin and Alaine,
with love and submarines.

Acknowledgements

Thank you to my Lyme Regis visitors: Jo Roberts-Miller for plot advice, and smoked anchovy sharing. Jo Paton Htay and Nic Boddington for old-lady seed-catalogue reading, a lot of red wine and a traditional Gilbert hangover to remind us of the bad old days.

Huge thanks to Lisa McCormack and Nikki Sopp whose work anecdotes I have shamelessly plagiarized throughout. And who gave me more excellent stories about Lagos than I knew what to do with. Sorry I had room for so few of them here.

Thanks to Nigel and Susie Cole in whose Lyme Regis studio I first had the idea for this book, and where much of it was written. And to the Town Mill Bakery and the much-missed Mill Tea and Dining Rooms for sustenance.

And finally, thanks, as ever, to all at Pan Macmillan and Aitken Alexander.

'Sometimes I wish we could rub out all of our mistakes and start fresh, from the beginning,' I said. 'And sometimes I think there isn't anything to us but our mistakes.'

The Paris Wife by Paula McLain (Virago, 2011)

I know she's told you everything. I don't expect you to forgive me — I'm not even sure I can forgive myself.

I'm not excusing what I did, but maybe something had to happen so we could stop making each other so unhappy. I suppose this was it.

I'm sorry.

1

Only an idiot would come to Lyme Regis to escape the past.

Lyme Regis *is* the past; it's saturated with it. Here, more than anywhere else I know, it is impossible to escape the heavy weight of time gone by. I don't mean the fact that I'm constantly bumping into people I went to school with, or friends of my parents, though there is that. It's not just personal history. I mean that you can't turn a corner without coming across some Jane Austen Society re-enactment of Louisa Musgrove falling off the Cobb into the arms of Captain Wentworth, or a troop of backpack-toting school-children heading off to East Beach, fossil-hammers enthusiastically, if inexpertly, in hand.

Of course nowhere is truly free from the past, but I wonder if anywhere else is so insistent on reminding you of it. Lyme presents the centuries gone by like a carpet seller laying out his wares in front of you, one on top of the other. Jurassic Period, madam? No? Cretaceous perhaps? Or does madam prefer later? Regency? Late Victorian? Mid-Seventies Postmodern? Layer upon layer of fossilized history, compacted over millennia, help-less creatures trapped in it, forever frozen in a moment not of their own choosing.

I am that idiot. I am that helpless creature. But it wasn't like I had an awful lot of choice.

At least I've ended up here in the autumn, just

as the town is winding down from the summer months. At this time of year it is perfectly possible to walk the length of Broad Street without becoming trapped in the middle of one of the innumerable walking tours (half of which are run by my parents), and I haven't yet seen a single coach negotiating the tricky bend in the road down by the museum. But the shops are still putting out hopeful signs advertising cream teas and other essential tourist purchases: fudge, Cath Kidston oven gloves and trilobite paperweights. Like there is a great call for paperweights these days. Still, I've managed to walk all the way along the Cobb this morning, the wind whipping my hair, wondering if I look a bit tragic and intriguing in the manner of the French Lieutenant's Woman, without having my moody reverie spoiled by hundreds of daytrippers. Although, to be honest, it's hard to retain an air of heartbroken mystery when you're accompanied, as I am, by an excitable puppy capering on the end of her lead and trying to fling herself off the sea wall in fruitless pursuit of seagulls.

And yet I am heartbroken; I don't have to act at all. It's why I'm here. Even if I'd thought I could escape the past, I should have known I wouldn't be able to. Not in Lyme Regis; not anywhere. You can't run away from yourself.

When she has exhausted herself sufficiently, I drag Minnie away from the seagulls to the Town Mill Bakery to share a warm, buttery croissant while the waitresses pretend not to notice. There is a sign that says dogs aren't allowed, but we all

2

pretend not to notice that, since it's the tail end of the season and there's no one else in here to complain, except for two older women sat on the trestle table behind me.

Just as Minnie licks the last crumbs from my fingers, I hear the women nearby adopt the tell-tale hissing whisper that indicates the imparting of gossip. Naturally, I lean backwards a little to earwig. Well, wouldn't you? I love an overheard conversation, and somehow it's all the more fascinating for being about complete strangers. I've passed many a slow afternoon listening in to the dramas of other people in Belsize Park cafes; it makes me feel better about my own. I catch the word 'divorcée' and listen a bit harder. Such an evocative word. It makes me think of Elizabeth Taylor, violet-eyed and be-turbanned, drying her post-Richard Burton tears with a handkerchief trimmed with diamonds.

I'm helped by the fact they're both hard of hearing enough not to realize how loudly they're speaking.

'Apparently,' the woman furthest away from me hisses, her voice penetrating through the empty cafe, 'her husband was — you know — playing away.'

I've hit paydirt.

'Nooo.' Her companion sounds scandalized. 'But she's so lovely, both of those girls are gorgeous, take after their mother, of course. And he always looked such a fine young man. Why would he do such a thing?'

'Well, you know what it's like in that *London*,' says the imparter of the gossip. Her voice sounds suddenly constricted and, though I can't see her, I can imagine that she has pursed her lips.

Interesting, I wonder who they could be talking about? I've so thoroughly shaken the provincial dirt of Lyme off my shoes since I moved to London myself that I haven't got any idea who else might have headed there in my wake.

'And in that world, too,' says the companion. 'All celebrities and parties and,' her voice drops lower as if she hardly dares speak the words, '*drugs*, I shouldn't wonder.'

'You can be sure of it,' says the gossiper with authority. I am even more intrigued. This sounds like someone I might know. Not that I'm a drug addict or a celebrity — far from it — but my working life was sometimes nothing *but* celebrities and parties and drugs. That's the music business for you.

'Well, she just walked out of the marriage, I hear. Gave up everything and came down to Barbara's old bungalow with nothing but a suitcase and the dog.'

I look at Minnie under the table.

'I thought they sold that place when she died?'

'Tried to, of course, but no offers. It's a dreadful time to be selling somewhere. The credit crunch, you know. I suppose she's grateful for that now, or where else would she have gone?'

'Terrible', says the companion, 'to be left with nothing.'

I can feel the croissant stuck somewhere in the middle of my chest, a hard unmoving lump, as if my insides have stopped working all of a sudden.

4

I look at Minnie again. *You're not nothing,* I think. *We're not nothing.* Don't listen to them. I try to swallow but my throat has turned to stone.

'Desperately sad,' agrees her friend. 'Sandy and David say she's devastated. Apparently he's been ringing their house all times of the day, but she won't answer his calls.'

Of course I can't answer his calls. I haven't spoken to him since the note — what is there left to say? Whatever he has to say to me, I don't want to hear it. How is talking about it going to make any of it better? It's finished. The only way I can keep myself together is to keep the shutters down completely. Impenetrable, closed off. If I let him in, even a little, I know we'll just go back to where we were. And I couldn't bear it. Not again.

'Hardly surprising she won't speak to him,' says the companion, tutting. 'No one should have to tolerate that sort of behaviour. It's disgusting. Does nobody take marriage seriously any more?'

I think I might be sick. I need to get out of here. I turn on the wooden bench, preparing to swing my legs over.

There is a sharp 'Shh,' when they see me move.

As I stand up the two women duck their heads, retracting into their coats like tortoises, as if I might suddenly grab a baguette from the nearby bread counter and swing at them with it out of rage. But I won't. I'm not angry; just stunned. I thought I'd get away from everything hidden here in Dorset, away from my real life in

London, but apparently not. Anyway, it serves me right for listening in to their conversation. Wasn't I intrigued and fascinated myself, until I realized they were talking about me?

Besides, I *am* devastated. It *is* desperately sad. But they don't know the whole story. They're wrong about everything. I didn't leave with nothing. What I left behind was nothing. That was the whole problem.

2

It turns out to be pretty easy to end a marriage, once you've got to the point where you know there's no going back. I read and re-read the note on the kitchen table until I realized I had it by heart, learned like a poem for school; I expected I would be able to recite it perfectly even in ten years' time. I turned off my phone and left it on top of my laptop, shut tight like a clam, so that Matt would know there was no way to contact me. I put my wedding ring on top of them both. And then I left.

In the months before I walked out, I'd found myself constantly fantasizing about splitting up. I obsessed over it with all the passionate intensity that I had once poured into planning our wedding. Just as I'd thought, not even two years ago, that the choice of wedding flowers was a huge signifier of who we were and what our marriage would be (glamorous, exotic, expensive, flown in from far away), so I felt that the manner of leaving the marriage would be some enormous statement that summed up everything that had gone wrong between us. I imagined tempestuous fighting, rows over who owned what, outrageous demands. Matt and I had always excelled at arguing, after all. I'd expected that it would be me who'd throw him out — it was his unreasonable behaviour that got us here after all — while I barricaded myself into the house, throwing his stuff out onto the pavement. I harboured dark thoughts of cutting up his suits, burning his stupid cricket memorabilia, clearing out our joint savings. I'd seen enough movies to know how it was meant to go. With the help of a brilliant, lawyer (I hadn't worked out quite how I'd pay for that, seeing as I hadn't worked for nearly a year, but surely it was a mere technicality?) I'd sue Matt for every last penny. Hadn't I given up everything for him? He owed me. And if he wouldn't pay emotionally, I'd bankrupt him financially instead.

What I'm trying to say is that, in my furious imaginings, I thought the arguments leading up to the end of a marriage would get bigger and more dramatic until they culminated in the mega-row that would end it all. What I hadn't expected was that they'd get smaller and smaller. As if neither of us was willing to waste energy that we might need, instead, for our escape.

By the time I left all I felt was a complete blankness. I knew it was going to hurt later, but at that moment what I felt reading the note was more like a grateful recognition — so here you are, at last, my way out. It was a safety net, unexpectedly appearing to someone trapped in a burning house. And, like someone leaping from the flames, it didn't occur to me to take anything with me; it was all too tainted by then. The bitter rancour of the last few months had seeped into everything.

I took a few clothes, though. There was making a point, and then there was being arrested for public nudity. People were going to

8

be talking about me enough without my being done for indecent exposure. By then I didn't much care about what I wore; my work clothes had hung, untouched, in my wardrobe for months, and there they stayed.

And I took Minnie, of course. I knew Matt would be upset about Minnie. Sometimes I thought that he had bought me a puppy just so he could guarantee there would be someone in the house to greet him with boundless enthusiasm when he got back from work — God knows I couldn't always manage it. I couldn't leave her behind. He was never at home anyway, so who'd have looked after her when he was away for work? And even when he wasn't away, she'd have been too lonely on her own in the house all day. I should know.

Perhaps if I'd thought a bit more about what I was running to, instead of what I was running from, I'd have brought a bit more with me. Perhaps I shouldn't have left with nothing after all; I hadn't even fought for any of it.

'Excuse me, are you okay?' asks a voice. I realize that I'm resting my forehead against the outside wall of the bakery, as if I'm trying to press my head through the grain of the wood. I've only made it a few feet away from the shop doorway. Minnie whines at my feet, confused by my immobility. I'm not sure how long I've been standing here.

'Thanks, I'm fine,' I say, straightening up and smoothing my hair away from my face. 'I just felt a bit faint, sorry.'

'Do you feel all right now?' the woman asks,

looking concerned. I see she has an apron wrapped around her hips, and I suddenly recognize her as the woman who served me coffee in the bakery. I feel mortified that she's seen me like this.

'Yes, fine, thanks, fine,' I repeat firmly. I cannot take sympathy at the moment, especially not from strangers. It makes everything worse, as if all of my problems are written on my face for everyone to see, visible even to a passing acquaintance. I take my sunglasses out of my coat pocket and put them on. I have a horrible feeling I might be about to cry and I can't bear that she might see me break down.

'That's a lovely little labradoodle puppy you've got there,' she says. I appreciate her attempt to change the subject, but I wish she'd just leave me alone. The painted wooden slats of the bakery wall had been cold and solid on my forehead. Comforting, somehow. I could have stayed there for a while.

'She's an Irish water spaniel,' I say automatically. I don't know why I always feel I have to correct everyone — it's not like Minnie cares what breed they think she is. Matt would say it's because I always have to be right. Maybe it is.

'She's lovely,' says the woman, bending to pat her. Minnie squirms with delight at the attention, rolling onto her back to present her fat round belly. 'How old is she?'

'Five months,' I say. I know, before the woman even opens her mouth again, that her next comments will be: what's her name? Hasn't she got enormous paws! Will she get much bigger?

There were days in London when I would

10

have this exact conversation five or six times. And I'd be grateful for it; that might be the most I'd speak all day, until Matt came home. And when he didn't come home? Well, then I'd just speak to Minnie instead. Poor dog. Sometimes I wondered if, behind that enthusiastic canine grin, she was thinking, Will she *ever* shut the fuck up?

But this woman is going off on a tangent.

'Aren't you Prue's sister?' she asks, looking up.

'Yes, I'm Kate,' I admit, slightly haughtily. Prue is eight years younger than me. I prefer to think that she is my sister, rather than I am hers. It's a minor distinction, perhaps, but one of those that matters a bit too much between siblings.

'I thought you must be,' says the woman, smiling. 'You look exactly like her. I'm Cathy, by the way. Friend of your mum's actually. You look just like her too.'

It's strange how in London people identify me by my unusually white-blonde hair — halfway down my back and untouched by hair dye. It's the one thing that makes me stand out from the crowd, which is helpful when you're only five foot two. But here it's simply the way that everyone can tell I'm one of the Bailey girls. There's no escape; it's like wearing a badge with my name, age and family history on it.

As a teenager I never managed to set foot in a local pub without someone immediately recognizing me as Sandy's underage daughter and officiously marching me out. And even though now I am back I can drink legitimately, clearly I

11

won't be able to do so without someone commenting on my family roots.

'Oh right, yes,' I say. 'Of course. How nice to meet you, Cathy.'

She stands up from petting Minnie and sets her hands on her hips, as if she's sizing me up. 'Sandy says you hardly ever come back to Lyme. Are you here on holiday?'

'In a manner of speaking,' I say stiffly. I wish she'd take the hint and leave me alone. Must everyone in Lyme have an interest in my private life? 'Just taking a break, you know how it is.'

Her smile suddenly falters. Obviously she's remembered what's really brought me home. Does everyone know? Has there been some sort of public announcement in the *Bridport and Lyme Regis News?* 'Kate Martell, formerly Bailey, formerly the one who got away and made herself a glamorous life in 'that London', has slunk back to Lyme in disgrace, her marriage over, her career finished.'

'Well, I'd best be getting on,' says Cathy, hurriedly looking at her watch. She attempts another bright smile, as if that will make everything better. 'I just wanted to make sure you were okay out here.'

I smile politely; I'm good at that. Keeping up the appearance that all is fine.

'Thanks,' I say.

'Send my love to your mum and Prue,' she calls as she turns away, heading back into the bakery, where I hope she might spill some hot tea on those gossiping old biddies who were sitting behind me.

'Mmm,' I say, non-committal, even though she's too far away to hear my answer.

To send her love to Prue I might actually have to speak to Prue, and so far I seem to be unable to do that without arguing with her. I wonder if I've grown so defensive and angry that I can't speak to anyone without ending up in a fight. But then we were always like that; I shouldn't have expected that anything would be different, even though fifteen years have passed since we last shared our home town.

This is Lyme. The only changes here happen at geological speed; imperceptible to the human eye. Everything is just as it always was, and that, for me, is very much the problem.

3

Minnie pulls on her lead towards the beach, in the opposite direction to the bungalow. I don't blame her for not wanting to go back indoors, but we can't hang around the town all day, purposeless. To be perfectly honest, we have been entirely without purpose since we arrived here a week ago, but the important thing is that we should be purposeless out of sight of people who will report back to my family, so I drag Minnie back towards the path along the river.

I already have a severe case of the guilts about my life of highly visible leisure. It wasn't so bad in London where no one was around to comment on what I got up to on my own all day. Sometimes the Turkish shopkeeper would pointedly ask, 'Busy day?' as I perused the newspaper headlines without buying anything, but it wasn't hard to ignore him. Anyway, he was nicer to me once I got Minnie — I could flick through the magazines as long as I liked while she sat on his lap and let him feed her bits of pitta bread. But yesterday Mum gently mentioned that her friend — Cathy, I now realize — had seen me in the Town Mill Bakery most mornings, which is about as close as my mother gets to openly criticizing my behaviour.

I know in Mum's eyes eating breakfast in a cafe is not only a wasteful extravagance tantamount to eating a five pound note that has

14

been spread with butter and jam, but also a symbol of the demise of the family unit, in which everyone should eat their meals together in happy harmony. But since there's no room for me and Minnie at their house, I don't see that it makes any difference to the social fabric of Lyme Regis whether I eat breakfast alone in my granny's bungalow or alone in a cafe. Although it can't be denied that my savings are being eaten up one costly croissant at a time.

Despite my gloomy mood, I have to admit it's a gorgeously mellow morning, there is a soft light on the turning leaves that hang over the water. A family of ducks huddles on a stony island in the middle of the flow, quacking and waggling their tails, jostling for position in the small space. I should have kept a bit of croissant to throw to them; I'll remember tomorrow. Lyme is beautiful on a morning like this. It's cool enough to be snuggled into my parka, but warm enough that I'm happy to linger, peering into the gardens that back onto the leat towards the Mill. There are apples lying in the grass, windfalls ready to be collected, heavy rosehips dragging down the trailing thorny shoots. It all makes me feel a bit D.H. Lawrenceish, admiring of fecundity and sumptuous fruity ripeness.

I should appreciate this. I could be stuck in an office, or in a meeting. This is freedom. I should be happy to be here, instead of feeling that I'm in exile, cast out from the life I've left behind. Perhaps I am doomed to wander the streets alone forever, while gossiping locals refer darkly to my past. I could become a tourist attraction all by myself; 'The Head of Marketing's Woman' or something. Catchy, no? Although of course I am not Matt's woman any more. The Head of Marketing's Estranged Wife-Soon-To-Be Divorcée doesn't sound like she'd offer the French Lieutenant's Woman much competition. Although I have always imagined it would be rather cool to swish around in a cloak.

We've reached the end of the riverside path. It stops at a bridge, which offers us two choices; one direction will take us back towards the town, the other leads up the hill towards Granny Gilbert's bungalow. Minnie looks up at me, unsure which direction to take. You and me both, I think. But we take the path most travelled; the one that goes back to the bungalow. The one that's not going to make any difference.

There's a reason why tourists don't bother visiting Hill View Close, where Granny Gilbert's 1960s bungalow faces its identically unattractive neighbours across bleakly paved low-maintenance, wheelchair-accessible front gardens. No one poses for family photographs outside the boxy glass porches; no one stops to admire the sickly fern turning yellow in Granny Gilbert's living-room window next to the Neighbourhood Watch sticker. No one wanders these Lyme Regis streets and dreams of escaping the rat race for a new life in this cul-de-sac. Which would be why Granny Gilbert's house has been on sale for over a year without a single offer. The estate agent's board gives the house an even more forlorn look, like a poster advertising a show that has long since left town.

This is the kind of home you move into not out of optimism and excitement and choice, but out of compromise. You move here when your garden has become too much for you, because your family's concerned that you are unsteady on the stairs these days, because you no longer need all that space just for yourself. Because you've split up with your husband and have nowhere else to go. I should be grateful for this. I am. It's a place to live, for nothing. But it's hard to see this move as the fresh start I thought I was running to. I feel quite far removed from the Liz Taylor-style glamorous divorcée I'd hoped to be, and a bit more like Liz Taylor in the declining wheelchair-bound friend-of-Michael-Jackson years.

The front door opens with a pop of insulation foam; Granny Gilbert liked her home to be hermetically sealed from every possibility of draught. I'd claim she was an early environmentalist if it weren't for the evidence in her under-sink cupboard of the world's largest store of aerosol cans, promising to buff every possible surface to a reflective shine. Although I've kept the doors and windows open every day since I arrived, the house still reeks of chemicals — Misters Sheen and Muscle are my new housemates — and both Minnie and I sneeze every time we step into the hall.

I head straight for the back door to fling it wide open.

Granny Gilbert's garden is nothing special, just a square of patio surrounded by some scrubby rose bushes that Mum has hacked down

17

to stumps, but I feel astonished every time I see the view. It's like walking through the wardrobe into Narnia. Fooled by the drab interior of the bungalow, you don't expect to be presented with a scene straight from a watercolour painting. The hill drops down towards the town, the streets as clearly laid out below us as if they were marked on a map, and beyond them the flat, grey sea stretches to the horizon, flashing and glittering when the sun breaks through the clouds. To the right, houses further up the hill block the view towards the Undercliff, but to the left the eye follows the rise of the cliffs up past Black Ven and Stonebarrow to the Golden Cap, its sandy peak yellow and bright against the dark sky.

I can feel my heart lift; it's strange how a view can do that to you. Maybe it's something that happens when you get older. I don't remember being awed by the scenery when I visited Granny Gilbert as a child — the biscuit cupboard was my main focus then — but every time I step into the garden now I understand all over again why someone would move to one of these plain, ugly bungalows. Once you're inside, you don't have to look at it, and from the garden you can feel like you're flying over the town.

'Sandy, dear? Is that you?'

Minnie starts as a voice calls out from behind the rose bushes. She runs back to hide behind my legs.

'Hello?' I say to the shrubbery. 'It's not Sandy, it's her daughter, Kate.' I haven't yet met a single neighbour but, to be honest, I have kept my head down every time I've left the house, unwilling to meet anyone's eyes in case I'm drawn into a conversation. I'd rather not have to explain my circumstances to everyone in Lyme.

I hear the harsh scraping sound of something metallic being dragged across paving stones, and then a muffled grunt. Two gnarled brown hands, a flaming red nail on each finger, grasp the top of Granny Gilbert's garden fence with purpose. Rising up behind them, like the sun over the horizon, is a lavishly rubber-petalled orange swimming hat. And finally, a face, wrinkled and tanned to the consistency of biltong, in which two dark eyes twinkle brightly.

'Now, you must be Kate! How lovely. Don't you look like your mother? I'd know you *anywhere.*'

'Hello,' I say, and I'm about to ask her name when there's a clattering sound and the swimming hat disappears from view. For a moment her fingers still cling to the top of the fence, knuckles blanching with the effort, and then they disappear too. I hear a worrying thudding noise, of something soft landing on something hard.

'Are you okay?' I call over the fence, but there's no answer. 'Shit,' I whisper under my breath. 'You stay there, Minnie,' I say. I sprint back through the house and out into the deserted close. Not even a net curtain twitches. There's no one to ask for help.

A high wooden gate blocks off the entrance to next-door's garden, and it's locked. I try to peer through the slats, but they're too narrow to see anything; all I get is a faceful of creosote fumes. From Granny Gilbert's garden I can hear

Minnie's high-pitched anxious bark.

I rattle the metal latch and call out again, 'Hello? Hello, are you all right?'

I can hear a faint groan from behind the gate — what if the old lady is lying there with her head split open on the paving? God knows what Neighbourhood Watch will think, but I can't just leave her. I step backwards and take a running jump to leap over the gate, which has clearly been designed with the specific aim of preventing someone from doing exactly that. Instead of clearing it, I hang by my fingertips from the top, my feet scrabbling for purchase against the bottom, achieving absolutely nothing. At this rate there will be two of us lying unconscious outside this bungalow.

Wait, though, is that a recycling box at the end of the drive? They're sturdy things, aren't they? I drag it to the base of the gate and make sure the lid is secured before I stand on it; it gives me just enough lift to allow me to launch myself over the top, swinging one leg over so I'm sitting on top of the gate. From this new vantage point, steadying myself by clamping my legs on either side of the gate, I can see into next-door's garden; a toppled stepladder lies on its side on the paving stones, but there is no sign of the old lady. She must be hidden from view by the house; she might be really badly hurt if the ladder's thrown her that far.

I'm about to swing my other leg over and jump into the garden when the gate rattles alarmingly, as if it's about to give way. Before I can launch myself onto the other side, a hand grabs my leg and a male voice demands, 'Care to explain what you're doing breaking into my grandmother's house?'

I'm so intent on not falling off the gate that I can't look down properly to see who has hold of my leg. 'I'm not — I didn't — I think she's fallen over in the garden. The ladder — the ladder.' I'm babbling incoherently.

'What is going on?' asks a querulous voice.

The swimming hat is gone, revealing a damp, wispy head of hair, like the down of a freshly hatched chick. And now I can see it wasn't just her face that was tanned. The old lady is burnished to a rich shade of mahogany, the kind of Seventies colour you rarely see in these days of SPFs and skin cancer warnings. I wonder if it can be real, but she looks far too no-nonsense to be messing around with fake tan or sunbeds.

'Are you okay?' I ask. 'It sounded like . . . I thought you'd fallen, I was trying to check . . . '

The old lady looks annoyed, her eyes flash at me. 'In the garden just now?' she says. 'I simply slipped. Nothing to worry about, I *assure* you.'

'Oh, it's just that you went so suddenly,' I say, clutching onto the gate with my knees. 'While we were talking. It made me worried when I saw your swimming hat disappear like that.'

'Swimming hat?' says the man, frowning.

'I wasn't wearing a swimming hat,' the old lady retorts. She glares at me pointedly.

'Have you been swimming this morning?' asks the man. He puts his hands on his hips and looks at her accusingly. 'I thought we'd agreed you'd only go when I can take you.'

'Honestly, I'm not some helpless little old lady,' says the little old lady, waving a dismissive hand in a way that is meant to include both of us. 'All of this fuss about *nothing*.'

Now the man's let go of my leg, I see my chance to get down at last; my thighs are beginning to protest at having to support me in this position. There is no elegant way to lower yourself backwards off a six-foot-high gate, let me tell you. I can only be grateful that I'm in jeans and not a skirt, though I can't help wishing they weren't tight ones; I realize my bum must look huge as I hang over the top of the gate, my feet scrabbling in mid-air for the recycling box below.

Suddenly the voices behind me stop. I feel hands around my waist and I'm lowered onto the ground.

'Thank you,' I say primly, trying to regain my dignity. My hair has been flying all over the place thanks to my exertions, and I pull it back off my face in an effort to look respectable, and not like a pensioner-robbing house-breaker.

'No way,' says the man, a slow smile spreading across his face. He is standing far too close to me.

'What?' I say crossly. I don't like the way he's staring.

'Kate Bailey, I don't believe it.' I haven't been called Kate Bailey for two years. I'm about to correct him — I'm Kate Martell now — but I stop myself when I realize that I don't really know what to call myself at the moment. Maybe I will go back to my maiden name. It's too early to tell.

'I'm sorry, I don't remember — ' I begin.

'Oh, of course you don't.' He laughs, stepping back to link his arm through his grandmother's. She pats the drying wisps of her hair, trying to style it. 'The famous Kate Bailey's forgotten all about Lyme, hasn't she?'

I look at him more closely. I'm sure I would remember if I knew this man, he doesn't look like someone who's easy to forget. He towers above his grandmother, his dark hair is closely cropped to his head and he has the kind of strong nose that would be a disaster on a woman, but which lends his face a certain character. It's the commanding sort of profile you would expect to see on an ancient coin.

His eyes begin to crinkle under my scrutiny, as if he's about to burst out laughing. 'Got it yet?' he asks cockily, but I can see his apparent confidence waver momentarily. He looks much younger for that second, and suddenly I know exactly who he is.

'Eddy *Curtis*? Dready Eddy?'

Suddenly I can see him just as he was all those years ago — his dark hair twisted into giant, matted patchouli-stinking dreadlocks, the sides of his head shaved.

'I knew you'd get there in the end.' He grins, ducking his head shyly.

'But, Eddy, give me a break.' I laugh. 'You look totally different. God. You used to have all that hair for a start.'

'Ugh that *hair*,' shudders his grandmother, grimacing at the memory. 'Quite disgusting.'

He rubs the top of his head ruefully. 'Not so

23

much any more.' I realize that his crop is designed to disguise the beginnings of a receding hairline. But who knew that underneath those revolting dreads, Eddy had been such a looker? In my memory he was little more than a lanky spliff-rolling hairball who held a massive party one summer night just before I left Lyme for good.

'Short hair suits you,' I say. He rubs the top of his head again, embarrassed, and I feel myself begin to blush in sympathy, as if I've just propositioned him on his grandmother's driveway, instead of idly commenting on his haircut.

Next to Eddy, the old lady speaks, 'Kate, dear?'

Eddy and I both turn to look at her.

'I do hope you don't think I'm rude not to have called round before. Only I've had a bit of a chest, you know.' She coughs once, primly, as if to demonstrate.

'It's all that swimming, Grandma,' says Eddy. 'I told you it might be time to pack it in.' She pulls away from him crossly.

'Don't be ridiculous. Nothing of the sort. Gets the blood pumping.'

'Till you're carted off in an ambulance.'

'That was only *once*,' huffs Mrs Curtis, thrusting her hands into the pockets of her cardigan. 'I'm not dead yet, you know.'

Eddy's expression softens, and he reaches out towards her.

'Hmm.' Mrs Curtis allows him to take her arm again.

Eddy raises his eyes to the sky in a way that only I can see. The whole exchange has an almost scripted feel, as if they have had this exact

24

conversation many times and now it is almost a pleasantry, drained of any actual meaning or expectation that the behaviour of either will change.

Mrs Curtis fixes her beady eyes on me, her fluffy head cocked birdishly to one side. 'Now I'm better you'll come round for tea, won't you? Or we could even go out for a cup?'

'Grandma,' Eddy says warningly. I wonder what objection he can possibly have to us sharing some tea.

'What?' she asks.

Oh God, am I going to get co-opted into the neighbourhood as a replacement for my grand-mother? Forced into bridge groups and RNLI coffee mornings? The thought makes me shud-der. In London I barely knew my neighbours, except to exchange curt nods and twice-yearly comments about the weather or the shortcom-ings of the local bin men. But Eddy's granny looks so pleased with her invitation that I can hardly refuse. I only have to go once, I tell myself.

'I'd love to,' I lie. She beams at me happily.

'Kate Bailey,' says Eddy, shaking his head, and I'm not sure if he's speaking to me or her. 'Kate Bailey is back in town.'

'Eddy, dear, did you bring my pills?' his grandmother interrupts.

Eddy confirms that he has brought everything she asked for, and begins to steer her back towards the front door. 'Come on, Grandma,' he says. 'Didn't you say something about a cup of tea?'

'Oh yes, dear, a cup of tea. What a lovely idea. Aren't you a thoughtful boy?'

'Bye, Eddy,' I say. I start to wave, but it feels stupidly childish somehow, so I shove my hands into my jeans pockets again. 'It's good to see you again.'

He looks up as he helps his granny up the step into her house. His smile is distracted; his thoughts already inside the house. 'Good to see you, too, Kate. I'm glad you haven't forgotten me.'

He shuts the door, but I can still hear their voices; hers high and questioning, his calm. He always was the kind of boy you could rely on, even back when we were at school. The boy who'd stay sober to drive everyone else home from a night out in Exeter; the boy who talked down Kim Dearborn when she'd started spinning out on acid at a party on the beach. It didn't seem like much, back then, being reliable — it's not a quality highly rated by teenagers. It's something you learn to appreciate only when unreliable men have stamped all over your heart.

I hadn't forgotten Eddy Curtis. Of course I hadn't. I'd tried, of course. I'd tried to forget about Lyme altogether.

But now I've come here to forget everything else.

4

Lagos, Nigeria

In my time at Hitz Music Television, I had arranged for the Red Hot Chili Peppers to play a set under the Arc de Triomphe in Paris during an electrical storm that threatened to electrocute everyone on stage. I'd battled German bureaucracy to shut down the centre of Berlin so that U2 could perform at the Brandenburg Gate with a fireworks display that cost over a million euros, conducted by a lunatic pyromaniac who spoke only in an obscure Sichuanese dialect that had to be relayed to us through two interpreters. I'd had to clear Bondi Beach of twenty-thousand pilled-up ravers after an Australian dance festival got out of hand. In short, I was used to dealing with a certain amount of drama. It was my job. But I'd never run an event like the African Music Awards before.

After two weeks in Lagos I'd begun to get used to Nigerian time, which made the Spanish idea of mañana seem like a model of ruthless punctuality. Nothing ever happened when it was supposed to, and not just because the traffic in Lagos was little short of diabolical, making it impossible to know how long it would take to get anywhere. A phone call from someone promising they were on their way meant they could be expected any time in the next six hours. 'They'll be out of the venue this morning,' meant 'Prepare to be able to unload your equipment no earlier than midnight'. 'We will provide a VIP backstage area for the artists' meant 'You will arrive to find the artists' dressing rooms only half built, with exposed wires hanging from the ceiling over a large pool of water in the middle of the floor.'

My team and I had worked twenty-hour days to whip the venue into some sort of shape, handing out bribes in thick wads of multicoloured notes, keeping the peace between our surly South African security team and the local crew, falling into bed at two in the morning after downing medicinal bottles of Star beer in the hotel bar.

And now, of course, the Hitz management had arrived, like the cavalry at the eleventh hour, here to take all of the glory without any of the graft.

'I put a spoon in that brown slop, and all these fucking googly eyes were looking at me,' whined Dean, our Head of Talent, as he lowered himself into a chair in the meeting room.

'Trippy,' said his assistant, Leila, encouragingly.

'Fucking fish head curry, they said,' Dean continued, glad of an audience. 'Fish heads! Not just eyes — teeth! I felt like Indiana Jones in the Temple of Fucking Doom or something.'

I didn't dare look at anyone across the table in case I burst out laughing. The idea of portly Dean, his stomach straining against his shirt buttons, vast continents of sweat blooming under his armpits, comparing himself to Harrison Ford would have to be savoured later in the bar.

'Yeah, man, I think the Temple of Doom was

actually in India,' suggested dimwit Leila, known to us all as the Tangent, partly, as demonstrated, for her uncanny ability to hone in on the least important detail of any discussion, and partly because she insisted on dyeing her skin a ferocious shade of orange. 'This is, like, Africa?'

Her starey blue eyes wavered for a moment, as if she was suddenly unsure of herself — maybe this wasn't Africa after all. Rumour had it she was only kept on by Dean because of her unfailing ability to score drugs anywhere in the world. And then to take most of them herself. I nodded at her in affirmation — yes, you're in Africa — and she looked relieved.

'I know that thanks, Leila,' snapped Dean, pulling his shirt down over his belly. If you asked me he could afford to miss a meal or two without too much suffering.

'Kate,' barked our boss Richard, entering the room and slamming his clipboard down on the table so that we all leapt to attention in our seats. 'Fish heads. Sort it.'

I nodded, mentally adding it to my ever growing list of things to sort before the show kicked off tomorrow. I would have sorted it earlier if I'd known, but I had lived exclusively on crisps and hotel sandwiches since I'd arrived, so the local delicacies had passed me by.

Richard held up his clipboard to the light and squinted at it. 'Perimeter road closed?' he barked.

'Yup,' I promised. 'Job done. I saw the governor this morning.'

'Good.' Richard wasn't one for effusive praise. 'Damage?'

'Ten VIP passes, personal intro for his daughter to Slender Dee. And we foot the bill for refitting backstage.'

'Yeah, Slender Dee won't do meet and greets,' said Dean with unpleasant satisfaction. If ever there was a spanner to be thrown in the works, you could bet that spanner would have Dean's fingerprints all over it. The man lived to annoy.

Richard glared at him. 'Who the fuck is Slender Dee anyway?'

Leila looked up, 'Oh he's huge here. Huge. He's, like, a DJ and singer, yeah? Blind. Cancer.'

'He has cancer?' my assistant producer Sarah asked anxiously. We'd already had to re-do the risk assessment to take on board the fact that he was blind, and I knew she was worried the insurance wouldn't cover him for a pre-existing condition.

'No, dude, Cancer, the crab,' said Leila. 'It's, like, his astrological sign? You know, hides in his shell, yeah? Reserved. Doesn't like the limelight.'

Dean held up his hands helplessly. 'I can't force him, Richard.'

'He is one blind fucking singer,' snapped Richard. 'He won't have a fucking clue where he is anyway — just tell him you're putting him in a taxi, point him at the governor for five minutes and then send him on his way.'

Leila and Dean exchanged pained glances, their standard response when requested to do anything other than gush over celebrities and submit enormous bills to expenses for 'fruit and flowers', which was accepted code for payments made to Leila's dodgy chemical associates.

'Do it,' warned Richard, in a voice that silenced all argument. 'Next.'

The meeting bored on, and my to-do list grew like a tropical fungus, spreading into the margins of my notepad.

The new head of marketing had missed his flight and was now stuck in traffic somewhere on the way from the airport. I was fairly relieved by this, as I'd been ignoring his emails for days. I'd had his predecessor perfectly trained up in how to deal with Production (a combination of bribes, flattery and outright begging), but this new guy was full of unrealistic expectations and he wouldn't take no for an answer.

However, as he wasn't present, it was easy enough to overrule Caroline, his young and inexperienced deputy. Even Leila managed to put her foot down about a meet and greet with the sponsors. I felt quite sorry for Caroline in the end, but if Matt Martell didn't know how to get what he wanted out of his colleagues without sending a junior to ask for it, there was really no hope for him.

If you ask directly for what you want, you allow the possibility that someone will say no. You have to be smarter than that, surely?

★   ★   ★

To absolutely no one's surprise, the show was running two hours late. The only saving grace was that we weren't broadcasting live. I was checking the running order backstage, and wondering how long it would take to get everyone out of there — the de-rig would start minutes after the last artist stepped off stage — when the mysterious head of marketing made his first appearance. I didn't notice him at first, but there was some whispering at the door and it was distracting me from my time-keeping, so I looked up to ask whoever it was to be quiet.

A tall man stood at the door, looking furious, as one of the South African security guys tried to stop him coming into the room. He was wearing a suit, which was enough to make him look out of place amongst the backstage crew in our jeans and T-shirts, but the lanyard around his neck told me he had to be part of the team. He had brows as dark as the hair that flopped down over his forehead, and they were pulled together in an expression of harassment and bewilderment that was painfully familiar to me after two weeks of dealing with the craziness of Lagos. It was almost enough to make me feel sorry for him. Until he opened his mouth.

'Kate Bailey?' He wrenched his arm away from the security man, and I nodded to let Dirk know it was okay to let him go.

I raised my eyebrows in expectation as he strode across the room towards me.

'Are *you* Kate Bailey?' As he got closer he looked uncertain.

'Yes,' I said, looking back down at my figures to let him see I was busy.

'Oh right. You're younger than I expected.'

'Really?' I sighed, looking up. I got this all the time; it was both a blessing and a curse to look younger than I was. Usually I made it work in my favour: either people underestimated me completely, or the fact that I'm small and blonde and young made a certain kind of man soften towards me — and I have no compunction in taking full advantage of that.

'Well, you don't look like . . . I mean, Ball-Basher Bailey; I just expected . . . sorry.'

He quickly held out his hands in supplication, as if I didn't already know that was my nickname at Hitz. To be honest I encouraged it: I found that having a reputation as a ball-breaker got half my job done by intimidating people in advance. Pre-warned to find me scary, people backed down without me even having to raise my voice.

'Now's not a great time,' I said, pointing at the paper-work that lay in front of me. 'I'm just trying to work out what time we're going to finish so I can brief the de-rig.'

'Then it *is* a great time,' said Matt, pulling up a chair and sitting down next to me uninvited. 'Because that's what I need to know. I've got ice sculptures melting all over the room and a load of angry sponsors.'

'And you are?' I said meanly. Of course I knew who he was, but it annoyed me that he hadn't even bothered to introduce himself, and had just launched in with complaints.

'Shit, sorry,' he said, slapping his palm to his forehead. He looked much younger when he laughed. The furrows on his forehead relaxed, and his eyes creased into a smile. 'Matt Martell, head of marketing. Sender of multiple emails. Bane of your life.'

I couldn't help smiling back, but I wasn't

33

going to let him off that easily.

'Purchaser of ice sculptures in the subtropics,' I said. 'I know you're new in the job, Matt Martell, but who in their right mind orders ice sculptures for a party with a start time that can best be described as flexible?'

'It wasn't me!' he insisted. 'It's the sponsor who's paid for them, and by the time their guests get there, the sculptures are going to look like Slush Puppies.'

'Well, I'm glad you're not as dumb as you look,' I said. Although he didn't look dumb at all, he looked pretty gorgeous, if you want to know the truth. He had that sort of blue-black hair that makes you think of Elvis, and eyes so dark I couldn't even see what colour they were. Isn't that always the way, though? The stupid ones are always the prettiest.

'Oh right?' said Matt, running a hand through his hair and leaning back in his chair. He gave a short, abrupt laugh. 'I thought you just had a bit of a brutal email manner, but now I'm thinking it might be more of a borderline personality disorder.'

'What, like efficient-and-good-at-my-job disorder? Effective diagnosis, doctor.'

'I was thinking more like unhelpful-and-obstructive disorder.'

'Also known as not-willing-to-waste-time-on-stupid-questions disease. Pity it's not contagious.'

Matt smirked. 'Look. Enough of the insults, Basher Bailey. I need to get people into my party before it's a complete disaster. Half the guests are there, but the staff say you've told them not

34

to open the bar until the show's over.'

'Yup,' I said. 'And?'

'And if they don't get a drink soon they're all going to leave before the rest of the guests arrive. When's this show going to end, anyway?'

'I haven't worked it out exactly,' I said, 'because I keep being *interrupted*, but I reckon we've got at least an hour till we're done. More if we get any encores.'

'An hour? But the party was meant to start an hour and a half ago.'

I shrugged. 'Yup, the show was meant to start three hours ago. I was meant to be drinking my way through your free bar by now. Lots of things were meant to happen. But this is where we are; nothing I can do about it.'

'But Airtel are going to be furious, they've spent a fortune on this party.'

'I'm really sorry, Matt. Sounds like a nightmare. But I'm not sure what I can do — the audience is going to go crazy if I pull any of the acts. The show must go on, right?'

'You don't have to pull any of the acts,' said Matt, leaning forwards intently. 'All you need to do' — I bristled instantly at his presumption — 'is open the bar and allow the sponsors out of the audience so they can come backstage early.'

'But, Matt,' I sighed, and spoke as slowly and clearly as I could to get the words through his thick head. 'The sponsors and their competition winners are taking up the whole six front rows of the audience. We're filming this — I can't have half the audience walking out of the room while the show's still on. And the artists will go mental

35

if they have to perform to a load of empty seats.'

'Can't you just get the cameramen to film different parts of the audience?' said Matt.

'No, Matt, I can't, actually. We've all had to work with these delays for weeks — now it's your turn. Deal with it.'

'But all the artists are leaving already,' said Matt. 'I've seen them getting into their cars as soon as they get off stage. There won't be anyone left to come to the party if it doesn't start soon.'

That got my attention. 'Which artists are leaving? Not Slender Dee?'

'Who?' Matt looked bemused, as well he might, not being as familiar with the cream of African musical talent as I'd become over the last two weeks.

'Shit, what are those useless idiots from Talent doing? They're meant to be making sure Slender Dee comes to the party.'

Matt grimaced. 'I'll tell you where Talent are — sitting at my party watching the ice sculptures melt and bitching about not being able to get a proper drink. They're the ones who told me where to find you.'

'Right,' I snapped. I threw down my pen and stood up. 'Follow me.'

Matt bit back a smile, but I wasn't laughing. Before I met the governor, I wouldn't have cared if all the acts had flown to Timbuktu as soon as they'd finished performing, but I'd promised his daughter would meet Slender Dee and I'm a girl of my word. Most of the time.

Matt hadn't been joking about the party; it

looked like your worst kind of social disaster. The few people who hadn't left already were standing around in angry clusters, sober and irritable. Leila sat at the bar, her slack black-pupilled gaze suggesting that, for her, the party had already started, and possibly nearly finished, too. The waiters were nowhere to be seen; I suspected they were having a smoke out the back as usual. The ice sculptures were so far gone it was impossible to tell what they had once been — their misshapen remains dripped into spreading puddles on the concrete floor.

The only person who looked like he was having any fun at all was Dean, who was sat on his fat arse on a cheap white leather sofa, with a local woman on his right hand side and another sat on his lap, teasing his hair with her fingers. Rather her than me, I'd always thought he used far too much gel for a man of his age. I got my phone out of my pocket and snapped a picture before he realized I was there.

'Hi, Dean,' I said loudly.

Hearing my voice, he hastily pushed his friend off his lap and stood up, distancing himself from both women as fast as he could. Classy.

'Kate, babe, how you doing? Great show, great show.' I knew he hadn't seen a minute of it, though that wouldn't stop him telling the artists — if any of them showed up afterwards — that they were amaaaaaaazing.

'Thanks. Now, look, we've got a bit of a problem. Matt tells me the talent are all fucking off back to their hotels when we need them to come to the party to meet the sponsors and the governor's daughter.'

'Oooh, the governor's daughter, you don't say!' Dean minced obnoxiously.

I stared at him, not blinking.

'Oh God, you're serious? Look, I've done my best, but what can I do? They don't want to hang about in that crappy backstage area for another hour and I don't blame them. It's a shithole. And Matt says you won't open the bar here until the show's done.' He shrugged. 'I know I'm pretty great at my job, but I'm not a miracle worker.'

I flicked my phone on and opened up the picture of Dean with the two women.

'See this, Dean? In one second I can text this to Marie.'

His eyes opened so wide I thought his eyeballs might plop out into the ice-sculpture puddle beside him.

'When did she give you her final warning, Dean? After Glastonbury, wasn't it? How long did you have to stay at Richard's before she let you come home?'

'Kate, seriously, you wouldn't. Nothing was going on, I swear.' Beads of sweat formed on his temples and he tugged at his collar.

'Doesn't look like it in this picture though, does it?' I said, waving the phone at him.

'I'll go backstage now. You'll have all the artists here for the party, I promise you.'

'Dean,' I grabbed his arm. 'Slender Dee. That's the important one. Get him to the party and you can delete this picture off my phone yourself.'

'I'm on it, Kate,' promised Dean, and scuttled

off down the corridor towards the artists' dressing rooms, casting backwards glances at me as if he hoped I'd burst into flames.

Next to me Matt rubbed his chin, considering me with a look that was somewhere in between admiration and horror.

'What?' I asked.

'You're a tough woman, Kate Bailey.' He smiled.

'I know how to get the job done, you mean,' I said. 'Nothing to it. You could've done it yourself if you'd only known Dean's weak spot.'

'Ouch!' He laughed. 'I don't know if I'd feel comfortable threatening a man's marriage just to get results.'

'Puh, I'd never have shown Marie that picture, and even if I did she wouldn't have cared less. She's under no illusions about who she married. She used to work in Production herself before she had children. She knows what it's like.'

'You're pretty cynical, aren't you?'

'Cynical?'

'Don't you believe in true love?' he asked, raising a mocking eyebrow.

'True love?' I scoffed. 'Not between Dean and Marie, I don't.'

'What about for you?'

I scowled at him.

'Look, Matt, I really don't have time for this. I've got to get back to the running order now that I've finished sorting out your little problem.'

'About opening the bar — '

'Matt Martell, if you ask me that again, I'll send a compromising picture of you to your girlfriend, even if I have to pose for it with you myself.'

I turned on my heel and stormed out of the bar. Behind me I heard Matt call out, 'I don't have a girlfriend.'

5

There's no need for an alarm clock when you have a dog, I've found. I wonder if I could market the woken-by-puppy alarm? It's indisputably more pleasant than the shrilling of a mobile phone next to your ear, though maybe not everyone would want to be jolted from sleep by a cold, wet nose on whichever part of their body is sticking out from under the duvet. In favour of my scheme is the fact that Minnie keeps time remarkably well; she likes me to be up by seven every morning or she makes her protests known. Now we're beginning to feel settled at Granny Gilbert's I've managed, a few times, to let her into the garden and sneak back to bed for a while, but Minnie does not approve of this laziness and will return persistently, like a living snooze button, to make sure I get up properly.

This morning I let her out and stay up, leaving the back door open while she snuffles around. Minnie leaps into the tiny patio garden with enormous enthusiasm every single day, as if it's the very first time she's ever encountered this incredibly exciting space. As if the decaying rose bushes and mossy patio tiles are a wonderful surprise, instead of exactly as she left them the day before. There is probably a great lesson there, if I could be arsed to learn it. But frankly I need a cup of coffee before I start tackling the grand existential questions of life. While I wait

41

for the kettle to boil, I switch on the radio: Granny Gilbert's ancient Nineties sub-woofer monster with its double-cassette player for the recording of mix-tapes that I am quite sure she never once considered making.

Of course I miss Granny Gilbert; I used to come here every day after school while Mum and Dad were still at the office. She used to look after Prue, too, when Prue was a baby. But she was ill for so long before she died, and so confused with it, that it was as if we did our grieving while she was still alive. For the last six months she wasn't even living in the bungalow; she had to go into a home in Bridport where they could give her round-the-clock care. If Granny Gilbert had been aware of what was happening to her, she'd have hated it. She'd have railed at the nurses, refused to leave her home, demanded to be allowed to feed herself. I suppose the only good thing about any of it was that by then, whatever was left of my mother's mother was entirely unresisting and uncomplaining. Which was how we knew that she wasn't really there at all.

The estate agent said that having someone living in the house might make all the difference to selling it. Not that there has been a single viewing since I moved in. Maybe seeing the house being used as a home, instead of as a mausoleum, will be what finally sells it. He did ask, hopefully, if I was going to be doing any redecoration while I was staying, as if I could effortlessly effect some Grand Designs-style transformation of an undesirable bungalow into a sumptuous show home. It would be hard to know where to even start. With the entirely blue bathroom, from tub to tiles right down to the colour-coordinated guest soaps in cellophane wrappers that have sat on the bathroom shelf since I was at school? With the rag-rolled walls of the kitchen — a paint effect that I'm told was quite the Farrow & Ball design statement of its day when Mum helped Granny Gilbert do it in 1986?

I'm contemplating what one would do about the swirly Artex living-room ceiling when I realize that the strange shrill noise I've been ignoring must be Granny Gilbert's phone. Or, more to the point, my phone. I hadn't even known it was connected. The house has been standing empty for so long I assumed it must have been cut off.

'Hello?' I answer warily, expecting it to be some kind of telemarketer.

'Hello yourself,' says my sister. 'Am I interrupting another hectic day? Got meetings lined up, people to see?'

'Very funny, Prue. What do you want?'

'Why would I want anything?' she asks, affronted. 'Can't I just give my sister a call to see how she's getting on? To see how things are?'

I'm instantly on high alert.

'Oh, right. Well, in that case I'm fine, thanks. It's good of you to ask.' Also extremely unlike you to ask, Prue, I think.

'Fine?' asks Prue. 'Just fine? Are you maybe . . . ' I hear her pause, and I know, without even being able to see her face, that this is a significant pause. A pause with an as-yet-unspecified purpose. 'Are you maybe a little lonely?'

43

'No,' I say quickly. I'm not sure what the trap is but I know there must be one. This is Prue. There is always a trap.

'Really? Because, wow, I don't know how I'd feel living in that sad old bungalow all by myself, with no one around to talk to, ever.'

'I'm fine with it, actually, Prue, just fine,' I say. 'I like living alone. I don't expect you'd understand since you've never even moved out of home.'

'No.' She laughs but it's a forced laugh; she doesn't like being reminded that she has never lived anywhere else but at Mum and Dad's. Even though she's the one who insisted she will only leave home when she gets married, it somehow doesn't fit with her forward-thinking ambitious-young-businesswoman image. 'No, I suppose you have lived by yourself before. But not for a long time. Not since you met Matt.'

My teeth are clenched, but I still spit out a bland reply, 'I suppose not.'

'But maybe there's nothing more lonely than living with someone when the love has gone,' offers Prue.

'Fucking hell, Prue, what is this?' I snap. 'Have I just received a call from Dial-a-Cliché? Is there an actual reason you've rung me at stupid o'clock, or did you just want to make me feel even worse about everything than I already do?'

'Keep your hair on,' says Prue with infuriating calm. 'I was just calling because I'm worried about you. I know you think I don't care, but I do.'

A lump rises in my throat. Even though I'm still suspicious of her motives for this unexpected call, lately even the most perfunctory offer of sympathy has me fighting back tears. 'Thanks, Prue. Sorry if I'm being snappy. It's just a difficult time.'

'And a lonely one,' she prompts persistently.

'Okay, perhaps a very little bit lonely,' I finally concur, defeated into agreement.

'I knew it. It's good you're admitting it at last. So why don't you bring your lonely self over for supper tonight? I'm cooking.'

It's not the most appealing invitation I've ever had, but let's face it, it's the only Saturday night invitation I'm likely to get in my self-imposed state of seclusion. 'Thanks, Prue, that would be nice.'

'Good. Be here by seven. Bring wine — white, four bottles. I've told Teresa at the wine shop which ones to put by, you can pick them up later.'

See? Of course there was an agenda here. I am willing to bet they'll be the most expensive wines Lyme has to offer.

'By the way,' Prue continues casually, 'Ben's coming.'

'Really?' I haven't yet met my sister's new boyfriend, and suddenly I feel much more interested in the evening ahead.

'Yes, really. For some unfathomable reason, he actually wants to meet you,' says Prue.

'He's coming all the way from Bristol?'

'Yes, from Bristol, where else would he be coming from?'

'Don't get chippy, Prue, it just seems like a long way to come for supper. Is he staying over?'

45

Granny Gilbert's phone is connected to the wall by a long curly wire. I stretch it to its fullest as I hold the kettle under the running tap while Prue continues to talk.

'Certainly not!' says Prue, adding proudly, 'He's staying at the Alexandra; I got him a room for half price because of his connection to Baileys'.'

The way Prue speaks of my family's business is as if it's some great colossus of commerce, instead of the three of them letting holiday cottages and running tourist events in a sleepy Dorset backwater. Prue's always had bold schemes for Baileys', despite Mum and Dad's lack of interest in becoming bigger, and has signed herself up to all sorts of mental local business organizations to further her ambitions. In fact, I'm pretty sure it was at some Young Entrepreneurs South West event that she first met Ben.

'Nice,' I say, flicking the kettle on. The Alexandra is the poshest hotel in town, and Prue knows I know it.

'They appreciate which way the wind's blowing,' says Prue.

'Er, what?'

'Now that Ben's getting involved in Baileys',' she says. 'They know we're going to be sending a lot of business their way. They'll want to keep us sweet, I can tell you.'

'Right,' I say. Prue's plans for domination of the Lyme Bay area could not be of less interest to me. 'Why couldn't he stay with you?'

I hear Prue inhale sharply before she answers.

46

'You know how I feel about that sort of thing,' she says primly.

'Well excuse me for suggesting that your *boyfriend* might possibly stay the night. It's not completely outside the realms of possibility.'

'Not everyone, Kate, has your London ways,' she snaps back, sounding seventy-five instead of twenty-five. 'I'll see you at seven.'

And then she hangs up.

Once, just once, I would like to have a conversation with Prue that doesn't end like this.

6

Lagos, Nigeria

'Here she is.'

'Someone get Kate a drink, would you?'

'Why don't you do it, Danny, you plonker?'

'Jay, it's a free bar, anyone can go up. You don't get extra chivalry points for it.'

If you want to know how to spot a group of cameramen at fifty paces, though I can't imagine why you would unless it was to avoid them, allow me to tell you what to look for. Firstly, they will be dressed identically, although they would be very offended to hear anyone say so. Being freelancers, they consider themselves individuals, mavericks even, but when you see them en masse their protests of individuality are like listening to a flock of flamingos affecting outrage that you can't tell them apart: 'But I'm a totally different *kind* of pink, and my legs are *miles* longer than his — and what? You think just everyone has a beak like *this?*' When it comes to the plumage of a cameraman, think dark T-shirt, combat shorts, usually camouflage (with plenty of zips for kit) and trainers.

And, in the case of this lot, they will stick together at all times, sharing laddish banter and in-jokes while trying to cop off with girls from the Production team. And, I can't deny it, frequently succeeding. Sarah had had a dalliance with at least two of these cameramen in the recent past and, in the interests of full disclosure, I will admit to a night spent with Chris after an event in Ibiza in the summer. But, frankly, you show me the Production girl who hasn't slept with a cameraman at one point in her career and I will show you a massive liar. It's practically part of the job description.

'It's okay,' I said, pushing my way past them towards the bar. The room was heaving now that the show was over, and Dean had excelled himself by dragging the talent to the party, as promised. 'I'll get it myself. Sarah, what are you having?'

'Bottle of Star,' she called, having 'accidentally' got stuck in the crowd right next to Jay, one of her cameraman conquests. He turned his shoulders towards her, blocking out his identikit friends. She lowered her eyes bashfully, and then looked back up at him through her lashes. I rolled my own eyes, guessing a replay was imminent.

Chris, obviously thinking that I, too, might be keen to revisit the past, broke away from the group to come and stand next to me at the bar. I craned my head over his shoulder to check out the VIP area, which was nothing more than a corner of leather sofas on which, I was glad to see, Slender Dee had been seated, awaiting the arrival of the governor.

'Hey, Kate,' Chris said, nudging me to get my attention. It hardly sounded like a declaration of true love.

I wondered if it was because Matt's words had

hit a raw nerve that Chris seemed so much less attractive than he had done in Ibiza. There was a time when the very sight of him, muscles flexed on his camera platform, his dirty-blond surfer boy hair in his eyes, had made my stomach flip over. Now I felt nothing more than a kind of indignant boredom at Chris's assumption that we'd just pick up where we'd left off.

I often wondered if my love life was confined to short-lived work flings because of my job — all the travelling, late nights and unpredictable hours were hardly conducive to domestic bliss — or if I had somehow chosen the job in order to avoid being settled in any way. Work was always my excuse to stay out of anything serious. I'd always preferred to keep my relationships short and easy — much like myself, ho ho.

But a girl can tire of the production merry-go-round. And I don't just mean when she runs out of options and is reduced to recycling available cameramen. Maybe I was getting old. But thirty wasn't old. Not compared to someone like Dean, who was still running around snorting coke with the riggers backstage and fooling around behind his wife's back when he's pushing fifty. I mean, that's old *and* pathetic.

'Hey,' said Chris, again. Mr Romance. It's not as if I felt he had to get down on one knee or write me a poem, or compose a song in my honour, I just felt like it would be good if he showed even a little effort. Standing next to me and repeating 'hey' until I got drunk enough to let him snog me was hardly appealing, and it certainly wasn't true love.

There was a stir over in a corner of the room, and the crowd of cameramen moved for a moment, as one, like a shoal of fish, for long enough for me to glimpse the governor entering the room, outfitted in a beige uniform that was ostentatiously draped with swags of gold braid. His teenage daughter held his hand, her skinny frame swamped in a patterned dress, biting her lip nervously in anticipation of meeting her hero.

'Excuse me,' I said, grabbing two bottles of Star off the bar and handing one to Sarah as I left Chris looking baffled.

It was a mere two minutes' work to introduce the governor and his daughter to Slender Dee, and I left them happily chatting in the VIP area, which suddenly looked more impressive for being surrounded by the governor's security detail. Dean nodded over to me anxiously from the buffet table where he was 'working', i.e., getting drunk with some artists, and I mimed deleting the photograph from my phone. He smiled back nervously, not quite trusting me. I'd never send anything like that to Marie, but maybe I didn't need to — maybe just the threat of it would make him keep it in his pants tonight.

Now, at last, I could relax. The show was over, the de-rig had begun, in just — I looked at the clock on my phone — in just nine hours I'd be on a plane home. And until then, I had a lot of drinking to do. The cameramen had parked themselves at a table and looked as settled as if they'd moved in for the night, leaning back in their chairs, empties already piling up. Sarah had moved off to sit in a far corner with Jay, knees touching as they sat opposite one another, talking intently. Leila was slumped on one of the white leather sofas, smiling benevolently at no one in particular. Danny was giving the eye to one of the singers from Gabon, a beautiful woman in a green printed dress who held herself elegantly on a high stool by the bar. I wondered when Danny would realize that she, like Slender Dee, was blind, rather than playing hard to get.

Matt was still working. I guessed that the people he was talking to must be the Airtel VIPs, judging by his pretty convincing look of absolute fascination at everything they said. He was aided in this by his height — he had to be well over six foot — which meant he had to incline his head to listen to most people. It lent every conversation a confiding air, a sense of real attentiveness, when he was probably bored rigid and wondering when they'd leave the party they'd paid for. Matt saw me looking and gave me a wink over the heads of the sponsors. I smiled back and turned towards the bar again.

I was halfway across the room, squeezing myself past the Lagos glitterati and Nollywood stars, feeling deeply underdressed in comparison with their platform shoes and towering head-pieces, when I felt a tug on my sleeve. What now? The sponsors may have thought this was their party, but as far as I was concerned, it was my reward for two weeks' hard slog and I wasn't about to be dragged into more work issues.

I turned to see Matt behind me, head inclined again in that confiding way.

'Cheers,' he said, clinking his bottle of Star against mine.

'Cheers,' I said, eyeing him warily. Behind him I could see the massed ranks of the cameramen watching our conversation, Chris in particular.

'I can see you want to get back to your friends,' said Matt, looking backwards over his shoulder at the table. 'I just wanted to thank you for helping me earlier — and sorry for hassling you, I know it's been a bit of a nightmare show. I didn't mean to make things harder for you.'

'It's fine,' I said. 'It's my job.' But I couldn't help smiling at him a bit. He was awfully good-looking. Now that I looked closer, his eyes were a dark, dark blue.

'Maybe I should get you a drink,' he offered. 'To say thanks.'

'Er, it's a free bar, Matt.' I laughed. 'And I've got a bottle of Star on the go.'

'Maybe I should take you out for a drink when we get home, then?' Matt suggested. 'I'm sure I can get some Star sent to London, what with all my great new friends at Airtel.' He waved over towards one of the sponsors, who waved back, grinning. 'See? Joseph over there would be only too happy to help.'

Matt made a thumbs-up sign, and Joseph signalled back. Matt raised an eyebrow at me.

'Star for life. Sorted.'

'Matt, sorry to disappoint you, what with your impressive Nigerian connections and all, but I'll be happy if I never see another bottle of Star for as long as I live,' I said.

'Even though it will always be a special

reminder of how you and I met?' Matt teased. 'Over a bottle of Star, some African superstars and a blackmail plot against the head of Talent?'

'Not even for that,' I said, grimacing as I drained the remnants of my warm beer. I was surprised to find that I was having fun. I guessed Matt was used to putting people at ease. He had an easy sort of charm that, while I could see it was practised, felt entirely natural. I was happy to let myself be charmed, for once, instead of being the one who had to smooth everything over.

'Ah, well, I guess it will only be meaningful to me, then,' sighed Matt. 'You're a tough woman to please, Basher Bailey. I guess it's a good job you're pretty enough to make up for it.'

I considered him from under my fringe, my eyes narrowed. 'What do you want?'

Matt looked momentarily startled, before bursting out laughing. 'Can't a compliment just be a compliment?'

'It so rarely is,' I said smoothly. 'Everyone's usually out for something.'

'Well, maybe I am out for something then,' said Matt. I suddenly noticed that by leaning in towards me he'd made me inch myself back into a corner that was slightly secluded from the rest of the bar.

'Oh yes?' I said. My voice was steady but I could feel a blush stealing up the back of my ears, threatening to give me away. Was Matt flirting with me, or was he about to hit me with another annoying request from his sponsors?

'Yes,' said Matt, moving closer. I stepped away

54

again and found the wall of a small alcove at my back. My heart started beating faster, as if I was trapped. Matt just gave me a lazy smile and raised his eyebrows.

'I need a drink,' I blurted, waving my empty beer bottle in front of my face.

'Okay,' Matt said, his easy grin unperturbed. 'Another Star?'

'No,' I said, flirtatiously challenging. 'Something else. You choose.'

I twisted around and put my empty beer bottle in the alcove by my head. As I turned back to face him, Matt lurched towards me, his eyes wide. I flinched backwards — was he really going to try to kiss me now? In front of everyone? But instead he pushed past me and caught the beer bottle just before it hit the floor.

'Reflexes of a ninja!' he exclaimed, straightening himself up, and pushing his hair out of his eyes. He'd moved closer to catch the falling bottle, but he didn't move away from me now that he had it.

'Impressive stuff,' I said, my heart beating faster. 'No wonder they made you head of marketing with skills like that.'

'Oh I don't put my ninja skills on my CV,' said Matt. 'I only show them to a select few.'

'Then I'm honoured.'

'Okay. To the bar. No Star. Are you saying you're ready to move onto the hard stuff?' Matt asked, raising an eyebrow. He was only saved from being off-puttingly cheesy by the spark of amusement in his eyes that told me he wasn't taking any of this too seriously.

Two can play at that game.

'Oh definitely,' I replied, holding his gaze. 'The harder the better, frankly.'

'Wait there,' said Matt. He'd only been gone a second when he returned, catching hold of my chin with the fingers of one hand and tilting my face up towards his. 'Promise me you'll wait?'

His conspiratorial grin was infectious. I felt drawn in to a secret exchange. 'I promise.'

'Good,' he said, 'because when I come back I'm going to kiss you, Kate Bailey.'

When I thought about it afterwards, it was the best line I'd ever heard. And of course it was a line. He'd stated his intention with the certain knowledge that if I was there when he got back from the bar, I was up for being kissed. And if I wasn't there — well, he'd have saved himself an embarrassing turn-down.

My head felt giddy, as if I'd had far more than one bottle of beer. *Did* I want to kiss Matt Martell? Only this morning he'd been nothing more than the annoying new boy who sent me too many emails. But now . . . He winked at me from the bar.

'Hey, Kate,' Chris appeared at my side, grabbing hold of my upper arm. ' 'Scuse me for interrupting your little conversation, but there's a whisky over at our table with your name on it.'

'Oh,' I turned to face him. I was embarrassingly aware that I couldn't wipe the smile off my face. A smile that had nothing to do with him. 'I'm okay, thanks. Matt's getting me a drink.'

'Yeah,' said Chris, frowning darkly. 'Matt.'

'What?' I asked crossly. It was a bit late for

Chris to start getting jealous. It wasn't like he'd made any effort until he saw Matt chatting me up. Chris's eyes flicked over to Matt, and then back to me.

'Look, Kate, no offence,' he said, lowering his voice. 'But that Matt Martell's a total wanker. He flirts with everyone, but you know he's going out with Ailsa Logan, right?'

'Ailsa Logan?' I echoed. This must be a mistake.

'Yeah,' said Danny, appearing at my other shoulder. 'Ailsa Logan off *Rise & Shine*. That fit TV bird.'

'Are you sure?' I said. 'He said he didn't have a girlfriend.'

The two cameramen exchanged a glance.

Chris scoffed. 'Well, he wouldn't, would he? But I saw pictures of them together at the British Television Awards just last week. It was in the paper on the plane over.'

I felt my cheeks flame with anger. As the queen of location flings, I should have recognized a kindred spirit. What happens on location stays on location, right? But a girl has to have standards. I'd never knowingly slept with someone who was in a relationship, and I wasn't about to start now.

Over at the bar Matt had worked his way to the front, his broad shoulders forcing a space in the crowd. He turned to look over his shoulder at me. When he saw that I was flanked by two burly cameramen, he looked puzzled and raised a hand in a hesitant half wave.

'The nerve of him,' said Danny, linking his arm with mine.

'That bastard,' said Chris, taking my other arm.

I couldn't disagree.

And I let them lead me away from Matt Martell and straight into a welcoming vat of appalling Nigerian whisky.

7

I can't deny that I am intrigued to meet the mysterious Ben. Although I suppose he's only mysterious to me, since Mum and Dad must have met him plenty of times. It's the first time a boyfriend of Prue's has taken an interest in the business, and for my parents to have allowed him to get involved they must think it's a serious relationship. They've been running the business ever since Dad gave up being a roadie when Prue was born; I don't think she understands that they'd already lived a big life by the time they came to Lyme. Their ambitions for excitement had been fulfilled by years of travelling and hanging out with rock stars. They moved to Dorset for the quiet life. I guess I got a little taste of the travel and glamour — I was six by the time we moved here, when they were looking for schools and stability. Prue, on the other hand, has known nothing but the quiet life, so she can't help but try to push Baileys' into the limelight all the time.

The back door is still open and I can hear noises from next door's garden; Eddy's granny must be up too. I'm wary of calling to her over the garden fence, since I have no wish to see her topple backwards off a ladder again. But the noises in the garden sound high-pitched, excited, not the usual mild chatter of an old lady talking to herself. I pour hot water into the cafetière and leave it to sit while I step outside.

'No, *you're* the nasty queen and *I* am the princess,' declares a voice that very definitely does not belong to Mrs Curtis.

'I don't *want* to be the nasty queen, I am going to be the prince who is going to save the princess,' someone else answers.

'You can't be a *prince*, stupid, you're a *girl*.'

'Then I'm going to be a *princess* who saves the princess.'

'It doesn't work like that, the princess has to be saved by a *prince*.'

'Says who?'

'Says everyone, actually, and anyway I don't want to be saved by you — I'm the oldest.'

'Girls?' says a man's voice from inside next door. Eddy's, I realize.

'Daddy,' the younger voice pleads. 'Daddy, we can both be princesses, can't we?'

I hear Eddy step out into the garden.

'You're both my princesses, Grace, course you are,' he says, affectionate but dismissive, not realizing the sisterly argument at stake.

How strange that Eddy should have children. Proper school-aged children, not the tiny, squalling babies that some of my friends have lately produced, but little girls who are old enough to have fights and opinions. Eddy, who used to scrawl band names on his school bag in biro, who used to drive a battered orange VW beetle with a bent wire coat hanger for an aerial, whose party piece was rolling a spliff with one hand. This is the Eddy Curtis that I knew; and now he's a father. A proper grown-up. I didn't even know he was married.

'Ow, stop it,' shrieks one of the girls, and Minnie, startled, begins to bark.

'A dog!' exclaims Eddy's younger daughter, Grace, I think.

'Kate?' Eddy calls over the fence. 'Kate, sorry, it's really early, did we wake you?'

'Hi Eddy,' I call back. 'You didn't wake me, I was already up, honestly.'

'Eight thirty on a Saturday.' Eddy laughs. 'Things have changed a bit since I last knew you.'

I hardly know how to answer that. It feels like everything has changed and yet nothing has at all. Here I am back in Lyme, chatting to Eddy Curtis. Next we'll be jumping into his car to go to some party we've heard might be happening outside Axminster.

'Daddy,' a voice whispers urgently. 'Has she got a dog?'

'Better than that,' I call over the fence. 'I've got a puppy. Would you like to meet her?'

Eddy's girls are in my garden before I've had a chance to remember that I am still in my pyjamas, without having so much as cleaned my teeth. Not that they would notice, they have eyes only for Minnie, who leaps all over them in excited welcome; she loves children. But Eddy looks embarrassed, and I'm not sure how to behave. My London manners feel all wrong — I can't air kiss him hello when I've most likely got morning breath. So much for the glamorous Kate Bailey he's imagined; I must look a right state.

'Sorry to barge in on you like this,' he says, avoiding looking directly at me. 'We collect my granny from swimming on Saturday mornings — it's a bit of an early start for all of us.'

'Is there a pool in Lyme now?' I ask. I wouldn't mind a swim myself once in a while. Something to pass the time.

Eddy grins and rubs the top of his head with his knuckles. 'Nope. Not for my Grandma. It's the sea or nothing.'

'The sea?' I gasp. 'But it's October! It must be freezing.'

'Bracing, according to her,' says Eddy with a wry smile. 'She used to go every day. Has done for years. But she got caught in a current a while ago — she's not as strong as she thought she was — and someone called the Coastguard.'

'Oh my God, was she okay?'

'She was completely fine by the time they arrived, just furious about all the fuss. Especially when they took her off in an ambulance for a check-up. The coastguards gave her a ticking off about swimming by herself at her age. You can imagine how well that went down.'

'But she still goes in?'

'We've struck a deal — she swims on Saturday mornings only and the girls and I go, too. To watch, you understand. Just spectators. Not in any way keeping an eye on an eighty-year-old woman submerged in the sea by herself.'

'Obviously.' I can't help but be impressed by Mrs Curtis's hearty ways, so at odds with her wiry appearance.

Eddy smiles. 'But I'm not totally sure she's

sticking to her side of the bargain, judging by what you said the other day about her swimming hat.'

'Unless she was just, er, wearing in a new one?' I suggest, suddenly overcome with belated neighbourly loyalty.

'Oh I see,' says Eddy, raising an eyebrow. 'I thought you'd be *my* ally in this, and here you are taking her side already.'

Eddy and I both watch the girls, shrieking as Minnie chases them around the garden.

'Eddy Curtis, a dad,' I say. 'I can't believe it.'

He looks at me quizzically. 'It's not that weird, you know. I'm thirty-four, not thirteen.'

'I know.' I laugh. 'I suppose I still think of you as a teenager. You're not weird at all. I'm weird.'

'Why are you weird?' he asks, looking amused.

I shrug. 'Oh, you know, *it's* weird, I mean. Life's weird. You're a dad; Dready Eddy is a dad. And I'm, well, I'm living in my granny's bungalow.'

Eddy shifts from foot to foot on the paving stones. 'Yeah, sorry, I heard about, er, your husband.'

'It's fine,' I say, glad he's brave enough to say it straight out instead of hedging with euphemisms and platitudes, like most people. 'Not every marriage is meant to last.'

He barks a sharp laugh, as if it's been punched out of him. 'No.'

The youngest girl comes running up to us, breathless and excited.

'Daddy, can we stay here with the puppy? Can we?'

Her sister, who can't be more than eight, rolls her eyes in a distinctly teenaged manner.

'Grace, we have *things to do*. Don't we, Daddy? It can't all be fun and games.'

I stifle a smirk at her world-weary air.

'Charlotte's right, sweetheart,' says Eddy, pulling gently on Grace's plait. 'I've got to get you back to Mummy's house by eight thirty so she can take you both to ballet.'

'But I don't want to go to ballet,' wails Grace, her eyes filling with tears. 'I want to stay with you, and with the puppy.'

Eddy tenses up next to me. Back to Mummy's house? He offers me a rueful half smile.

'Yeah,' he says. 'Life is weird. Come on, girls. We have to go and say goodbye to Great-grandma or we're going to be late.'

'Can we come and see the puppy again?' asks Grace, clutching at my hand and gazing up at me imploringly. Charlotte tries to look more aloof, as if she doesn't care, but I can see that she's every bit as keen to be invited back. Acting cool doesn't fool me; I've done too much of that myself to fall for it from other people.

'Of course you can,' I say. 'Next time you visit we can take her for a walk, if you like.'

Eddy's already at the side gate. 'Stop bothering poor Kate, girls,' he calls. 'Off we go.'

They run out of the gate, waving, and I have to catch Minnie by the collar to stop her from following.

'Sorry, Mins,' I say. 'You've got to stay here with me.'

She whines as the gate closes, and I feel like

64

whining too. I'd rather be off with Eddy and his children, chaotic and complicated as it all sounds, than here alone with another day to fill. I wonder how different things would have been if Matt and I had had children. We weren't torn apart by the pressures of a young family. No, we didn't have that excuse. We can't blame the failure of our marriage on anyone but ourselves.

8

When I left every means of communication on the kitchen table in London, it had felt like a dramatic statement of intent. Screw you, Matt Martell, you have no way of contacting me ever again. But, like most dramatic statements, one short week later it feels like lunacy. Of course it has kept Matt away from me, but it has also kept me away from everything else. It's not like I was expecting the emails to have built up or anything, or as if I had important business to attend to — let's be honest, the most urgent emails I receive these days are ones about the Ocado delivery — but I hadn't remembered that I'd need to check my bank account, if only to watch the money drain out of it, and pay bills and generally remember that I am actually a grown-up and not the Lyme Regis teenager I once was.

I left Minnie at home this morning while I trawled the streets of Lyme to see if I could find an internet cafe. Yes, I know, the internet cafe has gone the way of AOL and Yahoo Answers, but this is Lyme Regis and I lived in hope that there might be a fossilized millennial internet cafe somewhere around, even if it was just in the Senior Citizens' Centre. Mum offered me the use of one of the work computers, but when I realized she meant I'd have to come into the office I decided I'd rather take my chances elsewhere. Somewhere I might get a bit of privacy.

It seems there's no shortage of cafes offering WiFi, but everyone expects you to have your own laptop these days. Even here. I finally admit defeat in a chintzy tea house, and order a cup of tea to mollify the sullen teenaged waitress who has so grudgingly answered my questions. There isn't a single other customer in here, so it's hard to see from what urgent tasks I could have distracted her.

I've taken a seat by the window, even though it's steamed up so much I can hardly see outside. I pull my coat sleeve over my hand and use it to rub a little porthole on the glass, just enough to give me a view of the street. I've no sooner taken my hand away than two narrowed eyes appear, squinting in. There's a sharp knock on the window and then the eyes are gone.

Seconds later the door of the cafe swings open and Mrs Curtis appears, waving brightly.

'Yoo hoo,' she calls, approaching me determinedly. 'I said let's have tea, and here you are! What a *coincidence*.'

I stand up and pull out a chair for her, but she brusquely pulls it aside and settles herself in, fussing with a flotilla of plastic bags that must be arranged just so on the floor. She throws her coat off with the exuberant gesture of someone disrobing in front of an admirer, but keeps her pink knitted hat on.

'Left my wig at home,' she whispers.

She points to the pot on the table.

'Now then. What kind of tea are you having?'

'Earl Grey,' I say, stunned into monosyllables by this unexpected whirlwind of activity.

She grimaces. 'Can't stand the stuff. Emily! Emily!'

The teenage waitress ambles over, drawing her order pad out of a pocket in her apron. Although Mrs Curtis clearly knows her, Emily's red-cheeked face doesn't offer a flicker of recognition.

'Hello, Emily. One pot of Darjeeling please, dear. Three bags — not two, three. A jug of full-fat milk, none of that nasty skimmed. And I think a piece of the Victoria sponge, don't you? Wait, there's a fly in this sugar bowl, so let's have a new one, please.'

The waitress writes this down unhurriedly, and tucks the pad back into her pocket, before picking up the sugar bowl with a heavy sigh.

'Chop chop, Emily!' trills Mrs Curtis, drumming her red nails on the tabletop. 'I haven't got all day.'

As Emily leaves, casting dark looks behind her, Mrs Curtis leans towards me and confides, 'Of course I *do* have all day, don't I? But Emily's mother tells me she is a *terrible* dawdler, so I like to come in here every now and again and give her a bit of a *push*.'

The mutinous set of Emily's shoulders tells me she'd like to give Mrs Curtis a push right off the top of a cliff, but she does seem to have picked up speed, so perhaps there's a method in the old lady's madness.

'Now, Kate,' says Mrs Curtis, patting at her bags to check they haven't rearranged themselves while she wasn't looking. 'Why do I have the feeling you've been *avoiding* me? Hmm?'

'Oh! I haven't,' I say. 'That is, I'm sorry if it

68

seems like that. I just haven't felt very sociable since I moved in. I didn't mean it to seem rude, Mrs Curtis.'

I should have known that, in a small town like Lyme, hiding away only serves to draw attention to yourself. But if I had run all over the place telling everyone my problems I'd only have been criticized for making a song and dance of it. I can't win.

Mrs Curtis ducks down for a moment to pick up her handbag, and takes out a plastic packet of tissues, which she places on the table between us. 'I suppose this is because of *that man?*'

She nods pointedly at the tissues, as if even the mention of my husband will make me start wailing.

'I suppose,' I say weakly.

'Needless to say I've heard all about it, dear. People are *terrible* gossips, you know. But why should you be hiding yourself away when it was that man that caused all the problems?'

I remove a tissue from the plastic packaging, to Mrs Curtis's evident satisfaction. She pats the packet approvingly, as if it is a pet. I don't actually feel like I will cry, it's just something to do with my hands.

'It wasn't just him,' I say, picking at the tissue.

'Of course, I know it is very *modern*, dear, to say that both partners are to blame. Not like in the old days when there had to be a guilty party or you couldn't get a divorce. But I *do* think,' she leans forward with her elbows on the table, 'that when someone has been *unfaithful,* then it very much *is* their fault and there is simply no point

69

in pretending otherwise.'

The tea arrives and Mrs Curtis busies herself with sending back a cup, claiming to see traces of lipstick on it, and then trying to force me to eat half of her Victoria sponge. It gives me an excuse to change the subject and I manage to sustain a fairly lengthy conversation about how tea should be made, whether tea leaves are better than bags, and whether milk should be poured in before the tea or after. Mrs Curtis, I am unsurprised to learn, has strong opinions on all of these matters, and does not hesitate to share them.

But it doesn't take long before she turns her shrewd eyes on me again. 'I expect you think I'm dreadfully nosy, don't you? Asking about your husband. Believe me, I don't want to *upset* you. But it is one of the few benefits of being old — ageing is so full of *indignities* otherwise, dear — that you are suddenly allowed to say whatever you like. Everyone already expects you to be batty, you see.'

She waves a forkful of cake in my direction and I shake my head to decline it. Behind her Emily folds napkins, one at a time, placing them into a wicker basket with deeply felt resentment.

'I used to be much more polite, I can assure you. But where's the fun in that, dear? Anyway, I can see that you don't want to talk about it, and that is quite all right with me. God forbid I should be one of those *encroaching* women who can't take a hint.'

'Not at all,' I demur. I pick up my teacup, and put it down again when I see it's empty. It clatters loudly in the empty tea room. 'It's all just

70

. . . it's very raw. I'm not — '

'Quite understood!' She leans forward again, waving a red-painted finger commandingly. 'There will come a time when you do want to talk about it, dear. All the time, to anyone who will listen. Believe you me, I *know*.'

Before I can follow this intriguing line of enquiry, she looks up at the clock on the wall behind me and gasps. 'Goodness, will you look at the *time*, dear! I have bridge at four!'

She summons poor Emily over to the table to instruct her on how to package up the leftover tea leaves into a parcel that Mrs Curtis can take home to put on her roses. The plastic bags are mustered, the coat buttoned and offers of help with either are brusquely rebuffed. She is gone before I realize that she has left without paying.

Emily looks happy for the first time, a tight-lipped little smile spreading across her face as she watches the door swing shut.

'Thought you must be new in town,' she says. 'Her always does that. Famous for it. Never seen her pay for her tea once. She'll have followed you down the street.'

She presents me with a round silver dish containing the bill, the only time so far that I have seen her move with anything approaching speed.

'Service ain't included.'

I leave Emily a large tip for no other reason than she is the first person I've spoken to in Lyme who seems to have no interest in, or knowledge of, my private life. If only I could pay off everyone else so easily.

9

London

The Hitz Christmas party had been cut back that year, for reasons unspecified. It was as if they thought we wouldn't notice that we'd been relegated to a wind-battered marquee in London Fields instead of the ballroom of the Dorchester, as usual. Or that, rather than a sit-down meal, we'd be happy with a spread of sandwiches and sausage rolls, much as if we were attending a provincial wedding rather than a party held by a multinational corporation.

Some said it was because Leila had been cautioned for possession when leaving last year's do, and it had made the papers, which reflected badly on the company as a whole. But everyone knew that was rubbish as the scandal just made Hitz sound like a rock and roll sort of place, which in our line of work was a good thing. Also the publicity had brought Leila a lot more business, so she was delighted. Some said it was because our former head of marketing had woken up with a black eye and a missing tooth after last year's party, and had to attend a meeting the next day looking like a tramp. But he'd left now, so that couldn't be it.

I thought it was more likely that our head of finance had wielded the anti-fun scissors; no one had got a bonus this year, and it hadn't escaped

72

my notice that they'd failed to replace the last two people to leave the production team.

But there was one Hitz Christmas party tradition that would not die, no matter what cutbacks were forced on us. For the last three years, Sarah and I had pulled a stunt at the Hitz Christmas party. In truth I wondered if we'd ever top last year, when we'd stripped down to leotards and broken into the full 'Single Ladies' routine. But that had taken weeks of rehearsals. With Lagos having got in the way this year we just hadn't had the time to practice.

'But Sarah,' I said, pulling down the hem of my dress, which kept clinging to my tights in a way that spelled trouble for later that night, when I was bound to be less sober and therefore less attentive. 'We could get *hurt*. Can't we just take a year off or something?'

She stopped in the entrance to the marquee, grabbing my shoulders with both hands, her eyes glittering with determination. This year's cunning stunt had been her idea, which made her especially passionate about it.

'Kate, the cunning stunt must continue. Don't you see — they can take away our party, but they can't take away what makes it great: you and me. Everyone is relying on us. We're like . . . Father Christmas or something. We owe it to everyone.'

I must have looked dubious, because she shook me, 'Do you really want to deny everyone the full Christmas party experience? Do you?'

'I'm not denying anyone anything,' I began.

'That's what Chris said after Lagos,' Sarah sniggered, letting go of me.

'*What* did Chris say after Lagos?' I demanded.

'Oh, nothing,' she said airily, her back turned to me as she walked into the marquee.

'Whatever,' I said, trying to sound breezy.

To be honest I barely remembered what had happened after I'd downed a row of whiskys at the Airtel party. I'd found myself sneaking out of Chris's hotel room at stupid o'clock the next morning, staggered to my flight, and had tried very hard not to think of it ever since. I firmly believe that a bit of brazen denial is the best way to deal with such things. Who wants to sit around talking about the stuff you're ashamed of? Best to pretend it never happened and hope everyone else does too.

Sarah stopped in the entrance and took in the room. Smiling waiters greeted us with trays of champagne and dubious-looking bright blue cocktails. It was a given that at least half of the waiting staff were aspiring musicians and presenters who would try to thrust a demo CD into your hand, or turn the evening into an audition if the opportunity presented itself. It was important not to let yourself get into a conversation with any of them, or you'd never escape. Sarah and I, Christmas party veterans, took a glass each without making eye contact with the server.

Tables were laid out around an enormous dance floor where a few brave, or prematurely drunk, colleagues were already trying out their moves. Most people were, like us, just taking in the atmosphere, admiring each other's party outfits and initiating flirtations they hoped might

74

end in the chill-out tent later, aka snogging central. Over at a table in a dark corner of the marquee, Leila had already set up her dispensary; every few minutes a colleague would approach her and conduct a furtive transaction before disappearing off to the bathrooms.

Towering above all of us, beyond the DJ decks, past the buffet tables, stood a vast and imposing Christmas tree, its topmost branches brushing the canvas roof.

Sarah's eyes lifted to the top of the tree, where a white-winged decorative angel looked down over the dance floor. 'Look,' she said. 'I'm just saying that you and me, we've got reputations to uphold here. Bad ones.'

'Okay,' I agreed grudgingly. Over in a far corner, a familiar sight caught my eye.

'Oh crap, the cameramen are all here,' I muttered to Sarah. They stood in a huddled mass at the bar, in their best T-shirts and trainers. Jay had broken ranks to wear a festive jumper with a snowflake theme, and it was clear from the howls of laughter around him that his friends weren't about to let him forget it.

'Really?' Sarah asked, opening her eyes enormously and suspiciously wide. 'I wonder who let them in?'

I turned to glare at her. 'Sarah, no one ever looks that innocent without being very very guilty. This is your doing, isn't it?'

'Not exactly,' she lied, beaming over at Jay. He looked relieved to see someone who might save him from his piss-taking mates. 'But I might have mentioned that the party was on tonight.

And that they're not very strict on the door.'

'I thought you said you'd stopped seeing Jay after Lagos?'

'I have,' she said, not meeting my eyes. 'Except on special occasions. Parties.'

'Weekends?'

'And, er, week nights,' she admitted with a sheepish smile.

'God, I don't believe it. And you've kept it to yourself all this time?'

'I don't know what you're so annoyed about, just because you and Chris never turned into anything doesn't mean that Jay and I can't give it a shot.'

'Ooh, so it's Jay and I now, is it?'

'You can take the piss all you like, Kate,' said Sarah, giving Jay a flirtatious wave across the room. 'I really like him and you're not going to put me off him just because you're always running away from relationships.'

'Running away? Hardly. You would too if your only option was Chris, and you know it.'

Sarah shrugged. 'Fair enough. I've never known what you see in him; I've hardly ever heard him say more than five words in a row.'

I snorted with laughter. 'I don't even know if I have, to tell the truth.'

I looked over to where Chris was studiously ignoring me in a manner designed to draw attention to himself.

'Then aim higher, okay?' said Sarah. 'You deserve better than that. You deserve a proper relationship with someone who really likes you. It's about time you found someone nice.'

I started laughing. 'Jeez, Sarah is this like when you wouldn't get a tattoo unless I promised to get one done at the same time? Do I have to have a relationship just because you've got one?'

'You said you wanted a tattoo as well!' Sarah protested, punching my arm crossly. 'And fuck off, will you? I just want you to be happy.'

'I am happy, you lunatic. I'll be even happier when I beat you at the cunning stunt tonight, though.'

'You reckon?' said Sarah, looking at me challengingly. 'We'll see. I'm off to see Jay. Coming?'

I considered it, but once you got talking to the cameramen it was hard to get away, and it was best not to get trapped with them this early. Not when there were so many other people to talk to first. I needed to get a few words in with our boss Richard, who found this kind of work function — where he wasn't fully in charge — stressful. And my assistant Kirsty was still new enough to need introductions to people. I'd reached an age where the annual shindig was not just about getting hammered and getting off with someone. Times were tough at Hitz, and I knew I had to focus on the work part of the work party.

As Sarah joined the cameramen, disappearing amongst the checked shirts, I saw Chris look over at me and then quickly look away again, busily checking his phone as if he had lots to attend to. He didn't even offer a smile.

There was a time I'd assumed a deep soul lay behind his taciturn ways, but I seemed to remember I'd ended up snogging him in Lagos mostly because when he started talking he was so immensely dull.

Well. If I was Chris's last resort, then he was mine. Surely I could have much more fun tonight without revisiting my lazy cameraman? And I still had my mission to consider. This was going to require tactics. I squeezed my way past a crowd of people just coming into the marquee, and started weaving between the tables so I could scope out the room. It was too early for many people to be sitting down yet, though by the end of the evening it was a safe bet that the tables would be full of slumped Hitz staffers, snogging couples and glassy-eyed drunkards.

A movement caught my eye by the Christmas tree. Almost hidden by the branches, a barrel-shaped man stood, his back to the outside wall of the marquee. The muscles in his massive neck bunched and flexed as he chewed gum while surveying the dance floor from his half-hidden position. The tell-tale curly wire of a radio headset disappeared into the collar of his white shirt, suggesting hidden reinforcements close at hand. A security guard. This was a complication.

'What are you up to?' said a voice close to my ear. I turned around quickly and there was Matt Martell, looking far too gorgeous in a dark navy suit that made his eyes distractingly blue.

'Hello, Matt,' I said frostily. 'What makes you think I'm up to anything?'

'A little bird tells me you're pretty entertaining at the Hitz Christmas party. You and your friend

Sarah. I couldn't help notice you checking out the security arrangements over there. Are you sizing up some sort of misbehaviour?'

'You'll just have to wait and see,' I said, raising an eyebrow and hoping I looked mysterious and inscrutable. Although there was no hope of remaining mysterious and inscrutable once I was on the mission. Demented would be closer to the mark.

He smiled back with that confiding little head tilt of his. How did he manage to make every exchange feel like we were the only two people in the room? I could feel myself falling for it all over again. I felt like giving my own face a sharp slap. Or Matt's. Get a grip, Kate, I thought. Don't let your guard down.

'So it's funny we haven't seen each other at all since Lagos,' Matt said. 'I've been looking out for you.'

'Have you? Well, Hitz is a big place, Matt, and I'm a busy person.'

'It's not that big,' said Matt. 'And no one's that busy. I get the feeling you've been avoiding me, Basher Bailey.'

'I don't know why you'd think that,' I said hastily. Because of course that is exactly what I had been doing ever since we got back. I'd sent Sarah to meetings when I knew he'd be there. I'd avoided the third floor entirely. I'd even gone so far as to take the stairs instead of the lift for a full month to ensure I wouldn't bump into him, with the added and unexpected bonus of some impressive thigh-toning action.

'Oh, I don't know,' said Matt. 'I suppose for

you it's normal to flirt with a guy and let him think he's going to kiss you, and then when he turns his back for one minute you disappear off with another man?'

'That is not at *all* what happened, Matt Martell,' I snapped.

'Really?' he asked, his expression no longer amused. 'Because I went to get you a drink and the next thing I saw was you sitting on the lap of some cameraman downing shots. And it didn't look like you went home alone either.'

I felt my mouth opening and closing in rage, unable to spit out the words. I don't mind calling myself a party girl — I'm not about to deny it — but for Matt to use it against me like this, when he . . . when he . . .

'How dare you question my morals, when *you're* the one who had a girlfriend all along!'

'When I had what?'

'Oh did you think I didn't know about Ailsa Logan?' I demanded. 'Well, I did, Matt. As soon as Chris and Danny told me about her I knew exactly what sort of man you were. It may surprise you to know that I'm not the sort of girl who messes around with a man in a relationship. I *do* have morals, no matter what you might think.'

Matt raised a hand to the back of his neck, lifting his chin as if regarding the roof of the marquee. He let out a long, whooshing sigh.

'Ah, Ailsa,' he said. 'So that was it.'

'Yes,' I said triumphantly. That told *you*, Matt Martell.

'And if I told you that I'd split up with Ailsa

before I even started at Hitz?' he asked, lowering his eyes to meet mine.

'Well,' I said. 'That's not what the others said.'

Matt laughed, nodding towards the cameramen who stood, as ever, in a unified mass by the bar. 'Those guys? Kate, I don't even know them. Why do you think they'd know what's going on in my private life?'

'So you're saying they were lying?' I challenged him.

He sighed again, 'I'm saying they just didn't know. Ailsa and I kept it pretty quiet that we'd split up — she didn't want any bad publicity when she was about to renegotiate her *Rise & Shine* contract.'

'If that's the case, Matt,' I said, feeling like a detective in a murder mystery, whipping out a crucial piece of evidence at the eleventh hour, 'perhaps you could explain why you were seen with her at the British Television Awards just days before you came out to Lagos.'

Matt whistled through his teeth. 'You're thorough, aren't you, Basher Bailey? I like that about you. You don't let things go. If you must know, I agreed to go to a few events with Ailsa after we split up, just to stop people asking her questions. It was all pretty amicable between us, so it was no big deal. Do you reckon you can stop interrogating me now?'

'I wasn't interrogating you,' I said in a small voice. My bubble of self-righteous fury was deflating rapidly. Of course this could easily be another smooth Martell line; I wasn't about to trust him entirely. But I had to admit his

81

explanations did have the ring of plausibility.

Matt pulled a phone out of his suit pocket. 'Do you want to call Ailsa?' he asked, scrolling through the list of names on the lit-up screen and holding it towards me. 'Ask her yourself?'

'No!' I exclaimed, pushing the phone away.

He laughed and put it back in his pocket. 'Then maybe let your guard down just a touch?'

He nudged me with his elbow. I pushed back.

'I'm glad to hear you're a girl with morals,' he said, his lips twitching with amusement. 'I'd hate to think I might have tried to kiss a girl without them.'

'Oh shut up,' I started, but before I could say anything more there was a sudden commotion behind me.

A surge of Hitz staffers ran across the dance floor in the direction of the Christmas tree, which was swaying dangerously, as if a high wind had burst through the marquee. I could hear shouting and shrieks. Above the heads of the newly formed crowd, red-manicured hands grasped at the branches. Sarah was making her bid for glory — before the party was an hour old.

Matt started laughing. 'Oh God,' he said. 'Is this your mission? To climb the Christmas tree?'

'I didn't think she'd try it so early,' I gasped. The tree bowed down towards the dance floor and the crowd ebbed back, out of the way of its wildly swinging branches. The shaking suddenly doubled: Sarah had been joined on the tree by the security guard. I saw him grab her hands and try to pry them off. Decorations began crashing to the ground.

'Fucking hell,' said Matt. 'What was she *think-ing?*'

'It's a dare, Matt,' I said defensively.

'I know that, but the security guard. She needed a distraction first. She didn't think it through.'

'I suppose *you'd* have planned it a lot better?'

'Of course I would,' he grinned, leaning down to whisper in my ear. 'We would. That's why you're going to win this one.'

By now Sarah had been wrestled to the ground, where she struggled with the security guard, who was bellowing into his headset. The cameramen ran to her rescue, although Jay was restrained by Danny, who pulled him away. After a few minutes of confusion, Sarah was dragged up, both arms pinned to her sides by the security guard.

'Okay, Kate,' Matt hissed, 'this is your moment. I've got your back.' He took hold of my hand and led me round the back of the crowd that was still gathered around the commotion. No one saw us pass; all eyes were still on Sarah, who was loudly protesting her innocence and claiming to have slipped and simply fallen on the tree by accident.

I barely had time to notice how strange it was to be holding hands with a man whose presence, until that evening, I'd been actively avoiding. Matt was right; this was my best chance at getting to the top of the tree without anyone seeing. The security guard was marching Sarah towards the door, his face grimly set. Richard stepped in front of him to intervene on her behalf, trying to calm the situation.

The tree was upright again, invitingly unattended.

I snuck around behind it. Trying to climb up the front of the tree had surely been Sarah's first mistake. From underneath the tree looked enormous. It *was* enormous. What had I been thinking? But I had a reputation to uphold. Also, Matt Martell was watching. I had a sneaking suspicion he wasn't so much watching my back as watching my backside as I grasped the highest branches I could reach and hauled myself up. I hadn't considered that I'd be scaling a tree when I'd chosen such a short dress for the evening. The tree lurched from side to side and I glanced at Matt in panic — he gave me a thumbs up.

'No one's looking,' he hissed.

Why hadn't I ever considered before the extremely agonizing spikiness of a Christmas tree? The vicious needles pincushioned my hands and the tree wobbled precariously as I scrabbled for a pain-free hold. As my hands flailed amidst the branches I grabbed onto a steel wire that secured the tree to the floor, but my hands slipped and the wire burned a hot line across my palm like a festive Chinese burn. Ow! I clamped my legs around the tree trunk and felt the needles dig into my thighs. This was harder than it looked. At last I managed to get one of my feet onto the lower branches and push myself up — much easier than trying to drag myself by my arms. From there it took only minutes — teeth clenched to ignore the pain — before I got within reach of the top.

Sarah had decreed that just climbing the tree didn't count. The winner had to retrieve the white and silver angel that was attached to the topmost branch or the climb was invalid.

I looked down to where Matt stood, half-hidden behind the tree. He wasn't looking up, though. His attention was caught by something happening on the dance floor. So much for looking out for me, I thought. I should've known I couldn't rely on him.

I reached up to where the angel sat, balanced on the highest branch. She was tantalizingly close. I stretched my fingers and grabbed onto the hem of her dress. I pulled. She stayed firm. I pulled harder. She didn't budge. Was she superglued on there or what?

The tree lurched again, bowing down towards the crowd. I looked down and saw that no one was looking at Sarah now. All eyes were on me. Fuck.

'Get it, Bailey!' shouted a voice. Then other people joined in. 'G'wan, Kate, get the angel!'

Emboldened by their cheers, I took another reckless lurch towards the top. The dance floor seemed to swim before my eyes as the tree rocked from side to side. I could just see a blur of faces; it was impossible to distinguish any one in particular, apart from Matt, standing to the side. He was looking up now.

'Come on, Basher,' he shouted. 'Show us what you're made of.'

With a final push I grasped the angel around the waist and yanked her fiercely upwards. She flew off the top of the tree, and I swung back horribly. Only the fact that I had my legs wrapped around the tree trunk saved me. The crowd cheered. Once I realized I wasn't about to dash my brains out on the dance floor I felt a surge of elation. Victory was mine! I held the angel above my head in triumph.

The crowd went wild. At least, the security guard did. I hadn't spotted him breaking away from Sarah and Richard and storming to the bottom of the tree.

'Get down from there, you silly bitch,' he shouted, shaking the tree violently.

'Oi, careful.' Matt moved towards him, grabbing his collar. 'You're going to make her fall.'

'She should've thought of that before she climbed the tree, shouldn't she?' snapped the guard. I wanted to climb down, but he was shaking the tree like a bear and I was afraid to let go of my hold on the trunk in case I fell.

'Mate,' began Matt, trying to pull the guard away from the tree.

'Don't 'mate' me, you middle-class wanker,' the guard exploded. Even from my vantage point at the top of the tree I could see that his face was purpling with anger. The guard abruptly let go of the tree and wheeled around towards Matt. Matt looked up to check I was okay, which meant he didn't see the guard pull back his right fist.

'Matt!' I shouted, but it was too late. The security guard, enraged at the appalling behaviour of the Hitz staff, had taken it out on the head of marketing with an impressive haymaker.

Matt staggered backwards, clutching at his jaw. I scrambled down the tree, ripping my tights to pieces on the branches. By the time I reached the bottom I looked like a Goth who'd been pulled through a shredder.

The security guard was surrounded. Firstly by the cameramen, who'd formed a barrier around him, and then by a crowd of agog Hitz personnel. He kept trying to barge his way out, charging at weak points in the circle of watchers, like a goaded bull.

'You bastard!' Sarah shrieked at him from the fringes of the crowd, where Jay was holding her back. I started to feel a bit sorry for the guard. He probably thought he was in for a quiet night watching people get festively merry, not this carnage.

Matt had collapsed into a chair, still nursing his jaw. I pushed my way through the people who'd gathered around him.

'Matt, are you okay? I'm so sorry. It was all my fault.'

He winced, but his eyes crinkled into a half smile. His teeth stayed clenched as he hissed, 'Did you get the angel?'

I held it up, still clasped in my hand like an Oscar statuette. 'Course,' I said proudly.

'That's my girl,' he grimaced.

'I'm not your girl,' I said.

'You will be,' he said.

10

London

'Take off your tights.'

'What?'

'I said, take off your tights,' repeated Matt, his face hard to read in the darkness of the back of the taxi.

I may have made a mistake in telling Matt Martell that I liked how he took charge of a situation. It had felt impressive when he grabbed my hand and whisked me out of the emergency exit while the rest of the Hitz staffers were distracted by the police bursting through the front door of the marquee. A slight overreaction on the part of the security guards, but it would brilliantly bolster Hitz's rock-and-roll reputation.

My heels sank into the grass outside, but Matt didn't let up his pace until we were safely out of the park and standing on the main road.

'But . . . my bag, my coat!' I wailed, rubbing my arms in the cold.

Matt took off his jacket and draped it around my shoulders. 'Don't worry about it, Basher. Can't you get Sarah to pick them up for you?'

'What are we doing out here?'

Matt pointed to the angel, still clutched in my hand as if I was holding the Olympic torch.

'Do you really want to have to explain yourself?'

'I would have dropped it before the police saw,' I said.

'And lose your trophy?' Matt asked teasingly. 'I couldn't let that happen. Hang on.' He stretched out his arm and a taxi appeared out of nowhere and pulled up alongside the pavement.

I looked at Matt in awe. Getting a taxi in the middle of the Christmas party season was practically impossible. I wondered if he had some kind of magical aura that just made everything incredibly easy for him; he expected the world to arrange itself for his convenience and it did. No wonder he always seemed so confident and untroubled.

As the taxi hummed through the streets, Matt's face was briefly illuminated by flickering orange streetlights. He didn't seem to be joking about the tights.

'Er, I'm not taking off my tights,' I said, nervously.

'Calm down, Basher. I'm not threatening your virtue — I'm perfectly safe in taxis, you know.'

'Then — '

'Take a look at yourself,' he said, pointing to my legs, which his jacket didn't nearly cover.

Of course my tights were ripped to ribbons, but I hadn't fully appreciated until now that they also bristled with pine needles, poking out as if I had a serious problem with fierce green leg hair.

'But I'll be cold,' I objected.

'Are you seriously telling me those are keeping you warm? There's more hole than tights.'

I wriggled on the seat uncomfortably, which I regretted the moment a pine needle pierced the skin of my left thigh. I let out an undignified shriek.

'Take. Them. Off.'

'Well, you have to look the other way,' I said, conceding defeat. Now I'd noticed the pine needles I couldn't unnotice them; the adrenaline of our escape was wearing off and for the first time I was aware of just how uncomfortable I was in my pine-needle leggings.

Matt laughed and turned his head to look out of the taxi window. 'My eyes are averted, Miss Bailey. Your honour is safe.'

I'm sure that somewhere in the depths of the internet there must lurk tights fetishists, people who find the sight of a gusset and reinforced waistband erotic, but it seemed unlikely that Matt Martell would be among their number. It wouldn't have been so mortifying if I'd been wearing stockings — at least peeling off a single stocking has vaguely sexy connotations — but stockings make me feel insecure, constantly threatening to slip down to your ankles at the worst possible moment.

I've always felt that wearing stomach-taming tights is better than sporting those gigantic Bridget Jones holding-in pants. At least you can wear some vaguely attractive underwear beneath a pair of tights, and it's usually easy to whip them off in the bathroom or somewhere out of sight if you think you're about to get lucky. Trying to wrestle them off in the back of a cab, however, while a man you hardly know is almost certainly watching in the reflection on the window, is an entirely different matter.

I slid my hands up either side of my skirt and hooked my fingers into the waistband. A firm grasp was what was needed here. I hoped I'd be able to slip them off in one seamless movement, but they don't call them control tights for nothing. These babies weren't going to give up easily; they clung to my hips like a welded-on chastity belt.

'Need some help?' Matt asked, his face still politely averted. But I could see his shoulders shaking and I had no doubt he was fully aware of my difficulties.

'Don't look!' The fear that Matt might turn round and see the roll of stomach that was about to be released from the waistband gave me added strength, and in sheer desperation I lifted my hips off the seat and hauled the reinforced gusset down to my ankles. I kicked off my shoes and rolled the tights into a ball. Not sure where to put them, I slid them into Matt's jacket pocket.

'So are you cold now?' asked Matt, turning back.

'No,' I said, pulling his jacket tighter around me.

'I am,' he said.

I felt, with a shock, his marble-cold fingers sliding along the seat and onto my bare thigh. I watched his hand progress from the outside of my leg to the top of my knee. My hair fell over my face to cover my eyes; I wasn't sure I'd be able to look directly at him without blushing furiously. He pushed his hand gently between my thighs and I found myself primly clamping my knees together to stop his progress.

I could feel Matt's breath by my ear. He

whispered, 'I'm getting a pretty good idea of how you managed to stay on that tree, Basher. Impressive thigh action.'

I crossed my legs, trapping him further.

'Like that, is it?' he asked.

He suddenly pulled his hand towards him, but as it was still trapped between my legs, I was swung across the seat. Before I realized what was happening, he was lying on top of me so I couldn't move, his body heavy on mine.

I lifted my eyes to see him looking at me in barely disguised amusement.

'I thought you said you were safe in taxis,' I muttered, trying not to laugh.

'That's before you trapped me between your thighs, Basher Bailey,' said Matt. 'A man has to defend himself. Though there are worse places to be, I'll admit.'

He flexed his fingers, brushing the edge of my knickers, and I started to giggle at the ridiculousness of it all, our legs intertwined on the seat, his hand squashed, pine needles scattered all over the floor of the taxi.

'Bet you're warming up, though,' I said, squeezing my legs together even harder.

'Oh definitely,' he answered. He lifted his free hand to cup the back of my head and pulled me towards him, his eyes deep and dark.

His lips pressed onto mine for a moment and then he pulled back to look at me. I didn't expect confident Matt Martell to be so hesitant, so cautious. I thought he'd be the kind of man to crush me passionately, but he just held his face very close to mine and let a slow smile spread over his face, as if he couldn't quite believe what he'd just done. I could hear my own heart beating and wondered if he could hear it too.

The moment stretched out until I could stand it no longer. I grabbed his face with both hands and kissed him so hard our teeth clashed.

11

I know I'm late when I ring on the doorbell at Mum and Dad's; Mrs Curtis had spotted me leaving and insisted that I start the evening with a sherry at hers. 'Just a little sharpener, dear.' It felt unneighbourly to say no, even though I had to suppress a shudder as I forced down a sticky Harvey's Bristol Cream. I had thought sherry was a drink for lightweight old ladies, so I'd been surprised to discover, as Mrs Curtis lectured me about the benefits of cold-water swimming on the cardiovascular system, that one tiny glass had left me feeling decidedly tipsy.

Still, I'm only behind by half an hour or so. In London that's considered on time, but I should have known Prue would think differently. The front door has barely opened before she launches into her attack, voice lowered to a hiss so that it doesn't carry back into the house.

'I knew you would find a way to make this all about you!'

'Sorry — ' I say, not sure whether to explain myself.

'You always have to make an entrance, don't you? The great Kate can't just turn up when I ask her to. She has to leave us all sitting around waiting when we don't even have any *wine*.'

'Jeez, give me a break,' I say, handing over the carrier bag from the wine shop. 'I thought Mum and Dad would have some already. I didn't realize I was depriving you all.'

'They don't have the *right* wine,' Prue snaps. 'We were waiting for the *right* wine. To go with the canapés, actually.'

'Okay, I'm sorry, it was just — '

'Oh, spare me your excuses,' sneers Prue. 'God knows we've heard enough of them over the years. 'I can't help out with Granny Gilbert because I'm in Singapore for the Grand Prix'; 'I can't come to Mum and Dad's wedding anniversary because I'm in Ibiza'; 'I can't come to your birthday party because I'm hanging out with Beyoncé and Jay-Z in Los Angeles'.'

'Prue! That's not fair! That was work; I couldn't help being away. You know I'd rather not miss family things if I can help it.'

And frankly 'hanging out with Beyoncé and Jay-Z in LA' sounds far more exciting than the reality, which was discussing how many pounds of Beyonce's gigantic stage set can be permitted per square yard of hastily built stage, and rowing with the managers of Argentina's biggest tween boy band over child-labour laws in the state of California.

'Well, you haven't been working *lately*, have you? And it's not as if you came down to Lyme until you had no choice. You just don't have to make it so obvious that we're your last resort.'

I can see I could be stuck on the doorstep for a very long time if I try to defend myself. Prue's clearly taken my accidental lateness as a diss of enormous proportions, a statement about my lack of interest in her life, my failings as a sister and as a member of the Bailey family. I seem to be failing at quite a lot these days.

'Prue, I'm sorry,' I say. 'I'm really, really sorry. I know this evening's important to you. Are you going to let me in?'

'Okay,' she says, opening the door at last. 'Come in then. Everyone's waiting.'

My parents greet my arrival with an excitement that suggests a certain amount of desperation, springing up from their battered old sofa to hug me as if we haven't seen each other for weeks. Dad hisses into my hair that I had better have brought the wine. Even Mum ventures to ask if I came via the off-licence, and she thinks she's veering close to alcoholism if she has a second helping of sherry trifle at Christmas. Ben stands up from the armchair behind the fire and extends his hand towards me. I allow him to crush my fingers in greeting while I size him up.

He is not at all what I had expected from someone who Prue first met at a Young Entrepreneurs' South West conference. I suppose I had, snobbishly, imagined a mobile phone salesman type — all shiny suits and over-gelled hair. Instead Ben looks more like a refugee from a Young Farmers' meeting. He sports violently red trousers — to coordinate with his florid cheeks perhaps? Although that is unfair since sitting next to the fire could do that to anyone's face. His checked flannel shirt is open at the neck — intentionally, I assume — and by his stomach — unintentionally, surely? — exposing a small triangle of pale belly beneath his corduroy jacket. His thick hair grows in whorled curls flat on his head, like the hide of a young blond bullock, and his eyelashes are long and fair, which makes the bovine resemblance all the stronger. He's so thoroughly rustic that when he drags me into a bear hug I expect him to smell of hay. But instead he smells, strongly, of aftershave.

'Kate, hullo, very good to meet you,' he says, heartily slapping my back. 'I've heard an awful lot about you from Prue.'

I cannot imagine that she's said anything good, so I can do no more than laugh nervously.

'Wine. At last,' Prue announces tersely, depositing an opened bottle on the coffee table where five glasses wait expectantly. 'The canapés will be ready in five minutes, so if you need the loo then go now so you're ready for them.'

Dad grabs at the wine and pours out large glasses; I take mine gratefully. Ben lets out a loud 'Aaaaaah' after his first gulp and Dad looks at him murderously. Since Dad is not exactly a stickler for manners, and used to be famous for his ability to crush a beer can on his forehead, I wonder what Ben has done to ignite his wrath.

'Ben here has just been telling us all about his business plans for Baileys',' says Mum, her eyes swivelling nervously from Dad's face to Ben's. 'They're very, er, interesting. Aren't they, David?'

Dad mutters into his wine. 'Yes,' he says. 'They are very . . . interesting.' He takes a swig from his glass and slams it down on the table, staring challengingly at Ben.

'Lovely,' I say, trying to understand all that

remains unspoken here. I'm afraid to ask a question in case the entire room combusts. Only Ben seems immune to the atmosphere, smiling affably back at Dad in a way that suggests there is not an awful lot going on in that curly-haired head of his.

Prue bustles in from the kitchen, proffering a plate of wildly ambitious canapés.

'Mango, scallop and Thai basil skewer?' she offers, thrusting the plate at Ben. 'Mini timbale of oriental vegetables?'

Ben exclaims, 'Yum, yum,' like a little boy, as he accepts a mini timbale. He rubs his stomach appreciatively in anticipation and his face falls as he realizes his shirt is open. While he tries to button it up again with only one hand, the tiny timbale leaps out of his thick fingers, and lands, split in two, on the carpet. If only Minnie had been here he'd have got away with it. Her hoovering abilities beat any cleaner.

'Ben!' shrieks Prue, whisking the tray away from Mum, whose hand hovers in mid-air, halfway through reaching for a skewer.

'Gosh, sorry, Prue.' Ben's face goes even redder as he stands, frozen in shame.

'Please don't worry,' insists Mum, scooping up the canapé and flinging it into the fire. 'That rug's had everything you can imagine dropped on it over the years, a mini — what was it Prue, love? — a mini thingummy won't do it any harm.'

'It was a mini *timbale*, Mother,' says Prue. 'And I only made three each, so Ben you can only have two now.'

Dad raises his eyebrows at me, unseen by Prue. We are all a little terrified of my sister, and never more so than when she's playing the ungracious hostess.

'Mmm, scallop skewers, yum,' I say, reaching for one in the hope of mollifying Prue.

'Don't patronize me!' she hisses under her breath.

'I'm not — they look lovely,' I say, and it's true.

'Well, take one then,' she snaps. And I do. She puts the tray down on the wobbly wooden table by the side of Ben's armchair and stalks back to the kitchen.

'Wow!' I say. 'Prue never does anything by halves, does she? Did she dive for these scallops herself out in the bay, do you reckon?'

'Ah, no,' says Ben, with a look of polite condescension. 'Prue isn't a diver. She bought the scallops, actually. From the fishmonger down by the Cobb. But I'm sure they are just as fresh as if she had dived for them.'

'Right,' I say, not quite sure how to answer.

Ben grimaces at Mum, 'Awfully sorry about the carpet.'

'Really,' Mum insists, lowering her voice, 'it's not about the carpet; Prue's just a little stressed because she's spent all afternoon making sushi and I don't think it's gone awfully well.'

'She made her own sushi?' I ask. I'm astounded. Even at my most derangedly domestic goddessy, I have never attempted sushi.

Dad harrumphs; he's still looking at Ben with misgivings. 'I never knew rice could stick to a person like that,' he mutters.

'Oh dear,' I say. I have to bite my lip to stop myself smirking. I notice Mum can't meet my eye either.

I don't want you to get the impression that Prue is some kind of monster. She isn't at all, although I realize I've painted her as one so far. Maybe it makes me feel better to make her sound worse than she is. I mean, all she's trying to do is make a meal for her family and her boyfriend. It's not a crime. She just seems to get no enjoyment out of it, so it's hard for anyone else to enjoy it either. Sometimes it feels like we're separated by more than just eight years — sometimes it feels like we're doomed to be for ever distinct and separate; parallel — never meeting, like the layers of rock out on the cliffs.

'So, Ben,' I venture when the atmosphere has thickened to the point where I could scoop it up with a spoon and use it to top a mini timbale, 'you've been talking to Mum and Dad about your business ideas?'

Dad's face darkens.

Ben, on the other hand, beams delightedly, as if he's been waiting for just this question. His ruddy cheeks crimson further. 'Well, Kate, we were just discussing that when you came in. I've been looking for some time now for expansion, development and growth opportunities in the South West region.'

It sounds like he's reading from a press release.

'Oh right,' I say. I don't really understand when people talk about 'business' like that. It's like when someone says they work in 'systems' or 'analysis'. To be honest, when I hear any of these expressions, to me it's like someone telling me they're a fundamentalist Christian. I'll do my best to listen to what they say, but I've already pretty much switched off.

'Yuh,' says Ben, resting his elbows on the arms of the chair so that he seems to be sitting in state, like a Pope. I suppose commerce is the new religion, but he doesn't look especially Papal with his stomach still hanging out.

'Just been talking to your parents about developing some new revenue streams for Baileys',' he continues. 'Shaking things up a bit, you know?' He taps his fingers on the chair, contentedly beating a little rhythm.

It all sounds fairly boring to me; I can't understand why his uninspiring corporate speak has Mum and Dad seething on the sofa next to me. I can virtually feel their anger.

'Yah,' Ben says. 'What I'm aiming to do is turn the business around from a well-established but essentially moribund concern into something pretty exciting. Everyone thinks all the action is happening in London, but they couldn't be more wrong.'

Dad rolls his eyes and Mum smiles tightly by his side. I nod encouragingly at Ben, who ploughs on regardless of the fact that two thirds of his audience appear to hate his guts. And all three of us can *see* his gut.

'Yuh, consider Copella apple juice — old family business, stuck in the doldrums until it was given a proper kick up the arse by someone

101

who knew what they were doing. Now look at them — millionaires! Yeo Valley, too. The South West's full of chances for someone who's got vision.'

'Like you,' says Dad. The sarcasm in his voice is unmistakable. But not to Ben.

'Absolutely, Mr Bailey — or can I call you Dad?'

Dad is too surprised to say anything.

'That's why I'm coming to work with you, Dad. And Mum. To help you out. To inject a bit of fire into the business.'

'I'm not sure I feel quite comfortable with that, Ben,' says Mum. I don't know if she means she objects to him calling her Mum or to him injecting fire into their sleepy family business. I think either is a possibility.

'No, really,' Ben barrels on, beaming heartily. 'I insist. We're family. Practically. Right, Dad?'

By now Dad's beard is bristling, as if he's an animal readying itself for a fight. I can see he's about to blow, so I launch into another question to stop him having the chance to speak.

'So, Ben, you've already started working for Baileys?' I ask. I'd thought it was more something that was under discussion than an actual reality.

'Yup,' says Ben slapping his hands down on his thighs. 'All official. We were just hammering out the details when you arrived.'

'Now you listen to me,' Dad starts. But before he can really get going, Prue appears at the door that divides the kitchen from the living room.

'Everyone having fun?' she says, her smile so

102

brittle it looks like it might fall off and shatter on the floor. 'Dinner is served.'

Here is a piece of advice for you. Don't try sushi at home. And especially don't try it on your parents, however gamely adventurous they may be. Cold fish, glutinous rice and wads of slithery seaweed do not make for a comforting, relaxed family meal. Especially when Dad keeps asking, 'Is it *supposed* to be like this?' And if everyone's a little too afraid of the food to dig in with gusto, it stands to reason that they'll dig into something else instead. Namely the alcohol. I'd imagined the four bottles I'd brought were more of a gesture — we'd drink one, and the other three would probably be set aside for another time. But we are already halfway down the fourth bottle before Prue accepts defeat and clears the half-eaten leftovers from the kitchen table. She tops up my glass before she leaves — is it my imagination or have she and Ben made sure I drink more than anyone else tonight? Oh well, I'm not driving, so I don't suppose it really matters.

At least we've all been too busy comparing chopstick techniques and attempting to convey Prue's California rolls from mouth to plate without incident (again, Minnie's help here would have been most welcome) to engage in much more discussion about Ben coming to work with Mum and Dad.

Prue reappears from the kitchen with a tray of ramekins filled with a burned green sludge that she declares to be green tea crème brûlée. I hear Dad groan as he reaches for the wine again.

'Shh, David,' Mum whispers. 'I'll make you a sandwich later.'

'Before I pass round dessert,' says Prue, reaching out for Ben's hand. 'We have some news we'd like to share with you.' She nods at Ben, as if giving him a cue.

He stands up alongside Prue and clasps her close to his side; she gazes up at him with a kind of surrender that I've never seen on her face before. As if, for once, she is prepared to let him speak for both of them. But only, I think meanly, because she has probably already written the script.

'Mum, Dad, Kate,' he says, nodding to each of us in turn. 'I'm very, very happy to let you know that Prue and I are getting married.'

'No!' exclaims Dad in a strangled voice. He manages to recover himself quickly. 'No! What a wonderful surprise!'

'Oh Prue, love,' says Mum, her eyes filling with tears. 'My baby, getting married. I can't believe it.'

'You're not pregnant, are you?' asks Dad, his eyes narrowing.

'Dad!' exclaims Prue, scandalized. I'm not even sure if she has ever even shared a bed with Ben, although surely she must have done. They've been on holiday together, I know that much. But she's the most puritanical twenty-something I've ever encountered, and that includes the evangelical Christian ones at the Jesus Rocks! event in Colorado in 2002.

'Just joking!' Dad insists, though the relief on his face suggests this is not strictly true.

'Prue, that's amazing news, congratulations,' I say. I'm horrified to feel a tear sliding down my face as I hug her; it must be all the wine I've drunk. I manage to wipe my cheek surreptitiously on Ben's jacket as I hug him too. This is not the time for me to lose it. It's Prue's moment.

The disaster of Prue's dinner is forgotten in the triumph of her news. 'We haven't got a ring yet,' she says, her face shining with excitement. 'Ben's granny wants me to have hers but it's too big for my finger, so we're having it resized. It's a family heirloom.'

Ben looks down at his future wife admiringly. 'Worth a pretty penny, I can tell you. Prue's going to have to take very good care of it.'

'I will,' she says with mock annoyance. 'And because Ben's giving me something important and valuable connected to his family, it's very important to me that he joins Baileys' and works in the business with all of us.'

I'm sure she doesn't mean it to sound like a corporate merger — expensive family heirloom in exchange for stake in successful family business — but her announcement does sound a little like something one might read in the business section of the paper rather than the giddy gushing of a future bride.

'And', she continues, 'we've decided that we should use the wedding as an opportunity to show people that Baileys' can expand beyond just holiday cottages and tourist events — we should be looking at moving into other areas: weddings, parties, fêtes, that sort of thing. We can use the wedding as a showcase for our contacts and expertise. And of course we can get discounts from all of the suppliers if we promise to use them again for future events.'

'Gosh, you've given this a lot of thought already,' says Mum, looking somewhat stunned.

'Of course,' says Ben affably. 'Whatever my Prue wants, she gets. We think a wedding in the New Year should give us enough time to set it all up how we want it.'

'But that's only three months away!' says Dad.

'Plenty of time,' Prue dismisses Dad with an airy wave of her hand. 'The sooner the better, and it's not like we have that many events in the winter anyway. Don't you see — we can turn the business into a year-round concern, so we're not just dependent on the tourist season and visitor numbers?'

'I like having the quiet winter season,' says Mum gently.

'You can still have that, Mum,' says Ben. 'Of course you can. As you head towards retirement it's only natural that you'll want to play less of a role in the business. You too, Dad. Prue and I understand that. It's the natural order of things for you to step down and make way for the energy of a new generation.'

Dad moves as if he's going to stand up and I see Mum pull at the edge of his frayed jumper to stop him.

'We've thought of everything,' says Prue.

'You certainly seem to have done that,' Dad agrees bitterly.

'But Ben,' I say, spotting a small flaw in their

106

business plan. 'You can't be planning to stay at the Alexandra until the wedding, can you? Surely you can't commute from Bristol every day? Are you going to move in here?'

'No!' both Dad and Prue exclaim simultaneously.

She shoots Dad a warning look before answering. 'Of course not! You know I don't believe in living together before marriage.'

'Oh,' I say. I did know it, of course, but I thought it was less of a moral position and more a sign that she hadn't met someone she wanted to live with.

'I mean, Kate,' says Prue, frowning. 'It didn't work out so well for you, did it?'

'Prue, love,' admonishes Mum, 'that's unkind.'

'Not wrong, though,' I agree sadly. 'I suppose living together before marriage isn't a guarantee of anything really.'

'Exactly,' says Prue. 'Which is why Ben is going to move in with you instead.'

'With me?'

'That's right, sis!' grins Ben, as if bestowing his presence on me is a gift that he is certain will delight me. 'Prue said you've been lonely all on your own in the bungalow, and I need somewhere to stay while I whip Baileys' into shape. So it all makes sense!'

'Just wait a minute,' I say, holding out my hands as if I can ward Ben off physically. 'Wait one minute, you two. You can't railroad everyone into doing what you want just because it suits you. Why should I share my house with Ben? Why can't he move in here?'

'It's not your house though, is it?' snaps Prue. 'Granny Gilbert left it to both of us. And there isn't a spare room here, and there is at Granny Gilbert's. You mustn't be selfish, Kate. Try to think of what other people need.'

'Mum!' I plead, turning to my parents as if I'm a teenager again. My head swims with alcohol and I can't form my thoughts into coherent enough sentences to argue back. 'You can't agree with this.' They both stare at me, mute in the face of the force that is my sister.

Ben reaches over to nudge my arm chummily. 'Come on, sis, it'll be fun. Bit of bonding with the in-laws and all that. I promise I'm house-trained.'

'Ben, I'm sure you're a delightful housemate — ' I begin.

'Then it's all settled,' he beams.

'No, look, wait, we need to discuss this,' I protest.

'What's to discuss?' asks Prue. 'You said you were lonely — I thought I was doing you a favour.'

'You led me into that conversation!'

'Kate, Kate,' says Prue, shaking her head sorrowfully. 'We all know you've had a hard time lately, but don't let it turn you bitter. Everyone says you're spending too much time on your own. Mum and Dad are worried about you — don't you see? Ben and I are trying to help you.'

It's typical of Prue to present her best interests in a manner that makes it seem as though she is being the generous one. But to suggest that I am being selfish in my desire for a bit of privacy and peace in which to mourn the end of my marriage is too much. Not to mention that if Ben is living at the bungalow, Prue will be there all the time too. It's the worst of all possible worlds.

'Wait,' I say, an inspired thought finally fighting its way into my fuddled brain. 'Wait, I've had a better idea. 'Why don't *you* both live in the bungalow together and let *me* move into Mum and Dad's? Wouldn't that be a better plan? It's only a matter of weeks, really — surely even you can relax your principles for a few weeks, Prue?'

She smiles a tight little smile. 'Relax my principles? I might have known you'd suggest such a thing. You can't just switch your principles on and off like a tap when it suits you, Kate. Principles are something you have to stick to, no matter what. They're non-negotiable. You don't just drop them when they get in the way of what you want. It's like marriage — you take it seriously or you don't do it at all.'

She does, at least, have the grace to look momentarily sorry for what she's said.

'I took my marriage seriously,' I say quietly. 'I took it very seriously, Prue.'

'That's enough, Prue,' says Dad. 'There's no need to go dragging your sister's problems into this.'

'The way I see it,' says Ben, barrelling heartily into the conversation, as if we are all happily chatting instead of seething with anger, 'is that we will both be solving each other's problems. Right, sis? Right, roomie? I think we're going to have a lot of fun together.'

'So that's settled then,' says Prue.

12

Ibiza

The island was a different place this year. I'd always stayed right in the centre of San Antonio, sharing an apartment with Sarah, since we were on the same schedule and that meant we wouldn't end up waking each other up by coming in at different times. It wasn't as if we spent much time there anyway, just dropping down for a few hours' sleep in between running the Hitz Does Ibiza events and getting as much dancing in as possible as soon as our responsibilities were over. I'd seen too many of my colleagues go fully feral to countenance caning it during the working day — Sarah had lucked into her job after her predecessor had disappeared on a 24-hour bender some years ago — but at night pretty much anything went as long as you were able to get up in the morning. And no matter what, I did get up in the morning. As late as possible.

Matt had a totally different attitude to the island, though, insisting his team was put up in a villa outside of town, with verandahs, olive groves and a pool. I still had my San Antonio apartment, but I'd ended up spending every night at Matt's villa so far, and since the rest of his department seemed to be out all the time, it was almost like having the place to ourselves.

'Basher,' he whispered in my ear.

I rolled over onto his side of the bed. 'Mmm,' I said, keeping my eyes closed as I rested my head next to his. He slid his arm around me and pulled me closer.

'Get up.'

'What's the time?' I asked, opening one eye a crack. Matt had told me, in that annoyingly grown-up way he had of managing to know something about absolutely everything, that the Ibizan architecture is mostly white in order to reflect the heat of the sun, but jeepers it's a cruel, cruel thing to be exposed to that much stark brightness first thing in the morning. Even the inside of our villa was nothing but harshly reflective surfaces. It was like waking up under a spotlight in the dentist's.

'Six,' said Matt.

'Six! Ugh, what are you waking me up at six for, you mentallist? I didn't get in until two.' I pulled the covers over my head. The only time I'm interested in 6 a.m. is when I haven't been to bed yet. Otherwise I really don't want to know that such a time even exists.

'I know,' said Matt. 'You woke me up to bang on about some hassle with a presenter.'

'Sorry,' I mumbled into the covers, mortified. My memories of last night were a little hazy. I'd ended up in the bar with Sarah, Kirsty and the crew until far too late, ranting about the diva demands of a *Hollyoaks* actress with Hollywood pretensions. I thought I'd got it out of my system before I came home to Matt. Clearly not.

'Come on,' Matt insisted, tickling my ribs. 'I've got something to show you.'

I pulled the covers down from my face and squinted at Matt, who looked hideously fresh and awake, tanned against the white sheets.

'Matt, if what you want to show me is your cock, I don't want to see it until eight at the very earliest. Or feel it. Understood?'

'Believe it or not,' said Matt, grinning, 'it's not all about shagging.'

I snorted in disbelief. Since Matt and I got together at the Christmas party, it had been pretty much all about the shagging. I had been given a gold loyalty card at my local waxing salon, so frequent were my visits there of late. We barely went out, we didn't do coupley things, we weren't hand-holding at the cinema or whispering sweet nothings over dinner. We were just having sex. Lots of it.

'I mean it, Kate,' insisted Matt, yanking at the covers. 'Irresistible though you are in the mornings, that's not what this is about.'

I scowled. I'm not good at surprises, unless I'm the one in charge of them. 'What is it about then?'

'Get dressed and meet me out front in ten minutes,' he said.

I sighed heavily. 'I've got Sarah picking me up at ten,' I warned him.

'We'll be back in time,' Matt promised. 'Trust me.'

And strangely I did trust him.

So, despite it being 6 a.m., and despite my lack of interest in doing anything other than sleeping, I dragged myself out of bed and pulled on a denim skirt and a vest top. I scraped my hair up off my face, and covered my wincing eyes with sunglasses.

Outside, Matt sat on a scooter, revving the engine.

'Do you know how to drive that thing?' I asked nervously. Suddenly my outfit, which had seemed perfect for the warm morning, felt like insanity. As if I was offering up my bare arms and legs to be cheese-gratered by the Spanish tarmac.

'Nope.' Matt grinned. 'But how hard can it be? Put this on.'

He handed over a helmet. I took it reluctantly.

'Come on,' he said. 'I promise I'll be careful. I won't let you get hurt.'

'Oh, that's what all the boys say,' I teased, trying for a light-hearted tone to banish my fears. Matt patted the seat behind him and I told myself to get a grip.

Back home in London, if someone had said to me, 'Why don't you get on the back of a motor-bike with someone who's never ridden one before?' I'd have said no without even thinking about it. But Matt's boyish enthusiasm was contagious, and the morning was beautiful; bright and clear and still cool enough to raise slight goose-bumps on my arms. Fuck it, I thought.

I shouldn't have worried. God knows where Matt had borrowed the scooter from — for work we were all ferried around in expensive air-conditioned cars that were loaned to us by the sponsors — but it soon became clear we were in no danger of being done for speeding. The engine strained and spluttered as Matt urged the bike up the hill away from the villa, and by the time we'd got to the end of the long stony drive that led to the main road, I'd relaxed enough to stop gripping his waist like a terrified baby monkey.

Instead of turning right towards San Antonio town, Matt steered away towards Santa Inés, or so the sign said. It's weird, because I've been to Ibiza more times than I can count, but it's so much a place I come to for work that I'd never given any thought to exploring the island. I know there's meant to be this amazing hidden Ibiza outside the superclubs and foam parties and sunburned package trippers, but if I was going to go on holiday, there's no way I'd come back here to find it. I liked to get in, do my job, get wasted and get out. I could have been in Blackpool or Bognor for all the attention I paid to my surroundings.

As we chugged along at a comically slow speed I saw the island opening up before my eyes. Unable to speak to Matt over the sound of the popping engine, I let my mind wander along with my gaze. Stray goats chewed on desiccated branches by the side of the road, unconcerned at our passing. I saw one ruminatively working away on a plastic bag. I wondered who lived in the isolated houses up in the hills — not the glamorous gated villas for holiday visitors, but the whitewashed old ones with the washing pegged outside and a rusting water tank nearby. It seemed so remote and far away from everything that mattered. I had the former country girl's horror of life away from an urban centre.

My thoughts unfurled as the scenery spread out in front of me, the hypnotic buzz of the scooter drowning out any anxieties, and I'd entirely lost track of time when we started to descend again, down towards the startlingly turquoise sea of a small bay. The water was so clear I could see the rocks and corals beneath, and the skeins of seaweed rocking gently back and forth with the tide. Two small fishing boats were moored at buoys in the bay; paint peeled on their wooden hulls, and nets hung over their sides, drying in the sun. When Matt pulled the scooter up alongside a weather-beaten old hut, a table of fishermen looked up from their breakfasts and nodded acknowledgement.

'This is it,' he beamed, as proud as if he had created this picture postcard scene all by himself. 'What do you think?'

'It's amazing,' I sighed, drinking it all in.

The rocky shore rose up sharply all around us, so that we were hidden away from the rest of the island, protected in this tiny inlet. It was hard to imagine the high-rises of San Antonio were only a few miles down the coast. From here all that was visible beyond the stony embrace of the inlet was the sea, stretching out uninterrupted to the horizon, as if it went on forever.

Matt leaned over and dropped a kiss on the tip of my nose. 'You know, you even look cute in a bike helmet.'

'Oh shut up,' I laughed, taking it off as quickly as possible. No one looks cute in a bike helmet, and I knew it.

Matt grabbed my hand and led me over to the

only other table outside the hut, a rusting metal one with alarmingly rickety legs. Squinting inside the hut, dark and dim in contrast to the bright outside, I could see two more tables and a rough bar, at which a few more fishermen stood, their yellow waterproof trousers hanging over chairs behind them while they drank. Their work was already done for the day and their relaxation was contagious. I could almost forget I had a full day of work ahead of me; it felt like I'd left it far behind. I stretched my arms up over my head, yawning loudly in the sunshine.

'Bored already?' asked Matt, a slow smile spreading over his face as he watched me visibly unwind.

'Yeah, massively,' I said, smiling back. 'I can't believe you'd bring me somewhere so hideous. Look at this place. I mean, they don't even have a DJ.'

He laughed. 'I knew you'd love it. The food's pretty much fish or fish, by the way, with a side order of fish. But they do a ferocious coffee.'

'Sounds good,' I said. And though I normally ate little more for breakfast than half a piece of toast on my way to the bus stop, I could feel my stomach growling in anticipation as the smell of frying fish wafted over to us from the kitchen.

The patron stepped outside, wiping his beefy hands on the front of a stained apron. His darkly tanned face was wrinkled by the sun and wind, and he squinted at us underneath impressively huge black eyebrows. He didn't bother with anything like menus, just lumbered over to stand by our table, raising one heavy brow expectantly.

'*Si?*'

I smiled as winningly as possible, hoping a cheery demeanour would compensate for a complete lack of Spanish vocabulary. He merely raised the other eyebrow.

To my amazement, Matt suddenly began speaking in what sounded, to my uneducated ears, like perfect Spanish. He pointed over at the fishermen, indicated the two of us, and answered the patron's gruff questions with confidence. I stared at him open mouthed.

The patron's face broke into a vast smile, exposing a gold tooth that winked in the sun, like a shiny reward for Matt's unexpected fluency. He slapped Matt heartily on the back and burst into a torrent of words, of which I could understand not one. The fishermen over at the next table looked up, laughing, and one of them raised his glass to us.

'Since when did you speak Spanish?' I asked, as the patron retreated back inside, still chuckling.

'Impressed?'

'Of course I am,' I said. 'You're a man of hidden talents, Matt Martell.'

'I'm glad you're beginning to see it,' he said, leaning forwards. Our lips touched and the fishermen started whistling. We broke apart, grinning and holding hands under the table where they couldn't see.

'So what was your big drama last night?' asked Matt, tickling my palm with his thumb.

I squinted at him in the sunshine. 'I thought you said I told you all about it last night?'

'You did. I didn't say I listened, though.'

'Ugh, there was just a load of hassle with one of the presenters,' I said, pulling my hand away and leaning back in my chair. 'She had some eye problem — probably just one of her stupid false eyelashes got stuck in her eye, but she made a massive song and dance about it. Refused to go on stage without eye drops, but she didn't have any. And of course we couldn't give her any.'

'Why not?' asked Matt.

I stared at him. Sometimes I wondered if Matt and I worked at an entirely different company — he never seemed to understand the compromises and underhand manoeuvres that were second nature to me.

'Health and safety?' I said. 'Do you know how much we could get sued for if she had an allergic reaction to the eye drops?'

'Pretty unlikely, though, isn't it?' Matt scoffed.

'Well, you say that, but it's not you who's had to do all the risk assessments. It's more than my — ' I stopped myself.

Matt started laughing, throwing his head back in the sunshine. 'More than your job's worth? Were you actually going to say that?'

'Shut up,' I said, pretending to sulk. 'You don't understand.'

'Oh I try very hard to understand you, Basher Bailey,' he said. 'So tell me what happened next.'

'Well,' I explained. 'I sent one of the interns out to the pharmacy and got her to buy every single kind of eye drops they had.'

Matt nodded.

'And then I put them all in her dressing room

118

when she went to the loo. And when she came back I just said, 'Aren't those some eye drops over there?' And she used them and everything was fine.'

Matt shook his head, 'What a load of fuss over nothing. I don't understand why you couldn't just give her the eye drops without all the subterfuge. I mean, it's Hitz does Ibiza, not passing on microfilm in Cold War Berlin.'

'It doesn't work like that, Matt,' I said testily. I was rather proud of how I'd solved the problem; I thought he'd be impressed with my quick thinking rather than dismissive.

'It can work like that if you want it to,' he said. 'I think you get off on the drama of it all.'

'Oh fuck off,' I scoffed. 'I do not!'

He never understood that you couldn't say no to the celebrities directly. It didn't work like that. You had to find a way of making them do what you needed, while letting them think it was their idea all along.

Before we could really get stuck into an argument, the patron arrived with an enormous platter of tiny battered fish, fried whole, accompanied by nothing more than half a lemon and two cloth napkins.

I made a gesture for a knife and fork and the patron roared with laughter, slapped me on the back, and walked off, as if I'd made a particularly hilarious joke.

After we'd eaten, I sat licking the last few lemony, salty traces from my fingers. We were alone outside the shack now. The fishermen had left a few minutes ago, coming over to shake our hands farewell now that we were all best friends, clambering back onto their boats and motoring out of the bay with shouts of goodbye.

I stared out at the sea, watching the waves roll up onto the rocky shore. The sound of the stones being pulled back by the retreating water was restful and calming. The hectic pace of Hitz Does Ibiza seemed to belong to another island altogether.

The patron, clearing our plates, called out to someone behind the bar, and a moment later two tiny glasses, full to the brim with a suspiciously cloudy green liquid, were placed in front of us.

'Oh gosh, no, I really don't think — ' I protested, still suffering from the beers last night.

'Come on, Kate.' Matt laughed. 'I thought you were the hardcore party girl? Don't show me up in front of my new mates.'

'But it's *breakfast*. And you're *driving*.'

Matt shrugged, picking up his glass. 'It's just one; live a little.'

The patron nudged my glass towards me with a finger that shared the dimensions of a fatly stuffed farmhouse sausage.

'Hierbas Ibicencas. I make it myself,' he said, proudly pointing to his chest.

Matt held out his glass to me and I picked up my own. We clinked them together in the sunshine and downed our drinks in one. I felt a burning aniseedy flame rush down my throat all the way into my stomach, where it spread out until I swore I could feel it down in my toes.

The patron watched us eagerly.

'*Gracias*,' I coughed in my best Spanish, feeling my cheeks redden with the sudden rush of alcohol. '*Gracias*, it was, er, *muy delicioso*.'

He beamed happily and rubbed his stomach, saying something I couldn't catch, but the gist of it was that my digestion would be grateful for this early-morning shot of booze. My digestion, churning from last night's excesses, begged to differ.

'I'm just going inside for a sec,' said Matt, standing up and pulling his wallet out of his shorts pocket. He was sweet like that, he'd always step in and pay for things without even mentioning it. I'd objected for a while, but he told me he liked doing it, so these days I just let him. I watched him disappear into the cool darkness of the bar.

The patron collected our glasses in the palm of his meaty hand. '*Una mas?*' he asked.

'Oh, no, *gracias*,' I said, shaking my head.

'Your boyfriend?' he asked, nodding his head towards the shack. 'One more for your boyfriend?'

I looked up at him, squinting through my sunglasses. 'No, *gracias*,' I said again. I pointed towards the scooter, parked next to the shack. I mimed steering the bike. 'He's driving. And, er, he's not my boyfriend.'

The patron frowned, his vast eyebrows beetling together over his nose. 'No boyfriend?'

'No,' I said, embarrassed. 'We're, um, *amigos?* Just friends.'

The patron's frown deepened, but I couldn't decide if it was from my denial or from a lack of understanding. I wasn't sure why I'd felt I had to

121

explain it to him in the first place, and I suspected neither of us had the vocabulary necessary to discuss the exact nature of what was going on between Matt and me. How do you say fuck buddy in Spanish anyway? He shrugged and stacked the plates on top of each other. As he walked away, Matt appeared behind him, having been hidden from view behind the patron's bulky frame.

'Ready to go?' I smiled, pushing my chair back away from the table. 'Sarah will be coming to get me in a bit, we need to head back.'

Matt looked furious.

'What did you just say to him?' he asked.

'Um, I said the drink was nice?' I said hesitantly, starting to get up. 'But only because I don't know the Spanish for 'tastes like paint stripper'.'

'No, sit down,' said Matt. 'You know that's not what I meant. What did you say to him about us?'

I laughed nervously. 'Us? Oh come on, Matt, what do you mean *us*?'

'You said — I heard you — you said that we're just friends. Is that really what you think? That we've been seeing each other since *Christmas*, that we spend pretty much every weekend together and we're just friends?'

'Why are you doing this, Matt?' I asked. 'We've had a really perfect morning, why are you spoiling it all?'

'I'm spoiling it, am I?' Matt said bitterly. 'Kate, I keep trying to talk to you about our relationship, and you just bat me away every time.'

'Relationship?' I scoffed. 'Matt, all we do is have sex with each other. That's not a relationship.'

Matt looked thunderous. His hands clenched into tight fists by his sides. 'Is that all this is to you? Kate, I have tried and tried to get you to talk about things, tried to introduce you to my friends, get you to meet my family, and you fight me all the way. Don't you want this to be more than just sex? Don't you want to be in a relationship? Or do you just not want to be in one with me?'

I shrugged, scowling at my feet. The tangerine-coloured polish was chipping on my big toe. Why did he have to mess things up? Weren't we fine as we were? I felt trapped, penned in. The steep rocks around us suddenly seemed forbidding and dark.

Matt unclenched his fists and stepped towards me. I could hear from the slight tremor in his voice how much he was trying not to lose his temper.

'Look, I know you say you don't do relationships, but I'm sorry to break it to you, you're in one. With me. However you choose to define it — friends with benefits, whatever — we are in a relationship. Grow up and deal with it.'

'I am perfectly grown-up, Matt Martell,' I snapped, standing up to look him in the face. 'How fucking dare you?'

'You're not,' he said. 'You're like a teenager, making sure you get your kicks and forgetting about how anyone else feels. How do you think it makes me feel to hear myself dismissed like that? To hear you tell a total stranger that we're just friends?'

I could feel myself starting to tremble. I can

deal with confrontation at work without even flinching. I'd even admit to quite enjoying it — especially when I win, and I usually do. But this was a different kind of confrontation — it was personal, cutting straight to the core of who I was. A very small part of me did feel sorry for Matt, could see that his feelings were hurt, but a larger part of me felt utterly enraged at his accusations.

'For fuck's sake, Matt, where has all this come from? You've been perfectly happy with things for months, and now you're being a total girl who wants to talk about feelings and all that bullshit.'

'It's not bullshit,' said Matt. 'And maybe you should try being more of a girl, and actually having some feelings for once, instead of just treating me like some fuck buddy that you can take or leave. Sometimes I wonder if you even actually like me.'

'I don't think you're just a fuck buddy,' I said, feeling tears spring up in my eyes. My voice wobbled. 'I do like you.'

'Well, you've got a weird way of showing it,' Matt snapped. Behind him I could see the patron looking over at us, clearly wondering how we'd gone from two happy, hand-holding customers to a pair of furious shouty nutters in a matter of minutes.

I burst into tears.

'No,' said Matt. 'That is not fair, Kate, not fair.'

'I ca-ha-han't help it,' I wailed.

Matt ran his hands through his hair, as if he was about to pull it out by the roots. Finally he stepped over towards me and put his arm around my shoulders.

'Basher,' he said, into my hair. I let myself lean against him.

'I'm sorry,' I sobbed. 'I know I've been keeping you at a distance. I'm sorry.'

'I just don't get it,' he said. 'I like you, you like me. Why do you keep pushing me away?'

'I don't know. I'm just no good at this,' I said. 'It freaks me out.'

'I have always thought you're a bit of a freak,' Matt agreed, a little too readily.

'No, *you're* a freak,' I said, feeling myself start to smile.

'No, you are.'

I could feel Matt's chest shaking with a chuckle. I used the back of my hand to wipe the tears away from my face.

'Kate,' said Matt, holding onto my shoulders and pulling me away from his chest so that I had to look up at him. 'Let's get this straight. I'm your boyfriend. Understood?'

I nodded, my lips pressed tightly together to stop my chin wobbling.

'Not your fuck buddy,' he said. 'Not a fling. Not just friends.'

'Yes,' I said.

'And you're my girlfriend?'

'Ye-es,' I agreed, and tried not to squirm.

Here in the early-morning sun, full of fish and drunk on sunshine and Hierbas Ibicencas and hope, it felt like a promise I could keep. To be in a relationship.

Like something I might actually be able to do.

13

When I walk into the kitchen, Ben guiltily puts a hand behind his back, but it's too late. There's no mistaking the crust of toast that disappears down Minnie's throat. She licks her chops contentedly and looks up at him in the hope there might be more.

'Ben!' I say, trying to keep the nagging edge out of my voice. It's hardly the first time I've asked him not to feed the dog. Not that I don't feed her the occasional toast crust myself, but Ben has a way of using her as a dustbin for anything he doesn't want to eat. And he's always conveniently elsewhere by the time Minnie's stomach revolts against, for example, the half tin of sweetcorn that made a particularly unpleasant reappearance on the patio yesterday.

'It's only a bit of bread,' he mutters, lowering his eyes to the surface of the table.

Even on a flimsy kitchen chair, Ben likes to sit with his knees incredibly far apart, as if they repel each other by magnetic force. This wouldn't concern me if it weren't for his usual morning attire of a T-shirt and threadbare pyjama bottoms, so faded that they're like the ghost of a pair that has long since died. The material has become so thin that it is as if he is performing a dance of the seven veils each morning, threatening to reveal that which should remain hidden. He doesn't seem to notice, contentedly scratching at his crotch with as much self-awareness as an animal.

'I know it's only toast,' I say, sighing. 'But she's just a puppy. She has a bit of a delicate stomach; I've told you before.'

Ben can't disguise the small roll of his eyes.

'My mum's dogs can eat anything,' he says, planting his hands on his thighs and stretching his pyjama bottoms worryingly. 'That's farm dogs for you. Seriously. I remember this one time Patch ate an entire sheep's placenta. Down in one.'

I'm not ready to hear about a placenta-eating dog first thing in the morning. My stomach lurches.

'Not squeamish, are you?' asks Ben, seeing me clutch the kitchen counter for support. 'My mum says dogs pick things up from their owners. I mean, maybe you're projecting this delicate stomach onto your dog?'

It's far too early in the morning for this conversation. For any conversation, come to that. I'd grown used to mornings on my own — the only voices the ones on the radio that I could switch off.

'Yup,' says Ben. 'I mean, not to piss you off or anything, but Minnie's eaten my toast crusts every morning since I got here. No harm done.'

'Okay,' I say, weakly. I can't be bothered to have an argument. I have come to Lyme to get away from arguments. That was the whole point.

'I mean, Patch — the one that ate the placenta — there was one time when Mum caught him eating rat poison.' Ben beams, as if I might be

127

vastly impressed by his dog's cast-iron stomach. 'And not a whimper out of him. So I reckon your dog can cope with a bit of *bread*.'

'I suppose so,' I say. Pick your battles, isn't that what I learned living with Matt? 'But please be careful, she's only little. She's probably not at the cast-iron-stomach placenta-eating stage quite yet.'

'Whatever you say, boss,' says Ben, making a mock salute. He stands up and dumps his dirty plate and mug in the sink, where they join a stack of others. He wipes his face on the tea towel and leaves the kitchen, belching loudly. Two seconds later he peers round the kitchen door.

'Can I borrow that magazine?' he asks, pointing to an old copy of *Grazia* that's sitting in the recycling bin.

'Sure,' I shrug, surprised. I wouldn't have pegged Ben for a *Grazia* reader. He grabs it gratefully and is off down the corridor.

'Wait!' I call, as I realize what this sudden acquisition of inappropriate reading material means. 'Wait — I was just about to have a shower.'

But it's too late. The bathroom door is slammed shut. And I know that Ben won't be emerging in a hurry.

I never knew one man could take up so much space in a bungalow.

I mean, it's not like it's the first time I've ever confronted a pair of tired old pants hanging off the bathroom radiator, or a sports sock balled up behind a cushion on the sofa. I've lived with

Matt for long enough to be no stranger to male domestic blindness, or to the belief that laundry left on the floor will somehow migrate under its own steam towards the washing machine and magically reappear in the wardrobe, cleaned and ironed. But it would be true to say that sharing the marital home in North London with the man you've sworn to love and honour (though not obey) till death do you part, is not at all the same as sharing your dead granny's bungalow with your sister's future husband. I'm not saying that clearing up after Matt was an act of love — more like an act of tolerance — but at least it felt like something I'd gone into knowingly, for better or worse. Not like living with a man who is not only effectively a total stranger, but one who seems to be oblivious to any kind of hint or suggestion relating to the domestic sphere.

It didn't surprise me when Ben reluctantly confessed that, apart from a house share at university, he has, like Prue, always lived at home. Though he presented it as a carefully planned business strategy in order to save up a deposit for him and Prue to buy their own home, to me it seems more like a strategy for having his mum do all his dirty work for him.

Minnie is still sniffing for crumbs under the kitchen table, where Ben has left a jam-smeared knife sticking out of the butter. There's a splash of coffee on Granny Gilbert's oilcloth table-topper. Every instinct I have tells me to get a cloth and clear this up, but I resist.

'No,' I say, out loud, as if warning myself. Minnie looks up at me, half guilty, prepared to cower in case I'm speaking to her.

'Not you, Mins,' I say, pulling at her silky ear to reassure her.

No, I am not clearing this up. If I have learned anything from the failure of my marriage, it is that I should have been tougher with Matt from the very beginning. It starts with thinking that tidying up after him is just a little thing. That you don't really mind doing it, and anyway, it's quicker if you just get on with it yourself rather than make an issue of it. Anything for an easy life, you think, naïvely unaware that you are making your future much more difficult. And before you know it, those little moments of annoyance that you hardly even noticed at first, between all the sex and the laughing and the finding each other so generally delightful, become days and weeks of simmering resentment. Then one day your husband asks why he doesn't have any clean socks and you realize you have a very clear vision in your head of exactly how you are going to kill him.

So I leave Ben's dirty dishes where they are, as I have done for five days now.

I would like nothing better than to snap on a pair of rubber gloves and tackle the disgusting mess the kitchen has become. But I know I must resist if I am not to carry on cleaning up after him as long as we are forced to share this living space. I just hadn't realized that Ben's tolerance for filth would be so much greater than my own. There are fat flies circling the lampshade, and squeezed-out teabags rest in teaspoons on the work surface, which is liberally sprinkled with sugar crystals. The offending bag of sugar sits next to the kettle, the handle of a soup spoon poking out. For some reason this annoys me more than anything — who uses a soup spoon to put sugar in their tea?

I am not proud to admit that I have hidden a couple of clean mugs in my bedroom just to ensure that I don't have to resort to fishing through the mouldering pile in the sink whenever I want a cup of tea, furtively washing them up in the empty bathroom sink so as to remain undetected by Ben.

I know what you're thinking: that I am taking out on Ben my frustrations with my husband. But that's not it at all. The two men couldn't be more different. Although, come to think of it, if someone had taught Matt a few lessons before we moved in together things might have been very different. And if I were starting again with Matt, I'd be very different too.

There is a clanking sound from the hallway and Minnie's ears spring up. She barrels out of the kitchen, barking furiously, and I can hear the skittering of her claws on the parquet floor as she races to the front door. When I go into the hall to see what has caught her attention, it's just some post. A leaflet from the Co-op and something from the Royal Mail about delivery services. I'm about to put it straight into the recycling bin when a square of card falls onto the floor.

Minnie lunges for it, but I get there before her. It's a postcard from London. It's a postcard from Matt.

You won't answer my emails. You won't call me back. If I wrote a letter I don't think you'd open it. Will you read a postcard? Kate, please. You can't just cut me off like this.

I hate him for fooling me. For realizing I wouldn't be able to stop myself reading, even when I've made it so clear that I don't want to hear from him. I hate even more that there is a terrible part of me that leapt in gladness to see his handwriting — before I remembered. What does he think is left to say? Does he really think we can talk our way out of this? Sit in some marriage guidance counsellor's office and talk about our feelings? As if that would make a difference.

I stare at the postcard for so long, not moving, that when Ben comes out of the bathroom he asks if something terrible has happened. I say of course not, don't be silly, and tuck the postcard in with the leaflets to hide it.

I don't say that the terrible thing happened already, and nothing written on a postcard can undo it.

14

I have put the postcard in the recycling and taken it out three times. I know I am doomed to do this forever — well, until the recycling truck carries it away — unless I get a grip on myself, and so I put the postcard in my pocket and resolve to throw it away somewhere far from the house. Somewhere public, where I won't be tempted to fish it out again for fear of witnesses.

But here I am in the Town Mill Bakery, having walked past bin after bin, and the postcard is still in my hands. Like the note on the kitchen table, I can't stop myself from reading it again and again. Throwing it away is going to be an entirely academic exercise now that I can remember every word.

'Kate, hi, what are you up to?'

Eddy Curtis is holding a cup of takeaway coffee between both hands. He must have come in here and got served without my even noticing, so absorbed was I in Matt's card. Eddy pulls at the soft grey scarf wrapped twice around his neck. Although he's in jeans he looks business-like, as if he has to be somewhere important shortly and getting coffee is just the first step in a busy day rather than one of the highlights, as it is for me.

'Oh, hi, Eddy,' I say, tucking the postcard back into my coat pocket, out of sight. 'Nothing much, you know. Just, um, things. What are you up to? Not at work?'

I say this as if I have any idea what Eddy Curtis does for work these days. When I last knew him the only work he did was revision for his Geography A level.

'Heading there now,' he says, stooping to pat Minnie, who has greeted him like an old friend. 'But since the office is just my spare room I always like to get out of the house before I start work. Have to remind myself there's more than just the four walls pressing in on me.' He laughs.

I laugh, too, but I recognize the barely masked slight desperation of the person who spends too much time at home alone. I have felt it myself ever since I left Hitz; the feeling that the world is carrying on without you while you sit still in a room, slowly petrifying. The need to see people — even total strangers — just to remind yourself that you do exist.

'Tell me about it,' I say in sympathy. 'Why do you think I have breakfast here every day?'

'Every day?' he asks, and instantly I feel like I'm flaunting my flashy London ways again. The latte-swilling media bore, showing off in front of her home-town friend.

'Do you want to sit down?' I say, gesturing to the space in front of me. It's still early enough, and mid-week enough, to be quiet in the bakery.

Eddy looks at his watch, hesitant. Behind him the chefs are dragging trays of granola out of the industrial ovens, and peeling vegetables for this lunchtime's soup. Cathy is busy writing down a list of specials on a blackboard. I realize that I have adopted the reassuring rhythm of their workday as if it were my own, trying to fool myself that I am some kind of colleague, rather than a customer.

'Just for a minute, go on,' I press him. I am longing for a conversation with someone — anyone — who isn't Minnie or Ben or my mother.

'Okay,' he says, and slides onto the bench opposite me. 'Why not? What's the point in working for yourself if you can't start late sometimes?'

'So what do you get up to in your spare room then, Eddy Curtis?' I ask, and instantly feel myself begin to blush. 'Er, I didn't mean — that sounds . . . '

He splutters into his coffee and wipes his mouth with the back of his hand. 'Ha, well,' he says, reaching for a paper napkin from the stack on the table. 'Get your mind out of the gutter, Kate Bailey. I set up my own company a few years ago, helping local businesses use more renewable energy.'

'Wow,' I say. 'That sounds impressive.'

Eddy shrugs and looks embarrassed, rubbing the top of his head with his knuckles. 'It was more impressive when there were loads of grants for that kind of thing, but it's getting harder to bring the work in lately.' He continues, with a sigh, 'Most businesses round here are just hoping to make it through another year, people don't have a lot of money to invest in expensive new technology right now.'

'Sorry,' I say. 'That must be hard after you've spent all that time building it up.'

Eddy smiles and shrugs again, as if it's no big

deal. 'It's fine, I make enough to live on, and for the girls. Luckily I've never been someone who wanted a fancy big-shot career. Not like you.'

I snort with laughter. 'Hardly,' I say. Working in television is one of those jobs that impresses other people only because they know very little about it. Telling people you've just come back from running the African Music Awards suggests something exotic and glamorous, far removed from the Portaloo and fish-head curry reality.

'Come on, Kate,' says Eddy, his eyes crinkling as he grins. 'You were the one that got away, the golden girl, the TV superstar.'

'Eddy,' I say, sternly. 'Two months presenting late-night music videos at the tail-end of the Nineties does not make anyone a TV superstar.'

Eddy raises an eyebrow. 'It does compared to everyone else in Lyme,' he says.

I raise my coffee cup to my lips. 'I suppose; if you put it like that. But that was a very long time ago. I haven't been on telly for years. I haven't worked for a bit, actually.'

Eddy looks surprised. 'Really? I thought your mum said you were some sort of TV producer these days.'

'Um, not for a while,' I say, absently brushing away a scattering of crumbs from the surface of the table. I wonder if Eddy has spoken to Mum recently — has she been pretending that I still have a job? Has she been too embarrassed to tell people the truth?

'Get tired of the high life, did you?' he teases.

'Something like that,' I say.

'And now you're in Lyme again,' says Eddy. 'I

136

didn't think you'd ever come back.'

He looks at me for a little too long and I feel a chill run through me, as if someone has dropped a cold pebble down my back.

'Neither did I,' I say quietly, meeting his eyes.

Silence stretches between us. I can hear the tinny sounds of the bakery kitchen radio, tuned to some music station, and the low voices of the staff as they talk. A couple comes into the bakery, wrapped up in waterproofs, rucksacks on their backs, and Cathy goes over to greet them.

Eddy speaks first.

'You know Tim moved to Australia,' he says. 'And his parents emigrated out there too, a few years ago. None of them are here any more.'

'I know,' I say. And I do. Mum wrote and told me when it happened, casually dropping it into an email that was full of other snippets of Lyme news.

'Would it be better if I just pretended I'd forgotten about it?' he asks.

'No,' I say. 'I haven't.'

Eddy puts his hand awkwardly over mine, as if I might slap it away. But I don't, I let it rest there, heavy and warm.

'You left all of that behind a long time ago,' he says. 'Look at everything you achieved. You'd never have done any of it if you'd stayed in Lyme. You left and you really made something of yourself. You should be proud.'

'You're very sweet, Eddy.' Even though I mean what I'm saying, my voice comes out all flat and strange, as if I'm a robot who has been programmed to say it.

Eddy frowns. 'I should go,' he says. 'Sorry — I shouldn't have brought it up. It's just, I felt it shouldn't go unsaid. With you back here after all this time.'

He stands up, tugging again at the scarf around his neck. 'It's good to have you back, Kate. Whatever the reason. And if you need to talk, I'm always around.'

'In your spare room.'

'In my spare room. Or any time. I really mean it. You can count on me.'

I have very good reason to know this is true.

'Thanks, Eddy,' I say, and I really mean it.

15

The conversation with Eddy, so soon after the postcard from Matt, has made my head hurt. I pay my bill at the bakery and, to Minnie's delight, take her to the Undercliff for an extra walk to clear my mind. Although Ben will be at work by now, I'm not ready to go back to the bungalow. I think everyone in my family thinks I've come back to Lyme for something as self-helpishly cheesy as closure, or self-reflection. That's why they're tiptoeing around me, not asking what I'm going do to for money or work or what's going to happen between Matt and me. They're carefully respecting my space, as if I'm using this time to think through my options, to write lists of pros and cons. To work out what lessons I need to learn from the whole sorry experience of failing at being a wife.

The truth is, I have no idea why I'm here. I just ran away. Like I ran away from Lyme all those years ago. I hadn't even thought to connect the two until Eddy brought it all up again.

When I left Lyme I tried to close off my memories of the life I had here. Coming back, I'm a different person in every way. Not because I went off and got a television career, that's not it at all. I've changed, I must have. And yet Eddy's insistence that the past has been forgotten only serves to make me see that it hasn't at all. Not by the two of us, at any rate. And I should have

139

known that Lyme, clinging to its history as it always does, would have preserved it all, everything I've tried to bury, ready to expose it at any time.

Tim Cooper. I don't know if it's better that he's not here in Lyme any more or worse. Perhaps if I saw him again, as he is now, older and grown-up, it would erase the memory of him that I have in my head. But would I have come back if I knew he was here? Probably not. Even the idea of seeing him unexpectedly, impossible as it is, makes my heart beat faster — as if he will emerge from one of the Undercliff thickets, leaping out from behind a tree having tunnelled his way back from Sydney or Brisbane or wherever he lives now. Australia would suit him. The Tim I knew back then, anyway, all brawn and strength and surfing. Any excuse to whip his shirt off and show us his muscled chest. All the girls in Lyme were a bit in love with him, even the convent girls from St Mary's knew his name and called out to him from the bus stop where we all waited to be picked up for school. But he didn't wave back at them. Not even when they turned over the waistbands of their tartan skirts to show off their legs, giggling behind their hands. No, Tim waited at the bus stop with his arm around my shoulders.

Tim Cooper was a sex god. Everyone said so. When he walked down the hallways at school, the crowds parted for him like the sea in front of Moses. He hardly seemed to notice. He had this intriguing way of looking above it all; superior in a manner that didn't seem condescending, but

140

rather justified, as if he was just claiming his due. Like he was on a higher plane than the rest of us. He had a faraway look, as if his mind was on greater things. As if, while we mere mortals fretted over a spot on our chin, or a party we hadn't been invited to, he was considering the nature of time, or the infinity of space.

When he had turned his faraway look on me in the kitchen at Ally Baldwin's seventeenth birthday party, I had been struck dumb. 'I know you, blondie,' he said. 'I've seen you around.'

All of my usual smart retorts dried in my mouth with the shock of discovering that I had attracted the attention of this demi-god. I could hardly stammer out an answer. Which didn't matter much since Tim Cooper wasn't really interested in conversation. To my astonishment, what Tim Cooper was interested in was me.

It had taken me months to realize that Tim's faraway look did not hide a great and complex mind, devoted to deep thought. Months of furious snogging at the beach, and in the back of his car, and in whatever spare bedroom we could find at house parties, where we barely spoke to anyone else, just hid ourselves away to grab what little privacy is granted to a pair of hormonal teenagers. Months in which I'd lost my virginity without a backwards glance, glad to be rid of what I considered a shameful burden.

Being wanted by the most desirable boy in school was like being handed the keys to the kingdom. We were Kate and Tim, teenage celebrities. Your party was nothing until we'd made an appearance, glassy-eyed with lust as we stumbled down from your mum and dad's bedroom. If you were a girl, you wanted to sleep with my boyfriend. If you were a boy, you wanted to sleep with me — not because I'd suddenly become irresistible, but because going out with Tim had conferred on me the gift of his approval, and there was no higher accolade in the Lyme Bay area.

I walked taller, I dressed differently, I found that I'd adopted, without even meaning to, Tim's languid manner of movement. Because why would you ever rush anywhere when everything you wanted was coming to you?

It's impossible to know if I would have developed this kind of confidence without Tim, or if he was just the conduit for something that would have happened anyway. Years later I would read the famous Sophia Loren quote that sex appeal is 50 per cent what you've got and 50 per cent what other people think you've got. And I'd think that for me it was 50 per cent what Tim Cooper gave me.

And yet I haven't even spoken his name out loud for nearly fifteen years. Whenever Mum or Dad has tried I've changed the subject. I've always thought it's better to just move on, leave things behind, not dwell on them. What good does it do to rehash things over and over? It just makes people upset, brings up emotions that are better off buried. Last time it was easier though; I guess things are when you're younger. School was ending, everyone was moving on, it looked less like running away when I left Lyme for London.

No one questioned the fact that I left for university early — who wouldn't want to get to the big city as soon as possible? What eighteen-year-old wouldn't prefer to be in the middle of London than hanging out in Lyme for yet another tourist-filled summer working with their parents? When I wrote home, which was rarely in those days before everyone had an email address, I was sure to make my holiday job in a Covent Garden sandwich bar sound far more exciting than it was. I sent Prue a postcard especially to tell her about the time I'd made Liam Gallagher a bacon roll, brown sauce no butter, and he'd said it was 'sound'. I hoped the postman might read it and tell other people about my new big-city life.

By the time I started my university course in October, no one would have known I wasn't born within the sound of the Bow Bells. I'd dropped my provincial ways like I'd dropped my Dorset burr. Now I spoke the same chirpy Mockney as everyone else; I knew about cool bars in Brixton and went clubbing at Fabric. I used my Travelcard on night buses and tutted at tourists standing on the wrong side of the escalator. When people asked where I was from, I said Tufnell Park.

And as for the fact that I liked a party and wasn't too particular about the boys I took home, well, wasn't everyone the same in London? That was practically the definition of a student. It wasn't cause for gossip or disapproval. If anything it just consolidated my reputation at college. Who wanted to be one of those drippy wallflowers in the union bar, shyly sipping a single Bacardi Breezer and holding hands with your boyfriend, when you could be dancing on a table at the Bug Bar with a tequila in your hand? None of those shy girls got spotted by a TV talent scout; none of them got a screen test for Hitz Music Television, or became a VJ, and then turned that into a production career. Being a party girl worked out better for me than I'd ever dreamed. And even though by then I'd forgotten all about Lyme, even though none of it mattered any more, not at all, it felt like a massive two fingers to the lot of them.

It's harder to feel that sense of triumph this time; harder to disguise the running away. I'm not the triumphant winner, returning to show off the spoils of my exciting London life. It feels like everyone can see that I'm no better than they thought I was; that it was bound to all go wrong in the end. That the girl who had the great job and the husband and the big house was just play-acting; it was an illusion she couldn't maintain. And who is surprised that it's all come crashing down around her ears?

I hear barking in the undergrowth where Minnie is chasing rabbits; she whines with excitement, though she has never even come close to catching one. The Undercliff is a strange place — Prue won't walk here alone; she thinks it's too isolated, but I love it. I have done ever since I used to lead the Baileys' French Lieutenant's Woman tourist walk when I was in the sixth form, from the Cobb, up the hill into the Undercliff and back through the town to the museum where John Fowles's shabby old office chair, foam coming out of a rip in the seat, is preserved like a holy relic. The book was an A-level set text back then, so the groups of walkers swelled with students every summer, but it never felt like school work to me.

Inside the woodland, between the trees, time seems to slip away; with no visible buildings or roads or cars it could be centuries ago. Only the dim shadow of a tanker out at sea, interrupting the horizon, anchors me to the present. I read once that walking amongst trees was meant to calm you; psychiatrists recommend it to the depressed. Back in London I took Minnie for relentlessly long walks on the Heath, as if I was dosing myself up with medicine, downing the healing landscape one tree at a time. Maybe they were the wrong sorts of trees up there; either way it didn't seem to make much difference.

But here, in the quiet solitude, I feel as if I might believe it, as if the trees of the Undercliff are a benevolent presence, their mossy arms ready to embrace me, their unchanging stillness reminding me that everything passes in the end. These trees stood here before I was born, they were here when I was growing up, and they'll be here when I'm gone. I can allow myself to think about Tim and Matt without that feeling of dread and horror that threatens to overwhelm me most of the time. The mistakes that feel so enormous to me become somehow smaller here.

Though this stability is an illusion, too, of course. In reality the Undercliff is one of the least stable parts of the Dorset coastline. It owes its rugged wildness to the fact that nothing can be built on it for fear of landslips. Only a few years ago a huge chunk of the Black Ven, further down the coast, collapsed onto the beach below. The last landslip at this spot was back in Victorian times — an enormous piece of the cliff slid out to sea, the seemingly solid land buckling and sliding away. Farmland was destroyed, fields fell into the sea, and yet parts of the cliff stayed just as they were. Beyond the chasm, crops continued to ripen on fragments of land that were now isolated out in the water, like living fossils. Everything that seemed permanent disappeared without warning.

I suppose, though, that however it seemed, the landslip didn't happen in a moment. As shocking as it must have been, underneath the surface things must have been changing for some time. Little cracks and fissures opening wider, hidden tensions in the bedrock. After the landslip people knew what to look out for — the odd way a patch of grass seemed to have sunk, a bubbling spring where there hadn't been one before, the fence posts that had fallen for no reason. There were warning signs if only you knew what to look for. And now I do.

Minnie bounds back to me, her tongue lolling out of her mouth, eyes wild as if she hopes I'll share in her excitement, but I can see she's starting to tire. It's time we went back.

As my footsteps turn back towards home, I start to think again about Ben, and the mess I will have to face at the bungalow. It makes me shudder to think of it, but I know I am doing the right thing by refusing to clean up. And not just for me. As I follow the path back to Lyme I realize that, unbeknownst to him, I am doing Ben a huge favour here. There may be a few difficult months while I break him in, but it needs to be done for the sake of his relationship with Prue. He will thank me later, I am sure of it. It is as if he is a foster child that I've adopted in order to teach him, by example, a few important lessons about the co-habiting dynamic. No, a foster *husband*, that's better.

Wouldn't that be the perfect wedding gift to my sister and her future husband? A husband who is already house-trained, his annoying edges knocked off. Who needs a full set of champagne glasses, or teak-handled barbecue tongs engraved with Mr and Mrs, when they could have something truly useful? Something that will actually make a real difference to married life? I cannot wrap this gift, but surely it is far more valuable than anything I could buy?

If you know the warning signs in advance, you can do something about it. Fill in the cracks, move the livestock to safer ground. Not build your house on the fault line. Matt and I are like the crops still growing out at sea, too far away to be harvested, all that effort wasted. There's still time for Prue and Ben; I am going to save them both, even if they don't know it yet.

16

London

Matt truly believed that eight years of living in Bethnal Green had somehow made him more authentically urban than me, simply because my flat was within ten minutes' walk of Hampstead Heath. Even though he was the one who'd owned an entire house, while my flat was a minuscule one bedroom on the third floor of a purpose-built block. It was as if the very presence of grass, trees and open vistas on my doorstep, instead of abandoned mattresses and fried chicken shops on his, stripped me of my status as a true blue Londoner. As if the pair of us, white, university educated and working in television, weren't already stuffed into every middle-class pigeonhole imaginable, no matter what postcodes we inhabited.

It hadn't exactly been my intention to make Matt move to Belsize Park. In truth, I had been against us moving in together at all, but to say so directly sounded unnecessarily harsh, and I'd just delayed and hesitated and hedged my bets until he asked me outright if I just hated the idea of moving to East London. It was easier to agree that this was my worry than to admit to the churning sense of anxiety that filled me up every time I thought about where this was going. And when he offered to move in with me instead, my excuses ran out.

148

It wasn't that I didn't love him. Of course I did, though he was the one who said it every five minutes. Of course, that was why it was terrifying. It meant so much, you see. So much that I couldn't stand the idea of what would happen if it didn't work out.

But when he'd moved in to my flat, ruthlessly casting out the girly cushions in my living room, and cluttering up the hall with a ton of sports equipment that he never seemed to use, I wondered why I'd ever worried about it. Everything felt so easy. Even boring things, like trips to Ikea or the supermarket, felt fresh and new because we were doing them together. As if by choosing a curtain rail together we were investing in some sort of shared future. Though obviously I never said so to him; no need to tell him he was right, I'd never hear the end of it. But I was surprised by how this shared life, which I had thought would be all compromise and difficulty, turned out to give me far more than I had to give up. Matt always said I was an all-or-nothing girl; either entirely against some-thing or entirely for it, with no in between. And slowly, slowly, I was coming round to being entirely for a future that had Matt in it.

However. The ointment always has a fly in it, and ours was Matt's continued belief that he was somehow too 'street' for Belsize Park. Even though he was now a signed-up member of the Hampstead Heath massive, with a council tax bill and a parking permit, he couldn't resist reaffirming his bogus urban authenticity every time we went to the Heath.

It was one of those late September Sundays when the sun puts on one spectacular last show, as if trying to remind you that it will soon be gone. Even with the best efforts of the sunshine, there was an autumnal chill in the air that practically pulled the covers off you and begged you to get outside before winter came. Well, okay, the chill didn't do that, I did. But Matt, for all his urban warrior act, could always be persuaded out of bed by the promise of lunch at the Holly Bush.

On our walk across the Heath he insisted on playing the game that he called Hummus Bingo and that I, refusing to join in, called Class War. He racked up the points according to rules that seemed to be devised purely to afford him a maximum score.

'Regular, shop-bought hummus in a plastic tub — one point. Too easy,' he said, striding dismissively past the picnic of a young couple whose entire lunch appeared to consist of hummus, Doritos and White Lightning Cider. Ah, sweet youth, and sweet youthful metabolic rate that permits such appalling dietary habits.

Matt granted himself two points for spotting any variation on classic hummus — roasted red pepper, lemon and coriander, that sort of thing — three if purchased from a deli rather than a supermarket. But the true bonus points were earned by those picnickers who had expended a little more effort on their Middle Eastern dips.

'Now wait, wait.' Holding my hand, Matt led me on a determined detour towards a family seemingly dressed straight out of the Boden catalogue. 'Signs are good, very good. Yup, yup, here we go. Proper wicker picnic hamper, tick. Assortment of tartan rugs, tick. Kilner jars and proper cutlery — I feel some serious points coming on.'

We slowed our pace once we neared them, the better to spy on their lunchtime spread. Matt pretended to be looking for something on the ground, and I helped him. Half crouched in the grass, we crept closer, like ineffective and highly visible reconnaissance spies on Operation Hors d'Oeuvre.

'Linus, hummus!' called the mother, holding out a pitta bread to a small boy who was far more interested in shovelling handfuls of crisps into his mouth.

'Not hummus,' he sulked, pushing her hand away.

'Come on, darling,' she said, her face falling. She waved the pitta bread as if that would make it more tempting. 'Mummy made it especially.'

'Bingo!' hissed Matt, clutching at my hand for emphasis. 'Double points for homemade.'

'Not like it,' insisted the little boy, his lower lip stuck out rebelliously.

'Just try it, darling. Just a taste.' She tried to catch him with her free hand.

Linus had other ideas and wriggled away from her, grabbing another handful of crisps as he went.

His mother sighed and turned to her husband, her shoulders slumping in defeat. She looked tired. 'I don't even know why I bother. You shouldn't've let him at the crisps so early.'

Her husband grunted, not looking at her, his attention held by the sports pages of his newspaper.

'Charles, are you listening? I made this from the Ottolenghi book especially. I suppose you wouldn't have cared if I'd just gone to Nando's, would you?'

Charles didn't stir, not even when his wife began passive aggressively rearranging the picnic spread, as if weighing up each component as a weapon. If I were him, I'd have been worried, a thrown Kilner jar could do some serious damage, even to his thick head.

Matt and I grinned at one another, trying not to laugh out loud. Other people's domestics always seem completely risible, don't they? While your own are incredibly serious and complex.

'Nightmare,' I mouthed, rolling my eyes.

We stumbled to our feet and brushed the grass off our clothes. Charles and his wife were still not speaking, a frosty silence lengthening between them as we walked away from their waterproofed picnic rug.

'God, yeah, she was awful,' he agreed. His voice went high and mocking. 'Linus! Hummus!'

'What? No, *he's* awful,' I said, pulling on Matt's hand to make him stop and look at me. 'Just ignoring her like that when she'd made all that effort.'

'Is it any wonder, with her nagging at him?'

'She wasn't nagging!' I felt stung into defence of this stranger. Something about the droop of her neck told me Charles didn't pay her much attention.

'Basher, if you had nothing better to talk to me about than hummus recipes, I'd ignore you too,' said Matt, tapping me playfully on the nose.

I ducked my head out of the way, but it wasn't worth arguing over. Other people's problems didn't affect us. We'd never let ourselves get like that.

'Right. To the pub,' said Matt, setting a brisk new pace up the hill. I followed after him, trying to match his long stride.

'Wait, have you finished your Class War game, then?'

Matt turned around. 'Game over,' he said. 'Obviously.'

'Obviously?'

He shrugged. 'Sudden death. She said the magic word.'

I looked at him blankly.

'Ottolenghi. Patron saint of weird hummus. You lose.'

'But I wasn't even playing, you arse!'

'Them's the rules, Basher Bailey. If one of us wins, stands to reason the other one loses, right? I can't help it if that's you.'

At the time I thought very little of this game. It all just seemed like nothing, a silly diversion that kept us occupied on the walk towards our Sunday lunch. But afterwards I remembered it for two things: the opposing sides we had taken in an argument that had nothing to do with us. And the fact that only one of us could win.

17

The postcard is in a bin on the seafront. And I ripped it up into little pieces just in case the compulsion should come upon me to run back and try to retrieve it. Matt mentioned the emails I haven't answered. It's time to face these, too. And if that means going into the Baileys' office, one cramped room containing my entire family and my inescapable housemate cum foster husband, then so be it.

When Mum and Dad established the company, they rented the upstairs floor of a house just off Broad Street. I am sure the intention was to move to bigger premises as the business grew, but somehow they never got around to it. Nor had they ever thought about redecoration — it's not the sort of office where meetings are held, since holiday-makers either go directly to their rental cottages or meet in town or on the Cobb for one of the guided walks. No one visited, and nothing ever got thrown out. Like the striated cliffs of Lyme, new material was simply added on top of the old. Which meant that stepping back into the office was like revisiting my childhood. There was the supremely Eighties poster for the 'Do You Think He Ichthyosaurus?' fossil tour — all bubble writing and batwing jumpers (the latter on the tourists, I hasten to add, not the dinosaurs). There was the framed Austen Festival newsletter, featuring a furious six-year-old Prue, dressed up in an olde-worlde outfit very much against her will. At seventeen I had hated the picture of me leading the French Lieutenant's Walk; the photographer had caught me with my mouth hanging open in a weird way, and the wind had blown my hair into knotty tangles. Now I am just astonished at how young I look.

'What are you doing here?' says Prue, looking up from her computer. There's a pile of wedding magazines next to the monitor, each one bristling with multi coloured Post-its marking relevant pages.

'Hello, darling,' says Mum. She takes her glasses off and stands up, pushing them into the twisted knot of hair that is piled on top of her head. 'Come on in. I hoped you'd come and visit us.'

Dad waves hello but is busy scowling at a screen and obviously doesn't want to be disturbed. There is no sign of Ben, but then I hear a toilet flush and he appears behind me, wiping his wet hands on his trousers. Even here, it seems, there is no escape from his bathroom habits.

'Kate!' he exclaims. 'Just talking about you, weren't we?'

Mum quickly shakes her head at him, and Prue glares him into silence. Dad harrumphs behind the computer monitor. I suppose that means they weren't saying anything good. I should be used to people talking behind my back by now, but it always makes me feel sick to realize they have.

'Ben, I think we need some more milk,' says Prue, giving him a pointed look.

'Ah, not sure we do actually,' says Ben. He heads towards the office fridge to prove his point. 'Loads left.'

'No there isn't,' she answers, stepping in front of the fridge and blocking his way. 'I, er, I drank it.'

'All of it? A pint?' Ben rubs his blond curls, bemused.

'Yes. I just really fancied a big glass of milk. While you were in the loo just now. Lovely. But now there's none left for tea. So can you run out and get some? Just take some money from petty cash.'

Ben shuffles his feet, kicking at the corner of a desk as he looks at each member of the Bailey family in turn, sensing he is being banished. At last he grabs a handful of change from the red tin by the office door and stomps off down the staircase, his heavy footsteps reverberating through the building.

The sounds of his departure have barely faded before Prue crosses the room to point at me accusingly, her pale blue eyes so like mine that it's like being accosted by my younger self.

'Don't you think I don't know what you're doing.'

'Prue,' says Mum. 'This is not the way to — '

Prue interrupts. 'Ben's told us, you know.'

'Told you what?' I ask, wondering what Ben could possibly have to complain about since he's moved into Granny Gilbert's bungalow. That I don't allow him to use my dog as a waste

156

disposal unit? That I haven't bought the most recent copy of *Grazia* to accompany his morning poo?

'Darling,' says Mum, coming over to stand between me and my sister. She takes hold of my hand and squeezes it gently. 'What Prue is trying to say is that we are very worried about you. Ben has mentioned that the house has become rather dirty since he moved in. He says you never clean anything up, which is ever so unlike you.'

'Dirty?' I echo. I have the uncomfortable sense that I may have fallen on my own sword here.

'You're trying to drive him out, aren't you?' says Prue, hands on hips. 'I know your game, you were just like this when we shared a room. You think if you make it all horrible he'll just leave. Well, he won't.'

I start laughing at the idea that my cunning plan has been so woefully misunderstood, but I realize that to say it out loud — the house is dirty because I am training your future husband — cannot help but sound very wrong indeed. Prue has always resented any influence from me. In fact, it wouldn't be too much to say that her entire puritanical streak may have been formed primarily by her efforts to be as unlike me as possible.

'Oh you can laugh,' says Prue. 'But you won't drive him out of the house. No matter how filthy you are.'

'Filthy!' I say. 'Jeez, Prue, it's your stupid fiancé who doesn't even know how to put a plate in the dishwasher. I'm not filthy; I'm just not cleaning up after him. And if that's a crime then you can put the handcuffs on me right now, officer.'

Mum looks relieved. 'Oh dear, is that how it is? I must admit I did wonder, you've always been so neat and tidy.'

'Could never even put a bloody cup down at yours without you running for a coaster,' Dad offers from his corner of the room, as if this is a helpful comment.

'I haven't complained about Ben coming to live with me,' I say to Prue, 'but I'm not going to run around after him with a dustpan and brush like his mother.'

'It's not like you've got anything else to do,' mutters Prue.

'What's that supposed to mean?'

'Girls,' admonishes Mum.

But Prue can't stop herself. 'It's not like you're doing anything else, is it? Ben's here helping out with the family business — a family business you've never taken even the slightest interest in, I might add. He's planning a wedding, he's moving his entire life here. And what are you doing? Hanging out in cafes with old ladies. Oh yes, I saw you with old Mrs Klepto Curtis at the Bay Tea Shoppe.'

'Klepto Curtis?' I ask, looking from Prue to my mother.

Mum interrupts. 'Prue, really, it's not nice to speak about Mrs Curtis like that. She is not a kleptomaniac.'

'Mum,' says Prue, throwing herself down onto her office chair. 'She stalks tourists around town nicking free teas off them all summer long.

Someone even made a complaint to the police in June.'

'She doesn't actually steal anything though,' insists Mum. 'She's just a confused old lady.'

'She doesn't seem all that confused,' I offer. She seemed sharp as a tack to me, to tell the truth.

'Stop changing the subject,' says Prue. 'The point is that everyone else is working their arses off right now, and you're just swanning around town doing absolutely nothing. Would it kill you to be a bit understanding of how busy Ben is? Maybe he doesn't have time to, like, scrub down the taps to your satisfaction.'

'I'm not doing nothing,' I say.

'Yeah?' Prue sneers at me. 'Go on, what are you up to then? What's taking up all your time? Walking the dog? Thinking deep thoughts while you look out to sea? Don't think we haven't all noticed your French Lieutenant's Woman impressions. Everyone's seen you.'

I take a sharp breath in. It is typical of Prue that she should so ruthlessly and accurately summarize my aimless wanderings. I cannot deny that my daily schedule of dog walking and tea drinking doesn't stand up to outside scrutiny. I'm not getting over anything. I'm just wasting time.

Dad's head lifts up from his computer, waiting to hear my answer, and even Mum doesn't instantly leap to my defence, which means that they must in some way agree with Prue. Let's face it, even I agree with Prue. But if she thinks I'm about to admit it, she is very much mistaken.

'I'm decorating Granny Gilbert's bungalow, actually,' I say, lying quickly. 'I spoke to the estate agent about it.'

I can only hope Prue doesn't end up confirming this conversation with the estate agent as, while he would agree that we spoke about decorating, he would no doubt tell her, truthfully, that I had scoffed at the idea of doing it myself. We had decorators do our place in London, and my knowledge of DIY starts and ends at pointing to a colour chart to indicate which shade someone else should paint my walls.

But even as the words leave my mouth, I realize that this could be a great idea. I need a focus for my restless mind, and perhaps this will be it.

'You? Decorating? When did you decide this?' demands Prue.

'Um, recently?' I say. 'Very recently.' Like, five minutes ago.

'Well,' she folds her arms across her chest. 'You should have discussed it with me first. Granny Gilbert left that place to both of us. You can't go round painting it all weird colours and stuff. I mean, you're all depressed, you'd better not go doing the walls in black or anything.'

'Who says I'm depressed?' I ask.

'No one, darling,' says Mum, quickly enough that it's obvious she thinks I am.

'Well I'm not. And I'm doing this for our benefit, Prue, actually.'

'How?' says Prue.

'Well,' I am clearly going to have to freestyle this, but as I do, the mission becomes clearer and clearer, as if I truly had given it a great deal of thought and preparation. 'The estate agent said that Granny Gilbert's house might sell if it gets a bit of a facelift. And couldn't you and Ben do with the money for your deposit?'

I don't add that I could do with the money myself. My savings are running low, and there's no telling how long it will take for Matt and me to divide our assets. Granny Gilbert's bungalow isn't going to make anyone a fortune, but if it was sold at last the profit could be enough to give me a fresh start.

'You don't have the first clue what you're doing,' says Prue. 'What if you make it worse?'

I glare at her.

'Girls,' says Mum, again. 'I think it's a lovely idea, Kate, darling. And you are very clever to have thought of it. And Prue, I think as Kate is doing this partly for your benefit, you might have a quiet word with Ben about tidying up after himself. After all, the estate agents could send someone round to the house at any time.'

Dad snorts behind his computer. 'Going to take more than paint to shift that place,' he says.

'Shut up, Dad,' says Prue, on my side for once. 'I could invest my half of that money in this place. Actually put some of my plans into action.'

Dad looks alarmed. 'Already? Aren't you too busy with the wedding to start changing Baileys' right this second? I thought we'd agreed to take it all slowly?'

'You know my primary focus is always the business,' says Prue, her chin set determinedly.

Dad looks over at the bridal magazines and her eyes follow his pointed gaze.

'There's a reason they call it the wedding *industry*, Dad,' she says. 'That is research. You won't be making that face when Baileys' has a piece of the pie.'

She catches a glance between Mum and Dad.

'Pie. Wedding cake. Whatever. You'll see. I have plans for all of us.'

None of us doubts it for a moment.

While Prue and Dad debate the future of Baileys', I take the opportunity to check my emails on Ben's computer. But he is back from the shops with the milk before I can do anything more than see that Matt has sent me an email every single day since I left, and so has Sarah.

I select all and delete the lot. I have come to Lyme for a fresh start. It will do me no good at all to wallow in the past.

18

When Ben gets back from work, he stands with the front door open, his jaw hanging and the key still held in his extended hand. The hall floor is hidden underneath a patchwork of Granny Gilbert's old floral bed-sheets, in one corner of which Millie has made herself a nest to sleep in. The fringed lampshade has disappeared and a bare bulb swings from the ceiling like in a prison cell. From my vantage point at the top of a stepladder, Ben's face is a comical sight. It's good to know that he is capable of expressing an emotion other than just hearty affability.

'Hi, Ben,' I wave from near the ceiling, and he looks up at me with wide eyes.

'Wow, Kate, what have you done?' he asks.

'What does it look like?' I say, chirpily, brandishing the wallpaper stripper I've hired from the DIY shop in Axminster. 'Time to make some changes here, don't you think?'

Ben's forehead wrinkles. 'Do you know how to use that thing?' he asks, nodding at the machine in my hand.

'Oh yes,' I lie, pressing it against the wall so that clouds of steam obscure me from view. I can hear a violent bubbling inside the machine, but it's okay. I checked with the man at the shop and he told me it won't burn me; but it might sound quite bad if I use it wrongly. Which is perfect.

Ben drops his bag to the floor and takes off his

163

coat, shutting the door behind him. 'Ah, Kate, I'm not sure you're meant to just hold it in one place like that,' he says.

'No?' I ask, innocently, turning around so that the steam billows towards him.

'No,' he says, holding his hands up in front of his face. 'Seriously, have you done this before?'

'Well, not exactly,' I admit, pushing my damp hair off my forehead with the back of my hand. I'm sure I look convincingly hardworking. 'But I'm learning. See, I've done loads already.'

I indicate a small pile of peeled wallpaper on the floor. In truth, I have been toiling away for approximately fifteen minutes, having timed my efforts precisely to coincide with Ben's arrival home.

'Look, ah, Kate, let me — ' he begins, and I know I've got him already.

'Mmm?' I say distractedly, turning away as if I'm eager to get back to work. I half drop the steamer as I wobble on the ladder. I have choreographed this beautifully. Come on, Ben, I think. I'm not sure how much longer I can keep this up.

Out of the corner of my eye I can see Ben rolling up his shirt-sleeves.

'What you need to do,' says Ben, and I keep my face turned to the wall so he doesn't see me smile. 'What you need to do, Kate, is move the steamer slowly up the wall and then scrape the paper off immediately afterwards, while it's still damp.'

'Like this?' I ask, scraping at a dry piece of paper until a tiny fragment peels away. The steamer belches in my other hand, miles from the wall.

'Steamer first,' explains Ben, standing close up against the stepladder to look at my work. 'Use the steamer.'

I can tell he is itching to take it out of my hands and show me how it should be done.

'Mmm?' I say, waving the steamer around again while I continue to scrape elsewhere. I can hear Ben sigh in exasperation at my incompetence. Any moment now . . .

'Look, Kate, why don't you let me show you how to use it properly?' he says at last.

'Oh *would* you?' I ask, turning to him gratefully. 'I think I'm just quite hopeless at this.'

Ben chuckles as he takes the steamer out of my hand. 'Come on, off the ladder,' he says, looking far more comfortable now that he's in charge. 'Let me show you how it's done.'

He presses the steamer against the wall and follows it with the scraper, peeling away a thick, satisfying strip of Granny Gilbert's textured apricot wallpaper.

'See?' he says, with a triumphant note in his voice. 'It's not so hard — steamer first, then, like this, the scraper. Steamer, scraper. Just like that.'

'Wow, Ben. I didn't know you were so good at this sort of thing,' I say, admiringly.

I didn't — this is a total stroke of luck. Having pledged myself as the dedicated bungalow decorator, it occurred to me while choosing paint colours that the circumstances presented another excellent opportunity for training my foster husband. And it's already working better than I could have imagined.

'Well, I've done a bit of decorating for my mum,' says Ben, pulling away another sheet of wallpaper and depositing it on the floor next to the stepladder. 'Actually pretty good at it. Mum says I do a better job than the Polish decorator she paid for last year.'

'Gosh, isn't Prue lucky? I wish Matt had been a bit more handy around the house. It's such an attractive thing in a man.'

I can see a flush on the back of Ben's neck, and he coughs embarrassedly. Perhaps I am laying it on a bit thick. He might, oh God, he might think I'm actually coming on to him. Rein it in, Kate, rein it in.

'I think Prue will be really impressed when she sees you like this,' I say briskly, stepping back away from the step-ladder and crossing my arms. Textbook 'I do not fancy you' body language. 'It's a whole other side to the businessman she already knows. Every woman hopes her husband will be practical around the house.'

Ben chuckles again. 'I'd have thought she'd just tell me off for making a mess,' he says.

'Oh no,' I reassure him. 'Prue will be grateful. I know she will. I certainly am.'

Although I am a little concerned that, not seeing the bigger picture here, not knowing that Ben is in pre-husband training, Prue might mistakenly think that I am just getting him to do my dirty work for me. Which would be all wrong. Obviously there is a benefit to having Ben help with the decoration, but my motives are purely altruistic.

He seems to have got into a rhythm with the wallpaper steamer, running it up the wall methodically, and following it with the scraper. I can see he's actually enjoying himself.

'Shall I take it back now you've shown me how to do it?' I ask.

Ben pulls the steamer towards him like a child whose sole possession of a toy has been threatened.

'Tell you what,' he says. 'Why don't you let me get on with this for now? Quite like a bit of manual labour, you know. Using the old muscles after being in the office all day.'

I demur politely, insisting several times that he needn't bother, but I time it carefully to capitulate just as he's about to give up. I've managed to make him beg to do it, and he seems as pleased when I agree, as if it was all his idea in the first place.

'Well, if you insist, Ben,' I say, when we've finally established that the steamer is his and his alone. 'I feel bad that you're doing all this work for me.'

'Oh, not a problem,' says Ben. 'Least I could do.'

'Well, in that case let me make you supper,' I say. I've actually already made supper — a beef stew that cooked for hours this afternoon. It is all part of the plan, but he needn't know that.

'Right, well, right,' says Ben, looking delighted. 'Jolly decent of you.'

I pick up his bag and coat and take them through to the kitchen. Let Ben see that there are rewards for good behaviour. It's just like training Minnie — a matter of rewarding the good behaviour and ignoring the bad. And setting firm boundaries.

All the things I wish I'd done much, much earlier.

19

London

You know I'd really like to tell you all about our wedding. I really would. Because, despite everything that happened afterwards, I still think of it as one of the best days of my life. But listening to Prue's wedding talk has reminded me that even those closest to you really couldn't care less about the colour composition of the flower arrangements, or the menu tastings or the difficulty you had finding underwear that wouldn't show through your silk and chiffon dress. Let alone mentioning the speeches, which are bad enough to sit through at the time, and twice as bad second hand (sorry, Dad).

So I will spare you the details, and simply say that Matt and I got married, and it was everything I had ever hoped for. More than that, really, since I had never hoped for marriage at all.

What can I say? It turned out I did believe in true love.

Or maybe it was just the way he asked me.

We had been house-hunting for months without success. As much as we may have still been in the first flush of living-together love, it could no longer be denied that my flat was too small for both of us. The galley kitchen was so narrow that we couldn't pass in it without squashing ourselves up against either the counter or each other. Initially this was a charming novelty, an excuse for cheeky kitchen fumbles and misbehaviour. But early in the morning, with hangovers and slept-through alarms and disagreements about who had stacked the dishwasher like that (I am sure I don't need to tell you it was Matt), the charm quickly wore off.

They say that moving house is one of the most stressful events in one's life, and on the basis of our experience, I'd say they're right. First we argued about where to live; nothing was dragging me out East, not even Matt's promises that we could own a vast mansion in Mile End for the price of a Chalk Farm bedsit. I was too old to relocate to an edgy area — I didn't care about being cool, I cared about not being mugged when I walked home from the tube. And I knew exactly where I wanted to live. Matt's exasperation with my refusal to look anywhere else finally gave way to resignation.

Winner: me.

Then there was the garden or no garden discussion, which forced me into an indefensible corner from which I attempted to argue the passionately green-fingered case for, while Matt held in front of me the case against: the dust-covered remnants of a long-ignored African violet from a shelf in the bathroom, and the desiccated, leafless skeleton of something that had once been a fern. Not having remembered to water either for months somewhat weakened my argument that I'd be tilling the earth and growing vegetables in our new home.

Winner: Matt.

Flat-roof-gate was bad enough that the estate agent excused himself to make some phone calls outside, one of which was probably to a counsellor at Relate to see if they made emergency house calls. Matt, whose knowledge of DIY barely extended to changing a light bulb, claimed with all the blustering confidence of a building trade veteran that any home with a flat roof was guaranteed to leak and refused even to consider any property that had one. I wouldn't have minded so much if it wasn't obvious that he'd just heard something negative about flat roofs from a man down the pub and taken it to heart without having any knowledge to back it up. In addition to this his rigorous stance ruled out all the houses with lovely glass-fronted modernist extensions that I'd set my heart on. So who could blame me for resorting to hiding the particulars from him, and arranging to meet at a mystery house without revealing its dark flat-roof secret? I had hoped he'd fall in love with it — everything else was *perfect* — and overlook this one tiny flaw.

Only it turned out that this was typical of me, trying to get my own way through manipulation instead of respecting Matt's decisions. Which was typical of him, taking a unilateral position on something and refusing to budge, no matter how wrong he was. Which was typical of me, making out it was all his fault when I was the one who refused to contemplate moving outside a mile-wide radius. Which was typical of *him* because . . .

Winner: a surprise entrant, the estate agent.

It turned out he hadn't actually gone to call Relate. In sheer desperation he had called back to the office to be reminded of the absolute pointiest roofed homes they had on their books. And a property had been added that very day, only one street away. A tiny Victorian terrace with an undeniably slanting tiled roof and absolutely no extension on the back. It had a garden, but only a tiny patio, big enough for a table — Matt agreed this was acceptable. Okay, so if you stretched out your arms you could touch the walls in the second bedroom, and damp bubbled up the base of the kitchen walls, but it was a house, a whole house. And four months later it was ours.

The day we moved in it poured with rain, which I tried not to take as an omen. A box of crockery got smashed when the sodden cardboard gave way in the middle of the hall. The removal men somehow lost a kitchen chair, and it turned out — oh irony — that the pointed roof leaked into the second bedroom.

But Matt and I couldn't stop smiling. When we'd paid the removers we ran around the house, from room to room, up and down our stairs, into the garden and back again at great speed because of the rain. We sat on the sofa — our wet hair dripping onto the thick plastic wrap that we hadn't yet removed — and just grinned at each other. It was ours; we owned it together.

That night we sat on the living room floor eating fish and chips straight out of the paper since all the plates were smashed. It turned out that the former owner had mean-spiritedly taken out all the light bulbs when he left and, as we hadn't noticed until it was dark, we had to eat by the light of a hastily unpacked scented candle. Matt produced a bottle of champagne, and we drank it from plastic cups that he'd bought from the corner shop. I couldn't have been happier.

Or so I thought.

Matt got up to throw away the fish and chip papers and I could hear him rustling in the boxes we'd left in the kitchen.

'What are you looking for?' I called out. Surely there was no point in trying to unpack in the dark?

'Nothing,' he answered, but he carried on shifting boxes around. It started to annoy me. He'd only go putting everything in the wrong place. Why didn't he just sit down and enjoy our first night in our new home?

When he came back he held a book in his hand, which was odd, because I'd told the removals men to put all the boxes of books in the living room.

'This is for you,' he said, handing it to me. 'Present.'

'*Morality: An Introduction to Ethics*,' I looked up at him quizzically. 'Wow. Thanks, Matt. It's just what I've always wanted, you total fruit loop.'

He sat down next to me on the floor. 'Well, you once told me you were a girl with morals, so I thought it looked right up your street.'

He was trying to keep a straight face, but his

173

eyes gave him away. There was something weird going on. Had I moved in with a lunatic? Was he only revealing his true self now that we were locked together in a mortgage?

'I know all I need to know about morals,' I said. I put the book down and reached for his cheek to kiss him, but he pulled away.

'I don't think so,' he said, picking the book up insistently. 'You see, I've been thinking about what it means for a girl with your strong morals to be living in sin.'

'That's hardly troubled you before.' I laughed. 'Living in sin!'

'Well, it troubles me now,' he said gravely. 'Deeply and disturbingly. I can think of nothing else. Which is why I think you should read the section on the ethics of love.'

'Matt, are you drunk? Have you been taking some sort of mind-altering substance out in the kitchen?'

'Just read it.'

I sighed and took the book out of his hand. I could tell he wasn't going to let this drop, so I'd indulge him for now and get it over with.

'Page seventy-eight,' he prompted, as I scanned the contents page.

I turned to the page, but there was something odd. It had a hole in it. In fact the hole went through every other page after page seventy-eight, creating a hidden recess inside the book. And there was something in it.

I looked at Matt, who was trying to look cool.

'I'm pretty sure it's morally wrong to mutilate a book, Matt,' I teased. 'Let alone a book on morality.' I turned the book upside down and shook it. A small black velvet pouch, secured by two tightly pulled strings, fell out onto the floor.

I suppose if you were the kind of girl who had long dreamed of long-stemmed roses and sparkling diamond solitaires, you would have instantly known what this meant. But Matt and I had never once spoken about getting married. So, of course, I responded with the deeply unromantic, 'What's that?'

'For fuck's sake, Kate, will you just open it?' said Matt, picking it up with obvious exasperation.

I untied the strings and peered into the pouch. And inside was . . . you think I'm going to say a ring, don't you? But it wasn't. Matt knew me better than that. Inside, rolled up tightly like a tiny scroll, was a note, which said, 'I'd like to put a ring on it. But if you think I'd dare choose one without you, I wouldn't be your future husband. Marry me?'

I looked up, astonished. I'd never seen him look so nervous. He kept pushing his hair back over and over again with the flat of his hand. I was too surprised to speak.

'Well?' he said at last.

'For the sake of morality, Matt,' I said. 'Yes. Yes, I will, yes.'

And to celebrate I'm afraid we proved beyond doubt, on the plastic-wrapped sofa, that neither of us had any morals worth speaking of.

20

After days of endless rain — good for my decorating efforts, bad for my mood — Minnie and I greet the few isolated rays of sunshine that struggle through the clouds this morning with giddy enthusiasm, skipping along the beach by the Cobb as if we haven't been here for weeks rather than days. We celebrate the break in the weather by running up and down to the shoreline, throwing stones to skim on the surface of the water (me) and eating disgusting things discovered in the seaweed (Minnie).

I am reassured to discover that something as simple as a little sunshine can lift my spirits, despite my circumstances. It makes me feel as if happiness is still a possibility, even after everything. Or perhaps it's not the weather at all, but my newfound sense of purpose. My days are suddenly and satisfyingly full with transforming Granny Gilbert's bungalow. And all the while I am transforming Ben with my undercover training programme.

I will say this for my sister's fiancé. When he has learned a lesson, he doesn't have to be reminded of it again and again like some people. Now that we have established I do not clear up after him, he puts his own plates in the dishwasher every time. Admittedly, I have seen him allowing Minnie to lick them first, which is quite disgusting, but I feel it is better to praise the good behaviour than criticize the bad. Nagging never worked on Matt.

There is still room for improvement of course. The day before yesterday I overheard Ben on the phone, inviting a friend round to watch the football tomorrow night. I have waited patiently for him to tell me of this plan, since it means I am effectively banished from the living room unless I fancy spending the evening listening to the kind of tedious beery banter that greets a well-timed fart as the height of humour. As yet he has failed to mention it. But instead of finding this annoying, I can't help seeing it as another training opportunity.

Things are getting better. I can feel it.

Minnie and I pause our walk along the seafront to sit on the low concrete wall for a while, soaking up the weak rays of the sun. Well, I sit still, while she digs in the shingle for crabs to chase. Above us on the boardwalk, two old men lean on a painted rail, staring out at the horizon.

'Looks good out there, Bill,' says one.

'Depends what you're looking at,' says Bill tersely.

'Well, I'm looking at Pam Curtis, I don't know about you,' says the man who isn't Bill, and he points far out, towards an orange buoy in the water.

Only, when I follow the direction of his finger I see it's not a buoy at all. It's a bobbing swimming hat. And it's not a Saturday. Mrs Curtis is breaking the rules again.

As we watch, the orange hat zigzags in towards the shore, propelled by Mrs Curtis's impressively powerful breast-stroke. Her goggled face pulls above the water for each breath, and then sinks below the surface so the petals of her hat appear to float like lotus flowers.

'Morning, Pam,' calls the one who isn't Bill. As Mrs Curtis nears the shore, she stands up in the water to wave, exposing her dark green swimming costume as she shakes her head to one side to get the water out of her ears.

Minnie runs down to the waterline and then shies back, barking at this unexpected figure emerging from the sea. Mrs Curtis shoos her away from the pile of clothes she has left on the beach, and reaches for a towel to rub herself down.

'Morning, Bill, Peter! Hello, Kate, dear!'

She pulls off her swimming cap and replaces it with the pink knitted hat I have seen before. Holding the towel around herself, she wriggles out of her swimsuit and drops it on the pebbles, fishing with her hand for her underthings.

'Now I see why you're standing here, Peter, you dirty old sod,' says Bill with a chuckle.

'She's never dropped that towel yet,' Peter answers wistfully.

I hear Bill give a loud cough, and suddenly they both seem to realize that I am there below them, listening to every word.

''Scuse me, miss,' says Peter, and both of their heads disappear guiltily back behind the railing.

'Wasn't that Prue Bailey?' I hear Bill ask as they retreat in haste.

Mrs Curtis advances up the beach, waving; her towel rolled tightly under her arm. Minnie skirts her heels, sniffing suspiciously, still not convinced that she should trust this sea creature.

'It's glorious out there today. Glorious!'

She drops her voice to a confidential whisper as she reaches me. 'I'm sure I don't have to tell you that Eddy need know *nothing* about this, dear. What he doesn't know won't hurt him.'

I nod, but don't agree in so many words. I'm not one to tell tales, but I can't help agreeing with Eddy that it's probably not safe for his grandmother to swim alone each morning, even if she is watched over by a couple of elderly swains.

'You seem to have a few admirers, Mrs Curtis,' I tease. 'One of those chaps was watching you swim like his life depended on it.'

She shrieks with laughter and clutches at my arm. 'Not Peter Turner! Oh my good *lord*, no, Kate, dear. That silly old fool, he's been after me for *years*. But I have absolutely no interest in a *man* at my age.'

'Why ever not?' I ask. Surely your interest in the opposite sex doesn't just fade away with your hair colour?

Mrs Curtis shudders dramatically, grimacing. 'Oh dear, no. I had quite enough of *that* with Mr Curtis, thank you very much. Are you heading back home?'

I say that we are, and Mrs Curtis and I fall into step with each other, or I should say that I fall into step with her. I'd started off slowly to accommodate her advanced age, and the steepness of the hill that leads back up towards the cul-de-sac from the Cobb. But she is having

179

none of it, and sets a hearty pace that I struggle to maintain. Luckily my breathlessness is disguised by the fact that she does most of the talking.

'While there is much to be said for marriage as an *institution*, like all institutions, it is only when you are *out* of it that you realize how much *freedom* you have. Don't you think, dear?'

She turns her sharp brown eyes on me enquiringly.

I'm not sure if I would categorize my unemployed aimlessness as freedom, or even as an escape. It's far too soon for me to really know whether I have got out of the institution at all.

'Mmm,' I say, partly because I am unsure of my answer, and partly because I am having trouble catching my breath on the hill. But it's enough to encourage her to continue.

'Not that I don't miss Mr Curtis. He was a dear, *dear* man.' She sighs. 'And positively an *animal* between the sheets. Don't look shocked, dear, these things matter. As I'm sure you know. The only problem was that he was an animal between a *lot* of sheets, if you know what I mean. And I think you do, dear, judging by what I've heard.'

'I'm not sure I — '

Mrs Curtis holds out her hand to interrupt me, stopping for a moment to turn back towards the bay behind us. Wisps of hair have escaped from her pink knitted cap, and they curl around her face, lending her the appearance of a deeply tanned and wrinkled baby.

'You will find, dear, that these things hurt less

in time. Really. Of course the *sting* is always there. The betrayal, that is. But it fades. The question you must ask yourself is, is your marriage worth *more* than that?'

She fixes me with her beady gaze, head tilted as she waits for my answer. Minnie looks up at both of us as if she, too, would like to hear what I think.

'Well, dear, *is* it?'

I turn to look out to sea, leaning on the wooden fence posts that have supported many a breathless tourist halfway up the hill. We have climbed high enough to be able to see the bay spread out below us, all the way to Portland. Grey clouds are massing on the horizon; the break in the weather is already at an end.

'How do you know?' I ask.

Mrs Curtis leans on the fence next to me, though while my breath is still ragged, she doesn't seem to need the support. Her red nails trace an unseen pattern on the wooden posts.

'That is the question,' she says. 'How do you know?'

'With Mr Curtis,' I say. 'You forgave him. But you said the sting was still there. How can you move forward after something like that? How did you put it behind you?'

Mrs Curtis dips her head to pick at a knot in the wood. 'You just do, dear. Or you don't. You never *know*, you just *decide*. That's the hard bit. The *deciding*.'

'But what if you make the wrong decision?'

Mrs Curtis laughs brightly, as if I have said something funny. She pats my hand in a brisk fashion, more as if she's administering a gentle slap than reassuring me.

'I know you hope I will tell you what to do, dear. I was *just* the same. But there is no right answer. You decide, and then you do the best with the decision you've made.'

'You forgave him,' I say. 'But you wouldn't get married again. Is that because you wouldn't be able to trust someone else?'

'Oh no, dear,' says Mrs Curtis, hooting with laughter. 'Not to trust anyone ever again — what a sentence that would be. I'd be punishing myself if I thought *that*. Of course I could trust again. But dear, at my age — *eighty*! I know I don't look it — there are a lot of widowed men who simply want to be looked after. Well, I've done enough of that. I like to look after myself now.'

She spreads her hands out on the fence, and then tilts her head up to the sky, squinting at the clouds that are rolling in above us.

'That's all. Ooh, dear, was that a spot of rain? We should get back. Unless, dear,' she turns her bright eyes on me imploringly. 'I didn't bring my *purse* with me, but maybe you might treat an old lady to a cup of tea?'

21

Mum is on the doorstep on the dot of six, as I knew she would be. She's holding a bottle of wine and she looks so happy, her cheeks all pink and glowing from the cold, that I almost feel guilty for using her like this. But for all that Ben has been a tremendous help with the decoration, he still has several lessons to learn. And I am teaching him one of them tonight, with the unwitting assistance of his future mother-in-law.

'What a sweet idea to ask me round,' she says as she kisses me on the cheek. 'You know I've been longing to see what you've done here. Ben's been all mysterious about it at the office. Said I had to wait and see.'

She casts her gaze around the hall, and I'm alarmed to see tears spring into her eyes.

'Mum?' I ask anxiously, taking hold of her arm.

'Oh, it's nothing, really.' She puts her hand on top of mine and squeezes it reassuringly. 'Just, I suppose it's looked the same for years. And now — goodness, it looks so different, doesn't it? You've made such an improvement.'

She runs her free hand over the new, smooth wall. No more textured wallpaper, dented by Prue's and my childhood bikes, or the scuffmarks from Granny Gilbert's walker. No more stained beige carpet. Now the walls are a cool pale green, soothing and welcoming. A mirror hangs by the front door, and the coat cupboard has been painted a matt white. The parquet floor has been buffed to a brilliant shine thanks to the machine that Ben discovered in the hire shop; his passion for a new gadget has transformed the floors throughout the entire bungalow. It is also now impossible to walk anywhere in socks without incurring a serious and painful fall, and Minnie tiptoes around the house with extreme caution, but it seems a small price to pay for the improvement.

'Not just me, Mum,' I say, giving credit where it's due. 'Ben's done a lot of this. He's been really great; I couldn't have done it without him.'

Mum suppresses a laugh. 'Well, love, according to Ben this has all been his idea. He's ever so proud of it all. As far as he's concerned you've had very little to do with it.'

I grin back. 'I love it when a plan comes together,' I say. Allowing Ben to think everything was his idea was part of the training. No need to spell it all out for Mum, she's a married woman herself. She gets it.

'I wish I could have persuaded your father it was *his* idea,' she says. 'I've been on at him all year to do something about this place. Well, whoever did it, it looks wonderful, Kate.'

'Ben's really gone for it, Mum,' I say. 'Honestly, last night he woke me up at half eleven to ask me if I thought he should paint the radiators in gloss or eggshell. Now he's on it, he's impossible to stop. I had no idea he'd be this easy to train.'

Mum gives me a quizzical look, her forehead creasing. 'Train?'

I laugh dismissively. 'Oh not *train* train — you know, I just didn't think he'd turn out to be such an, erm, asset as a housemate.'

'Hmm,' says Mum, her eyebrows lifting a fraction, but she's looking at me in that way only a mother can: as if she can see deep into my worst possible self. It makes me want to fling myself on the floor and tell her everything. All the things I haven't told anyone. But I know she will disapprove of my interfering in Prue's relationship, so I keep my mouth shut.

'You haven't seen the living room!' I exclaim, ushering her in the direction of the door.

She allows me to steer her away, although I can feel a certain steeliness in her shoulders, as if she is tensed for something. She peers into the living room and gives a little gasp.

'Do you like it?' I ask.

'It's lovely,' she says. 'Just lovely.'

'Okay,' I say, clapping my hands together purposefully.

Mum starts in surprise, her hand flying to her throat. 'I've got another surprise for you tonight. We're going to have a spa evening!'

Mum looks rather more baffled than thrilled. 'Spa?'

'Yes, you know, mother-daughter bonding, beauty treatments, that sort of thing.'

'Oh right,' says Mum, for whom painting her toenails is a once-a-year event. 'Lovely, darling.'

'I thought it would be fun,' I say, ushering her into the bathroom where I've laid out a dressing gown for her, and a pair of slippers. The lights in the bathroom are off and I've lit a tea light in a

185

jam jar for atmosphere. We haven't done anything to the bathroom yet and the candlelight also hides the hideousness of the blue plastic suite.

Mum hesitates in the doorway, resisting me. 'Do I really have to get changed?' she asks. 'Kate, it's a sweet idea, but I'm not sure . . . '

My plan will not work unless Ben has a very good reason to turn around and go straight back out again as soon as he arrives home from work. I believe the sight of his future mother and sister-in-law in a state of undress will be that reason.

'I'm getting changed too, I'll get into mine in the bedroom, Mum,' I say, forcing her into the bathroom. 'It's more relaxing this way. Trust me. I've been to loads of spas.'

Mum allows me to shut the door behind her. When she emerges she is hesitant, gripping the collar of the dressing gown anxiously, as if it might fall off and expose her.

'Right, put this on,' I say, sliding a towelling headband over her head. 'It'll keep your hair off your face for the masks and creams.'

'Masks and creams?' Mum echoes uncertainly.

'Let's have some wine,' I carol, determined to remain relentlessly cheerful in the face of Mum's lack of enthusiasm. She will enjoy this in the end, I'm sure of it.

It takes a while — and two glasses of wine — but Mum finally relaxes into the spa experience. I've got us a DVD of *The Notebook,* which I think Mum will like. More importantly, it's the girliest film I can think of, and guaranteed to send any red-blooded male screaming out of the house. I've dimmed the lights and lit candles, and Mum is reclining on the sofa, both of us sporting livid green face packs, while I paint her toenails a pretty pastel pink.

'Darling, this *is* a treat,' she sighs. 'I can't think when I last indulged myself like this.'

'You deserve it, Mum,' I say. My ears are tuned for the turning of a key in the lock, and at last, there it is.

'Christ!' Ben exclaims, as he steps into the living room from the hall. Two full Tesco's carrier bags hang from his hands. 'I mean, sorry, er, Mum. I just — '

Mum shrieks and pulls her foot out of my hand, smudging her nail polish all over my dressing gown.

'Oh hello, Ben,' I say smoothly, turning around. 'How was your day?'

'H-hello, Ben,' stammers Mum, clutching at her robe again, although she is hardly in a state of total undress. I may be using her a little, but I'm not about to humiliate her.

'Ah, Kate, I didn't know you had company tonight,' says Ben, a scarlet flush rising up his neck. He shifts his feet uncomfortably, the plastic bags rustling with each movement.

'Oh sorry,' I say innocently. 'Didn't I mention it? How rude of me. I really should have told you my plans in advance. I didn't mean to give you a shock.'

Ben coughs in embarrassment. 'Not a shock, Kate, Mum. Not a shock at all. A lovely surprise.

But — ah — I had made plans for this evening myself.'

'Had you?' I ask innocently. As if I didn't know exactly what he had been planning.

Mum stands up suddenly. 'I think I need to wash this off,' she says, pointing to her face. She scurries away to the bathroom. My own face mask is tightening on my skin, but it is constricting my face in a way that only helps me look innocently blank.

'Look, Kate,' says Ben, looking at his watch. 'This is bloody awkward. I've got a friend coming round to watch the football in about ten minutes.'

'Oh dear,' I laugh airily. 'I hope he won't mind us being here as well. I'm sure we can keep quiet during the important bits. Mum and I can watch *The Notebook* afterwards; I'll pause it.'

I reach for the remote control.

Ben drops the bags and I hear the clink of beer bottles hitting the floor. A packet of Kettle Chips falls out onto the parquet.

'Christ, Kate, I can't have James round here with you and your mum half dressed! It's bloody not on. He's come all the way from Bristol to watch the match with me.'

I feel a creeping sense of guilt. I didn't realize his friend had travelled so far. Ben has worked so hard on the house, and he must miss his friends since he moved down here. But, I think, no, he should have told me about his plans. There is an important lesson to be learned here, and though Ben looks distraught, I cannot back down.

'Well you can hardly cast us out of the house

188

dressed like this,' I say. 'And Mum's been looking forward to this evening. If I'd known you had a friend coming round I'd have gone over to theirs so you had the place to yourself.'

'I thought you'd heard me on the phone,' Ben says, petulantly kicking at the door frame. 'Thought you knew I'd invited him.'

'Oh I don't listen in on other people's conversations,' I lie. Of course I do when they concern me — who doesn't? 'Sorry, Ben, if you wanted me to know your plans, you should have shared them with me in advance.'

Ben picks up the bags furiously and makes for the kitchen. Halfway across the newly buffed floor he stops and turns back.

He opens his mouth to speak. I stare at him with my green masked face, which is becoming seriously uncomfortable. He thinks better of it and retreats into the kitchen. I'm surprised to find myself feeling a bit trembly now that I'm on my own in the living room. I know I've done the right thing. He has learned a lesson this evening in the best way: painfully, and at personal sacrifice. Those are the learnings that last, if you ask me. The carrot is far less mighty than the great big stick.

I hear Ben muttering in the kitchen, either to himself or on the phone, I can't tell. I don't need to listen in this time, the point has been made. Unless I am much mistaken he will be changing his plans right now.

When Mum comes back into the living room, her face pink from the washed-off mask, she has taken off the robe and is back in her own clothes.

She sees this disappoints me and shakes her head firmly.

'No, love, I'm not staying in that when Ben's here. So embarrassing. Poor chap, he looked horrified.'

There is a cough from the doorway into the kitchen, and Ben reappears, his face no longer flushed. He has his coat buttoned up to his chin.

'No need, Mum,' he says jovially, and if there is a forced edge to his cheery demeanour we all pretend not to notice it. 'No need at all. You make yourself comfortable here — James and I will be at the pub. Much better idea all round. Should've thought of it before.'

'I do feel bad,' says Mum. 'Kicking you out of your own home like this.'

'Not at all,' Ben insists. 'Own fault. Forgot to tell Kate. Not used to her having visitors, I suppose. Bit of a surprise it should be tonight of all nights.'

His gaze flicks to mine and away again so fast that I'm not quite sure if I saw a glint of rebellion there, as if he knows exactly what I'm up to.

'I'm really sorry,' I say. 'If only I'd known.'

Ben's bonhomie seems to desert him for a moment. 'Point taken,' he says sternly, before remembering himself and reinstating his cheery smile. 'Anyway, Mum, Kate, have a good evening, won't you? I expect I'll be back late. G'night.'

'I do feel guilty,' says Mum as we hear the front door close behind him.

'Don't,' I say. I have enough guilt for the pair

of us. I thought Ben too thick-skinned to see through my scheming. Clearly, he's not as biddable as I'd first thought. 'Really, Mum, it's just a mistake. And anyway, it's my home, too.'

'Of course it is, darling,' says Mum. She eases herself back onto the sofa and picks up her wine. 'But you know, he's with the family all day at work, and then with you when he gets home. It can't be easy for him never having any space to himself.'

'He didn't have to move in here,' I say sulkily.

'No,' Mum agrees. 'It was rather thrust on you. But that's life. And it does rather feel like you're making him do all the fitting in with you, rather than compromising on both sides.'

'I need to wash this off,' I say, indicating the face mask, which is setting rock hard.

'Of course you do,' says Mum. 'I'll pour us some more wine.'

22

It's not that I haven't spent much time with Mum over the last few years, because she came up to London fairly often, but I hadn't realized she could be such relaxed and fun company. It occurs to me, as we drink our wine together, and snigger over *The Notebook,* which turns out to be pretty preposterous, that she is quite different in Lyme to how she has been as a visitor to our house in London. Because my trips to Lyme have been so sporadic and rushed, fitting in a visit with Granny Gilbert and my parents and making sure Matt wasn't too bored, and trying to squash down the panicky feelings that often rose up in my chest when I came home, I'd seen Mum here as part of a whole rather than as an individual. She was Mum-and-Dad-and-Prue-and-Granny-Gilbert rather than someone in her own right.

When she came to London, she was someone else altogether. All the calmness that I see in her now seemed to desert her as soon as she stepped off the train at Waterloo. Suddenly she became anxious and fretful, confused by the ticket machines at the tube station, so worried about being in the way that she was, inevitably, always in the way. Even once we got home she'd be unable to sit still — constantly offering to make tea or do the gardening, even though there were hardly any plants on our patio. I knew she meant it kindly, but when I came into the kitchen to find that she'd helpfully rearranged the fridge it made me want to scream — it felt as if she was telling me I wasn't any good at this business of making a home. Sensing my annoyance would make her try all the harder, so she'd refuse to make any decisions in case they might be wrong.

Every treat and outing I had planned would be spoiled by my expectations and her hesitations; her insistence on not being any trouble becoming more troubling and infuriating by the hour. By the time I waved her off at the station at the end of each trip, both of us would be tense and snappish. As soon as she'd gone I'd be devastated; angry at myself for not being a better daughter, for not being more patient and kind.

Matt despaired. He didn't understand how I could long for my mother's visits, and then allow them to be spoiled by insignificant incidents. He couldn't see that it was because we both cared too much about it all, because there was so much we wanted to say to each other and couldn't, or didn't, that the smallest decisions became freighted with vast importance. That Mum's inability to choose between a latte and a flat white — 'Whichever one's the least trouble, love.' 'But neither of them's *trouble*, Mum, we're in a *shop*, which one do you want?' 'I don't mind, whatever you think.' 'I'll get you a latte, then.' 'Oh, I didn't realize it would be so milky.' — was only the vessel for all the complex feelings we had about each other. Her wanting to mother me, me insisting on my independence, her trying to let me be the grown-up.

Here in Lyme it was different. I felt bad that I hadn't noticed it before. In her own environment Mum was relaxed, certain of her place and less concerned with getting things wrong. Here she was confident about her opinions and not afraid to express them. If I'd put her in a dressing gown in London, she'd have forced herself to stay in it even if Matt's entire cricket team had come round unexpectedly; she wouldn't have wanted to upset me by going against my suggestion. Here she changed out of it the minute she felt uncomfortable. I wonder if I am different here, too. Perhaps I have less to prove to her — to everyone — now that I don't have anything left of my own, except Minnie.

Even while we're snorting with laughter at the cheesy lines on the screen, I can see Mum's mind is on something else. She keeps glancing over at me, and I remember the set of her shoulders when I first led her into the living room this evening. She wants to talk to me about something. I know it must be Matt. She always had a soft spot for him; she told me I didn't know how lucky I was to have found someone like that. Well, I wonder if she thinks that now.

When she starts to speak, I'm already gripping the stem of my wine glass with tension. But she doesn't want to talk about Matt at all, it's far worse than that.

'Love, I saw Eddy Curtis yesterday,' she says.

'Did you?' I keep looking at the television, but it's a little too late to claim to be gripped by the film. I wish I hadn't been quite so quick to insist it was rubbish.

'He told me he'd had a chat with you the other day. About Tim.'

I feel bile rise up into the back of my throat, burning.

'That was all a long time ago,' I say. 'It's in the past now.'

Mum shifts on the sofa, trying to look at me properly, but I won't meet her eye. I can't believe she's brought this up now, after all these years of never mentioning it. Like I don't have enough to deal with.

As if she senses my anxiety, Minnie gets up from her bed and comes to sit next to me, nudging my fingers with her nose, which is dry from sleep. I stroke her soft head and it is a comfort.

'I wonder if it is, Kate,' says Mum. 'In the past, I mean.'

'Of course it is, Mum,' I snap, furious at her for ruining our evening together. I thought things had got better between us and now I realize they haven't in the slightest. 'What good is it, raking it all up again? Tim's in Australia, I don't ever have to see him again, I'm over it.'

Mum is quiet for a while. I can feel my heart beating wildly in my chest.

'I'm sorry,' I say eventually. 'I don't mean to be cross with you. I just don't understand why you want to talk about it now.'

Mum's expression is cautious, prepared for me to snap again. 'I always thought we should have talked about it. You just never wanted to, and I thought it was better to let you deal with it in your own way.'

I run Minnie's silken ears through my fingers as I let Mum speak. Concentrating on the dog makes it easier to hear the words.

'But, Kate,' she continues gently. 'You're not talking again. And I know you only do that when something terrible has happened. This time I can't let you shut yourself off, love. I'm sorry. I know you want us all to leave you alone, but I can't. I'm your mother.'

I bite my bottom lip, chewing until I can taste blood.

'I can't, Mum,' I say. 'I can't.'

I hear Mum sigh next to me, a slow sad exhalation. 'I'm sorry, love, but you're going to have to. You're not a teenager now. You're an adult. You can't just run away from things. You have to face up to them. Face up to yourself.'

I turn my head slowly in her direction, suspicious. I know she has been speaking to Matt; she's told me he's called them. What stories has Matt been telling her to ingratiate himself with her? To make her take his side?

'What do you mean face up to yourself?' I ask, my voice very quiet.

'No matter what happened, it takes two people to make a marriage. Or to break one. But you need to deal with this, not just hide from it. I let you do that with Tim and . . . ' she hesitates.

'Tim has nothing to do with this,' I say.

I am trying to persuade myself as much as my mother. I don't want to think about Tim Cooper any more. I have successfully buried that memory beneath my many accomplishments — my fabulous job, my lovely husband, my wonderful life. It horrifies me to discover that the memory had not been obliterated, only suppressed, ready to emerge again when my accomplishments had proven to be an illusion, no more substantial than dust.

'Your refusal to talk about it has everything to do with this,' says Mum, gently.

I shake my head.

'Please don't,' I whisper. 'Please don't, Mum, I can't bear it.'

My shoulders start to shake and, for the first time since I left my husband, I start to cry. Fat tears slide down my nose and drop onto Minnie's fur. She wags her tail and looks anxiously from me to Mum. I feel Mum's arm around my shoulders, her hand stroking my hair, and I let myself sob until my breath comes in shuddering gasps.

I cannot say it is a release. I cannot say I feel better for it. All I can say is that I don't feel any worse, which is more than I expected.

23

London

'Kate,' said Richard.

My pen traced the same words over and over on my meeting notes, shading in the spaces in the letters, adding a few hearts and flowers to break things up. I was so jetlagged from the overnight flight that I could hardly focus on the letters, let alone on the meeting which seemed to have been discussing the same tedious point, round and round without any conclusions, for twenty minutes.

'Kate,' said Richard more insistently. Sarah knocked my ribs with her elbow and I jumped.

The whole meeting was staring at me expectantly. Oh shit. Richard had been in a vile mood for over a month now. The fact that I'd been flying to Singapore for a few days each week had kept me mostly out of his firing range, but the emails I'd received from the office had given me plenty of warning that he was not to be displeased. Fifteen people had lost their jobs in the last two weeks, and everyone was nervous.

'Richard,' I said briskly, noticing that he was drumming his fingers impatiently on the table. The first rule of defence: attack. 'Can you clarify exactly what you're asking? I'm afraid I may have misunderstood the question.'

Richard glared at me. His fingers stilled. I

smiled back steadily.

'I can *clarify* that I was asking, Kate, if you were fucking listening to a word I said.'

Ah. No escaping that one. Dean from Talent smirked happily at my discomfort; he was just glad to have someone else face the wrath of Richard ever since Leila had done one illicit deal too many and been kicked out of Hitz. My kinder colleagues averted their gazes out of solidarity, but Richard continued to stare me down.

'Of course, Richard,' I said, trying not to blink. 'Sorry if I didn't seem to be paying attention, I was just thinking through a few things for Singapore. Got distracted by — ah — the budget.'

'Oh really?' Richard reached across the table and snatched my meeting notes out from under my hand. I scrabbled to get them back, but my hand just clutched at empty space. He squinted through his wire-framed glasses and an unpleasant smile spread across his face. 'How sweet. Mrs Kate Martell. Mrs K. Martell. Kate Martell. Mrs Matt Martell.'

A small squawk of glee escaped from Dean's throat before he could stop it, but as soon as I whipped my head round in his direction he dropped his eyes to the table, his shoulders shaking. Richard pushed the paper back to me, a sardonic expression on his face. This from the man who'd cried drunkenly at my wedding and told me the sight of me and Matt together made him believe in true love.

'Well, Mrs Martell,' Richard sneered. I folded

my meeting notes over and over, as if by hiding them I could erase everyone's memory. 'Do you think you might turn that fluffy little newlywed head of yours back to the matter in hand? Which is how many days of prep you and your useless team will need in Singapore?'

I had to bite my lip to stop myself from snapping back at him. I'd been working twenty-hour days, flying halfway around the world so often that I knew most of the stewardesses on Singapore Airlines by name, barely seeing my new husband, and Richard was bawling me out in front of everyone for a moment's inattention. I didn't work that hard to be patronized like some idiot.

'Ten days of prep, Richard,' I said carefully, keeping my voice steady. The person who loses their temper is the person who loses the argument. 'I can forward you the spreadsheet after the meeting. The local crew is on the case with the preliminaries, we need one week with just a skeleton crew, then three days with the full team and we're there.'

'How skeleton can you go on the crew?' asked Richard, frowning. In front of him was a sheet of figures highlighted in neon yellow and pink. No iPad for Richard, he was proudly old school, as he often liked to tell us. Acoustic, not digital, as if it made him more authentic rather than just out of date. He waggled his pen impatiently between his fingers, so that it was a blur of movement.

'Well, probably just me, Sarah and Kirsty initially,' I said. 'Plus the local team, that's about eleven.'

'And for the full crew?' He peered at me over the top of his glasses.

'Well,' I said, trying to remember the figures off the top of my head. 'Thirty? I think. I can send you the proper numbers after the meeting.'

Richard lifted the top sheet of figures and underlined something on the paper below. He looked up.

'Do you really need everyone out there for three days? Can't they get it done in two?'

I sighed and rubbed the heels of my hands against my red-rimmed eyes before I realized I was probably smudging mascara all over my face. Not that you'd probably notice — the bags under my eyes were multiplying as rapidly as my airmiles lately, and the skin there was already grey.

You'd think I was asking Richard for holiday time rather than begging to be allowed to fly thousands of miles to work like crazy, far away from my home and my husband. Everyone wanted to get the job done and get home, didn't Richard see that?

'Richard, every time I get back from Singapore you've changed the parameters again. It's making so much extra work. It was meant to be five days with full crew, then three and now you want to cut it again? Do you want this event done properly or do you just want it done cheaply?' I put my palms flat on the table. 'I can do either, but I can't do both. It's impossible.'

Richard scowled. 'It is your job, *Mrs Martell*, to get it done properly and not to spunk Hitz money all over the place while you're doing it.

Do you think that's impossible? Because there are plenty of people who'd leap at the chance if you think so.'

I knew exactly who he meant. If he thought he could go out to lunch with Jennifer Heston without my knowing about it, he was very much mistaken. Meeting the former MTV Production Manager in the Delaunay was about as subtle as setting up a table for the two of them next to Lindsey's desk in Reception. I don't know if Jennifer was touting for freelance work, or if he was trying to lure her over here above my head, but either way it had made me even more anxious on top of the jetlag and the stress.

I pushed my plastic cup of stale meeting coffee away from me. I thought it would keep me awake, but it was just making me jittery and paranoid.

'When have I ever gone over budget?' I demanded, hoping that he wouldn't remember how much petty cash I spent on bribes in Lagos. I was sure I had hidden it well enough that it wouldn't immediately come to his mind. 'You know I can deliver exactly what you want for exactly how much it needs to cost. It's just driving me demented that the budget keeps changing every five minutes.'

'Everyone is having to make compromises, Kate,' snapped Richard, throwing his pen down on the table with a clatter that made us all jump. 'Everyone. And when I have to make them, you make them too, do you understand?'

His face had become mottled with purple, as if all the blood vessels had rushed to the surface waving flags in solidarity with his argument. A vein stood out alarmingly on the side of his neck, pulsing like it was trying to break out of his skin and escape to somewhere calmer.

'Yes, Richard,' I said, bobbing my head down obediently. I didn't want to be responsible for him having a heart attack. 'Sorry.'

'Good,' said Richard, his colour diminishing slightly. He ran a finger round the edge of his collar, pulling it away from his neck as if he needed air. 'Get it right. I don't want to see Ball-Basher Bailey turning into Ball-Dropping Bailey, is that clear?'

'Yes,' I said meekly. I didn't feel it was quite the right time to correct him about my new last name when he'd seen it written out six times only minutes earlier.

★ ★ ★

When I got home Matt was already on the sofa, staring at his laptop, elbows on his knees. A half-empty beer bottle sat on the coffee table next to him and his face glowed a ghostly blue as he scowled at something, his nose only inches from the screen.

He'd changed into the old grey sweatshirt and pyjama bottoms he wore after a heavy day at work. I always teased him that they were his grotty equivalent of a Hugh Hefner-style smoking jacket — the items of clothing that announced a man at leisure. And I can't deny that I've worn that sweatshirt myself when he's been away on a trip for too long, just to remind myself of him.

'You'll go blind,' I said, from the doorway.

He turned his head and gave me a faint, tired smile. The bags under his eyes were almost a match for my own. 'I thought that was masturbation?'

'Are you watching porn again?' I teased. I leaned on the door frame. 'Put your hands where I can see them.'

'Yeah? Put your arse on my lap, Basher,' said Matt, leaning back and slapping his thighs. His wedding ring winked on his left hand. I still wasn't used to it. Matt Martell, my husband.

I hovered at the door, I hadn't taken off my coat yet and I felt grimy from the overnight flight and the commute home.

'Come on, my wife,' he said, stretching out his arm to beckon me over. 'Come here and make your old man very happy.'

I dragged my feet as I crossed the floor, dropping my bag from my shoulder. Matt's dark hair stood up in tufts on his head — he only twisted it like that when he was stressed. He didn't even know he was doing it, but it was one of the things I'd learned living with him. When his hair went like that it was best to tread carefully. I cast a quick glance at his laptop screen as I lowered myself onto his lap — no porn, just another spreadsheet. Lately I saw spreadsheets as I drifted off to sleep, columns of figures leaping over fences, the way other people counted sheep. Hitz was in trouble and we were all feeling it.

Matt let out an ungentlemanly 'oof' sound as I leaned into him.

'Matt Martell, are you implying that I am anything other than a sylph-like featherweight?' I asked indignantly.

'Not for a minute,' Matt promised, his face solemn. 'Have you even sat down yet? I can't feel a thing.'

'That's better,' I said, slipping my arms around his neck.

'Because my legs have gone completely dead,' he said, grimacing. 'I may never be able to feel them again. No, no don't get up, stay here. I've missed your face.'

I rested my head on his shoulder and inhaled. Matt didn't wear aftershave, but I loved the mingled scent of his shaving cream, the moisturiser that he insisted was actually a very manly 'face protector', and something indefinable that was just Matt. His hair; his skin. I traced the tip of my nose along the side of his ear.

'I missed yours, too.'

'How come you're so late home?' he asked.

'It's only eight,' I said. 'I just stopped off for a drink with Sarah. Richard's being a total bastard at the moment and we just needed to let off a bit of steam.'

'Get drunk, you mean,' said Matt, pretending to sniff my breath.

'I had one glass of wine, Matt,' I said, warningly, looking over at his open beer bottle. 'And then I left them to it.'

I didn't tell Matt that I'd been roundly berated for leaving so early. Jay had turned up at the Crown and Two Chairmen to meet Sarah, with Danny and Chris in tow, all ready to settle in for a session. Their disappointment at my leaving was mostly because I held the Hitz credit card that usually paid for several rounds. But we'd been told to cut expenses lately and I didn't dare use it unless it was legitimately for work. Instead I bought a round with my own money — tactical, since the three of them were coming out to Singapore in a few weeks — and left them to it. Ignoring all the calls about the ball and chain at home.

'I know, I know, it was work, right?' Matt laughed. 'You weren't enjoying yourself at all, it was a struggle and a trial forcing that wine down.'

'Oh, shut up. Why are *you* still working, anyway?' I asked, glancing over at the laptop glowing on the coffee table, an unwelcome intruder into my homecoming. It wasn't like I'd expected Matt to meet me wearing an apron and brandishing a casserole dish — unless he'd had a personality transplant since I'd been away in Singapore — but when I'd longed for home it was for more than a stressed-out husband and his computer.

Matt pushed himself forward, so that I nearly lost my balance on his knees and had to tighten my grip around him. He slammed the laptop shut. 'I'm not,' he said, squeezing me back. 'I'm spending the evening with my lovely wife.'

He kissed me, his hand reaching around to stroke my bottom.

'I've missed this arse,' he said. I tried to look at him seductively but my stomach gave a loud gurgle and he broke into laughter. 'Hungry?'

'Yes,' I said.

'For me,' said Matt, kissing me again.

'For you, but also, I am genuinely starving, Matt. Sorry. Can we eat first?'

'Sure,' said Matt, picking up his phone from the sofa beside him. 'What do you fancy? I'll order in.'

I took the phone from him and switched it off. 'I don't want a takeaway,' I said.

Matt looked puzzled. 'It might be a bit late, but we could head to Pizza Express or something?'

I shook my head, my hair falling out of the ponytail I'd pulled it into when I got off the plane. 'Matt, I haven't had a meal at home for a week. I just want something that hasn't been fiddled about with, heated up on an airplane, or garnished with two crossed chives and a kumquat. What's in the fridge?'

Matt made a face that told me not to expect much. Even though we'd spent a fortune on an American-style two-door stainless-steel fridge, there wasn't often anything decent in it — usually little more than a few beers, a half-open bottle of wine and an optimistically purchased bag of salad mutating from a solid into a liquid in the vegetable drawer — but it was always especially bad when I'd been away.

'Is there any bread?' I asked. Matt considered, his eyes rising to the ceiling thoughtfully and then he nodded. 'Cheese?'

'Think so,' he said. 'Cheddar.'

I rocked myself up off his lap and straightened up my skirt. 'Tonight, Matt, I will be serving my speciality, fromage au pain.'

Matt clapped his hands together in mock delight. '*Avec le sauce de Worcestershire?*'

'*Naturellement, monsieur,*' I said, with a little curtsey.

'Good job I didn't marry you for your culinary expertise,' he grinned.

'Fuck off,' I said affectionately. 'You could always make it yourself, you know.'

'You know I don't mean it, Kate,' he said, opening up his laptop again. 'You're everything a wife should be, and more. I'll be down to the kitchen in ten minutes, just need to finish this off first.'

He picked up his beer and took a long gulp, while I headed down to the kitchen and hoped there were more where that came from.

24

I know what people in Lyme think about the sort of person who wears sunglasses on a grey morning in November. Chanel sunglasses. Inside the bakery. But the choice is to either be considered a pretentious urban idiot or have everyone witness the fact that my eyes have swollen up into puffy slits from crying, like the freshly risen dough on the racks behind me, and I know which one I'd prefer. I expect they already think the former, so let them think it. I don't need to be the subject of more gossip.

'Are you all right there, my love?' asks Cathy, kindly, as she brings over my coffee.

'Fine, thanks,' I say, turning my covered eyes in her direction and offering her my brightest smile. 'How are you?'

'Oh I'm fine, my love,' she says, staying nearby while she adjusts the position of a sugar bowl and moves the butter dish by a few unnecessary centimetres. 'Got a bit of a hangover this morning, have you?'

I seize on the excuse instantly. 'Yes, gosh, half a bottle of wine with Mum last night and I'm a proper state today.'

'Thought so,' she says, nodding her head in satisfaction. 'Your Mum stopped in this morning for a Danish pastry and I'm not betraying any confidences if I tell you she only ever does that if she's got a sore head. She said she'd been visiting you last night, so I put two and two together.'

'I suppose the sunglasses gave it away a bit,' I admit.

'Oh, my love, I don't judge. Whatever gets you through. A coffee will sort you right out. Go and get yourself some toast, that'll help.'

A family comes into the bakery, parents and children, all anoraks and walking boots and glowering teenage resentment, so Cathy leaves me to show them to the far end of the trestle table. I go to the counter and cut myself two thick slices of heavy sourdough bread, and drop them into the toaster, watching the filaments glow hotly as the toast browns.

When I go back to the table, one of the teenagers is crouched down by my seat, her sulkiness forgotten, stroking Minnie's eager little face. The girl blushes as I approach, and stands up, flustered.

'S-sorry, I should've asked,' she says, stepping backwards.

'It's okay,' I reply, smiling. 'She loves a bit of attention. Her name's Minnie.'

The girl hesitates, looking back at her parents. 'They said I shouldn't disturb you,' she says, and I'm not sure if she has come over here to see Minnie because she wanted to or because she wanted to defy them. They smile at me apologetically. I expect I do look quite forbidding in my harsh sunglasses.

'Oh it's fine,' I say, and sit down on the bench next to her. 'You're not disturbing me at all. Are you on holiday?'

The girl crouches down again, and starts scratching Minnie's chest in a way that makes her puppy eyes glaze with contentment.

'Yeah.' She sighs. 'Lyme fucking Regis with my parents. Seriously. I'm too old for this.'

I hold back a smile. She looks impossibly young to me, with her gangly limbs and heartbreakingly studied attempts at nonchalance.

'How old are you?' I ask, before remembering how much I hated being asked that when I was her age. Every year gained felt so significant back then that it astonished me people couldn't tell exactly how old I was. How mortifying to be taken for fifteen (silly, schoolgirlish) when one was seventeen (about to leave home, grown-up).

'Sixteen,' she says, a challenge in her up-tilted chin, as if I might dispute it.

'Oh, I thought you were older,' I say. This is quite untrue, but I feel I owe her a favour after asking the dreaded question in the first place.

She ducks her head, blushing again, but not before I see a glimpse of the smile that shows her delight.

'I found Lyme pretty boring when I was your age too,' I admit, buttering my toast. 'There's not a lot here for teenagers.'

She looks up at me witheringly, clearly unable to believe I might ever have had anything in common with her. It's strange how coming back to Lyme has made me feel like I'm the same insecure eighteen-year-old who ran away to London, and yet to this teenage girl — nearly the age I was then — I am just another tedious adult who can't possibly understand her angst.

'Yeah, anyway, thanks for letting me say hi to your dog,' the girl says, standing up. 'Bye, Minnie.'

'Bye,' I say. 'Enjoy the rest of your holiday.'

She rolls her eyes. As she goes back to her parents I hear her mother tell her to wash her hands after stroking the dog. The girl refuses — 'It didn't even lick me!' — and they begin bickering in fierce whispers, as if we can't all tell that they're arguing. To my surprise, it's the mother I feel sorry for. She's only trying to look after her daughter, to protect her. I feel a sudden pang for my mother, and how she must have felt when I shut her out of my life back then.

My throat constricts and I feel blood rush to my cheeks. I can't start crying again; God, I won't be able to see out of my eyes at this rate. All of this reminiscing is turning me into a lunatic. This is why it's better not to dwell too much on the past.

'Yoohoo!' calls a voice, jolting me out of my thoughts. Mrs Curtis bustles through the door of the bakery determinedly.

Cathy suddenly steps into her path and there is a heated debate, conducted mostly in whispers. Cathy grasps Mrs Curtis's elbow and starts to steer her towards the door.

'Pam, it's nothing personal, but if you can't show me you've got enough money to pay for your tea — '

'Dreadful woman!' exclaims Mrs Curtis, slapping ineffectively at Cathy's hand.

I stand up and join them, lowering my voice to the same whisper, even though every eye in the bakery is already on the three of us.

'Cathy, it's okay. Mrs Curtis was going to join me, weren't you?'

Mrs Curtis straightens her fleece and pink knitted cap, sniffing in outrage. 'Thank you, dear. Is there *no* respect for one's elders these days?'

Cathy and I exchange a look that tells me I, too, may be persona non grata here if I don't watch it. But Mrs Curtis has already moved on and, with blithe unconcern, is helping herself to a plateful of pastries from the counter.

When she sits down opposite me her plate is piled high, and she begins to wrap each pastry in a napkin before tucking them into a plastic bag that she has pulled out of the pocket of her fleece.

'For later, dear,' she says. 'So kind of you. One small *misunderstanding* over my bill — so long ago! — and Cathy simply will *not* let bygones be bygones.'

I decide that now is not the time to tackle Mrs Curtis's free-and-easy attitude towards other people's money.

'Have you been for a swim this morning?' I ask.

'Ooh, *no*, dear,' she says, with an elaborate wink. 'Of course not. Now, I have been meaning to *ask* you . . . '

I steel myself for another round of questions about Matt. Mrs Curtis seems determined to draw parallels between her life and mine and, although I have grown pretty fond of her, I have to admit to resisting comparisons to a nearly bald kleptomaniac with a taste for sea water and rubber hats.

'That young man who's living with you — Prue's fiancé, isn't he?'

'Yes, Ben,' I say. 'They're getting married on New Year's Eve.'

'My dear he looked *ever* so cross last night. Not that I'm a curtain-twitcher — far from it! — but I just *happened* to see him leaving the house at about half past seven and he seemed in a *fearsome* mood. Muttering to himself, you know.'

I had thought Ben seemed far too accepting of my lesson last night. And now here was the proof that he wasn't accepting at all. How strange to realize that Ben, who I had considered to be so transparently obvious in all things, is able to hide his true feelings after all. But at the same time, it shows that the lesson must have gone in at some level. He needed to feel the bite of it to remember for next time.

'Just a bit of confusion over visitors, Mrs Curtis,' I explain. 'Nothing to worry about. You know how it is when you're living with someone new, takes a bit of getting used to.'

Mrs Curtis nibbles thoughtfully on a pain au raisin, chewing all the way around the outside in little bites.

'I suppose it is rather *strange*, to have to accommodate someone else in your own living space,' she says. 'I'm not sure I could tolerate it.'

'Well, you know,' I answer. 'It's just a matter of expectations, really. And training, ha ha.'

She looks at me shrewdly over the top of her

pastry. 'Training, dear?'

'Just joking,' I say, picking up a napkin and wiping at a non-existent spot of coffee on the table.

'*Are* you?' she asks.

I fold the napkin up into a small square and tuck it into my empty coffee cup. Mrs Curtis continues to wait for my answer as she picks at her pastry with her red fingernails.

'Mrs Curtis,' I say. 'Can you keep a secret?'

'No, dear,' she answers frankly.

But I decide to tell her anyway. Who's she going to report back to, after all? And even if she does go blabbing, everyone thinks she's crazy. No one would believe her. I feel a compulsion to have a witness to my mission — someone to observe the progress that would otherwise go unmarked by anyone but me.

'Mrs Curtis, what would you think if I told you that Ben is my foster husband?'

25

The doorbell rings early on Saturday morning. I'm still in my pyjamas since Ben woke early and decided to rip out the blue bathroom tiles before I could have a shower. Sometimes my good intentions are my own undoing, but it's the last room to be done up. The plumber arrives on Monday and in a week the whole house will be finished. I try not to think what will happen if the redecorated house sells as quickly as I assured Ben it would. It might force me into making some sort of decision about where to go next.

Through the frosted glass I can see two small figures, and a taller one. Minnie barks at the door, and I see the letterbox flip open and five little fingers poke through the bristle strips, a pair of eyes searching behind them.

'Well, good morning,' I say, opening the door to see Eddy and his girls standing there expectantly. Grace hops from foot to foot, one hand hidden behind her back.

'We've got a present for the puppy,' she shrieks, unable to contain herself any longer. She thrusts out her hand towards Minnie, who sniffs at the haphazardly wrapped package.

'Oh wow, aren't you sweet?' I say. 'Thank you.'

Charlotte plays it cool. 'Grace, Daddy says we're not to give it to Minnie unless Kate says so. You shouldn't feed other people's dogs without asking.'

'You know, you're absolutely right, Charlotte,' I say. 'You're very good to ask. Why don't you come on in and then you can give Minnie her present in the garden in case she makes a mess opening it?'

Eddy smiles at me over the heads of his daughters as they race past me towards the back door.

'Seem to always catch you in your pyjamas,' he says, embarrassed. He suddenly starts as he hears a sound from the bathroom.

'Er, Kate, have you got someone here? Should we — '

I snort with laughter. 'God, Eddy, no! It's my sister's fiancé.'

Eddy's eyes widen still further, and his eyebrows shoot up towards his hairline.

'Not like that! He's just moved in for a while, before the wedding — he's helping with decorating the place so we can sell it faster,' I explain. Eddy looks reassured, but still suspicious.

'Bit weird though, isn't it?' he says, tilting his head towards the bathroom.

I shrug. It's come to seem totally normal to me now, or as normal as things get in my family. From the garden we can hear the girls shrieking with excitement, and Minnie's sharp yaps. Eddy follows me into the kitchen, and I'm putting the kettle on when Ben appears, wiping his hands all over his sweatshirt, his hair and eyebrows white with plaster dust.

'Hi,' he says, confidently striding towards Eddy with his wiped-clean hand outstretched. 'How do you do? Ben Truscott. Prue's, er, betrothed.'

Eddy looks bewildered at the formality of the introduction. 'Eddy Curtis,' he says, looking at me for his cue. 'Kate's, er, schoolfriend?'

Ben beams at both of us. 'Kettle on?' he says, unnecessarily since he must be able to hear it clunking away behind me. 'Mine's white, two sugars.'

I give him a look that he chooses to ignore, staring instead at Eddy. It doesn't escape my notice that the arrival of another man in the house has ramped up Ben's testosterone levels considerably. He wouldn't dream of expecting me to make him tea without asking nicely if he wasn't showing off. I find myself wondering, as I open the cupboard for teabags, how effective Ben's training truly is if it all falls apart in front of other people.

As if reading my mind, Eddy asks, out of nowhere, 'My grandma says to ask you how the training's going?'

'What?' I exclaim, spinning around from the cupboard. But he looks perfectly innocent.

'Training,' says Eddy. 'The dog, I supposed she meant.'

'Oh yes,' I say. 'Minnie. Of course. Well, you can tell her it's going fine. A few wobbles, but a firm hand is all that's needed. The results are worth it.'

'So, Eddy,' says Ben, standing with his legs improbably far apart in what I can only assume is an effort to look more macho. 'At school with Kate, eh? I bet you've got a tale or two to tell, ha ha!'

Eddy mutters something about the girls, and

strides over to the back door to look out at where they're playing.

Ben, as oblivious as ever, ploughs on. 'Prue says she had a total mare at school being known as Kate's sister. Everyone always expected her to blow up the chemistry lab, or deal drugs behind the languages block.'

Eddy coughs and glances at me quickly.

'Reports of my wildness may have been exaggerated,' I say, smiling and letting Eddy see that I'm not bothered by it. 'And sharing the occasional spliff hardly counts as dealing drugs. Prue makes it sound like I was selling crack on the playing fields.'

Ben sucks in his breath audibly, shaking his head. 'You say that, Kate, but it's pretty well-documented that marijuana is a gateway drug. I'm no authority, but I believe I'm right in saying that the occasional spliff, as you so casually put it, can lead to much more dangerous drugs.'

I smirk down at the kitchen counter, plopping two teaspoons of sugar into Ben's milky tea as he continues his lecture. From over by the back door, Eddy catches my eye and flashes me a conspiratorial grin. Us against Ben. It feels strange — I'd almost forgotten how it felt to be anything other than me on my own against everything — but welcome to be silently sharing a joke across a room like this, not having to say a word to be understood.

Our eyes stay locked for a fraction too long to be comfortable, and Eddy breaks away first, stepping out into the garden, claiming to hear the girls arguing. Ben continues regardless.

'I'm sure you're right, Ben,' I say, eventually, to shut him up. I have a feeling he could go on for hours about the dangers of 'hard drugs', which is an expression I have only heard on the lips of people who've never taken any. 'It's only a matter of luck that I didn't end up as a crack whore, or worse.'

'Well,' says Eddy, coming back into the kitchen with a glint in his eye. 'I don't know about luck. Everyone knows that Manda Clarke had the crack-whore thing sewn up back then — she'd never have let you on her patch. And Davy Mason was running Lyme's heroin supply from the bike sheds. Not sure there was room for another dealer in town.'

'Heroin?' exclaims Ben, his eyes nearly popping out of his head. 'Crikey!'

'Well,' I say to Eddy. 'Until Davy got turned out of the bike sheds by Manda's underage prostitution ring, of course. No one wanted to cross the Big Mama of the Fourth Year.'

'Of course,' says Eddy gravely, shaking his head. 'Tough times. They'd cleaned the school up a lot by the time Prue got there, Ben. Don't look so shocked.'

Ben looks from me to Eddy and then back again, his forehead contracting with the effort of thinking. Then he reaches over and slaps Eddy on the back so heartily that Eddy has to take a correcting step to steady himself.

'Ha! Nearly had me then! Prostitution ring!' Ben's booming laugh fills the kitchen.

'Here's your tea,' I say, holding out a steaming

220

mug. 'Watch out for the heroin. I'm not sure I stirred it in properly.'

Ben scoffs and takes the mug out of my hands, still chuckling.

'So you've made this place look amazing,' says Eddy. 'Grandma said you'd been working like mad.'

'Thanks,' Ben and I say in unison. He looks embarrassed to have been caught taking all the credit.

'All Kate's idea,' says Ben graciously.

'But I couldn't have done it without Ben,' I say, equally gracious. I feel like we are an advert for cordial relations between in-laws, at least, now that he's forgiven me for turfing him out of the house when the football was on.

'Yeah,' he agrees. 'Kate's more of the foreman type. You know what women are like, mate. Just give the directions, ha! Leave all the grafting to us, right?'

Eddy laughs uncomfortably, and Ben adopts an even more wide-legged stance, as if to assert his manliness despite admitting he obeyed my orders. At this rate he'll soon be on the kitchen floor in full box splits.

'Well, it looks great,' says Eddy, politely tactful.

Ben claims that it's because he and I are a dream team, which is news to me. I suppose it's true that I think of myself more as the foreman than part of a team. But someone has to be in charge, surely? Otherwise you just drift, never achieving anything, never going anywhere. There has to be a direction in life, or where do you end up?

I excuse myself to use the bathroom while Ben is on a break from ripping up the tiles. I've hardly left the kitchen before I hear his next question to Eddy, announced in his foghorn voice as if he's projecting out into the street.

'Seriously, though, mate, I heard Kate was a right goer back at school. Did you and she ever — '

I slam the bathroom door before I have to hear any more.

In the half-destroyed bathroom, plaster dust settles in my hair as I pick my toothbrush off the side of the sink. Considering my reflection, I seem to have a touch of the Miss Havishams — if she had lived in a Sixties bungalow. It's less romantic than a crumbling old mansion, and the bright blue bathroom suite doesn't really lend itself to an atmosphere of tragedy, but we definitely have something in common. Our pasts weigh too heavily on the present. If I don't escape from mine soon, I may as well stay hiding in this bathroom forever, shrinking away from conversations, avoiding contact with the outside world.

Is that what I want? To hide out in Lyme for ever, slowly mouldering, my hair greying with age and dust? If the best revenge is living well, I'm not doing a terribly good job of it.

26

London

Although Matt frequently accused me of living there, I'd never been in the Crown and Two Chairmen in the middle of the day before. I suppose it had never crossed my mind that people might sit in a pub on a workday — don't they have places to go? Money to earn? But the pub was busy. Not like on a Thursday or a Friday night when the afterwork crowd was four deep at the bar, and punters took over the pavements outside, but tables were occupied, the quiz machine was in use, the barman rushed from customer to customer. I had thought it was only tragic, unemployed alcoholics who found themselves downing their third drink of the day by 3 p.m., but this afternoon I was well on the way to becoming one of their number.

Richard had called us in the moment we returned from Singapore. We thought, naturally, that it was for the usual wash-up session: going over what had worked and what hadn't, discussing what we could improve for the next time, making sure all the figures added up. He should have been out in Singapore to oversee everything, but at the last minute he'd had to stay in London. Even without him, the event had been a triumph — everyone said so — and through the jetlag and exhaustion we were proud of the job we'd done. Striding through the office after two weeks away, trailing our wheeled suitcases behind us, Sarah and I had greeted our colleagues, ready for the praise we were sure must be coming our way — and the compliments on the tans we'd managed to get by the hotel pool on the last day. But people seemed to be avoiding conversation beyond a brief hello.

When we got to the meeting, Sarah and I sniggered over Richard's new dye job — raven black — which, instead of making him look younger, gave him the look of an aged Elvis impersonator. It must have been the dark hair that made him look so grey; the colour had drained out of his skin completely. No longer was he the red and angry shouty boss at the head of the meeting table; this morning he looked like he was auditioning for the role of an undertaker, his face immobile and drawn.

'Sit down,' he said, and we all exchanged amused looks. What had got into him all of a sudden? Still in our post-show bubble, none of us could imagine what was going to happen next.

'You did a great job, everyone,' said Richard. I couldn't help but notice that he didn't have his usual list of figures in front of him, which made me instantly suspicious. He never went anywhere without those highlighted spreadsheets, I swear he slept with them clutched to his chest like a security blanket. 'Great job. No one could have asked for more of you. Not even me.'

Sarah's expression was quizzical, and mine must have matched it. The wash-up meeting wasn't about praise — we'd congratulated ourselves enough in the hotel bar after the show — it was about picking holes in the event so they didn't happen next time. Working out what went wrong, apportioning blame. I fidgeted on my chair. Something was up.

Richard cleared his throat and continued. 'I'm just going to come out and say it. They're shutting us down. That was our last event for Hitz. I'm sorry.'

We were all too surprised to speak. Sarah's jaw hung open as she stared at him. Richard looked anxiously from face to face, as if concerned we hadn't heard him properly. I felt like an utter fool. How had I not seen this coming? Being alert to the grapevine at Hitz was the only way to survive — I'd seen other people lose their jobs and wondered how they could have failed to see it coming. And now here I was, blindsided. Being away in Singapore was no excuse.

'The whole department?' I asked at last. 'But they cut us in half last year. I thought that was it.'

'I thought that was it, too, I'm sorry. They're taking event production out of house. Jennifer Heston is setting up a new production company and they're going to take over all ongoing events. What happens after that is anyone's guess.'

'How long have we got?' I asked.

'Three months,' he said. 'You all get three months — you can carry on working here until your notice period is up, or you can go home today and not come back. You'll get paid either way. And you each have a meeting with HR to discuss the terms of your redundancy.'

'I don't believe it,' said Kirsty.

'It's not as bad as it seems,' said Richard, in a tone that suggested he was trying to persuade himself of this as much as the rest of us. 'The package they're offering is very generous. And Jennifer's going to need experienced staff — and freelancers — to keep these projects running. There will be plenty of opportunities for you all. You're talented and smart. I've loved working with all of you. I know you'll be fine.'

His voiced cracked and he dropped his head down, so that all we could see was the improbably glossy hair with his pale scalp shining through, ghostly white.

Sarah spoke. 'What about you, Richard? What's happening to you?'

Richard dismissed her with a shake of his shoulders. 'Oh, I'll be okay, I'm having a lot of meetings. Something will come up.'

'The fuckers,' shrieked Sarah in the pub six hours later. 'The fuckers. Like it's not bad enough they kick us all out, they get fucking Richard to tell us when they're kicking him out too. Gerald should have had the balls to stand up and tell us himself.'

'Yeah,' said Jay. 'Like in the war, making a man dig his own grave. Nazi bastards.'

The news of our redundancy had spread beyond Hitz within hours. Like a bat signal of distress, audible to those whose working hours were flexible to nonexistent, those who were perfectly familiar with the inside of a pub mid-afternoon. The cameramen were all here, their numbers buoyed by other freelancers who'd leapt at the opportunity of an impromptu session.

'Dunno that Gerald's a Nazi, mate,' said Danny uncertainly. 'Bit strong.'

'Wanker then,' said Jay.

'Yeah, definitely a wanker,' Danny granted.

'I mean, Richard's got no chance,' said Sarah. 'How old is he? Fifty-five? And that terrible dye job — he must have thought it would make him look younger for interviews. But he just looks ridiculous. Oh God, I could cry.'

'Don't cry, babe,' said Jay. 'It's not your problem. He'll be fine. They've probably paid him a fortune — enough to keep him in hair dye for the rest of his life.'

Across the table Chris stayed apart from the banter, looking over at me every now and again in a way that I once used to find knicker-melting and now just found irritating. A sort of 'you and me, we're above all this, aren't we?' expression. I deliberately picked up my wine glass with my left hand and made sure the diamond solitaire caught the light. I didn't need solidarity from an ex-shag. I was going to be fine. Just as soon as I'd got completely shitfaced.

By the time the rest of the Hitz office started coming into the pub, we were all well on the way to annihilation. After we'd bought several rounds, I had ceremonially burned my Hitz corporate credit card with Pete's lighter, which had nearly got us thrown out of the pub. In the end the barman had been persuaded that he'd be losing a great deal of custom by banning us and had allowed us to stay. Kirsty had had her bag stolen, which had added an extra layer of drama to the afternoon. I began to see how delighted everyone around us was — though they would have denied it immediately — by the excitement and outrage of it all. The theft, the redundancies; it was all the same to them, as mere spectators. We were the centre of attention, the focus of all conversation, our most banal utterances treated as fascinating. Everyone wanted to be near us, to have some of the glamour rub off on them.

I knew it wouldn't last — that soon we'd just be four people out looking for work, like everyone else, no longer the centre of anything. But for now I was fired up with adrenaline, righteous indignation and at least a bottle of Pinot Grigio.

'I'm really sorry about it all, yeah?' said Chris, sidling up to me. He pulled up a small upholstered stool slightly away from the table, so that I had to turn my back on the others to answer him.

'Dunwurry about it,' I slurred, spilling wine on my skirt and rubbing it in. It was white, it wouldn't show. 'I'm gonna be A-OK.'

'I know,' said Chris, placing a reassuring hand on my thigh. I looked down at it, but wasn't sure I had the coordination required to push it away. 'You'll get a new job in no time, Kate, you're brilliant at what you do.'

'Manks, I mean, fanks,' I mumbled. The room was refusing to stay still. The pictures on the wall behind Chris seemed to be tilting at all sorts of strange angles. The flashing lights of the quiz machine throbbed in my head.

'I know you think I was just some casual shag,

Kate,' said Chris, his voice low so that the others wouldn't hear. 'But that wasn't how it was for me. I was just — I guess I was just a bit intimidated by you. Never dared talk to you unless we were both pissed. I wish I hadn't been now. You're an amazing woman.'

I tried to focus on his face, but I couldn't do it. I closed one eye to see if it would make it better, and angled my head like a dog sizing up a toy.

'Well,' I said, wobbling on my chair. 'Its a good job I'm totally sober now, isn't it?'

'I mean it,' said Chris. 'Don't let this get you down. You're going to get another job in no time.'

'Of course she is,' said a voice behind him. I squinted up to see Matt looming over us both, his eyebrows raised sardonically. He seemed to find the sight of the two of us slightly ridiculous.

'Matt,' I squealed, lurching up and throwing myself on him. 'Matt, where have you been? I've been here for ages.' I leaned on his broad chest and sighed happily.

Chris stood up quickly and stepped backwards. 'Hi, mate,' he said. 'All right?'

'Yes, thanks,' said Matt icily. 'You?'

'Yeah, great,' said Chris. 'I'm off to the bar. Drink, Kate? Matt?'

I looked unsteadily up at Matt. 'I think it's probably time I took this one home,' he said.

'Matty, don't be like that,' I pleaded as Chris scurried away. 'I don't wanna go home. Wanna stay here with my friends and get drunk. Don't spoil it.'

Matt's brows creased as he looked down at me. 'Seems like you *are* drunk, Kate. And it looks like things are probably winding up anyway.'

I looked over to the table, past the silver foil of the opened crisp packets, past the scattered peanuts and the empty glasses, past the upended wine bottle in its metal cooler. Sarah lay slumped with her head in Jay's lap while he gesticulated over her head, sharing stories with Pete and Danny. Kirsty was on the phone in tears for incomprehensible reasons, mo st likely to do with her stolen bag. Dean from Talent had muscled his way in to drink to our departure, like the bad fairy at a christening, toasting his own survival against the odds. The party was in full swing but we, its ostensible subjects, were no longer a part of it. Matt was right, it was time to say goodbye to them all. Everyone else was going to carry on without us.

27

Ben has excelled himself, truly, by volunteering the information that he and Prue will be having a night in at the bungalow tonight. Usually they watch television at Mum and Dad's, or they go out for quiet meals together, both going home separately before 11 p.m. I do not even pretend to understand their relationship. Where's the mad passion? The spontaneity? The can't-keep-our-hands-off-each-otherness of the soon-to-be-weds?

'Just, ah, wanted to let you know,' Ben says. 'In advance. So you can, well, just so you know in advance, Kate.'

'That's really good of you, Ben, thanks,' I say, suppressing the wish to pat him approvingly on his eager blond head, or give him a dog treat for good behaviour. I feel a maternal pride at his continued development — in my head there is a chart full of gold stars awarded for improvement.

This morning he asked me if I'd like to use the — new, shining white, pristine — bathroom before him. And when I came out from having my shower I saw him actually brushing toast crumbs off the kitchen table. Okay, he brushed them straight onto the floor, but it is definite progress.

'What are you two going to get up to, or don't I want to know?'

Ben flushes ruddily. 'Oh, ah, nothing like that.

I mean, Prue's going to cook us up a brace of pheasants and we're going to talk about the wedding over a glass of wine or two.'

See what I mean? A brace of pheasants? A glass of wine or two? At their age? It's not normal. My idea of a balanced meal when I was in my twenties was a slice of leftover pizza with a handful of crisps on the side for roughage. Washed down with a bottle of tooth-dissolvingly rough wine from the corner shop. And that was before I went out. The idea of spending an evening in with a brace of pheasants — well, at twenty-six I'd have imagined A Brace of Pheasants must be a really rocking new band, frankly.

'Sounds lovely,' I lie.

'Actually, ah, Kate.' Ben shuffles from foot to foot, hooking his thumbs into the belt loops of his chinos. 'Was going to ask your advice, if you — I mean, could you?'

I stare at him. I thought Ben was convinced he knew everything already. I'm not used to seeing him so uncertain and hesitant.

'Of course, Ben, fire away,' I say, settling myself at the kitchen table to dispense advice. Who'd have thought Ben would be so well-trained that he'd be positively begging for my thoughts?

'Thing is, Kate, Prue's asked me to book the honeymoon.'

I raise my eyebrows at him, waiting to hear the quandary.

'Said it's my responsibility, you know. She doesn't want to get involved.'

Ben pulls on his belt loops, looking strangely like a male stripper who's about to whip off his velcro trousers. I hope sincerely this is not the case.

He continues, 'Only, ah, she keeps asking me questions about it. And getting cross. And I don't know what I've done wrong because I haven't even booked anything yet.'

'Wait,' I say. 'Did you tell her this?'

'Tell her what?'

'Tell her you haven't booked the honeymoon yet?'

Ben looks stricken. 'Yes.'

'And it's how many weeks until the wedding — five?'

'Six,' Ben mumbles indistinctly.

I resist the temptation to shriek in horror. Why has he left it to the last minute? Why has Prue put something like this in Ben's clumsy hands in the first place? But panicking won't help. This must be handled with calm.

'So where does she want to go?' I ask, keeping my voice as steady and soothing as if I were talking someone down from the edge of a tall building.

Ben frowns. 'Ah, no, Kate,' he explains carefully. 'She said it was up to me to book it. Surprise.'

'Honestly? You really think that?' I try not to laugh. Poor Ben, and just when I thought he was doing so well. The man has no idea. And there I was thinking I was helping Prue out by training him up in advance — the truth is she's going to eat him alive.

'Well,' Ben looks indignant, his cheeks flaring red again, 'don't see why she wouldn't just say if there was somewhere she wanted to go. Said it was up to me.'

'So she hasn't dropped any hints lately? Not said anything generic about holidays or that sort of thing?'

'No,' says Ben, crossing his arms defensively. 'Only, well, she did say something about should she buy a new bikini.'

'And what did you say?'

'Said there was no need, she's already got one. Then she got all annoyed and went off in a huff.'

'Right, Ben,' I say, wagging my finger at him before I can stop myself. 'Clue number one: she wants to go somewhere hot.'

Ben's jaw drops open. He gazes at me in astonishment, as if I have revealed previously unknown psychic powers. 'Hot?' he echoes. 'How do you know?'

'She hinted about bikinis, so she wants to go somewhere she can wear one. At this time of year that means long haul, right? So you can rule out skiing holidays, ice hotels, Northern Lights, and pretty much all of Europe, okay?'

Ben runs his fingers through his hair, grasping his curls. 'Long haul. Hot. Should I write this down?'

'I think you can remember that, Ben,' I reassure him, trying not to sound exasperated. 'Now has she mentioned anything about, I don't know, trying different food, like has she said she's got a hankering for enchiladas or something? Or has she been looking at travel

234

websites at work that you've noticed? Left travel magazines lying around?'

Personally I would consider these tactics pretty obvious, but it is becoming very clear to me that Ben is someone who needs clear signposts if he is to be led in the right direction. I am surprised Prue hasn't resorted to hanging around the office wearing a sandwich board that spells out Thailand, or wherever it is she wants to go. Though I wouldn't put it past Ben to assume this is just a new fashion of which he was previously unaware.

'No,' he says. 'I'd have noticed. Sure of it.'

Somehow I doubt that very much. There is no question in my mind that Prue, who plans everything, will have a definite destination in mind. It is up to me to help Ben identify that destination before there is another relationship breakdown in the Bailey family.

'Okay, here's what you need to do,' I say. 'This lunchtime you're going to buy some magazines — go to the Post Office, they've got the biggest selection. You're going to buy *Condé Nast Traveller*, *Wallpaper*, *Red* and *Marie Claire*. Got that?'

Ben's forehead furrows with perplexity. He looks back over his shoulder at the kitchen counter several times until I divine his purpose.

'You can get a pen and paper now,' I say, and he scurries gratefully over to the pad where I write my shopping list.

' . . . *Traveller*, *Wallpaper*,' he enunciates, writing each one down carefully, his tongue poking out of the side of his mouth in concentration.

235

'Okay, when you get back from work, you're going to open them all up at the travel pages and have a look at what's there. When Prue arrives you're going to pretend to hide the magazines by the side of the sofa.'

'Pretend . . . to . . . hide,' Ben writes. He looks up, confused. 'Won't that spoil the surprise, though?'

'Ben, are you listening to me at all? The surprise Prue wants is the surprise that you've booked the place she wants to go to. That is the only acceptable surprise, don't you understand? I'm trying to help you here.'

'Just seems like she shouldn't see it all, though,' Ben sulks.

I try not to shake him. 'Ben,' I say, as patiently as I can manage. 'Remember at school, in maths, how it wasn't enough to have the right answer?'

Ben nods hesitantly.

'You remember how you had to show your working out as well as the answer? Right? To show how you got the result?'

'So?'

'So this is exactly the same. You get bonus marks for showing your working out. You have to demonstrate to Prue the trouble you're going to — let her see that you're putting a lot of time and effort into this.'

'But I haven't yet,' says Ben, honest to a fault. And dim to a fault, too, it cannot be denied.

'That's not the point! The point is that you'll get credit for showing that you're making an effort — do you see?'

'Ye-es,' says Ben, slowly.

'Okay, so you let her see the magazines, and then you point to something like, well, like an eco-lodge in Namibia, and you say something along the lines of 'I like the look of that, don't you?''

'Not sure she would, actually,' says Ben, shaking his head thoughtfully. 'Not sure that's her sort of thing, come to think of it.'

'There you go,' I say. 'You do know what she likes after all — or what she doesn't like. But look, that doesn't really matter — it's about starting a conversation that helps you to see that what she really wants is two weeks in the Maldives.'

Comprehension begins to dawn across Ben's troubled face. 'Right. Do you think that's what she wants then? The Maldives?'

I feel like someone who has led an extremely slow and decrepit horse to a drinking trough, only to have it leap in and take a bath, scrubbing merrily at its hooves.

'I don't know if she wants the Maldives, Ben,' I say through gritted teeth. 'That is what you will have to find out this evening.'

I see on the pad that Ben has written MALDIVES in capital letters, and I suspect that this is the only thing he will take away from our entire conversation.

'You'll be here though, right?' says Ben. I wonder if he thinks I will hide behind the sofa, offering clues Cyrano de Bergerac-style.

'No, actually,' I tell him. 'I'm going out.'

Ben looks as surprised as I feel. But I can't stay in moping for ever. It's time to move on.

28

London

'Steady on,' said Matt when I greeted him at the door, flinging my arms around him.

It had felt like days since I'd seen him rather than hours. It was strange how the days themselves, from saying goodbye in the morning to the key in the door that told me he was home, passed so interminably that I had found myself crying from the sheer boredom of filling another solitary hour. And yet the weeks of unemployment had piled up behind me with astonishing speed — it made me shudder to realize it had already been three months since I left Hitz.

'Can't a wife say hello to her husband with a little enthusiasm?' I asked, hanging off his neck.

Matt kissed me perfunctorily, a kiss that was designed to make me let go rather than ignite my passion.

'Notice anything different about me?' I asked, twirling round in the hallway. I liked having little surprises for him when he came home from work. It made things more fun.

Matt froze with his suit jacket halfway down his arms, like a straitjacket, trapped. 'It's a bit dark in here,' he said. 'I can't see properly.'

I pouted. He was clearly playing for time and hadn't noticed at all. Sometimes I didn't know why I bothered. He'd already told me I wasn't allowed to attack him with questions about Hitz the minute he came through the door, and I'd stuck to my word, even though I was bursting with things to ask. The least he could do was show some interest in my life.

Matt threw his jacket over the post at the end of the banister.

'Can you put it on the coat rack?' I asked. He sighed extravagantly, as it was an enormous effort to move his jacket two feet to the left, where it should have gone in the first place.

When we got downstairs to the kitchen I turned around again, grinning expectantly.

Matt looked me up and down. 'Er, new — apron?' he offered.

I looked down at my chest, which was covered in a yellow and green checked apron with white lace frills. 'It's not a new apron, Matt, I've had this for weeks. Honestly, are you completely blind? I've had my hair highlighted!'

'Have you?' he asked, his eyes narrowing as he tried to see the change in my hair. I turned my head from side to side so he could admire me. 'It looks lovely, but you always look lovely to me, Basher.'

It was hardly the most heartfelt compliment he'd ever paid me, but he sounded weary, so I decided to accept it gracefully and not push him. Matt's back was already turned as he crossed the kitchen to pick up a bottle of wine. I fetched a corkscrew out of the drawer and hovered at his elbow, ready to hand it to him when he'd peeled the foil from the neck of the bottle.

'Yes, I went to this place on the high street

— it's a new hairdressers, I don't know if you've seen it, but it probably opened up about three weeks ago? Not far from that cafe that does the breakfast you like? Although they've changed the menu since you went last, so maybe they don't do it any more. Anyway, they had a special offer on for cut and colour for a hundred pounds — the hairdressers I mean, not the cafe — I know I'm not earning any money lately, but really, Matt, it was such a bargain and I really think it's made all the difference. Don't you?'

He took the corkscrew from me and started to twist it into the cork with a methodical rhythm. 'It looks good, Kate, really.'

I opened up the cupboard and took out two wine glasses, buffing them to a shine with a tea towel before I put them in front of Matt.

'There you go,' I said. 'Perfect. Now, supper's going to be ready in an hour. I hope you're going to like it; it's one of those new Waitrose recipe cards I got the other day. Do you remember, you said you thought it looked nice, so I went back and got all the ingredients. But it takes ages — three hours in the oven! And that's not even counting all the preparation — so I can make you a snack first if you're hungry? I've got some hummus and breadsticks — shall I do that?'

Matt put down the wine bottle. He rubbed his chin with the heel of his hand and gave me a slow smile. 'Come here,' he said.

I let him pull me into his chest, crushing my ribs with his embrace. When Matt hugged me, really hugged me I mean, he reminded me of that song about how we're all two halves of a whole, searching for the missing half and trying to crush ourselves back together. It was as if he was trying to draw me into himself so that he never had to let go. Sometimes it almost hurt, but I never wanted him to stop. It let me feel small, protected, looked after.

He rested his chin on the top of my head.

'Oh my God,' he said, drawing in his breath in a gasp.

'What?' I started, muffled in his chest. Was the casserole burning?

'These highlights — you were right, they're the most amazing highlights I've ever seen. You're — you're glowing. These are job-getting highlights, that's what they are. Your luck is about to change, I can feel it. What kind of a pig of a husband am I not to have noticed before? Please forgive me.'

I swatted at him ineffectually, my hands still pinned to my sides. 'Fuck you.' I giggled.

He let me go. 'Sorry, Kate, it's been a long day. You're sweet to have made supper. But you don't have to do this every night. I bumped into Sarah this afternoon. She was in Hitz for a meeting.'

I moved away, around the kitchen island to check the oven timer. 'Oh yes? How's she doing?'

'Not bad — she's quite enjoying working with Jennifer, I think.' Matt regarded me over the top of his wine glass.

'Good for her,' I said, studying the Waitrose recipe card in case I'd forgotten anything. I was still quite new to this home-cooking thing and I had to check and double check constantly to reassure myself that I was doing everything right. It was hard to relax when I might unwittingly be cocking it all up; I wanted to get it all right.

I knew Matt was feeling the pressure of being the only one bringing in a salary, and I was determined to do everything I could to make his home life perfect. I'd given the cleaner her notice, partly to save money and partly because, if I was at home anyway, shouldn't it be me keeping things looking nice? And I was saving us a fortune in takeaways now that I'd started making our meals from scratch every night.

Matt put his glass down on the counter. He opened the fridge and took out the hummus, which I'd bought from the local deli — three points. I hadn't yet reached the stage of making it myself, but I will admit to going as far as looking up a recipe.

'I offered to do that,' I said, rushing over and taking the tub out of his hand. I knew he'd get it all over the work surface if I didn't put it on a side plate first. 'You sit down.' I got the bread-sticks out of the cupboard and tipped them into a bowl for him.

Matt, sitting down obediently at the table, raised his eyebrows, amused. 'Do you think I can't manage it myself?' he asked.

I made a face at him, and bustled past to take a packet of green beans out of the vegetable drawer, where they were hidden under a pillow of packaged spinach.

I'd spent ages laying the table, and had even bought some pink and white scented stocks, which I'd popped in a jam jar for that perfect insouciant oh-I-just-picked-these-up-on-my-country-walk vibe. Assuming that a country walk took one past an expensive Highgate florist who wrapped them in cellophane and handed one a sachet of plant food in exchange for a tenner. Also I will confess, though not to Matt, that, lacking an empty jam jar for the necessary *laissez-faire* look, I had scooped out the contents of a full Bonne Maman apricot confiture and stashed it in a plastic pot in the fridge. Still, it created the right effect, and that was what mattered.

Not that Matt seemed to notice, obliviously tucking into his breadsticks.

'Yeah, so Sarah said she's been trying to get you out for a drink and you keep telling her you're too busy.'

I shrugged and ripped open the plastic packaging, lining the beans up on the chopping board. 'Just diary clashes,' I said.

I chose my sharpest knife from the magnetic strip next to the oven, and sliced the ends off, brushing them onto the kitchen counter. I'd put them in my new composter later — though I had no idea what to do with compost it was something I felt I ought to learn. There was no point sitting idle while I looked for work.

'You know how it is,' I said. 'She's busy too, with her new job and all.'

Sarah had managed to get a new job with Jennifer Heston's start-up, and Kirsty was freelancing with them on a couple of projects, but it had been made clear to me that I was surplus to requirements. Jennifer and I had competed for the same jobs too often for her to feel comfortable about welcoming me into her new business.

Matt poured more wine into his glass and held the bottle out to me. I shook my head and put my hand over my glass. I was trying to cut down these days.

'Okay,' he said. 'She just seemed to think you might be avoiding her. And I thought so too. You haven't been out with your friends for weeks.' He offered me a gentle smile of sympathetic enquiry, of 'asking you this hurts me more than it hurts you'.

Except it didn't. It hurt me more. I just didn't want to let him see.

When I was at Hitz I used to get approached at least once every few months by some production company trying to lure me away. I thought a new job would be mine for the asking within weeks. But for all the lunches and phone calls I'd initiated, for all the meetings I'd had and the Christmas parties I'd attended, full of networking ambitions and hope, no actual offers had come up. Plenty of people had told me they'd love to have me on board, but cutbacks were making things difficult. Several told me they couldn't afford me, as if I was wandering around with a price tag on, refusing to get out of bed for less than a hundred grand. Everyone assured me I'd find something soon, that someone with my experience wouldn't be unemployed for long, but it felt as if they were only saying it to absolve themselves from any obligation to exert themselves on my behalf.

Now the calls had dried up completely. I tried to assure myself that I hadn't been forgotten. It had been Christmas, then New Year — people were just busy, that was all. And in fact, having this time to myself at home had made me do some serious thinking about work. Isn't that what a crisis was meant to do? Shunt you out of the life you took for granted and show you other possibilities?

'Why would I be avoiding my very best friend?' I asked, keeping my face fixed in a neutral mask. I had to keep my chin up. Stay positive.

I didn't want to confess to Matt that it was easier to do that when I wasn't directly confronted by all of my Hitz friends flaunting their new jobs in my face. The last time Sarah and I had met up she'd insisted on paying for everything, forcing my wallet back in my bag before I could even open it. I felt like a poor relation being taken for a treat by her indulgent benefactor.

'Yeah, why would you?' asked Matt casually, snapping a breadstick in half. 'I told her that, so she says she'll ring you this week.'

I didn't tell him that she already had. I'd let it go straight to voicemail. It was easier that way. Sometimes it just felt like the most extraordinary effort to be perky and cheerful when Matt came home, let alone having to put it on for other people.

'Great,' I said.

'So, what else have you been up to today?' asked Matt, scooping hummus onto his bread-stick.

'Oh, you know, stuff,' I said.

I knew he didn't think the things I did around the house really counted — those were just domestic distractions, not actually important. He meant, how many jobs have you applied for, did you rewrite your CV and have you sorted out the car insurance like I asked? Quantifiable achievements that he could understand and praise me for. He didn't appreciate how demeaning it was to have to offer up my day for approval, like a toddler presenting her finger paintings to an indulgent parent.

He looked up, frowning a little as if he didn't quite recognize me. 'I was just thinking on the way home, maybe it would be a good idea for you to, I don't know, join a gym or something. Get a bit of an exercise routine going.'

I turned around to face him. 'Matt Martell, that is fighting talk to a woman with a large knife in her hand. What do you mean I should join a gym?'

How dare he? I may have put on a few pounds since I'd given up work, but he didn't have to make me feel bad about it.

'Calm down,' said Matt mildly, not even slightly perturbed by my brandished weapon. 'I just meant it's good to have a routine, isn't it? Something to structure your day around. And endorphins, you know, a bit of exercise might cheer you up.'

I gripped the handle of the knife until my knuckles turned white. I seriously thought I might use it on him — or maybe on myself — if he carried on talking that way.

'So you're saying not only that I've got fat, but

that I'm a moody cow? Is that right? Anything else you'd like to offer an opinion on?'

Matt just laughed. 'Don't be mental, I'm not saying anything like that.'

I turned my back on him and savagely cut the French beans in half. A handful of them fell on the floor, but I didn't pick them up. My spine was so rigid with fury that I felt as if it might snap in two if I tried to bend.

'Kate,' Matt's voice adopted a pleading tone. 'Why are you taking this the wrong way? I just want you to be happy.'

I spun around, pointing the knife at him. 'No you don't. You want *you* to be happy. And you think if I was just a bit more *cheery*, just a bit less *fat*, a bit less *unemployed*, that you'd be happier. Well, it doesn't work like that, Matt. So maybe keep your stupid suggestions to yourself.'

Matt's face fell. 'You're not fat,' he said quietly.

There was a long pause while we both stared at each other. I felt like I knew every millimetre of his face. The tiny mole by his right ear, the faint lines that starfished out from the corners of his eyes. But I could not have told you what was happening behind those eyes, and that was new and alarming. I had thought I knew him better than I knew myself. I was used to his admiration, to his adoration even. Now I was horrified that what I saw in his face might actually be pity.

'You seem unhappy,' he said at last. 'I wish you'd stop pretending you're not. And then maybe we could do something about it.'

I felt my face go hot, and my throat tightened,

as if there was a hand around it. I wouldn't let myself cry — how could I defend myself against being unhappy by bursting into tears?

'I'm not unhappy,' I said. My voice was unconvincing, even to me.

Matt's eyes were sad. He didn't push it, which made me feel even worse. Once we'd have had a passionate row, now he treated me gingerly, as if I was no longer his equal, capable of standing my ground, but someone to be accommodated; the weaker partner whose fragile emotions must be protected.

I didn't push it either. Not because I was about to agree with him, but because it was an impossible argument to win. To insist in anger that you are happy only serves to make you look miserable.

So in the end I let him buy me a gym membership, and I pretended that it didn't make me feel like a surrendered wife; the kind who has manicures and coffee mornings and thinks the maintenance of her appearance is her primary duty to her husband.

I never went, of course. Sometimes just getting out of bed took all the energy I had. I was more likely to climb to the base camp of Everest than set a foot on a stairmaster. But it made Matt feel better and, as that was the only reason I'd allowed it, the gym membership fulfilled its function for both of us.

29

I'm sat in the pub nursing a vodka and soda and trying not to feel conspicuous. Which is hard to do since I'm the only woman in here other than the teenage girl behind the bar, who I have already flustered and alienated by asking if she had a piece of fresh lime to go in my drink. Lime is, it seems, a rarity in Lyme except in the form of cordial — no lime in Lyme, how ironic. It reminds me of the first time I came back from London in the late Nineties, and made the mistake of asking for a vodka and cranberry juice in Mum and Dad's local. Frankly I was used to drinking Cosmopolitans back then — we all were, perched uncomfortably on bar stools, flicking our hair, self-consciously trying to pretend we were Carrie Bradshaw — but I thought a vodka cranberry would suffice while I was in the sticks. It took years before I could venture in there without all the regulars falling about laughing at my pretensions. Cranberry juice! Can you believe her? Whoever heard of such a thing?

Of course, now that you can get cranberry juice in Lyme's Tesco Express, no one I know drinks it any more.

The other customers — all six of them — are men in unwittingly matching holey jumpers, like a Lyme Regis version of the cameramen I used to work with. As well as the jumpers, they share a certain hoary charm, the kind that makes dirty fingernails and muddy shoes seem like signifiers of earthy toil rather than a lack of hygiene. They all seem to know each other, and they are clearly intrigued as to what I am doing in the bar by myself. I can tell this because it's quiet enough that I heard the man in the most holey of jumpers (not the most holy of jumpers, that would be weird) say, 'I wonder what she's doing here?'

I start humming under my breath, no tune in particular, just trying to make a noise so that I can't overhear anything. It's not like I think I'm especially fascinating — although my question about the lime should give them cause for amusement — but I know what the gossip is like here. Either they will know I'm Sandy and David's errant daughter — in which case I don't want to hear it — or they won't — in which case I don't want to hear it either. No good ever comes of listening to what people say behind your back.

Tra-la-la, I hum to myself, trying to peer through the window, but it's hard to see out of glass that's as thick and swirled as the bottom of a bottle. Figures pass indistinctly, impossible to identify except as a brief blotting out of what little glow from the streetlights penetrates inside. I hadn't considered before how pubs in London tend to be more bright and open, their big windows and well-lit interiors designed to appeal to women who want to see what somewhere is like before they venture inside, rather than having to duck into a shadowy room hoping for the best. But I guess the holey jumpers like it like this — dark and cosy for hiding away. And if your wife walks past she won't even be able to see you're in here, which I suppose is the point.

Anyway, it wasn't my choice, Eddy suggested it. And as I'm hardly an expert on Lyme's nightlife, having spent most of my recent nights here watching television with Minnie, I wasn't in any position to suggest somewhere different.

I don't even want to think about the last time I went out for a drink with a man who wasn't either my husband or a work colleague. No, seriously, I really don't want to think about it. It will only make me either nervous or hysterical, which is silly, because it's only a drink with Dready Eddy. Which is weird in itself. He says he's 'made plans'. I wonder briefly if we'll be sharing a bottle of cider on the beach, or laughing uncontrollably from too much dope, which was pretty much the level of plan we achieved before I fled Lyme for good.

When he finally arrives, full of apologies for his lateness, he is welcomed as a friend by all the holey jumpers. They slap him on the back as he greets them at the bar, guffawing loudly at something — I am sure I heard the word lime, but it could have been Lyme, so I try not to take it personally.

He returns with a pint and a rueful smile.

'Sorry, got waylaid by the guys from the boatyard. And now I'm even later. Gaby didn't pick up the girls until seven — I should have called but I was in a hurry to get here.'

'I don't mind,' I say. 'There's no rush.'

And I really don't mind at all — why would I? A man can talk to his friends. No matter what Matt thinks, I'm not one of those women who demands a man's attention all the time. If you ask me, it would be pretty wearing to be under that kind of constant scrutiny anyway. Everyone needs their own space.

'Well, there kind of is,' says Eddy. 'Because I've booked us a table for dinner.'

'Have you?' I ask.

'Yeah, there's a place in the old Mill complex that I think you'll like. Really amazing food,' says Eddy. 'I've booked us in for eight.'

He sees my eyes flick to my watch.

'It's okay, I'll down this quickly,' he says, picking up his pint. I must look apprehensive because he starts laughing. 'Don't worry, I can handle it — they don't call me Steady Eddy for nothing.'

'They don't call you Steady Eddy at all,' I say. 'You will always be Dready Eddy to me, Eddy Curtis. No matter how many buzz cuts you get.'

He rubs the top of his head, as if he's stroking the ghost dreads from long ago.

'Dready Eddy.' He chuckles. 'That feels like a long time ago.'

'When did you shave them off?' I asked.

He thinks, sipping his pint. 'Last year of university. It was a fairly lame sort of hair rebellion in the end — I was happy to be Mr Counterculture until I got turned down from three jobs in a row, and then off they came.'

'You crazy anarchist, you,' I say.

'My girlfriend cut them all off one night after

we'd been out,' he says, remembering. 'Her hands went completely green afterwards. It didn't come off for two days.'

'That is disgusting,' I grimace.

'She certainly seemed to think so,' he says, laughing. 'She dumped me a week later.'

'Didn't like what she'd uncovered under all that hair?' I tease.

'Something like that,' he agrees.

'Well, I think she was a fool, Eddy,' I say kindly. 'Who knew Dready Eddy would scrub up so well?'

Eddy scoffs and finishes his pint. 'Come on,' he says. 'Let's go.'

We wave goodbye to the holey jumpers and step outside onto Broad Street. Even though it's dark now, and the moon is obscured behind silvery clouds, there is a very faint blue line on the horizon that shows where the sea ends and the sky begins. I like how the horizon makes me feel small in the best way — as if my problems are insignificant and fleeting. The perspective seems to promise possibility and escape. That's what I always thought when I was younger, and even though I've run back here with my tail between my legs, the sight of the horizon still pulls at my heart with hope. Which is an unfamiliar feeling to me these days.

The restaurant that Eddy's chosen is tiny, hidden behind an art gallery in the old Mill complex. There are barely ten tables and only one waiter, behind whom the solitary chef can be seen at work. Unlike the pub, however, this place is rammed. Every table is full and we have to squeeze our way apologetically past the other diners to get to our seats at the back of the room. There's a proper hum of conversation — the kind where you can't hear what other people are saying, so you're free to say what you want in return — and an air of eager anticipation about the food in store. I'd expect it somewhere like the posh Hix restaurant up near the Cobb — full of visitors from London since the locals blanch at paying twenty pounds for a piece of fish — but this bustling little corner of the Mill has the buzz of somewhere twice its size.

Eddy picks up the menu, while the waiter pours water for us.

'It's really nice in here,' I say.

Eddy's eyes twinkle with amusement. 'No need to sound so surprised,' he says. 'Lyme's changed a lot while you've been away.'

'I did used to come back, you know,' I say, on the defensive. 'It's not like I never visited at all. I just, well, I was always visiting family. I guess my parents don't know about this place.'

'Oh no,' says Eddy with confidence. 'They've been here plenty of times. Gaby and I saw them in here at least twice, and they seemed pretty familiar with the place.'

'Sandy and David?' asks the waiter, reappearing with a notepad. 'Oh yes, they're in here all the time. They often talk about you — Kate, isn't it? From London?'

He cocks his head to one side sympathetically. The expression on his face conveys not only pity, but full knowledge of my tawdry circumstances.

I do wonder how anyone in Lyme would ever

manage to have an affair or keep a similarly life-affecting secret. It seems I can barely step out of the front door without a total stranger revealing that they're entirely up to date on who I am and what's going on in my life. And to think I was just beginning to believe that Lyme had changed.

'I'm Stephen,' he says. 'Anyway, can I get you some wine?'

'Kate?' says Eddy, offering me the wine list.

'You choose,' I say, studying the menu.

'Oh, well, I don't know much about wine,' says Eddy.

'Me neither,' I smile at him. 'Whatever you pick is fine with me.'

Stephen purses his lips and whisks the wine list out of Eddy's hand. 'Well I do know about the wine, so how about you tell me what you're going to eat and I'll choose for you, hmm?'

Eddy grins with relief, and Stephen promises he'll bring us something we'll both like. Frankly as long as it's alcoholic I'm going to like it, but I don't tell him that as he seems to relish making the effort.

'It's so weird to be sat here with Kate Bailey,' says Eddy, breaking off a piece of the warm bread that's been placed in front of us.

'Oh stop it,' I say, keeping my tone light and breezy. 'Honestly, Eddy, if we're going to be friends you're going to have to stop going on about the past all the time. We're both different people now. Let's talk about other stuff.'

'Like what?'

'The present,' I say firmly, buttering my bread and taking a bite. The butter is rich and creamy and flecked with tiny salt crystals that crunch between my teeth.

'Hmm,' says Eddy. 'I suppose my present's a bit fucked, to be honest. That's probably why I keep talking about school and stuff. Everything was a lot simpler back then, wasn't it?'

I shrug. 'I suppose so, in some ways.'

Eddy looks at me quizzically.

'The present,' I repeat. 'Let's talk about the present tonight. Tell me what happened between you and your wife. Gaby? How long were you married.'

Eddy lets out a long breath, less of a sigh than an expellation of everything inside, as if he's trying to get rid of it all. 'Ten years?' he says, and I wonder why he's posed it as a question, as if he isn't sure of the answer. As if he can't believe it's over, or as if he can't believe it happened?

'Wow! Ten years. Jeez, Eddy, you were a child groom. If that's even an expression. I know you get child brides, so you must get child grooms.'

Eddy laughs. 'I was twenty-three. Yeah, it's pretty young I suppose. But we thought why wait? We were in love — all the usual bollocks. It was going to be different for us, you know?'

'I do know,' I say.

'You?'

'A year and a half,' I say. It doesn't sound long at all. Not in comparison to ten years. And no children, either. 'Yeah, we were just beginners really. But I think when it's finished, it's finished — you cut your losses and move on. No point dragging it out for years when you both know it's over.'

Eddy pinches a piece of bread between finger and thumb, pressing it into a tight ball.

'It's different when you have children,' he says, his voice tight in his throat. 'I'd have dragged it out forever to stay at home with them. But Gaby, yeah, she thought like you. Thinks like you. Move on.'

He makes a pathetic little mime of his hand taking off from the table, like a plane.

'Um, sorry,' I say. 'You were right. We should've stuck to schooldays. I suppose the present *is* pretty fucked, isn't it?'

'I'll drink to that,' says Eddy and lifts his glass to mine.

By the time the waiter arrives with our starters we are well on the way to being drunk. I don't know about Eddy but I'm actively pursuing it, doggedly downing my drinks as if they were prescribed medicine. I feel like I've been tightly wound up for weeks, and the alcohol spreads welcomingly through my veins, loosening everything, making me feel like everything will be okay. I'm sure I won't feel like that tomorrow morning, but tonight I don't care. It feels good to be out, to have a friend in Lyme, to have a life again instead of hiding from the one I used to have.

'These anchovies are amazing,' I say, taking another tiny battered fish from my plate with my fingers. It reminds me of something, but I can't think what.

'Told you the food here was good,' says Eddy.

'It's not just good, it's unbelievable,' I say. 'This is the best meal I've had in years.'

257

'Oh, that's the company,' he says. 'The food's pretty average, actually, but the company just makes it seem unbelievable. I have that effect on women all the time.'

'I'm surprised you didn't just take me to McDonald's in that case,' I say. 'If it would've tasted amazing wherever we went, you should've taken me somewhere way cheaper.'

Eddy snorts and grabs his wine glass. 'Yeah, I can just see Kate Bailey slumming it in Maccy D's. I know what you're like — a different fancy restaurant every weekend, I bet. Wine list as long as your arm. One of those little scrapy things for taking the crumbs off the table.'

'I carry my own, obviously,' I say. 'In my handbag. I like to be prepared.'

'Seriously, though, you must be finding it so quiet in Lyme after what you're used to.'

I consider. Quiet? After what I'd grown used to it's quite the opposite. I smooth out the tablecloth under my fingers, the thick weave of the linen is rough and scratchy, like a hairshirt. There's something pleasing about the texture — I wonder, briefly, if it would be so bad to wear a hairshirt anyway. Having a tactile reminder of your sins always with you might be better than being ambushed by the memory of them when you least expect it.

'Once upon a time, maybe,' I reply. 'But to be honest I wasn't going out much by the time I left. I — well, I stayed in a lot. Matt bought me Minnie — the puppy — and that kind of tied me to home a bit. I didn't like to leave her on her own at nights. She'd chew things, and I could

258

tell it distressed her to be left alone.'

'Do you think he did it on purpose?' asks Eddy.

My eyes widen. 'Bought me a dog to keep me at home you mean?'

Eddy nods.

'No!' I start laughing at the idea. As if Matt had tied me to a chair with a dog lead and forbidden me to ever go out again. 'No, I mean — God, I never even considered that. Totally the opposite, I think; he thought it would get me out of the house more, and then he got frustrated when it did the opposite.'

Eddy wipes a finger along the side of his plate, scraping up the last of the horseradish sauce.

'Why did he think you needed to get out of the house?' he asks.

'Oh, it's a long story,' I say.

'I don't mind,' says Eddy.

It is on the tip of my tongue to tell him that I do mind but — maybe it's the alcohol, maybe it's the unaccustomed night out — instead I start talking.

'He just couldn't accept that things changed,' I say. 'He thought I'd always be the party girl who was out all night and working like a maniac. He couldn't deal with me growing up and calming down.'

Eddy's forehead creases. 'So he got angry with you for calming down?' he asks, as if he's heard wrong.

I know in Eddy's eyes I will forever be the wild girl he knew back in the day.

'Oh you should've seen me, Eddy,' I tease.

259

'Apron on, dusting the banisters. I even did a cordon bleu cookery course. I don't do anything by halves, you know.'

Eddy chokes on his wine. 'Seriously?'

'I know! I thought, Whatever it took to be a good wife, I'd do it. I gave up everything. My career, my friends, my social life.'

'He asked you to do that?' Eddy looks dumbfounded.

'He didn't ask,' I admit. No matter how angry I am with Matt I can't pretend he was some kind of prefeminist-era caveman, dragging me into the kitchen by my hair and chaining me to the stove. 'He didn't have to. You know how some of the most important stuff in a marriage is what isn't said.'

Eddy nods sympathetically.

'He was always saying how I put too much time into work and not enough time into our relationship. So I did it for us. For our future together. And then he turned around and said I'd turned into someone else. After everything I'd done for him.'

'It hardly seems fair,' says Eddy loyally.

'He just didn't appreciate any of it. He kept saying I'd changed, but he didn't see that relationships have to change if they're going to move on.'

Eddy's lips twist into a rueful smile. 'Children have a way of forcing that change on you,' he says.

I pick up my wine glass and hold the bowl of it in both hands, as if I'm trying to absorb the wine through my palms. I stare into it, watching the reflections of the candlelight shift and flicker on the surface.

'Yeah, well, that didn't happen for us,' I say. Light again, light as air. 'There was a time when it seemed like a tragedy, but now I wonder if it was a sign, you know? That this wasn't going to work out. We weren't going to get what we wanted from each other.'

Eddy looks bewildered, unsurprisingly, considering I have veered off into dangerously alcohol-fuelled philosophy — next I will be claiming something weird about the Law of Attraction or some other woo-woo nonsense.

'Or perhaps it was just my hostile womb,' I say, forcing a smile.

I know the best way to get Eddy off the subject of my failed marriage is to lead him into a conversational dead end. A dead end with a man-terrifying gynaecological reference. Womb is hardly the worst I could say — especially to a man who has witnessed the birth of two daughters — but, as I had hoped, Eddy blanches, changes tack entirely and the evening is saved.

It's fortunate for both of us that the food is extraordinary and, like most of the other diners here, we can content ourselves with marvelling at it instead of talking about ourselves. The fish arrives with a bowl of buttery samphire, in whose branches rest the palest pink curls of shrimps. It's so rich that I can barely eat half of it, but somehow we both find space for pudding, too: a shared bowl of homemade vanilla ice cream, served with a warm salted caramel sauce that I expect to see again in my dreams.

I like talking like this, just being in the present moment, appreciating the food, with no agenda or issues bubbling under the surface. Mealtimes had become so fraught before I left London.

I was always so anxious to please, to know that Matt appreciated my efforts, understood the exact technique I'd used for the zabaglione. After all, wasn't the cordon bleu course I'd done for his benefit, too? Matt thought it was hilarious to buy me an apron with a Masterchef logo on it, and I laughed along with his impressions of the judges, though it seemed to me that he wasn't taking me very seriously. I didn't find the culinary dramas of those contestants ridiculous — I cried along with them when their soufflés failed, when they dropped the tray of cakes two minutes before service, when the lamb was cold and raw in the middle. I understood what it meant to put everything you had into a plate of food, to hold your breath for the reaction of the person eating it. But unlike those chefs on the television, for whom the praise of the judges got greater with every episode, it seemed that the harder I tried, the less Matt noticed. Or the less he cared, I should say. But isn't that the same thing anyway?

And after a while he just stopped turning up at all.

30

London

Curled up on the sofa, my head resting on Matt's knees, I let my eyes close. I don't think he was really watching television either. I could feel his hand gently stroking my hair. I wondered if it was a bad thing that the only time I felt really close to Matt these days was when we were silent like this.

Our conversations lately had taken on an almost sitcom feel; it was all 'Hello, darling, how was work?' 'Fine thank you, darling, don't you look nice?' Skating politely over the fact that I still hadn't got a job and that Matt had given up asking me about it. Even though we were arguing less it made me feel worse, as if we'd become polite strangers in a house share; considerately accommodating one another for reasons of domestic harmony rather than love.

'This is nice,' I murmured, as his fingers combed through the hair at my temples.

Matt grunted, which I took as agreement.

'Matt?' I plucked at a thin grey thread that was poking out from the seam of his trousers. It stayed firm.

'Mmm?'

'Matt, do you like that I've started cooking more?' I twisted the thread around my fingers to get some purchase on it.

263

'Yeah,' he said. 'Who knew you had it in you? You do a great job.'

'I like it,' I said as the thread snapped. 'I never thought I would, but I do. And it's nice how the fridge is always full these days, isn't it? And that there are fresh flowers every week.'

'Umm, yes,' said Matt. I suspected he hadn't noticed either of these things, but if I had to point them out to him, then so be it.

I sat up and crossed my legs on the sofa. 'I just think the house is more of a home since I left Hitz,' I said. 'Don't you? It's more welcoming, not just the place we dump our suitcases before the next work trip.'

'The house is great, Kate,' said Matt dutifully.

'Only it's made me think,' I said. I twisted a strand of hair in front of my face.

Matt stretched an arm along the back of the sofa and leaned backwards into the cushions. A slow smile spread across his face. 'Spit it out.'

'What?'

'You're building up to something. I can tell.'

'I'm just saying that I think there's a silver lining to redundancy. It's made me appreciate what we have at home. I'm really grateful for it.'

Matt raised an eyebrow. 'And?'

I picked up a cushion and held it protectively against my chest.

'And, well, okay, you know how I stopped taking the pill a few months ago . . . '

Matt looked incredulous, then delighted. 'You're pregnant?' he exclaimed. 'Oh my God, you're pregnant!'

'No!' I said quickly. It broke my heart to see

how Matt caught hold of himself, trying not to let me see his disappointment. But it also made what I wanted to say next that much easier. Asking for things directly had never been one of my strengths.

'No, of course you're not. Bad timing,' he said.

'Do you think so?' I asked, clutching my cushion more tightly and letting my highlighted hair fall across my face. 'Because I was thinking that maybe . . . maybe not getting a job is, I don't know, a sign or something. That maybe I don't need to get another job straight away.'

'It's not exactly straight away,' said Matt. 'It's been six months.'

'I know,' I said, not rising to the bait.

'I'm not having a go,' Matt said. 'I just mean that I know you miss work, it's obvious.'

'I don't know if it's work I've missed,' I said, 'or just having a purpose. What if I made my purpose something different from now on? If I'm going to have to give up work for maternity leave anyway, why don't I just take some time out now, while we've got the rest of my redundancy money to fall back on?'

Matt poured himself another glass of wine. The bottle was nearly empty now.

'That money won't last for ever,' he said. 'What's wrong with taking on a few projects here and there in the meantime? You don't have to commit to a full-time job again, I know it's hard to find one, but are you sure you want to give up completely?'

I sighed. 'It's not giving up, Matt. It's giving us a chance. Don't you see? We hardly ever saw each other until I lost my job. We were always on different continents, in different time zones. I couldn't do that if we had a baby. I'm trying to think of the future here.'

Matt looked unconvinced, his forehead wrinkled in consternation.

'Come on, Matt, you told me you wanted me to give my all to you, instead of to work. That's what I'm trying to do.'

'I don't know,' said Matt. 'I didn't mean you had to give up everything else. You love your work; you've always lived for it. I'm just worried you want to have a baby for the wrong reasons.'

'Don't you *want* to have a baby?' I snapped. 'I thought this was what we both wanted?'

'Kate,' Matt said gently. 'Of course I do. I'm not saying that. But are you sure this is the right way to go about it? Are you sure you're not just getting freaked out by not getting any work for a while? It doesn't have to be a choice between a job and a baby; there could be a balance here.'

See what I mean? Every time we moved away from our sitcom script, it turned into an argument. He always challenged my decisions, even when I was making them for the best reasons, for both of us.

I kept my voice calm and patient. I had rehearsed this the entire week he'd been away.

'I just think that if you're going to do something, do it properly. What's the point of being half arsed about this? Come on, Matt. This is what we both want. Let's be serious about this and really try to make it happen, instead of just hoping.'

Matt stared at me in silence for a moment, then his lips twisted into a half smile. 'Are you asking me this, or are you telling me?'

'Asking?' I said carefully.

'Oh good,' he smirked. 'I'd hate to think you'd already made up your mind about this without any kind of discussion.'

I wondered if he'd found the folic acid tablets in the bathroom. I was sure I'd hidden them behind the toilet cleaner where he'd never see them.

'Matt,' I insisted, taking his hands in mine. 'I'm doing this for us.'

'Are you going to keep me to a very strict procreation schedule?' he asked, his eyes crinkling at the corners.

I knew I had him now.

'Very,' I said, sidling up next to him on the sofa.

'Will you have a doctor's coat? And a clipboard and glasses?'

'Do you *want* me to have a doctor's coat, clipboard and glasses?'

'Oh yes,' he nodded. 'Essential. We must take this seriously, after all.'

'Very seriously. I wouldn't want you to think this might be *fun*,' I teased. I shifted myself up onto his lap, and put my arms around his neck.

'Absolutely not,' he agreed, his expression comically grave.

I moved my face closer to his and grinned. I knew I'd make him see it my way. Turning my head, I licked slowly along the edge of Matt's left ear and began kissing his neck.

'Well, if you put it like that,' he said, 'I think we'd probably better get on with it, don't you?'

And we got on with it right there on the sofa, if you must know.

31

When we come out of the restaurant, clutching each other for support after Eddy has taken an unintended detour into a hatstand by the door, the freezing night air hits my face like a slap. The clouds have gone, and the cold is so sudden and brutal that we both burst out laughing in surprise. But the reward for this drop in temperature is a sky full of stars, the Milky Way twisting through them all. With our arms interlinked we look up, our faces turned towards the crescent moon. The cold is sobering, exhilarating. Inside, full and warm, all I had wanted to do was go home to sleep. Now I feel like I could run all the way to London. But what would I want to do that for?

The night is so still and clear that the boom and wash of the waves can be heard, pounding against the walls by the museum.

'Let's go and see the sea!' I exclaim.

Eddy grins at me, bemused. 'I see the sea every day, Kate. So do you.'

'Every *day*,' I say. 'Not every *night*. Come on. Race you up the steps.'

Before he has a chance to answer I unlink my arm from his and run towards the wooden steps that lead over the mill stream, taking them two at a time. I can see my breath coming out in puffs of white against the cold air. Behind me I can hear Eddy catching up, and a kind of excitable panic makes my heart beat faster, as if he's really in pursuit of me.

At the top of the steps I stop, panting.

'I won!' I announce, arms held triumphantly over my head in a victory salute.

'You always do, Kate,' says Eddy, pulling himself up the last few steps and leaning on the handrail.

It's weird to see myself through Eddy's eyes — the confident winner that he thinks I am; the girl who left Lyme and made something of herself. I think spending time with him is good for me, after the last few months. To be with someone who likes me, admires me even.

'I'm not sure it counts if you don't even tell me we're playing until you're halfway up the steps, though,' he teases.

'Don't be a sore loser, Eddy,' I say. 'How am I meant to win if I don't make up the rules?'

And then I take off across the car park, hearing his shouts behind me.

We run through the alleyway that brings us out to the seafront, where the water, lit by the moon, shines like the scales on the back of a giant, restless creature. There is no one else around on this freezing night. We have the seafront to ourselves. I breathe in a deep lungful of night air.

When Eddy catches me up he throws an arm around my shoulders. 'Won't you stay still?' he begs, his breath coming in ragged gasps. 'Jeez, you've nearly killed me.'

I elbow him in the ribs. 'You're getting old, Eddy.'

'What's got into you tonight?' He laughs.

'You're like a teenager.'

I start laughing. I *feel* like a teenager, full of hope and possibility. Maybe it's the ozone from the sea, or the unaccustomed night out. Maybe it's the attention from Eddy. I don't know. I just like how I feel.

Eddy turns to me. 'This is how I always think of you, Kate. Always laughing, always running, one step ahead of everyone else. No one could ever catch you.'

His arm feels heavy on my shoulders, and I feel it tighten and tense. I turn my head towards him, and he pulls me closer so that we're facing one another. The wind whips my hair across my face, covering my eyes, and Eddy uses his free hand to push it behind my ear. He keeps his hand there, cradling the back of my head.

I feel a fluttering in my chest, and I can't decide if it's excitement or panic. Or if there's any difference between the two.

'Eddy, I — '

He bends his head and kisses me once, drawing away almost immediately, as if he has made a mistake.

'I didn't want you to talk me out of it,' he says quickly. 'I knew you'd make me lose my nerve. But I wanted to kiss you, Kate. I'm glad I did it.'

His speech entirely disarms me, and my protests stop in my throat. I feel my lips lift into a smile that Eddy takes for encouragement; he presses my head towards his again and I let him. His mouth is warm against my cold face.

'Oh God, Kate,' he moans into my neck.

I press my body against him, his hot breath

against my ear. He is trembling — from the cold, I think. I am trembling, too.

I know I'm safe with Eddy. He'd never hurt me. It's me I don't trust.

But I kiss him back anyway.

32

The lights are off when I let myself into Granny Gilbert's bungalow, so I take my boots off at the front door and tiptoe into the hallway, risking going flying in my socks on the slippery parquet. But of course Minnie has heard me come in and skitters through from the kitchen, excitement overcoming her usual caution on the treacherous floor.

And then someone calls out from the living room and I realize that Prue is still here.

'Hi,' I whisper, peering into the living room, where Prue is illuminated by the flickering light from the television. It makes her seem as if she is moving, though she is sitting quite still, pinned down to the sofa by one of Ben's sprawled legs. He lies next to her, fast asleep, his head hanging back on the arm of the sofa, his mouth wide open.

'Hi, yourself,' she says in a normal voice, looking me up and down. 'Ben can sleep through anything, don't bother whispering. What have you been up to?'

'I've just been out with Eddy Curtis for a bite to eat,' I say.

Prue stares at me, squinting through the half dark, her eyebrows knitting together. 'Get over here.'

I hesitate in the doorway. When Prue was little we all thought it was funny that she bossed us around. We obediently lined up where she told us to and played at schools with her teddy bears and dolls, reprimanded if we dared to step out of line. I don't think any of us expected that she would continue to treat us like underlings once she'd grown up, but I guess old habits are hard to break.

'I'm going to bed,' I say, mutinously refusing to move.

Prue tosses her head at my refusal to play by her rules. 'I can see from here anyway,' she says. 'You've been kissing.'

'What?' I exclaim, my hand flying to my lips as if they've given me away somehow.

Prue smirks. 'You used to look exactly like this when you snuck in from seeing boys. Don't think I don't remember.'

'Well in that case you were staying up way past your bedtime,' I say, pathetically struggling for a comeback.

'Yup, definitely kissing,' says Prue. 'I remember that expression, all dreamy and cat that got the creamish.'

'Yeah, okay, thanks, Prue,' I snap. 'Thanks for noticing.'

Prue's smirk drops. 'I was only joking, Kate,' she says. 'Jeez, you're so touchy. Whatever. Don't tell me about kissing Eddy Curtis then.'

'I won't,' I say, dropping down into the chair next to Prue. 'I'd rather hear all about your exciting night. Ben really knows how to romance a lady, eh?'

Prue looks over at her fiancé and sighs heavily. 'He's just exhausted, poor man. With all the work you've had him do on this place, and the stuff he's doing for Baileys', and the wedding things. Is it any wonder he can barely stay awake?'

'Did you, er, talk about the honeymoon at all?' I ask casually.

Prue's head whips round instantly. 'Yes,' she hisses. 'What is this about you telling Ben that all I want is to go to the Maldives? I couldn't care less about the Maldives. Why would you interfere like that? Are you trying to make trouble between us?'

'I never said you wanted to go there, Prue,' I say steadily, under her fierce glare. 'I said he should try to find out where you *did* want to go. Since I thought you probably had an idea or two.' Or forty-eight, but obviously it would be more than my life is worth to wind Prue up further.

'Well, God knows what you actually said to him, but he was in a complete state when I got here. Surrounded by women's magazines all over the floor and waffling on about luminosity and spa retreats as though he'd been brainwashed. He barely touched his pheasant, just drank a stupid amount and passed out before I'd even managed to tell him that I want to go to Barbados.'

'Really? Barbados? Do you want me to drop some hints?'

Prue sighs again. 'Judging by how well your helpful hints worked last time, maybe you should just stay out of it.'

On the floor by her feet are the magazines Ben

had obediently purchased. I can see that he has ringed certain pictures in magic marker — palm trees and beaches. So he was listening a bit.

'Right,' says Prue, pushing Ben's leg off her lap and getting up. 'If you're not going to dish about Dready Eddy then I'm going home. I will get it out of you, though.'

'I don't doubt it for a moment,' I say, resigned to my fate. She will surely force a confession soon.

She surprises me by bending down to kiss me on the cheek. 'Good for you,' she says unexpectedly. 'It came out all wrong when you came in, but what I meant was, it's good to see you back to yourself a bit. Happier, I mean. I know things have been a bit shit for you lately.'

'Thanks, Prue,' I whisper, my voice unsteady at her sudden kindness.

'I told you,' she says, striding to the door, her voice ringing through the living room. 'Nothing wakes Ben when he's like this. No need to whisper. Night.'

She slams the door behind her. Minnie and I both jump, but Ben doesn't stir. He is breathing in that heavy way that's always threatening to turn into a snore without ever doing so. It used to drive me insane when Matt breathed like that, I'd find myself unable to relax, lying there rigidly awake, furiously anticipating the moment he'd start snoring properly.

I pick up the magazines from the floor and stack them in a pile next to the sofa so Ben doesn't slip on them if he wakes in the night. As I'm walking over to turn off the television I tread on the magic marker and let out a yelp. Again, Ben remains motionless.

I bend down for the pen and twist it between my fingers, thinking for a moment. I feel giddy and mischievous after my night out, and not a little tipsy. I tiptoe over to Ben's prone form and pop the lid off the marker, catching that pungent chemical scent as I inhale. My first stroke of the ink on his forehead makes him shake his head very slightly. I hold my breath until he stops moving.

But he sleeps peacefully through the rest of it, until the job is done.

33

London

'Fuck's sake,' exclaimed Matt, leaping back onto the bed as if the floor was electrified.

'What?' I muttered, from under the covers. 'Get off, you're squashing me.'

'Your dog's puked on the floor again,' he said.

'My dog?'

'Our dog,' he conceded.

'You'd better not be getting sick on the duvet,' I warned.

'Cold sick,' said Matt, holding his ankle in both hands as if his foot belonged to someone else. 'It's all between my toes — it's fucking disgusting.'

'It's even more disgusting when she eats it, believe me. Anyway, it's your turn to take her out.'

'What do you think I was trying to do?' snaps Matt. 'I was about to do it before I stepped in a pile of cold sick.'

'Don't get cross with me about it,' I said, rolling over. 'It's not me who puked on the carpet. It wasn't me who — '

'Yeah, I know, it wasn't you who bought a puppy in the first place. You've told me that a million times. I thought she'd be company for you. I thought it would make you happy.'

She *had* made me happy, for about two

seconds when I first saw the tiny chocolate brown face peeping out from under Matt's coat. And, okay, for another half an hour playing with her on the kitchen floor while Matt watched over the pair of us; and then she peed on the floor and he made himself scarce, and that is really how it's gone since then. He was all about the fun and the exuberance, while I was the one who had to sort out training, and walks and cleaning up. Minnie was a gift that came with a hefty side order of responsibility.

'You didn't think at all,' I mumbled into the pillow.

'What did you say?' Matt demanded, pulling on my shoulder.

'Matt — get off! You're going to get dog puke on the sheets and I only changed them yesterday.' I batted his hand away without turning over. He carried on talking but I pulled a pillow over my head and pressed it down over my ear so that all I could hear was a muffled commentary I'd heard a hundred times before.

The next thing I heard was the sound of the ensuite shower kicking in. I knew it. No matter how many times I told Matt we had to let Minnie out as soon as we got up, he always thought he knew better. If he'd got up on time — it was his turn, after all — she probably wouldn't have puked on the carpet in the first place. It wasn't fair on the dog to make her wait any longer. If I knew Minnie — Matt didn't, that much was obvious — she'd be cowering with guilt in the kitchen, aware of her vomiting *faux pas.* Or peeing on the doormat in desperation.

I swung my legs out of bed, on the sick-free side, and grudgingly pulled on my jeans and a T-shirt. I slid my flip-flops onto my feet and pulled my hair up into an elastic band without even looking in the mirror. Once upon a time I'd have been ashamed for the neighbours to see me like this, but now I hardly even noticed, and I'm sure they didn't either.

'Fine, Matt,' I shouted at the bathroom door. 'You win. I'll do it.' Like I always do.

Downstairs in the kitchen Minnie had curled herself up into a tight ball in a corner of her bed, as if I might not see her there. I crouched down and cupped her little face with both hands, tickling under her chin. As soon as she realized I wasn't going to tell her off, she wriggled up to stand on her hind legs, her front legs scrabbling at my knees as she tried to lick my face.

'Don't you worry, Minnie,' I said. 'As long as you puke on Daddy's side of the bed, Mummy doesn't mind.'

I clipped the lead onto her collar and straightened up, ready to take her outside. I noticed an empty bottle of wine by the sink, and the glass beside it, with the sticky dregs clinging to the side. I'd heard Matt come in last night at half past ten, but I was already in bed. After half an hour of waiting to see if he'd come upstairs, I'd turned out the light. He never tried to wake me up when he came to bed these days. A good thing too, I didn't want him to if he was going to be drunk again. But it felt like the distance between my side of the bed and his was growing, as if there was someone or something else lying there between us, holding us apart. Something neither of us was prepared to look at too closely.

Matt was reading the paper when I got back, hiding behind it like a shield. Probably to hide the sight of the mess he'd made having breakfast. A toddler would have been tidier — there was jam on the table, and a crust under it, which Minnie snaffled before I could pick it up. No wonder she kept being sick.

'I was going to take her out,' he said, turning down a corner of the sports page to look at me accusingly.

'Yeah?' I asked, picking up his dirty plate and knife and heading towards the dishwasher.

'Just because I'm not doing it exactly to your timetable doesn't mean I'm not going to do it.'

I rolled my eyes. 'Matt, it's not my timetable, it's the dog's. She doesn't care if you've had a shower or not, she just needs to go out.'

Matt put down the paper and glared at me, his eyes hard and challenging. 'I had to wash the sick off my foot — or do you think I should have just pulled my socks on over it? You'd only have had a go at me about the extra laundry.'

'When have I ever had a go at you about the laundry?' I demanded.

He started mimicking me in a high-pitched sing-song. 'Matt, you never take the laundry basket upstairs. Matt, would it have killed you to bring the washing in. Matt, don't you know not to put wool on a hot wash.'

'Fuck off, Matt,' I said. 'Just fuck off. You have no appreciation of what I do for you.'

'You don't do it for me,' he sneered, standing

up. 'You do it for you. I just get in your way, and you couldn't make it more obvious.'

He pushed past me, ignoring Minnie, who tried to jump up for attention.

'Where are you going?' I asked.

'Out.'

'Matt! We've got Sarah and Jay coming round for lunch. You can't go out!'

Matt turned back. 'Can't I?'

'You invited them,' I hissed. 'You insisted they come — it wasn't my idea! — and now you're fucking off to leave me to do everything, just like you always do.'

He braced himself against the kitchen door frame, his hands on either side of it, as if he was about to burst it apart Incredible-Hulk style. His voice was a fierce whisper, somehow more frightening than if he had shouted.

'I *said* let's just have a picnic on the Heath. I *said* let's just buy some stuff from the supermarket. I *said* don't make a massive production out of it, let's just catch up with our friends. *Your* friends. You were the one who said you wanted to do everything from scratch, spend hours in the kitchen. You can't blame me for that.'

'But you're not even helping,' I protested.

'Because I can't do anything right for you, Kate. Everything I do is wrong. You're impossible to please right now, and do you know why? Because you're miserable. You're miserable and you're lonely and you're bored, and I am sick of trying to make it all better for you.'

'Oh really?' I snapped. 'So it's all my fault, is it? I work and I work for us, for this marriage,

282

and you turn it all around and use it against me.'

'Seriously, Kate?' Matt sighed, rubbing at his forehead, pinching up a frown between his thumb and forefinger. 'Take a look at yourself. You've turned into some kind of fucking domestic martyr and you expect me to suffer for it. You're always spoiling for a fight over totally trivial shit — '

'It is not trivial — our marriage is not trivial!'

'Kate, I know that. But marriage is about more than just who picks up the towels off the bathroom floor you know. Or cleans up the dog sick.'

'Me!' I screamed, a sob rising in my throat. 'It's me, it's always me. It's always always me.'

'And you won't ever let me forget it, will you?'

When the front door slammed behind him I sank down onto the floor and put my head on my knees. Minnie nudged at my hand with her nose, and leaned her small warm body against me. I wondered if I was going to have to take her to puppy counselling; if she was already traumatized by living in this household.

Household? What a strange choice of word. Already, you see, I was beginning not to think of it as home.

34

I remember reading a book once where a woman cooked all of her emotions into the food she created. When she was sad, everyone who ate her food would cry. When she was happy, they'd laugh. If I had been that woman then everyone who ate the lunch I served that day would have become bitterly resentful. But because life doesn't really work like that, it seemed that all the bitterness ended up on my plate instead.

Perhaps Matt had staked out the front door for their arrival, or perhaps, as he claimed, it was a total coincidence, but when the doorbell rang he was standing there with Sarah and Jay, laughing and joking, his black mood entirely gone. He had a carrier bag full of bottles, his ready excuse for why he'd been out, though Sarah and Jay would not know that rather than just popping out to the off-licence he'd been gone for three long hours. It seemed there was some big joke about the event they were all working on, a model-turned-presenter who was in way over her head, but the nuances were lost on me while I was occupied with getting the chicken in the oven on time.

'But the best thing is,' said Sarah, 'the runner went over to her house, right, to drop off the schedules, and she invited him upstairs — '

'Oh yes?' leers Matt inappropriately.

'He's totally gay, Matt, get your mind out of

the gutter. She just had to get something, and apparently she has this sort of mini-fridge thing by the side of her bed.'

'A mini-fridge?' said Matt, wrinkling his nose.

'Yeah, Paul said it's sort of a cross between a fridge and a bedside table — it's got a lamp built into it and stuff. Kind of cool, actually,' said Jay.

Sarah grimaced at him. 'Only it's not very cool at all, it's completely tragic. Because what do you think she keeps in there? Kate, what do you think she keeps in the mini-fridge?'

I looked over from the sink, where I was peeling potatoes. 'Um, I'm not sure who you're talking about?'

'Yes, you are, you know, Minty Alexander. The supermodel — she presented part of the roadshow we did last year?'

'The dark-haired one? Wasn't she one of *The Times* Young Media Faces? That one?'

Jay scoffed. 'Young Media Face, my arse. That woman is pushing thirty if she's a day. The number of fucking filters we have to use to stop her looking like Zelda from Terrahawks, you wouldn't believe.'

Sarah was getting annoyed now; we were all drifting too far off topic. 'No, but listen, what would you imagine a glamorous supermodel and television presenter might keep in the fridge next to her bed?'

I looked blank.

'Come on,' urged Sarah.

'Eye masks?' I suggested. 'Moisturiser? Coconut water?'

'Eye masks and moisturiser — cold. Coconut water — warm.'

'What?' asked Jay. 'I thought it was a fridge — isn't everything cold?'

'Get with the programme, Jay,' said Sarah. 'I mean, she's getting warmer when she says coconut water.'

'So you mean it's a drink thing?' asked Matt as he opened a bottle of wine.

'Hot,' said Sarah.

'Champagne,' I suggested.

'Warmer.'

'Vodka,' offered Jay.

'Same temperature,' said Sarah.

'Oh come on then, what?' Matt asked.

Sarah left a dramatic pause, looking at each of us in turn.

'You'll never guess,' she said. 'Cans of Stella. Cans and cans of wife beater, lined up in the mini-fridge by the side of her bed, ready for her to crack one open first thing in the morning.'

'Eurgh, that is fucking grim,' said Jay. 'First thing in the morning?'

'Now you know why you need all those filters.' Matt laughed.

'I know!' said Sarah. 'If only all those fashion magazines could see her downing her morning lager, I don't reckon they'd be so keen to call her a style icon.'

'Yeah, well that runner also said — ' Jay began, and he launched into another story of scurrilous celebrity gossip.

This used to be my meat and drink. When I talked about work on my fleeting visits to Lyme

Regis, Prue accused me of being a name-dropper, which had astonished me. Everyone talks about the people they work with, and in our case it was famous people. Gossiping about our encounters with celebrities wasn't showing off, it was just what we did. But now I felt I had nothing to contribute. Who wanted to hear about what Minnie had done on her walk that day when Sarah had stories of supermodels and Jay and Matt were falling over themselves to compete with tales of their own.

Matt poured out more drinks for our guests and raised the bottle in my direction. I shook my head and stuck to my glass of mineral water. He started telling a story about someone new in the Marketing team — Olivia, a girl who'd joined from MTV and who Sarah and Danny seemed to know already. I hadn't heard him mention her before. But then, he didn't talk to me about work very often these days. I wasn't sure when I'd stopped asking him about it.

When they all roared with laughter at yet another reference that sailed over my head, I just joined in politely, then excused myself to go and attend to the food.

I didn't think they'd even noticed I'd gone until, a few minutes later, Sarah appeared at my elbow.

'Kate, you look so well,' she said, picking up a wilted piece of watercress from the bowl of salad leaves I was arranging. She put it in her mouth and chewed, looking at me expectantly as if I was about to admit something.

'Do you mean fat?' I asked warily. I think we

all know that 'you look well' is code for 'haven't you porked out lately'.

'No!' She laughed, leaning on the kitchen counter. She seemed taller than I remembered, and I realized she was wearing expensive new pointy-toed snakeskin heels — the kind I rarely bothered with now that I had nowhere to wear them.

'Just *well*. It's the not-working-in-an-office glow — it suits you. You look so fresh-faced and lovely. I guess it must be really relaxing being at home instead of at work. A slower pace of life. Just having time to chill out and stuff.'

'Yes, it is,' I lied. 'It really is.'

Sarah looked out of the kitchen window into the garden. 'I really miss you, you know. Not just at work, though God knows, Jennifer is no Kate Martell when it comes to keeping everyone in line.'

I kept looking down at the salad leaves, turning them over and over with my hands in exactly the way I'd been shown on the cookery course I'd attended last month. People didn't know that even a salad should be made a certain way. I had to concentrate.

'I miss you, too,' I said. 'I'm sorry I haven't been in touch much. It's just . . . '

Sarah looked back at me. 'It's just what?'

'Stuff, you know. Work feels really far away for me right now. Even going into town — I don't know. It's just not where my head's at.'

Sarah regarded me searchingly.

'I never thought you'd be able to just drop work like that,' she said, real concern in her eyes, as if I'd been diagnosed with a terrible illness instead of just released from the drudgery of office life.

I had been like that once: unable to imagine a life that wasn't defined by schedules and budgets and deadlines. Thinking that if you weren't working you were hardly worth a place in the world. I shrugged. 'I've moved on. I didn't expect it either, but maybe I've just realized that no one can sustain the kind of job we do for ever. All that travel — the pressure. It was horrible to be made redundant, but maybe it's worked out for the best in the end.'

'I know you've moved on from work, Kate,' she said, 'I just hope that doesn't mean you've moved on from me. I thought we were proper friends, not just people who used to work together.'

I made myself laugh brightly. 'Sarah! As if I'd think that!' I screwed the top onto the jar of dressing I'd made and shook it hard. Sarah stepped back cautiously, flinching away from the flying jar.

'I've just been busy,' I continued. 'You have too. Don't go reading too much into it. It's not some massive diss, honest.'

She smiled. 'God, sorry, I didn't mean to lay a guilt trip on you. I only realized when Jay and I were coming here that I hadn't seen you for months. I counted. Four months, Kate! I used to see you every day. It's just weird.'

'It's weird for me, too,' I admitted.

Sarah looked over at the table where Matt and Jay sat. 'That's why I was so glad Matt said you wanted us to come over for lunch. It really means a lot that you asked us over. And Matt has been going on and on about your amazing cooking these days.'

So Matt had presented this as my idea, had he? I wondered what he was playing at.

'I'm really glad you're here,' I said. 'Don't expect too much on the food front, I think Matt's probably been embellishing a bit.'

'No I haven't,' he called over from the table. I could see by the slight glassiness in his eyes that he'd already had too much to drink. Again. Lunch wasn't even going to be ready for an hour. 'My wife is an extraordinary cook, I'll have you know. She's extraordinary at everything.'

I wondered if he thought that complimenting me extravagantly in front of my friends was the way to get back into my good books, or if he was drunk enough to believe his own words. As far as I could see, he mostly just thought I was extraordinarily annoying.

'Don't go getting any ideas, Jay,' warned Sarah, sauntering across the kitchen, wagging her finger at him. Somehow the way she did it managed to be teasing and sexy instead of nagging. I could see Matt looking at her admiringly, the glamorous high-heeled professional compared to his stay-at-home wife in her apron. Well, there was no point in taking the apron off now, I'd only get spattered with hot fat when I took the chicken out of the oven.

Sarah sank down onto Jay's lap, crossing one elegant ankle over her knee. 'Kate might have transformed herself into some domestic goddess, but she is a way better person than I am. You can dream on if you think that I'm ever going to be fannying around in the kitchen on your behalf.'

Jay tickled her ribs, making Sarah shriek and writhe so that her wine sloshed perilously close to the top of her glass. I picked up a cloth from next to the kitchen sink, ready for it to spill.

'Yeah, right, Sarah,' he said, rubbing his stubbled chin into her neck to make her laugh. 'The day you make me a meal from scratch, like Kate's done, is the day I make an honest woman out of you.'

Sarah snorted with laughter and leaned back over her shoulder to kiss the top of his head. 'That's enough of a threat to keep me single for ever, babe. Anyway, I scratched that curry out of the takeaway packet last night, you've got nothing to complain about.'

'God, takeaway curry.' Matt sighed with patent longing, and then he flinched guiltily, catching my eye. I turned back to the kitchen counter and wiped at a spot of water by the sink with the cloth I was holding tightly in my hand.

'Anyone want more wine?' I heard him ask. I felt his presence as he crossed the kitchen towards me, putting both hands on my hips. It felt like a sort of apology. I leaned my head back, about to rest it on his shoulder, when he moved me bodily out of the way, and I realized he was just trying to get to the cutlery drawer.

'There it is,' he said, picking up the corkscrew and returning to the table to open another bottle.

'Kate?' he waved the bottle at me again. 'Just

one won't hurt, will it?'

I shook my head. When Matt said it wouldn't hurt, he meant it wouldn't hurt *him*. He didn't understand that I had committed to this. Everyone said giving up alcohol increased your chances of getting pregnant. If it didn't happen this month — again — it wasn't Matt who'd blame himself.

'You're no fun,' he said. I could tell that he was trying for the teasing tone Sarah had adopted, but instead he just sounded petulant.

'Maybe it's not all about being fun,' I snapped, unable to stop myself.

Matt barely reacted, but I saw the swift, anxious look that Jay gave Sarah, and the way she squeezed the arm he had wrapped around her. It was typical that it would seem like me who was being unreasonable, when they knew nothing of how he'd behaved before they arrived. I looked like the shrewish, sober wife, while he was Mr Good Times.

'Did I tell you what happened last week with Randy Jones and the sixteen-year-old intern in Talent?' asked Sarah valiantly.

We all turned to her gratefully, gladly, trusting her to lead us to safer conversational ground.

35

I don't hear the exact words of Ben's reaction to my handiwork, but I get the general idea from the shouting and crashing noises that emerge from the bathroom first thing the next morning, shortly followed by the man himself. He stumbles into the kitchen, his face bright red and dripping with water.

'Why the fuck,' he stammers, pointing to his forehead. 'Why the *fuck* does it say Barbados on my forehead in giant letters? *Backwards?*'

'Well, otherwise you wouldn't have been able to read it in the mirror, Ben,' I say sweetly, trying not to laugh. It is one thing to play a practical joke, but quite another to guffaw out loud in the face of your victim. That would be cruel.

'It won't come off! Been scrubbing at it with a flannel for ten minutes!'

'Oh shit,' I say. I had assumed it would wash off straight away, once the joke was over. 'Ben, I had no idea it was permanent.'

'Did you use the permanent fucking marker in the living room, by any chance?' he asks. 'Because that might have given you a clue.'

'I'm so sorry,' I say. 'It was a joke, I thought you'd see the funny side. Look, why don't you try some of my exfoliating scrub, that might do it.'

'Already used half a tub of it,' he barks. 'Face is totally flayed.'

He rubs at his forehead with the sleeve of his dressing gown, as if the soft terry towelling will succeed where Dermalogica has failed.

'I've got a meeting today,' he wails. 'Who is going to take me seriously with the word Barbados on my face? Backwards? Why Barbados? Why?'

'Because of the honeymoon?' I say cautiously.

Ben spins round, his eyes narrowed. I never knew his affability could turn to pure rage like this. It almost makes me like him more to know that he's not as one-dimensional as I'd feared.

'Honeymoon?' he asks, in much the same way as a fundamentalist Christian might say 'abortion?'

'You wanted to know where Prue wanted to go on honeymoon,' I titter nervously. 'Umm, now you do.'

Ben growls something under his breath and storms out of the kitchen. When he returns, dressed in a suit, he has engineered a strange, thin fringe over his forehead by straightening his curls with what looks like a great deal of hair product. He scowls out from under the wispy curtain that entirely fails to obscure the faded blue letters.

'Well,' he says, 'if you set out to humiliate me, you've done a great job. Good for you. Hilarious. Now if you'll excuse me, I have to go to work, which is something you clearly know little about, or perhaps you would have thought more carefully about this.'

He points to his forehead as if I might have missed it.

'I'm sorry,' I say. I really am sorry. I didn't think it through at all. It seemed funny at the time. Surely the ends justify the means?

'Prue said I should look out for this,' Ben says. 'I said, no, Kate's a good egg, don't know why you've got such a problem with your sister. But Prue said you just use people, only think of yourself. Don't care how you affect anyone else. Now I see she's right.'

I stare at him with my mouth open, winded by his accusations.

He produces from his coat pocket a knitted hat that he pulls down over his hair. Blond curls escape at the front, but the offending letters are hidden.

'Good day to you,' he says, bizarrely, as if we are in a Victorian novel. Good day? I suppose he thought it would sound cutting.

After Ben is gone I hear a noise at the door and I wonder if he's coming back to shout at me again. But no, while I was steeling myself for another blow to my core, a knife has been slipped between my unsuspecting shoulder blades. On the doormat lies a letter from my husband.

At the sight of his handwriting my first emotion is pure guilt. I know rationally, of course, that I have no reason at all not to have been kissing another man last night. Some people might say that it's inappropriate to fool around with Eddy when I'm still married, but even puritanical Prue seemed to grant me an amnesty on that one, so some people would have to have incredibly high and unrealistic standards.

But it is impossible to see Matt's cramped scribble on the envelope — the messy writing of one accustomed to texts and emails rather than penmanship — without feeling a lurch of shame and horror. Perhaps I will always feel like this in some way: guilt at having let our marriage fall apart, at not being stronger and more resilient.

When couples who have been married for years and years share their secrets, they all seem to say the same thing: that it's hard work, and that there has to be forgiveness on both sides. I don't know if I am good enough at either of those things. I worked hard, of course, I worked harder on my marriage than on anything. When I think of how I used to complain of my long hours at Hitz, I realize how easy I had it. Those hours raced by in a blur of activity and appointments and teamwork. There were tangible results — a show produced, a budget finalized. Far harder was the painful stretch of time alone between nine and six when you were working working working for the happiness of someone who not only wasn't there, but who seemed to actively resent the things you were doing when he finally returned home.

And forgiveness. That is the hardest thing of all. I honestly don't know if I have it in me to forgive everything that happened. To stare it in the face unflinchingly and take the consequences. Because to forgive is to accept, isn't it? To accept what happened, instead of resisting it and running from it. That is what I'm not sure I can do. Reading Matt's letter instead of throwing it away would be a start.

Before I do that I need coffee. I take my time grinding the beans and letting the boiling water steep. I heat up a pan of milk, a refinement I rarely bother with because it will take more time. All the while the unopened envelope sits on the kitchen counter, all the more obvious because I am trying so hard to pretend I am unconcerned by it.

When my coffee is made, I take my cup and sit down at the kitchen table with the letter. Minnie settles herself by my feet, sighing heavily at this interruption to her morning routine. We should be out on a walk by now; there are seagulls unchased down on the rocky shore, lampposts unsniffed.

I use a knife to open the envelope; it makes a snickering sound, as if someone was laughing at me.

I don't know if I should read anything into the graduation from a postcard to two pages of actual watermarked writing paper. Even through my guilt and confusion, I am oddly touched by the idea of Matt going to the trouble of buying paper on which to write to me. I know we have nothing like this at home — who does, nowadays? I shake my head crossly — why am I wasting time on considering the medium when I haven't even read the message?

Of course, forgiveness is what Matt wants. As if it's as easily given as it is asked for.

Kate,
What is it going to take to get you to answer me? I've got in the car again and again ready

to come down to see you. But I know you need space. I'm trying to give you that.

There has to be room for mistakes. Neither of us is perfect. But you can't throw everything away without even talking about it.

I've got to go away for work tomorrow — Dubai, one week. I won't be at home if you call. But I'm on my mobile, I'm checking email. I'm waiting to hear from you. Please.

Matt

Maybe it is because I am a little hungover this morning, so my brain isn't ready to spin straight into its accustomed fury against Matt. Maybe it's because last night I was kissing another man. Or maybe it's knowing that my insistence on having things on my terms has sent my sister's fiancé to an important meeting with magic marker all over his face. Whatever the reason, I find myself contemplating how it would feel not to be angry with Matt.

I can't say I am going as far as thinking about complete forgiveness. But, like someone probing a sore tooth with their tongue, allowing themselves to measure the pain in careful, self-prescribed intervals, I consider reacting differently.

Running away, blaming, hiding. These have always been my solutions to everything. But where have they got me? When I think about it in the bright, sober morning, it is less of a surprise that I found myself snogging Eddy Curtis last night, leaning against an ice-cream-coloured beach hut on the seafront, like my teenage self. Because I may be running away from adult problems now

— from marriage and responsibilities — but my reaction is still that of a frightened adolescent. Afraid of facing up to actual emotion, preferring to bury it in new experience and hope that the bad feelings will just go away.

Suddenly kissing Eddy feels less the action of a free-spirited woman reasserting herself after the failure of her marriage, and more the regressive step backwards of someone who has failed to deal with her past in any way. To my creeping discomfort, Ben's words come back to me, again and again, more insistent even than the letter in my hand.

Prue said you just use people, don't care how you affect anyone else.

I let Ben move in here, wasn't that selfless? It's not like Prue was about to put herself out, even though he's her fiancé. And did I sulk and moan about it? No, I dedicated myself to making him a better person — for Prue, not even for myself! He may be annoyed about the magic marker — and I admit it was a step too far — but hasn't it had the desired result? He wanted to find out Prue's preferred honeymoon destination and I have delivered it to him — in black and white and scrubbed red skin.

So why do those words keep coming back? Why won't they leave me alone?

Matt said similar things to me, that I manipulated everything so that it was how I wanted. But like Prue, he never understood that it was for his own good. For *our* own good. But was it? When I think about us lately, I have the strangest feeling: that while I was trying to get Matt to change, he was trying to change me too.

But those words sting more harshly even than that, because they're pretty much exactly what Tim Cooper said to me just before I left Lyme for good.

36

That summer started early for all of us, in a bright, brilliant May of blue skies and sunshine. Exams were over, and while the rest of the school was shut indoors, staring out of the window at the sea, we were free. There were parties nearly every night, and we'd meet up in the late mornings to dissect the evening before over bacon sandwiches and Cokes on the seafront, playing frisbee down on the beach in the afternoon. I think we knew it was all about to be over — some of us had places at university, some of us were interviewing for jobs — but in that early part of the summer, it was all about possibility; it felt like the sunny days would stretch out in front of us endlessly.

It is hard for me to remember if I was already desperate to leave Lyme. My memories of that first part of the summer are so golden that I have almost convinced myself I would have stayed there happily for ever if things hadn't gone wrong. But that can't be right, since all the universities I applied to were in London. I remember dancing around the living room with Prue the day I heard I'd got into Imperial, her joy, even at ten years old, less for my achievement than out of delight that she would soon have our shared bedroom to herself.

Some of the boys had cars now, crappy rustbuckets purchased with the proceeds of summer jobs, and the novelty of being driven around by friends rather than parents made us all shut our eyes to the terrifying recklessness with which we hurtled around the country lanes. Nothing bad would happen to us — we were invincible, independent. While living at home with everything paid for by our mums and dads, of course — we didn't even know that this was something to be grateful for. Instead our parents were a terrible burden and we spent hours discussing how little they understood our lives, and what it was to be young.

Adding to my giddy sense of freedom that summer was the fact that I'd dumped Tim Cooper. Yes, I, Kate Bailey, had broken up with the undisputed sex god of Lyme Regis.

He hadn't seen it coming. Possibly because he'd been too busy looking in the mirror, but it wasn't his vanity that had finished us off. It wasn't just one thing; it was everything. The protective way he hovered around me at parties, never joining in a conversation, just waiting for me to get bored or drunk enough to go upstairs with him; it began to annoy me. I hadn't noticed how little he contributed, as if his beautiful face should be enough of a reward for those of us near him. He was an object to be admired, and when my gaze turned elsewhere, even momentarily, he was at first baffled, then angry.

And the more I pulled away, the closer he clung. Turning up at my house when I didn't answer the phone, pinning Kerry Walker's fifteen-year-old brother up against a wall for talking to me. Once your party wasn't considered a success until Tim and I had christened one of the bedrooms, now an evening was complete only once Tim and I had had a shouting match in your kitchen, or back garden, or wherever I happened to be when Tim lost patience with waiting for me to turn to him, only him and no one else.

'I don't understand you,' he bellowed. 'What do you want?'

But I didn't know what I wanted. I was seventeen, for crying out loud.

Though it was unknown to me then, some examination board somewhere was about to give me an A in English for my ability to debate the motivations of literary creations. I could see the subtext and the foreshadowing in novels, accurately predict the weakness of character that would lead to disaster (it always ended in disaster for women in those nineteenth-century novels), but when it came to myself I entirely lacked the emotional vocabulary to tell Tim what I wanted. I didn't know how to establish a boundary between him and myself when I wasn't sure if this new, confident, popular me was really me, or just the temporary gift of Tim, as easily withdrawn as it had been given. And because I didn't know how to discuss it, I ended it. Abruptly and badly. Tim couldn't believe it.

Nor could anyone else. There was a collective breath-holding from everyone around us for days. Tim Cooper had been dumped. One of the immutable laws of the universe had been broken — would others follow? Would the sun start setting in the east? Would the waves stop rolling

303

up onto the shingle?

He tried to get back together with me by blasting out No Doubt's 'Don't Speak' from his car stereo outside our house — don't judge him too harshly, it was 1997 after all. It didn't work, not least because Dad threatened to turn the hose on him if he didn't fuck off out of our drive. And also because we were at that age where music really means something, is your entire identity, and I couldn't help feeling that if Tim had known me at all, he'd have tried to woo me back with a band I actually liked.

This is not to say I didn't mourn the end of our relationship. Of course I did, I was a hormonal adolescent, so I seized on any excuse for dramatics. It was the perfect excuse to refuse to eat for days, to sulk around the house and to claim that no one appreciated the depths of my suffering. But underneath, I at least had the self-awareness to realize that my overwhelming emotion was one of relief.

And on the seventh day, I heard that Tim had shagged Manda Clarke up against a tree in the Undercliff. All was right with the world. He had moved on.

So when Dready Eddy announced that his parents were going away to Spain for a week, leaving him in charge of their enormous hillside house, I didn't think twice about turning up at his party, even though I knew Tim would be there.

Eddy's parents were architects, which to we unsophisticated children of Lyme Regis, brought up before the advent of *Grand Designs* and its ilk, was an almost mystical profession. Entering into their starkly modernist home, built high up on the hill, glass-walled and steel-timbered, was like stepping into the future. And in the future, of course, they played the Chemical Brothers at ear-splitting volume, and had a dustbin full of ice and beer in the middle of the balcony.

Eddy was taking his duties as host pretty seriously, which is to say that he had moved all the furniture out of the way and was offering bucket bongs in the bathroom. Beyond that it was a total free-for-all. I arrived at nine, backed up by Ellie Morrison and Jo Winters, who were ostensibly my greatest friends, but who couldn't disguise the fact that they were buzzing with the possibility of being self-appointed handmaidens to any Kate and Tim gossip that might occur that night, our first social encounter since we'd split up.

I considered myself lucky they'd come with me. I'd noticed that a few of my supposed friends had already started subtly distancing themselves from me, obviously hoping that doing so might increase their chances of being the next girl Tim took to the Undercliff. Well, good luck to them, if that was what they really wanted. For me it was enough to be at a party without my usual glowering shadow trailing me from room to room.

Of course the glowering shadow was already there, leaning against a kitchen counter, his arm around a triumphant-looking Manda Clarke. Once he was sure I'd seen him, he bent his head to mash his mouth on hers, looking at me the whole time. I would like to say that I walked over there with total confidence and said hello, taking the moral high ground and being an adult about it. But come off it, I was seventeen. Of course I didn't. I ducked behind my hair, pretended I hadn't seen him and went out onto the balcony instead to get drunk.

Eddy had set up speakers on the wooden decking and the bass pounded under my feet as I stepped outside, flanked by Ellie and Jo. It was still light enough to see the ocean, where the sun hovered above the horizon, casting us all in its reddish glow. It was the magic hour, when everything looks illuminated and beautiful, before darkness and cold descend. Someone put a Bacardi Breezer in my hand and I downed half of it in one go.

Ellie giggled in my ear about a tall boy who was sitting on a railing on the other side of the balcony — none of us had seen him before, which, in our incestuous small-town group of friends, lent him an air of celebrity. Even though the balcony dropped at least twenty feet behind him, he sat on the railing with complete unconcern, swinging a beer bottle by its neck. I saw him look over at us, and he caught my eye and smiled.

Eddy ambled over to us, affectedly casual, his dreads falling down over his face dangerously close to the glowing end of his spliff. ''S Will's cousin, Max,' he said, nodding over at the new boy. 'Come down from London — he's at Imperial. Um, hey, isn't that where you're going, Kate?'

'Yes, it is,' I said, barely registering the fact that Eddy knew where I was going to university. I couldn't have told you what he was doing after the summer if my life depended on it. So the dark-haired boy over there was going to be at my university, was he? Interesting.

'Ooh,' said Jo. 'He's looking at you, Kate. It's like it was written in the stars. How romantic.'

'Shut up, Jo,' I muttered, elbowing her in the ribs. 'You're so embarrassing.'

'He's coming over,' she hissed.

'I need another drink,' I said, nonchalantly walking over to the dustbin full of ice where all the bottles were hidden. I bent down to pick up another bottle, and looked back over my shoulder. 'Anyone else?'

'Yeah, great, thanks,' said Eddy. 'Beer, please, Kate.'

Ellie shook her head fiercely, indicating her Bacardi Breezer, which was nearly full. Her expression clearly said to slow down. Whatever; she wasn't my mother. This was a party. It was practically obligatory to get drunk.

'I'll have a beer, thanks,' said Max. Our fingers touched as I passed him the ice-cold bottle, and I dropped my gaze, knowing he was still looking at me.

In my memory all the parties that summer meld into one — even this one. I can't be sure how clearly I remember it now that I see it all through a haze of nostalgia. I do know that I spent a lot of the evening talking to Max, but I can't remember what we spoke about. I don't suppose it matters, since frankly in those days all a boy had to do was have a Britpop haircut and a decent pair of trainers and he was halfway there as far as I was concerned. With the glamour of coming from London, Max could have spoken to me about sewerage works or stamp collecting and I'd have been impressed.

I do remember feeling like I was flexing my muscles, having a sense of myself as attractive, to this stranger, just for being myself. He didn't know me as Tim Cooper's girlfriend. He didn't even know who Tim Cooper was. I felt I was being granted a glimpse of my future self, the girl I might be once I'd left Lyme behind. All at once I couldn't wait to escape this golden summer. Life seemed to be beckoning to me from London, calling me away. Max was just the personification of everything that was waiting for me.

The rest of the group drifted back indoors as the night got colder, but the two of us stayed there, leaning against the balcony railings, talking, talking. Every now and then someone would stumble out onto the balcony for a cigarette or a beer from the dustbin, but no one approached us.

I was going to kiss him. I was going to grab my future with both hands. But first I needed to go inside and use the bathroom.

Max helped me stand up, I told him my head was spinning, which wasn't a total lie as I'd drunk way too much, but it was mostly an excuse to hold onto his hand, flexing my fingers against his. I pulled away reluctantly and told him to wait there for me. He grinned and I felt my heart do a skip of anticipation inside my chest.

I slid open the glass doors back into the Curtises' house and was hit by a wall of body heat and music now that the speakers had been moved inside. People were dancing, and Ellie was asleep on the sofa. I stopped to check on her, but she pushed my hand away and rolled over, mumbling something about elephants. I couldn't see Tim anywhere. Maybe he'd gone already. As I walked through the room I felt like I was gliding above them all, aloof and apart. I had Max from London waiting for me outside. The future.

There were voices inside the bathroom and when the door opened a thick cloud of dope smoke rolled out, closely followed by one of the boys from the Lower Sixth.

'He's pulling a whitey,' someone shouted, and I stepped quickly out of the way, just in time to avoid being splattered with vomit as he buried his face in a potted palm on the landing.

'Hey, Kate,' called Eddy, from his position crouched by the bath, a cut-off Coke bottle suspended in the water. 'Want some?'

'She's already getting some from what I heard,' sniggered someone I couldn't see.

'Is there another bathroom?' I asked, pretending not to have heard.

Eddy pushed his dreads off his face, and frowned as he tried and failed to focus on me. 'Yeah, use the one in my mum and dad's room. Top floor. No problem.'

The bathroom door swung shut again.

'Are you okay?' I asked the boy who'd puked in the plant pot.

'It's cool, I'm cool,' he insisted, waving me away as he slumped against the wall. I shrugged and left him there, his head hanging between his knees.

The sound of the music was fainter as I went up the stairs to the top of the house. I could still hear laughter from the bathroom below, but up here it was hushed. Eddy's parents' room was almost monastic, all whites and greys, with a concrete shelf running above the bed. Expensive art books were arranged in tasteful piles, one each for Eddy's mum and dad. It was so different to my parents' cluttered terraced home. This was just how I would have my bedroom when I was grown up, I decided. I couldn't wait.

When I came out of the bathroom, turning off the light, I was temporarily blinded by the sudden darkness in the bedroom. As my eyes adjusted, I realized I could see hundreds and hundreds of stars through the huge window that made up an entire wall of the room, facing seaward. I gasped a little and stepped forwards, craning my head to look up. My breath misted on the glass.

'Hello, Kate,' said a voice.

I spun around in shock.

Half hidden in the dark, Tim lay on the bed, feet stretched out. Entirely bizarrely, my first thought was to tell him to get his shoes off Eddy's parents' immaculate bedspread.

'What the fuck, Tim,' I said. 'You nearly gave me a heart attack.'

He nodded smugly and stretched his hands behind his head. 'Where's your boyfriend?'

'Where's Manda Clarke?' I retorted.

'Oh, you don't need to worry about Manda,' he said.

'I'm not worried about her,' I snapped. 'I couldn't care less about her.'

Tim sat up on the bed and pouted like a child. 'Is someone a bit jealous?' he asked.

'Oh yeah, massively,' I said. 'I came up here to cry and cry. Or to use the bathroom. And now I'm done, so if you'll excuse me.'

Tim jumped up from the bed so fast it made me start, standing between me and the stairs, his arms folded across his broad chest, blocking my way. He smiled at me, but it wasn't the smile I was used to seeing on his beautiful face. This smile almost made him look ugly.

'Tim, just grow up.'

'Just grow up,' he mimicked. 'Is that guy downstairs grown up? Is he? Because he's from London, and he's going to university and all that shit. Is that what impresses you?'

'Tim.'

'Is it? Is *he* good enough for you, Kate? Since I'm not?'

'It's not like that.'

'Isn't it?' he sneered. 'You just used me, Kate. Used me and then dropped me when you'd had enough. You never gave a shit about me. You were only interested in what I could do for you. I made you popular and then you dumped me.'

'Tim, I'm going downstairs now,' I said. There was no point to this conversation. What good would it do to tell Tim I found him boring and possessive and clingy? He might think I didn't care about his feelings, but it would hurt him more to hear the truth.

He took one step towards me and clutched my wrist. I tried to pull away but he held on so hard that I cried out.

'No you're not,' he said from between clenched teeth. He was close enough that I felt flecks of saliva on my cheek as he spoke. 'You're not.'

He grabbed my other wrist and pushed me down onto the bed. I tried to kick at him with my feet, but he lay on top of me heavily, so that I was pinned down. I had always loved how strong Tim was; it had made me feel delicate in comparison, fragile. Now it made me feel scared. I knew that no matter how much I struggled, I didn't have the strength to get him off me.

'Tim, please,' I begged. 'Please. We can talk, is that what you want? Let's talk.'

Tim's eyes glittered in the faint light. 'Shut up,' he said. His voice was thick in his throat.

'Really, Tim, please.'

Without letting go of my wrist he bent his elbow so that his forearm pressed against my throat. My mouth opened and closed as I tried to draw in air to scream, but all that emerged was a rasping whisper.

I knew as soon as he pushed my legs apart with his knee what he planned to do. And I don't know if I will ever forgive myself for letting him do it. No matter how much I tell myself that I was scared, or drunk, or physically overpowered, the truth is that there came a point when I thought that the more I resisted the worse it would be. And so I let him.

It wasn't as if he was a stranger. A few weeks ago I'd have done it willingly. In some way, I did think I was better than Tim. I did. This was my punishment. These were the things I told myself to justify lying still. To justify lying.

When I came downstairs, hours later, the music had stopped. Everyone had gone. Except Eddy, of course. He looked shocked to see me appear in his living room; he must have thought he was alone in the house. He just looked at my bruised throat and my tear-streaked face and offered to walk me home, keeping a solicitous distance between us as we stumbled silently down the hill to my parents' house.

I always knew he must have guessed what had happened, but he never said anything about it and neither did I. My parents tried to get me to talk, but I wouldn't. No, more than that. I couldn't. Every time I tried, my throat closed up again, as if Tim's arm was still there pressing on it, stopping the words from coming out.

A few days later I left Lyme for good. And I never looked back until now.

37

'You're late today,' says Cathy at the bakery, bringing over my coffee. 'Big night?'

She lingers hopefully and I wonder if she's already heard something about me and Eddy. It's only to be expected that we'd have been seen on our night out — two single people in Lyme, hanging around in public. The holey jumpers probably texted the entire town with an update as soon as we left the pub. We were asking for it. But before Cathy can press any information out of me, the man himself arrives, his cheeks flushed from the cold outside.

'Brr,' he says, stamping his feet on the mat by the door. 'Freezing out there.'

'Going to snow, apparently,' says Cathy, looking from me to Eddy with blatant interest.

'Is it now?' says Eddy affably, rubbing at his short hair. 'White Christmas, maybe?'

'That would be nice,' I say. 'Prue would love snow for her wedding.' I'm surprised by how calm and collected I sound, idly chatting about the weather with my local friends, when inside my stomach is churning with guilt and panic. Not the kind of excited panic that had me kissing Eddy last night, but the far more familiar kind that makes me want to flee the bakery as fast as I can.

There was something about the way Eddy acted last night that makes me think for him last night was a little more meaningful than a drunken kiss. I don't know exactly how I feel about it yet, but I do know that I'm in no way ready for a relationship — haven't I proved that I'm no good at them? — and it terrifies me that Eddy might want that.

Eddy seems entirely unaffected by what happened, asking after Cathy's granddaughter, and wondering if someone called Bill will be selling Christmas trees out front again this year. While Cathy launches into a long description of the terrible chilblains that may affect Bill's seasonal business, I look at Eddy with new eyes.

If anything he seems less nervous than usual, more relaxed, laughing at Cathy's gossip. But perhaps he's just faking it, like me. His eyes flick over to me as he listens to Cathy, and I drop my gaze back down to my coffee in embarrassment. I only realize after I've looked up again how flirtatious that seems.

Cathy watches the two of us and wipes her hands on her apron briskly. 'Can't stand here chatting all day, can I? You stop distracting me, Eddy Curtis, you bad man.'

She flicks him with a tea towel as she leaves.

'I think she fancies you,' I tease, as Eddy sits down opposite me at the trestle table. He leans down to pat Minnie hello.

'Pheromones,' says Eddy, his eyes twinkling. 'She can't help herself. Neither could you.'

'Eddy!' I laugh. My face burns so hotly you could probably pick up a slice of bread off the counter and press it against my cheek to make toast.

'What?' he says, sliding his leg alongside mine under the table, unseen by Cathy or any of the other customers. 'Come on, you're not going to pretend it didn't happen.'

I realize as he says that that it is pretty much exactly what I was going to do. I shift my leg very slightly away from his, and his forehead contracts into a quizzical frown.

'Course not,' I say carefully.

'Kaaaate?' says Eddy, drawing my name out so that it lasts for ages. His lips curl up into a little smile. It is impossible not to smile back a bit.

'Look, I just don't know if that was such a great idea,' I say. 'I mean, I had fun and everything, but Eddy, you're great, but . . . ' My words peter out slowly.

Eddy raises his eyebrows. 'Well, I'm shocked,' he says teasingly. 'I was wondering when we were going to post the banns.'

'Very funny,' I mutter.

Eddy clumsily puts a hand over mine. 'Kate, just chill. It's no big deal. I know you're not ready to rush into anything. But let's not pretend it didn't happen. That's never a good thing to do.'

Oh Eddy, I think. If only you knew. Pretending things didn't happen is practically my way of life.

'God, this is embarrassing,' I say. 'Sorry.'

Eddy shrugs. 'I don't think it's embarrassing,' he says gently. 'I like you, Kate. I always have done. Last night was fun. But if you just want to be friends, then that's okay too.'

I lift my head to look at Eddy properly. His face is so open and clear, it's as if I can see right

316

into his thoughts, and they're all ordered and rational and sane.

'Jesus, Eddy,' I say. 'When did you turn into such a grown-up?'

He laughs, throwing his head back, as if I've said something completely hysterical. But I mean it, I really do. How did he get to be so sorted and straightforward, when he's messed up his marriage just like I did? Where's his self-doubt? His crushing sense of worthlessness?

'A grown-up?' he scoffs.

'You really are though, Eddy,' I say. 'You're so sorted. How do you do it?'

I can see that Eddy is a little bemused. 'Everyone seems sorted from the outside, Kate,' he says. 'You seem sorted to me. Sad at the moment, but sorted in lots of ways. You should stop being so down on yourself.'

That's easy for Eddy to say. I expect if you opened him up to expose his darkest secrets they'd be something like 'nicked a fiver off my mum when I was twelve' or 'failed to renew my car tax disc on time.' No wonder it's easy for him to open up about his emotions; they're so simple and clear. He's Mr Brightside; he always was, even when we were younger.

I don't even want to think what you'd find if you opened me up, but it wouldn't be pretty.

'You're sweet, Eddy,' I say.

It's weird, though, he's spent all this time thinking I'm so sorted and glamorous, successful Kate in London. But really the one who's got himself together — set up his own business, had two beautiful little girls, is at peace with himself

— is the one who stayed in Lyme all along.

He doesn't seem to feel that restless need for change and improvement that has always driven me. To prove myself. To make everything better. To improve everyone around me. I had thought I was doing a good thing, trying to make the world a better place. What if really I've been doing the wrong thing all along, refusing to see the world as it is, to accept people the way they are instead of how I want them to be?

'Kate?' says Eddy. 'You're miles away.'

'Sorry,' I say. 'Thinking.'

'Look, it's bound to be strange for you right now,' says Eddy. 'The end of a marriage is hard. I know you're probably not ready for anything else. But I'm here for you as a friend, okay?'

'Thanks, Eddy,' I say. 'You're a good person.'

He's a better friend than I deserve.

38

London

I'd been sitting on the edge of the bath staring at the pregnancy test in my hand for five minutes, willing it to form into the words that would change my life. Our lives. It wasn't just a plastic stick, it was a magic wand.

My period was two days late. I'd retched over my breakfast that morning, and my breasts were tender and painful enough that I had to hold onto them when I went down the stairs. These should have been encouraging signs, but I'd learned already the cruel irony that the symptoms of early pregnancy were pretty much indistinguishable from those I got before my period, so I wouldn't allow myself to believe anything until that test was positive. The doctor said there was nothing wrong with me, nothing at all. He just said something about not stressing too much, which was ridiculous. Hadn't I chosen not to work for that very reason?

The doctor said it would happen when I least expected it, which is what everyone used to say about falling in love. I supposed it might be true. It didn't stop me wanting to punch the doctor in his smug, unconcerned face though. It didn't stop me wanting to say, 'If this goes on much longer I am going to have to turn into a sperm snatcher, because my husband will barely sleep with me as it is.'

Matt and his super sperm. Oh yes, he'd had the tests too. Only after I'd badgered him for weeks. If I was being kind, which I was actually quite capable of being no matter what my husband said, I would have acknowledged that he was terrified by the tests. He knew how much this meant to me and he dreaded the possibility of being the one at fault. He should have been used to it.

But oh no, Matt Martell, for whom everything always came easy, excuse the pun, turned out to have super swimmers. When the doctor told him the results, I swear I thought Matt was going to do a victory lap around the clinic's waiting room, hands held high above his head.

'Nothing wrong with these babies,' he said, proudly, on the way home. 'Nothing wrong at all.' And when we got back, he initiated sex for the first time in weeks.

I don't think he realized that the only possible conclusion that left me with was that the person who had something wrong with them was me. It didn't just taint the present, it stained backwards into the past. I found myself recalling all the times I'd taken risks, not bothered with the morning after pill, crossed my fingers after opening my legs and greeted the arrival of my period like a benediction. What if all along I hadn't been able to have children? What if that proved I couldn't get pregnant at all?

I wasn't reassured by the doctor. If there really was nothing wrong, then I'd be pregnant by now. I'd done everything right. Everything. There had to be a reason.

'What do you want?' Matt demanded, when I tried to talk about why it wasn't happening for us. 'We've had the tests, everything's fine. You just need to stop obsessing about it.'

So I stopped talking about it, which, as far as Matt was concerned, was the same thing.

Now I think of it, I stopped talking about most stuff. Big stuff, I mean. There just didn't seem to be much point. Matt seemed to take this as a good sign, and I could see that our superficial little chats over supper pleased him — what was on the television that night, the cute thing Minnie had done that morning, the latest client he'd brought to Hitz. It was all so much better than the angry resentment I usually served up.

But then he started coming home later and later and I realized that he was avoiding me. It says a lot that by that time I didn't really care. As long as we had sex when I was ovulating, he could do what he liked.

I shook the stick, in case that might make it show its result earlier. And there it was. Not Pregnant. Again.

The stick didn't say 'Again'. I should make that clear. But it might as well have done. It might as well have said 'You, Kate Martell, are a complete failure. You can't have a baby. Your husband thinks you're going mad. You don't have a job. You barely have any friends left.' It would have been a lot to fit on a plastic stick, I admit. But just because it wasn't there didn't mean that I didn't feel every word of it in my core.

I heard my mobile start ringing in the bedroom, but I didn't make any effort to answer.

I felt too numb. And I wasn't even sure my legs would carry me there. I knew who it would be anyway — Sarah.

Her self-appointed pity mission had intensified in the last few weeks. Since I never came out, she'd invited herself over for a night of DVDs and popcorn, during which she'd drunk way too much and told me that she and Jay were having problems and she didn't know if she loved him any more. I was sympathetic, but it felt as if there was a glass wall between us — I was sympathetic, but I didn't tell her anything about me and Matt. To say it out loud, to tell her how strained everything had become, would be to make it real. And because I was keeping everything in, it made me seem distant. I could see it hurt her that I was so remote, but if I started crying I wasn't sure I'd ever stop.

I threw the test stick in the bin and covered it in tissue paper so that Matt wouldn't see it. As if he ever investigated the contents of the bathroom bin. Judging by the old razor blades and empty shampoo bottles he left lying around the bathroom, he probably didn't know there was a bin there at all. But it made me feel safer to know it was hidden. Maybe, too, I didn't want to see it again myself.

The cardboard packaging I took with me; I'd tuck it into my handbag and dispose of it later. I'd taken to hiding the packages from Matt since they only gave him ammunition against me, a reason to accuse me again of being obsessive and neurotic. The first time I just casually dropped the packet into next door's recycling bin, but I hadn't foreseen that this would cause an almighty row between the Palmers, since they already had four children and Mr Palmer had had a vasectomy. From that time onwards I had made sure to get rid of it further afield, in an anonymous municipal bin.

My phone buzzed again to tell me I had a voicemail. Of course it was Sarah, who else was it going to be? If my phone rang these days it was always either my mum, Matt or Sarah. Where once I'd fielded hundreds of emails a day and spent half my life on the end of a phone, now the arrival of a single text could startle me.

'Hey, Kate, it's me. Just calling to say we're going to be in the Crown tonight for a drink after work. Jay's working, so maybe if you came we could go for pizza after? Everyone says they'd love to see you. Just let me know, okay?'

She wasn't really expecting me to turn up. She'd be waiting for my excuse. I didn't dare confess that I'd become a little afraid of Soho. It was so full of people rushing to the next important meeting, everyone was busy, hectic, taking calls as they hurried along the pavements. I didn't feel I belonged any more. I didn't understand why Sarah wouldn't take no for an answer — the more I refused her invitations, the more frequently they came, until I felt besieged by them.

I texted back quickly — easier than phoning and getting dragged into a conversation.

Sorry, got to make supper for Matt tonight. Lots of love.

Her reply came immediately.

Oh right, I thought he said he was out. My mistake. Next time. Xoxoxo

Why would Sarah think that Matt was out? He hadn't said anything to me about it, not that that was particularly unusual. He didn't say much lately. We didn't often eat together any more. I'd taken to eating earlier, and he often wasn't home until nine. But he usually told me if he was going to be properly out for the whole evening, if only to save me the trouble of cooking for him.

Suddenly I was furious. All my stale resignation drained away and in its place was cold rage. Who did Matt think he was? Taking me for granted like this. Not even bothering to tell me where he was going or what he was doing. Just expecting me to sit at home on my own, like always, waiting for him to come back whenever it suited him. But even in my fury I didn't want to be the one who initiated an actual conversation. That might turn into an argument. And I might lose the argument. So instead I texted:

'Sarah says you're out tonight. Were you planning to tell me?'

Of course Matt didn't reply, which made me even angrier. By the time three hours had passed without a response, I was ready to explode, pacing the kitchen, running vicious conversations out loud with an imaginary Matt. Imaginary as in, he was here for me to converse with, unlike my actual husband who never was. Minnie cowered in her basket, but I was too furious to be able to stop myself.

When four hours had passed, I got changed. I put on make-up. I blow-dried my hair. I took Minnie round to the Palmers' house and asked them to look after her for a few hours.

Fuck it. Two could play at that game. I was going out.

39

It's not until I come out of the estate agents late one afternoon, having agreed a time for them to take new photos of the redecorated bungalow, that I realize the Christmas lights have gone up on Broad Street. They're hardly going to rival the Regent Street display, but the twinkling snow-flakes and trees look pretty in the fading light. The sight of them makes me stop for a moment in surprise. Christmas is coming. Soon. And then it will be a new year. I suppose I had forgotten that, while my own life might be on hiatus, for everyone else it is moving forwards just as it always has.

I can't help but think of last Christmas back in Belsize Park. Matt and I had decided to spend it just the two of us, no family visits, no belting down to the West Country on clogged dual car-riageways, eating a giant grab bag of Maltesers and arguing about whether it would be quicker to freestyle it cross-country with the satnav. I always voted for sticking it out on the main roads, while Matt was like a shark and felt he had to keep moving at all times, even if that meant detouring at five miles an hour down a single-track road in the wrong direction. This time there would be no fights about our route; we'd made our excuses about always travelling for work and needing some time at home, and our families indulged the romantic whims of the newly-weds and made no objection.

We didn't get out of our pyjamas until twelve o'clock on Christmas Day. It surprises me to look back and realize this was before I got into cooking, and nearly everything we ate that day came from Selfridge's Food Hall, where I'd spent a fortune on Christmas Eve on smoked salmon, ready-made blinis, stuffed turkey breasts and prepared vegetables, plus a football-sized pudding, even though the raisin is my sworn enemy and I knew I wouldn't touch it. Tradition must be upheld. I have grown so used to thinking that cooking and domesticity is how I expressed my commitment to our marriage that it's almost shocking to remember that our perfect Christmas — only a year ago — involved no more effort from me than waving my credit card at a shop assistant and getting a taxi home.

Of course I was flush with redundancy money then, and sure a new job must be round the corner, so it was different. Everything was different. We stayed in bed all morning, opening presents, eating toast and half watching — Matt's choice — Dan Akroyd falling all over the place with a side of salmon tucked into his stained Santa suit in *Trading Places.* Matt declared this a tradition that must endure for all Martell Christmases evermore. Neither of us could have imagined we would have only one.

I shake my head, trying to rid myself of thoughts of Matt. That part of my life is over now and I shouldn't dwell on it. I realize I have been staring into the window of Boots, where a woman turns and looks at me quizzically, as if

I'm criticizing her arrangement of scented talcs into a festive tinsel-swagged pyramid. Startled into a response I give her an overly enthusiastic double thumbs-up, which just confuses her even more. I expect she thinks I'm being sarcastic.

Minnie strains on her lead, impatient to get moving again instead of standing around in the cold. Suddenly she yanks away and leaps up on a man passing by.

'Sorry!' I exclaim, but when I look up I see that it is just my dad.

'Well, well,' he says. 'My two favourite girls. What are you up to?'

'Oh, just things,' I say. Now that the bungalow is all but finished, my sense of guilt about doing nothing has redoubled. If a new year is coming, it's going to have to bring with it some resolutions. If only I could work out what they should be.

'Tell me you haven't started your Christmas shopping?' Dad sighs, looking into the window, where the shop assistant is now winding fairy lights around the triangular stack of talcum powder. 'Your mum's on at me to write a list — I told her, just get me what you got me last year. And I'll get you all what I got you.'

I smile. 'Dad, don't pretend you do your own Christmas shopping.'

He looks embarrassed. 'Your mother likes doing that sort of thing,' he says.

'Does she?' I ask, raising an eyebrow.

Dad harrumphs crossly, tucking his chin into his chest. 'Look, Kate, we may not have one of those modern marriages, like you young people, but it works. Your mother and I are very happy.'

His words seem to hit me in the solar plexus like a physical punch. Who am I to judge their marriage? They've made it work for over thirty years. I couldn't even manage two. I must look stricken because Dad starts to look apologetic, his cheeks flushing in the cold.

'Now, don't tell your mother,' he says, suddenly conspiratorial. 'She thinks I've just popped out for stamps, but actually I wanted to get away from your sister's bloody fiancé for a while. Keeps ruddy going on about mission statements and training away-days. I can't bear it.'

Poor Dad. He looks worn out from resisting the twin forces of Ben and Prue on their mission of modernization.

Dad sighs. 'I'm too old to be making changes like this. Just makes me want to leave them to it and, I don't know, bugger off somewhere.'

'Go back to being a roadie?' I tease.

He looks thoughtful, as if he's actually taking me seriously and is considering offering his services to Lady Gaga first thing tomorrow morning.

'I do miss the travel,' he says wistfully. 'Anyway, I was going to sneak to the pub for a quick one. Why don't you come with me?'

I feel oddly shy at the idea. Me and Dad having a drink, just the two of us? He usually can't pass the phone to Mum fast enough when I call from London. He must be feeling really bad about that marriage comment to even suggest it.

But he looks sincere, waggling his eyebrows in the direction of the pub in comedy 'Shall we?' fashion.

'I don't know what Young Entrepreneurs South West would have to say about this, Dad,' I say, linking arms with him. 'Is this the behaviour of a thrusting captain of industry?'

He grins. 'Screw 'em.'

Sometimes it's hard to remember that Dad was once a roadie — he's so gentle and affable now, all twinkly eyes and bushy beard — but my first memories are of him roaring drunk, shouting and singing, while Mum shushed me and told me to go back to sleep. He hardly ever gets drunk these days, but the legacy of his years on the road is that he can drink more than anyone I know.

His first pint barely has time to wet the glass before he's finished it. And he's at the bar ordering a second while I'm still sipping my white wine. It feels decadent drinking in the middle of the day. When I lost my job I made myself two strict rules. No daytime television and no drinking until Matt was home. I will admit that often meant I greeted my husband at the front door with a wine bottle in hand. And when Sarah pointed out to me that wasting hours on the internet was my generation's version of daytime television my achievement in never watching *Cash in the Attic* did seem less impressive.

But still. I'd never wanted to be one of those people you saw staggering out of the pub in the middle of the afternoon, having totally lost sight of the normal rhythm of the working day, hungover by supper time.

Dad comes back from the bar and settles

himself in the chair opposite with a contented sigh.

'Drink up!' he says, nodding at my wine glass as he raises his pint at me in a toast. 'It's Christmas.'

'It's November,' I say.

'Nearly Christmas, then,' says Dad. 'Got to get in a bit of practice.'

'Dad,' I say. He looks instantly wary at the tone of my voice.

'Ye-es?'

'Dad, do you think that Prue and Ben are a good match?'

Dad snorts into his pint glass. 'Puh! Who knows? He's got a skin on him like a rhinocerous. But he's going to need it being married to your sister. He stands up to her, though. I like that. He might be a pain in the arse to work with, but he seems to make Prue happy. I suppose that's what counts.'

I consider him carefully before I ask my next question. I want to be sure that I'm ready to take whatever answer I am given.

'Did you think that Matt and I were a good match?'

His eyes widen in alarm, and he looks around the room as if someone might come to his rescue, but there are only two old men sat in the corner, quietly scolding each other about crossword clues in the paper spread out between them. Minnie is asleep under the table.

'Well,' he says, finally. Carefully. 'I don't know, Kate. Other people's relationships are always a mystery, aren't they? No one really knows what happens between two people except those two people. But yes, I did think you were a good match. I thought he was a good man.'

'I thought he was too,' I say. The Christmas lights have made me maudlin. Or maybe it's the wine in the middle of the day. Alcohol sometimes hits me like that — sends me down instead of bringing me up.

Dad clears his throat a few times. 'You know, er, Kate. I — I've spoken to Matt a bit over the last few weeks.'

My head snaps up. 'You've what?'

Dad leans back into his chair, out of my reach, as if I might be about to belt him one.

'I know — your mother said I should stay out of it, but Kate, he keeps ringing the house and saying should he come down here and . . . God.' Dad sighs helplessly. 'I just felt sorry for the man. No matter what he's done.'

I feel like I might be sick. The wine churns in my empty stomach. I can hardly look Dad in the eye, but since he's avoiding looking at me, too, it's not much of a problem. The two of us stare around the room as if we're doing random eye exercises or something.

'He . . . he said he wanted to come down here?' I ask.

Dad sighs deeply and turns his pint glass round and round on the beer mat, as if he's trying to screw it into the tabletop. 'I told him not to, Katie-bird. I hope that wasn't wrong of me, but your mum and I thought you needed some time to think by yourself.'

So Matt has wanted to come down here all

along? My parents have told him not to disturb me? I can't be angry at them when I know they were doing it with the best of intentions, but my emotions are all over the place at the idea that Matt hasn't been staying away because he wanted to, but because he was told to.

'Did he . . . ' I push the wine away from me. I know I won't be able to drink it. I can feel it curdling the contents of my stomach already. 'What did he say . . . about it all?'

Dad frowns and looks me directly in the eye. I don't rate his acting ability in the slightest. That look alone tells me that Matt hasn't told him the half of it.

'Katie-bird,' says Dad gently. 'It's not for me to go prying into the details, you know that. The problems you have are between the two of you.'

I smile at him gratefully, glad that he hasn't been burdened with all the sordid details. But if Matt isn't calling to put across his case, tell his side of the story, explain everything, then what is he calling for? Surely he knows I can't speak to him?

'But, what have you been talking about then?' I ask.

I feel a strange anxiety that my dad is in danger of taking Matt's side over mine. This is the first time I've sat down and spoken to my father about my relationship since I got to Lyme. And yet it seems my husband has been in regular contact, calling up for intimate family chats. Trying to win over my father, a man who has probably spent no more than an hour on the phone to me in total in his entire life.

'Well,' says Dad, tapping his fingers on the table. 'Cricket?'

'Dad, it's November,' I say.

'Well we have, actually,' harrumphs Dad. 'And his work and that sort of thing. Just, God, it's not like we're crying into the phone, Kate. But the man sounds desperate. He just needed to talk to someone.'

We sit in silence for a few minutes.

'He just wants to know how you are,' says Dad. 'I don't think it's disloyal to tell him.'

I consider Dad carefully. The two old men in the corner squabble over the clue for four across. It isn't disloyal of Dad. I know that. But what is Matt playing at? That is what I would like to know.

'What did you tell him?' I ask nervously. Of course I hope Dad has presented me as radiating good health and beauty, plus a serene maturity and composure, but with an added side of hysterical good humour and happiness.

'I said you were doing pretty badly,' says Dad.

'Jeez, thanks, Dad,' I say. 'Solidarity and all that.'

Dad's face darkens suddenly and he looks like he's about to start shouting, but when he speaks his voice is dangerously low. 'What did you want me to say to him, Kate? That your mother and I lie awake at nights worrying that we have no idea what is going on in your head? That you don't speak to anyone about anything? That you've hidden yourself away here and none of us seems able to reach you?'

I bite my lip and feel tears spring up into my eyes.

'It's like the shutters have gone down, Katie-bird,'

says Dad. 'You're keeping all of us out. You were just like this when you were a teenager. When you came back from that party at Eddy Curtis's and didn't speak for two days.'

'Dad — ' I say, but it comes out as a strangled sob.

Dad presses on. It's as if he can't stop himself from talking now he's started. The words are pouring out of him and every one seems to cut me like a blade.

'We let you run away that time. We didn't press you — we thought it was for the best. Whatever happened, you wanted to leave it behind you and we let you.'

I sniff and wipe my nose with my sleeve.

'It was a mistake,' says Dad. 'We thought we were being kind, but we weren't. And now you're doing it again. And,' I hear his voice begin to waver, and his chest starts to rise and fall fast as if he's trying to catch his breath. 'And, sweetheart, it breaks my heart to see you do this to yourself all over again. Why won't you let us help you?'

And to my utter horror, my big, brave, bearded father starts to cry, his head bowed into his chest, his eyes squeezed tightly shut. His shoulders shake and he puts a hand over his face as if he's ashamed for anyone to see him cry.

But it's me who is ashamed. That I've brought my father to this. The old men in the corner stare at me accusingly, or at least that's how it seems. I want to go and hug Dad, but I'm too scared that it will make him break down even more. It seems kinder to sit still and let him have a moment.

'Dad,' I say, trying to keep my own voice steady. 'You and Mum — you have helped me. You have, really. Just because I don't want to have big chats about everything doesn't mean I'm not grateful for you being there for me.'

Dad looks up angrily. 'No, Kate,' he says. 'It's not good enough.'

I hear, You're not good enough. I know it.

He continues. 'Kate, we're a family. What happens to you happens to us — do you understand? Not to the same degree maybe, but if you're sad, we're sad. If you're happy, we're happy. Your mother always says a parent can only be as happy as their unhappiest child.'

He wipes his eyes and blows his nose with a thunderous noise. The thought of my concerned parents sitting together discussing their wayward elder daughter makes my heart crack right down the middle.

'I'm sorting myself out, Dad,' I promise. 'Everything's going to be okay.'

Dad's eyes are red-rimmed as he contemplates this. He blinks several times. Then he shakes his head harshly. 'No, Katie-bird, it's not enough. You don't have to talk to me if you don't want to. You can talk to your mother, or your sister — yes, I know, what she's like, but she might surprise you. You just need to talk to someone, do you understand?'

I nod, dropping my chin down so that I don't have to see Dad's pleading face, which, for some strange reason, reminds me at this moment of Matt's.

I know my father must be desperate to initiate

this discussion in the first place, let alone insist on pursuing it when I am offering him no encouragement. He stays silent, waiting for my answer. Half of his second pint disappears while we sit together in the quiet of the darkened pub.

'I just don't know what good it will do, Dad,' I whisper at last. 'What's happened has happened. Talking won't change it.'

'It can't change what's happened, no,' Dad agrees slowly, 'but it might change what you do next. Because your mum says I have to be patient with you, but, Kate, I can't understand what you're playing at. You're just living in Barbara's house doing nothing all day every day — '

'I decorated the house!' I protest.

Dad laughs scornfully. 'Kate, you know what I mean. Decorating the house is a good thing, and I'm sure it was satisfying for you, but what do you want long term? Are you going to stay there for ever? What are you going to do for money?'

'Dad, my whole life's just fallen apart. I'm just giving myself some breathing space. Of course I'm not going to stay at Granny Gilbert's for ever.'

Dad persists. 'Your life won't just put itself back together while you hide away. You have to put it back together yourself. Refusing to talk about everything isn't healthy, Katie-bird. You're worrying us all.'

'Dad, please,' I say. 'Don't push me. It's not like you're Mr Emotional yourself. Don't you understand, I just need to get things straight in my own head before I go sounding off to other people.'

'Like you did about Tim Cooper?' says Dad. 'Did you ever get that straight in your own head?'

All the breath leaves my body, as if I've just fallen from a great height. I stare at Dad as if he has taken off a mask to reveal himself, *Scooby-Doo* style, as the evil villain of the piece.

'Don't talk to me about Tim Cooper,' I warn him, my voice shaking. I pull my wine glass towards me. Even though I know it will make me feel sick to drink it, I lift the glass to my lips and sip with revulsion, as if I am drinking poison.

'Your mother and I waited. We waited for you to tell us about it, Kate. And you never, ever did. I can't let that happen to you again. Or to us. It's affecting all of us, can't you see?'

'What do you think you know about Tim?' I ask.

Dad's face hardens and he seems to shrink in his chair. 'Kate, I'd have killed him with my own hands if I'd known at the time. You know that, don't you?'

I nod, my lips pressed tightly together. I did know. That was one of the many reasons I had said nothing.

Dad sighs deeply, and shifts so that he is leaning forwards across the table. He lowers his voice still further. 'You know that Tim moved to Australia, don't you? Your mum said she told you.'

I nod again.

'Well, I don't think she told you why, did she?' Dad sinks the rest of his pint. I offer to go up to the bar to get him another, but he sees straight

338

through my ruse and bids me to sit still while he talks.

'Tim was accused of assaulting his girlfriend,' says Dad. 'She'd tried to break up with him and they had some sort of a fight that got out of hand.'

I freeze in my seat. I'm not sure I could move if I tried.

'Did she . . . was she okay?' I ask.

Dad looks at me. 'Physically she got better. I don't know if you ever get over something like that — from someone you trusted,' he says. 'Anyway, it didn't go to court. It was her word against his, and he had no previous history of abuse.'

I can feel myself start to shake a little, not so much that Dad would notice, but a light tremor that runs through my chest, as if the rhythm of my heart has been disturbed. I knew Tim would get away with it. I knew it would be his word against mine. Hadn't everyone known I'd been sleeping with him for months and months willingly? Didn't every girl in town want to sleep with Tim Cooper? There was no point in saying anything at all.

'Kate?' says Dad, interrupting my thoughts. I look up. 'Kate, the thing was that his girlfriend said he talked about you. That after he attacked her he was full of shame and remorse — he was crying and saying he knew he'd done something bad. That he'd done it before. To you.'

My eyes widen at the idea that Tim felt anything other than that he'd got away with it.

'Why didn't you say anything?' I ask.

'Katie-bird,' says Dad, exhaling in exasperation. 'Why didn't you?'

There is a long silence during which we both studiously avoid looking at one another. When I finally speak, the words emerge croakily, as if I haven't spoken for hours. But perhaps it's because the words are coming out of a part of me that's been quiet for a very long time.

'I just wanted to get away, Dad,' I say. 'I didn't want to see Tim or anyone ever again. I knew he'd get away with it. I knew no one would believe I hadn't slept with him willingly.'

'We'd have believed you,' says my dad gently. 'Your mum and I. We'd have believed you.'

'But, Dad,' I say. 'I was drunk, I was stoned, I let him do it — don't you understand. I could have fought back, but I didn't. It was my fault too.'

'It wasn't,' says Dad angrily. 'He was a dangerous, violent man, and it wasn't your fault.'

'But what if it was?' I ask, my voice dropping to a whisper. 'Could you forgive me then?'

'Forgive you?' says Dad, choking on a sob. 'What do we have to forgive you for, Katie-bird?'

'Oh God,' I cry, burying my face in my hands. 'So many things, Dad. So many things. I don't even know where to start.'

40

London

Going into Soho felt bizarrely daring, as if I'd leapt onto a plane and flown to Buenos Aires on a whim. It had been so long since I'd gone out in town — or gone out at all, come to think of it — that I felt my heart race nervously in anticipation. It was hard to remember that going out had been practically a daily occurrence for me once; that I'd never have imagined feeling anxious at the idea of it. I hadn't called Sarah to tell her I was coming; I was sure she'd tell Matt, since he seemed to be telling her what he was up to these days. I didn't want him to know. Let him worry when he got home and found I wasn't there. Maybe a taste of his own medicine would be good for him.

I knew Sarah would be in the Crown, but my stomach tensed at the idea that Matt might be there, too. I had no idea where he went when he was late home. He could have been in the office, or he could have been at a work event. He rarely bothered to share any information with me. It was perfectly possible he would be in the Crown and I almost hoped he would be. Perhaps it would be better to confront him like this, dressed up, made up, to remind him of the girl I used to be. To make him see what he was missing by never coming home.

Across the tube carriage I could see a man looking at me, checking out my legs in the short dress I was wearing. It was nearly too cold to get away with not wearing tights, and a little voice in the back of my head warned me that bare legs and high heels looked more than a little slutty, but I wanted to be looked at. I'd had enough of being invisible. I stared back at the man, who quickly looked back at his newspaper, probably alarmed by the challenge and confrontation in my face. See, Matt? I thought. Other men find me attractive. Other men don't ignore me. True, I seemed to have terrified this man rather than enticed him, but I didn't care.

I had fortified myself with a large vodka and tonic before I left the house, and the unaccustomed alcohol coursing through my bloodstream had given me a dose of confidence to match my rage. Why had I ever stopped drinking? I had forgotten how alcohol loosened me up, made me feel as though I had something to say, like I was someone. And it wasn't as if giving it up had made any difference to trying to get pregnant.

I squashed that thought down. I was going out to forget all about it. Except, I suddenly remembered, I still had the pregnancy test packaging in my handbag. I would have to get rid of it as soon as possible.

Stepping out from the underground into the chaos of Leicester Square made my confidence waver momentarily. Everyone was moving so fast; there were too many people crowding around the tube exit, pushing and shouting.

342

Young, anoraked men outside the station tried to push free magazines into my hand. Music blared from a stretch limo that was pulled up by the pavement. I was shocked to realize how unaccustomed I was to the pace of the centre of town. Belsize Park was hardly the arse end of nowhere — it was still Zone Two after all — but it was residential, slower. No one was in a desperate rush on the Heath, or in my local cafe.

I felt as if I'd been recently released from an institution, afraid of the everyday. Once I'd despised tourists, stopping slack-jawed in the middle of the pavement, blocking everyone's way with their small-town awe at the bright lights of the city. Now I felt like one of them, hesitant and uncertain.

Come on, Kate, I told myself, squaring my shoulders, and flicking back my hair. Pull yourself together. Remember who you are. That didn't help. Remember who you used to be, then. That did, a bit. I ducked back behind the station, avoiding Leicester Square and taking a less busy route through the alleyways of Chinatown. This was more like it. See how I remembered the back streets and the shortcuts? See how it was all coming back to me with every step I took towards the Crown, towards my old life?

I'd taken the longer route, rather than changing tubes, because I wanted to give myself a few minutes to reacclimatize to Soho, instead of just rocking up to the pub straight away. Walking through the streets was like going on a tour of my past. Here was the tiny Italian-American diner where Matt and I had sat at the bar for hours drinking Old Fashioneds and ignoring the pointed stares of the people queuing behind us. Here was the cafe where I used to buy my lunch every day, four salads for a fiver, plus a pitta bread for free if you smiled sweetly enough at Stelios. I even felt a fond pang of recognition for the sex shops; the same thick-necked bouncers stood outside impassively regarding passers-by.

And yet even in the short time I'd been away there were changes. A long line of hipsters, all coloured jeans and oversized spectacle frames, waited outside a restaurant I'd never heard of. Further up the road a new bar was already turning people away. Soho was moving on.

Just around the corner from Hitz, I caught sight of myself in the window of Nan's Fish Bar, the greasy spoon caff where Sarah and I had often retreated for bacon sandwiches and builders' tea after a heavy night. I hardly recognized myself out of my usual jeans and sweatshirt. When had I stopped making an effort with how I looked? It had happened almost without my noticing it. And now that I saw myself as I used to be, striding down a pavement in Soho, with a place to go and people to see, I suddenly missed that girl and the life she'd had. The sadness of it made me pause.

What if Matt was right? What if I'd gone too far with trying to be the perfect wife, and forgotten about being the person Matt had first fallen in love with? The person I actually was.

I stared at my reflection until it seemed to dissolve in front of my eyes, and found myself looking through the glass and into the cafe.

It was nearly empty of customers, and a waitress was wiping down the tables purposefully, in a manner that suggested closing time was imminent. But there were two customers still there. At a formica table that was bolted to the wall, on red plastic moulded chairs, sat my best friend and a man. His back was towards me, his head bowed, but I didn't need to see his face to know it was Matt. She held one of his hands in hers. There was an intimacy to the way they sat, an understanding that told me this wasn't the first time they'd met like this.

I thought my heart had stopped. I couldn't breathe. And then my mouth started to water in the way that means you're going to be sick. A tremor ran up my legs until my whole body was shaking. My husband and my best friend — what a fucking cliché! They still hadn't seen me. I watched as Sarah rubbed her thumb across the back of Matt's hand. His head was tilted towards her in that confiding gesture I knew so well.

I opened my bag. There sat the empty package from the pregnancy test. With trembling hands I took it out. Here I was trying to hide my perfectly innocent attempts to have a baby with my husband, secreting the evidence in my bag as if I was guilty of something terrible, while all along he was the one with something to hide.

The door of Nan's Fish Bar opened and the waitress came out, carrying a heavy black bin bag that she dropped at the kerb.

'Excuse me,' I said.

The waitress turned around. Her stringy blonde hair was pulled back into a greasy ponytail, and her entire body seemed to be slumping towards the ground, as if, at the end of her working day, gravity was too much for her to resist.

'Yeah?' She looked at me suspiciously, with narrowed eyes. 'What?'

'Could you do me a favour?' I asked. 'Could you take this' — I held out the empty pregnancy test — 'and give it to those two in there?'

She frowned. 'Serious? What for?'

'That man is my husband,' I said.

Her face lit up with interest and she spun around to look into the window. 'No!'

I started to shake again. 'Just, please, give it to them and say it's from Kate.'

'That's all, lovie? You don't want to go in there and have it out with them? I'd cut his balls off, I would.'

I handed her the packet. 'What good would that do?' I asked.

'I'll do it!' said the waitress. 'Give him this, I mean, I won't cut his balls off. Not yet anyway. I'll do it, just you watch me.'

But I didn't watch. Instead I did what I always do. I ran away. As fast as my heels would let me.

41

Granny Gilbert's bungalow is finished at last. Or as finished as it needs to be. I resisted the temptation to spend my savings on the expensive wallpapers and cushions I indulged in at home in London. Here it's all neutral and simple, renovated just enough for someone to see the potential, without feeling that it's been stamped with someone else's identity. The finishing touches must be left to the new owner.

Just like Ben.

He still puts the milk back in the fridge when it's empty, I've noticed. That is something to be worked on. He seems to think the toilet brush is some sort of bathroom ornament that he need not trouble himself with. And he told me we were out of biscuits yesterday, as if it was my responsibility to do something about it. But these are small things. I can't give him to Prue entirely knocked into shape. That would be wrong, even if it were possible.

But though the improvements to my foster husband may not be as immediately obvious as those to the bungalow, it's hard to know which makes me prouder. When the estate agent brings the first people round for a viewing on Saturday morning — a middle-aged man and his mother — it is Ben who shows them round and offers to make them tea before I can even suggest it. The mother is visibly impressed, to the point of suggesting, with an acid look at her own son, that if the young man comes with the bungalow she'll take them both.

The estate agent leaves us, promising he'll be back for more viewings in a couple of hours. It seems there is an entire list of potential buyers who have been easily seduced by a few coats of paint and a new bathroom. He has barely left before the front door opens and Prue lets herself in.

'Since when did you have a key?' I ask, as she strolls into the living room with the assurance of one who belongs there.

She shrugs. 'Since I made one. It's my place, too, don't forget. I can come in any time I want. Just checking on my investment.'

Prue kisses Ben on the cheek and settles herself next to him on the sofa. It is not immediately clear from her words whether the investment is the bungalow or her future husband. Either way, I am helping her realize the full potential of both, and either way, she doesn't seem particularly grateful.

When the doorbell rings, she turns to me in surprise.

'Who's that?'

'What am I, psychic?' I say, getting up and trying not to trip over Minnie. 'Maybe the estate agent forgot something.'

But when I go to the door, Mrs Curtis is stood there, beaming with expectation.

'Oh my dear, I didn't want to interrupt, only I can't help having an *interest* in who buys Barbara's house since they'll be my new neighbours. Who *was* that sour-looking woman?'

As she speaks, Mrs Curtis edges past me into the house and goes straight to the living room, where Prue and Ben are in the middle of a disagreement about what shoes he will wear with his wedding suit. Ben doesn't see the need to buy new ones, but Prue very much does.

'Prue! What a delightful surprise!' says Mrs Curtis, as if she is welcoming Prue into her own home instead of inviting herself into mine.

'Hi, Mrs C,' says Prue, not getting up from the sofa. 'Come to cadge a cup of tea off us, have you?'

'What a lovely idea, thank you. Strong, two sugars.' Mrs Curtis wilfully ignores Prue's tone and instead fixes her with a stare that suggests she should get off the sofa and into the kitchen to put the kettle on.

But Prue is not easily moved. Instead, Ben rises and says he'd be happy to do it. He ambles into the kitchen and we can hear him humming happily to himself as he puts on the kettle. Prue doesn't seem to question Ben's domestic transformation, but Mrs Curtis settles herself in his vacated seat on the sofa and smiles at me approvingly.

'Well, dear, you certainly do have him well trained. I can only admire it.'

I shake my head at her, but she is too busy leaning over to poke a bony finger into Prue's thigh.

'Yes, dear, aren't you lucky that your sister has worked so hard on your husband-to-be?'

'What?' says Prue, flinching from Mrs Curtis's

hand. She rubs at the seam of her white jeans in case Mrs Curtis's red nails have left a mark.

'You are funny, Mrs Curtis,' I say quickly. 'We've been talking about Minnie's training and I think Mrs Curtis has somehow got it into her head that it's Ben I've been training. Imagine!'

'Yes! Imagine!' says Mrs Curtis, her eyes sparkling with mischief.

'As if Ben could learn anything from Kate,' says Prue. She looks around the newly decorated room, and I can see from her searching expression that she's just trying to find fault with it.

'You'd be surprised,' I say, suddenly overcome with annoyance. I have worked so hard on the bungalow, and on Ben, and it's obvious to everyone but her, the direct beneficiary.

'I would,' she agrees, before turning to shout into the kitchen. 'Ben, can you bring biscuits?'

She kicks off her shoes and leaves them in the middle of the floor. With a sigh I pick them up and move them next to the sofa, out of the way.

'No biscuits in the living room!' I say, loud enough for Ben to hear in the kitchen. 'There are more people coming round in an hour, I don't want crumbs on the sofa.'

Prue lifts her chin, challenging. She keeps her eyes on me, but directs her voice at Ben.

'Biscuits!'

'I said, no biscuits in the living room. You can eat them in the kitchen if you want to.'

Ben appears in the doorway, wiping his hands on his trousers, looking flustered. His cheeks have gone the mottled red that indicates a rare

350

show of emotion. That or alcohol, but I doubt he's had time to neck a bottle of wine in the five minutes he's been in the kitchen.

'Ah, Prue, no eating in the living room. It's a house rule, actually.' He looks anxiously from me to Prue.

'Whose rule? This is my house, too, you know. You mean it's Kate's rule. If I want to eat biscuits in here I will. Bring them in.'

'Ben,' I say warningly, putting my hands on my hips.

Mrs Curtis's head follows each of us in turn with great interest. Her feet don't reach the floor and she swings them contentedly, like a child, watching us as if we are putting on a show purely for her benefit.

Ben shuffles his feet, kicking at the skirting board. He mutters something.

'Speak up, dear!' says Mrs Curtis. 'I missed that.'

Ben looks up, resentful from under his knitted brows. With his curled blond hair and pale eyelashes he is more like an obstinate bullock than ever. An obstinate bullock that's been goaded beyond endurance.

'I said, I'm sick of being bossed around! That's what I said, Mrs Curtis. Sick of being bossed around by everyone — by you women! All the time!'

Prue turns to me accusingly. 'This is all your fault! Ben said you'd been nagging at him ever since he moved in.'

'Nagging! I have not!'

'You have,' mutters Ben.

351

It's outrageous. I have put time and effort into making Ben a better husband and this is the thanks I get? Accusations of bossiness from the bossiest Bailey of all?

'Not nagging, dear. Training,' pipes up Mrs Curtis from the sofa.

'Mrs Curtis,' I say, willing her into silence.

But Prue has caught something this time, and turns to her sofa companion. 'Training. You've said it twice now. You're not as daft as you look, are you?'

Mrs Curtis bridles. 'Daft? I should think not, dear. And nor is your sister. She's been — '

'I haven't been doing anything!'

But there is no stopping her now. She holds up an admonishing finger to silence me. Prue and Ben are agog.

'Kate, dear, it's time you got some credit for all your hard work. Prue, your sister has been very thoughtful. Very thoughtful *indeed*. She has put a lot of effort into training your fiancé to be a better husband. Domestically, that is — don't make that *face*, dear. Not bossing — training.'

'Has she?' says Prue, turning towards me, her eyes narrow dangerously.

'Yes, dear, he's her *foster* husband, you see.'

'I'm her what?' gulps Ben. 'Crikey.'

There's a long silence while I try to think of what to say. Mrs Curtis swings her legs, satisfied with her defence of my methods.

'I just wanted to help,' I stammer at last. 'There were things I wish Matt had known before we got married — just little things, a bit of guidance about stuff. I didn't want you to have the problems we had. I thought I was helping. I did help!'

Ben scowls at me from the doorway, his face a picture of wounded betrayal. It sounds so wrong when I say it out loud. I was so sure I was doing the right thing.

When Prue answers her voice is dangerously low. 'And what would you know, Kate, about what makes a good marriage? Who are you to lecture my fiancé on how he should behave? You didn't even make it to your second anniversary.'

'I know about mistakes,' I say, stung. 'I wanted to save you from them. I thought I was doing a good thing.'

Prue rises from the sofa and steps towards me, squaring up as if we are going to have a physical fight. 'You were interfering. Trying to get everyone to behave how you want them to. Just like you always do.'

'I — I wasn't!'

'You were!' she snaps. 'You're always like this, always think your way is the right way and everyone else is wrong. A foster husband! For fuck's sake! Is it any wonder your actual husband got sick of it and went off with someone else? Is it?'

Mrs Curtis gasps from, the sofa, her legs stuck out mid-swing in shock.

I feel as if the breath has been sucked from my body by a punch to the stomach. 'That is not what happened,' I say.

'Well, who could blame him?' sneers Prue.

I feel the trembling sensation start in the middle of my chest, fine tremors radiating outwards so that my arms hang uselessly by my sides. My words are stuck in my throat.

'You don't understand,' I say. 'None of you understands. It's not what you think. It never was.'

42

London

I was too shocked to cry as I stumbled through the streets, unsure where I was heading. I just wanted to get away from the cafe before Matt and Sarah had time to react. Instead of glamorous, I suddenly felt foolish in my too-short dress and fuck-me shoes. I pulled at the hem, trying to drag it down my thighs and cover up the fact that I was nothing but a silly housewife whose husband preferred to fuck someone else.

Of course it explained everything. The late nights. How he'd stopped talking to me. How Sarah knew what Matt was up to when I didn't. That bastard had even got me to cook lunch for her — her and her cuckolded boyfriend — in my own home. I had thought I was furious before, but it was nothing compared to the trembling, nauseating emotion now gnawing at the very core of my being.

I had given up everything for what? It wasn't an investment at all. It was as if I'd entrusted my life savings to a bank that had just gone bust.

I hardly registered where I was going as I pushed past people on the pavement, powering forwards as if I could walk away from this sick feeling of betrayal. But a crowd blocked my way ahead and I realized, to my horror, that my angry strides had led me straight to the Crown,

355

which was as busy as ever on a Thursday night. Before anyone from Hitz might notice me, I stepped into the road to cross over to the opposite side.

A taxi blared its horn and, unaccustomed to high heels, I lost my footing as I lurched back onto the kerb. My hands flailed, preparing to fall, and when I felt someone grab my elbow I clutched gratefully onto their arm to regain my balance.

'Thanks,' I mumbled, and went to cross the street again.

'Kate, wait, it's me,' said a voice. The hand on my elbow didn't let go.

I looked up into Chris's ice-blue eyes; his intense stare was made even more so by the concern written all over his face.

'Are you okay?' he asked. 'What are you doing here?'

'Nothing,' I said. 'Nothing, I was just — I was on my way home.' I struggled for composure. I didn't need to have my business discussed by everyone at the Crown. I wasn't some show for everyone's entertainment.

'Thanks for helping me,' I said stiffly, pulling my arm away. 'It was nice to see you.'

Chris smiled. 'It's been a while,' he said. 'You look great.'

'Thanks,' I said again.

'Hey, come on, let me buy you a drink. You can't be in that much of a rush. Some of the guys are in the Crown, everyone would love to see you.'

Everyone. I felt the bile rise in my throat

again. How many of them knew about Sarah and Matt already? Was it common knowledge? Was I the last to know? I had thought I'd make a triumphant entrance tonight, the long-lost colleague out on the town, fronting it out about being unemployed, telling everyone how great life was without a job. But now that I was a sadder figure, I couldn't face them.

'Um, look, I just don't feel like hanging out with a big crowd. Sorry, Chris. It's sweet of you to ask. I'm,' I pointed up the street to where double-decker buses shuddered past in a slow-moving line, 'I'm going to head off.'

Chris took hold of my arm again, gently but firmly, as if he was restraining a skittish animal.

'Are you sure you're okay? Because we don't have to go in there if you don't want to. If you need someone to talk to we could just go somewhere the two of us. If you'd rather.'

I thought of my house, emptily awaiting my return. Of going back alone, sober, sitting and waiting. Like I did every night. For what? For Matt to arrive and tell me what I already knew? For my husband to come back from fucking my best friend?

'Yes,' I said. 'Yes, I could do with a drink. Let's do it.'

Chris grinned and linked his arm with mine. 'Hold on tight. Easier this way, isn't it? In case you get the wobbles again.'

'Thanks, Chris,' I said, accepting it. Who was I to turn away from the only support I was being offered?

As we left I thought I heard someone shouting

after Chris, but it's a common name. He didn't turn around, so I guessed they must have been calling to someone else.

★ ★ ★

I hadn't been to the Spanish bar on Hanway Street for what felt like decades. It was always somewhere that we rocked up when the pub had shut and we weren't ready to go home yet. At the time of night when a pitcher of Sangria sounds like the best idea in the whole world, and everyone in the bar is your new best friend. The hour of the evening when dancing feels not just possible but actually necessary and incredibly vital (in a way that will make you die of mortification when recalled the next day). I don't think I had ever walked down those narrow wooden steps sober before.

It seemed like no one else visited the Spanish bar before closing time either; it was practically empty except for me and Chris. I let him go to the bar and took my pick from the tables — just being able to sit down felt like an exotic novelty — usually we were standing, crushed up against the stairs. The only seat at my preferred table was a wooden bench, tucked into an alcove underneath a particularly garish painting of a flamenco dancer, who sported a Sixties beehive hairdo with her traditional dress.

Chris came back from the bar with a bottle of Rioja and two glasses. I think my eyes must have widened at the idea of drinking that much after months of near sobriety, because he looked from

358

me to the bottle and back again.

'I just thought it would save us going up and down to the bar?' he said, anxiously posing his statement as a question.

'No, it's cool,' I reassured him. 'Good idea.'

Why shouldn't I have a drink, anyway? It's not like I was going to be having Matt's baby now. In fact, I'd probably had a very narrow escape. Imagine if I'd been pregnant when I heard about him and Sarah. Matt and Sarah. I wished I hadn't thought of that again.

Chris passed me a glass of wine and I gulped down half of it in one go.

'Jesus, you really needed a drink,' he said, his eyebrows raised in amusement.

'Yeah,' I said.

He left a long pause, during which we both refilled our glasses. I wondered if I should be making more of an effort to make conversation, but it wasn't like my friendship with Chris had been defined by a real meeting of minds. And I didn't want to talk about what had happened. I just wanted not to be on my own, and to get drunk. Chris was the enabler, rather than my chosen confidant.

He broke the silence first.

'So,' he said, hesitant and cautious, as if he was about to ask me something immensely personal. 'Have you seen much of Sarah lately?'

I turned to look at him, suspicious. 'Why do you ask?'

Chris shrugged. 'Just, Jay said they're having a few issues at the moment. Thought she might have mentioned it.'

I left another long pause. Was Chris trying to tell me he knew something about Matt and Sarah? I always thought coming at a problem obliquely was a female trait; most men just jump straight in and ask the inappropriate question. Maybe Chris was more emotionally intelligent than I'd given him credit for.

'Yeah, she's mentioned it,' I said, carefully. 'What does he say?'

'Not much.' Chris laughed. 'Typical bloke stuff, keeps getting drunk instead of actually addressing it. Just thought you might know a bit more. Don't like seeing one of my friends down, you know.'

I laughed back, filling my glass for the third time. 'What's happened to you, Chris? When did you turn all caring?'

Chris winced a little. 'You never did have a very high opinion of me,' he said.

'Oh, Chris, I did,' I said, guiltily, since he was perfectly right.

Chris lifted one corner of his mouth into a wry smile. 'You didn't. But that's okay. I guess I wasn't very good at talking about things. I've grown up a bit since then.'

'Me too,' I said, sadly, staring across the empty room.

'Shit, isn't it?' said Chris, comically mournful.

We both burst out laughing. I was almost sobbing, holding onto my stomach. I had the sense I might burst into tears at any moment.

'It is shit! It is! It's all shit,' I said, in between spluttering. 'Let's get drunk.'

By the time the bar started filling up, Chris

and I were on our fourth bottle. I'd like to say I remember it all perfectly, but the truth is it has come back to me in snippets over the last few months, and I don't know how accurate any of it is. Although some things I know beyond doubt.

We were knee-walkingly drunk. I had fallen over on my way to the bar, and had to be helped up by some concerned students. I ignored their pitying looks, and just took my shoes off and stumbled on to buy another bottle.

I remember that my phone rang, buzzing loudly on the table. The display showed that it was Matt, and Chris saw me choose to ignore it. And then my phone rang again, two minutes later, and it was Sarah. Chris saw me ignore it once more. He said nothing. I felt more certain than ever that he knew what had been going on behind my back. When my phone rang for the third time I switched it off decisively, if somewhat fumblingly. I dropped it in my bag and Chris smiled at me with what I felt was approval.

I remember the way we were sat on the narrow bench, turned towards each other our knees touching, I remember wondering why I had ever thought he was boring. Why had I given up all the excitement of the chase and the pursuit for something as tedious and soul-draining as marriage? I'd always said I didn't do relation-ships. That long-term love was stifling and limiting. And hadn't I been right? Wasn't this more who I was? Look what had happened to me when I'd been trapped by domesticity. I'd turned into someone I didn't recognize.

But I remember most of all the feeling of Chris looking at me the way Matt used to — amused, admiring, like he didn't want to be anywhere else, or with anyone else. As if I was someone worth knowing, worth being with.

I had grown so used to the way Matt and I were with each other these days — sniping, defensive, always ready to take offence — that Chris's undivided attention was as intoxicating as the red wine that was now, oops, spilled down my front.

'Oh God, look, I'd better go and wash this off,' I said, sloppily indicating the front of my dress.

I rose from my seat unsteadily. Chris slipped his arm around my hips to support me — and also to cop a feel of my arse; I wasn't so drunk I didn't notice that. 'Woah, I feel really wobbly all of a sudden.'

Chris stood up, his hand resting on my waist. He scanned the room. 'Want me to come with you?'

'Umm,' I said, trying to focus on his face. I had a vague feeling this was a bad idea, but at the same time I really wasn't sure if I was going to make it to the bathroom without embarrassing myself.

He pushed me gently towards the back of the bar.

'Won't we lose our table?' I said anxiously, looking around the crowded bar.

'Don't worry about it,' said Chris, and he propelled me across the floor, his hand in the small of my back.

43

When we burst into the Ladies' three girls were doing their make-up by the mirror. They all sniggered and exchanged glances with one another. I supposed we probably did look a bit of a state.

Chris just grinned at me — in the fluorescent tube-lit bathroom I could see that his teeth had gone purple from the red wine and I wondered if mine were the same. Suddenly I didn't feel fun and exciting, I felt a bit sordid and sad. But I smiled back at Chris anyway — it wasn't his fault.

He pulled a big old man's-style handkerchief out of his jeans pocket and pressed it to my chest, dabbing at the stain. The three girls pushed past us to get out, leaving us alone in the too-bright bathroom. I took hold of Chris's hand, holding it there, his fingers brushing the tops of my breasts. He looked up at me, and then he kissed me.

It was as though something was unleashed in me — I don't think I could truly say it was lust, because it was more like anger and rage and a bitter, bitter need for revenge. It is cruel to say it, but Chris could have been anyone. I just needed to feel something — anything — that wasn't betrayal and sadness and failure. I needed to blot out what was happening, to replace it with something else.

I dragged him into a cubicle and he slammed

the door behind us, locking it. His hands were all over me, pulling up my dress as he buried his face in my neck, breathing heavily. I kept my eyes closed; I don't know why. I wanted this, I knew I did. I'd started it.

The bathroom door opened with a blast of noise from the bar — music and laughter and shouting. Chris hooked his thumbs into my knickers and pulled them down to my thighs. I was horrified to feel tears on my cheeks, and rubbed them away with the back of my hand before he could see. But he stopped for a second, and when I opened my eyes a fraction I could see he was looking at me anxiously.

'Just do it,' I hissed.

I suppose we weren't aware of how much noise we were making; let's face it, when your judgement is sufficiently impaired to think that shagging in a toilet cubicle is a good idea, you're not really in a state to be worrying about what other people think. It is safe to say that, by this stage, I wasn't thinking of very much at all.

But outside in the bathroom I heard voices and stifled laughter. Then someone started banging on the door. Chris froze.

'Kate!' called a voice from outside. The banging on the door got more fierce. 'I know you're in there.'

I looked at Chris in astonishment. How the fuck had Sarah found me?

Chris and I looked at each other in horror. I pushed him away from me, pulled my dress down, and kicked my knickers to the floor. Sarah kept banging on the door.

'Kate! I know you're there! Danny saw you going off with Chris. I've tried every bar in Soho.'

Chris's eyes were wide with panic. But something steely and cold descended on me all of a sudden. Why should I feel guilty about this? What could Sarah possibly have to say to me that would make me feel worse than I already did?

I reached for the bolt on the bathroom door. Chris tried to stop me but as he was also trying to simultaneously pull up his trousers he was ineffective. I opened the door.

Although I was aware that there were plenty of other people crowded into the bathroom to enjoy the show, I was focused only on Sarah. Her face was red and shiny, as though she'd been running, and she looked on the verge of tears.

'Chris,' she spat, looking over my shoulder. 'I might have known. You always were a vile little opportunist, only going after girls when they're too drunk to say no.'

I felt Chris shrink behind me, as if I might protect him from Sarah's wrath.

'As a matter of fact,' I said, concentrating on not slurring. I wanted to sound haughty, distant, superior. 'As a matter of fact, *Sarah*, this was all my idea.'

Sarah tried to take my arm, but I stepped backwards onto Chris, who yelped and fell down onto the toilet seat.

'Don't touch me,' I hissed, flinching away from her reach. 'Don't you dare touch me. I know exactly what you've been up to — don't think I don't.'

Sarah took another step towards me, her hands held out placatingly. 'Kate, whatever you think I've done or haven't done, I just think I should get you home, okay? You're not in any state to be out.'

'Oh that's right,' I sneered. 'I'm not meant to be out, am I? I'm just the boring little housewife who stays at home every night, cooking dinner. While you fuck my husband.'

The crowd behind Sarah gasped. They were getting far more than they expected from a visit to the bathroom.

'While I . . . fuck your husband?' she asked, her voice faltering. Her hand rose to her chest in a masterful attempt to appear entirely innocent — who me? 'Is that what this is about?'

'You thought I didn't know,' I said. I made my voice sound strong, but my legs were buckling and I was leaning on the side of the cubicle for support. 'You thought you'd carry on pretending to be my friend. When were you going to tell me? Were you going to wait until I was pregnant so you could really twist the knife?'

Sarah shook her head. She didn't even try to deny it. She looked back over her shoulder at all the people trying to crowd into the bathroom.

'Will you all just fuck off out of here?' she shrieked. A few people looked guilty, but no one moved.

'No, stay,' I shouted. 'I don't care if they all know about it. I saw you. I saw you in Nan's Fish Bar tonight. You were holding hands. You weren't bothered about hiding it then, were you? Own it, Sarah, own it. Admit it.'

Sarah's eyes were suddenly full of tears. For one horrible moment I actually felt sympathy for her, before I remembered that she deserved to feel terrible.

'You really thought . . . ?' She gestured limply towards the toilet, where Chris cowered in silence. 'Oh God, Kate, what have you done?'

'Don't you dare judge me,' I stammered, stuttering over my words with rage. 'Don't you *dare*. How can you stand there and judge me after everything you've done?'

Sarah's lip trembled. She dropped her voice to a near-whisper.

'Kate, please, let's not talk about this here. Let's go home. I'll get us a cab.'

'I'm not going anywhere with you,' I spat. 'If you have something to say to me, you can say it here — in front of everyone.'

'Yeah, sister,' shouted a voice from the back of the crowd. I felt absurdly powerful. The audience was with me. I had the moral high ground. Even if I had just been caught shagging in a toilet cubicle, I had turned it around.

I lost the moral high ground just slightly with a loud hiccup, but I thought I got away with it.

Sarah tried to keep her voice low, but everyone had hushed so much, so as not to miss a thing, that her words carried as clearly as if she'd spoken into a microphone.

'Kate, nothing is happening between me and Matt. Nothing.'

'Oh really,' I sneered. 'So you were just holding hands for no reason, were you?'

Sarah looked over her shoulder again,

probably fearing the crowd was about to lynch her and brand a scarlet A onto her chest.

'Really, let's talk about this outside,' she said.

'No.'

Sarah sighed and her shoulders slumped. She pulled her bag across her body as if she was preparing to make a run for it.

'Kate, I was holding Matt's hand because he was crying. About you.'

I blinked at her.

'And you expect me to believe that?' I asked.

The faces of the crowd swivelled towards Sarah, like spectators at a tennis match.

'Yes, I've been meeting up with him,' Sarah confessed. 'More than once.'

I knew it.

'But only because both of us are so worried about you.'

'How ridiculous,' I said scornfully. 'Are you actually trying to blame your affair on me?'

'There is no affair!' shouted Sarah. 'Don't you see, you fucking idiot? You've turned into a total crazy person. Matt and I have tried to be sympathetic — it's obvious you're depressed — '

'Matt and I?' I sneered, in a sing-song voice. 'Matt and I? Oh, how cosy it sounds.'

Sarah threw her hands up.

'Kate, I don't know how to get this through to you. But if I have to shout it in front of a room of fucking nosy strangers' — she glared at the crowd behind her — 'I'll do it. You've gone completely insane about the most mundane things — fucking aprons and casserole dishes. You're always angry, you never want to go out,

368

you won't even consider getting a job, you've stopped speaking to me, to Matt, to anyone except that dog. You're obsessed with getting pregnant.'

Behind me, Chris stood up in alarm. 'You're trying to get pregnant?' he squeaked.

'Fuck off, Chris,' Sarah and I chorused.

He sat down again and dropped his head in his hands.

'Kate,' said Sarah. She was crying again. 'I promise you, I promise. Nothing is happening with me and Matt. But we've both been so worried about you. Worried you'll do' — she let out a loud sob — 'something stupid.'

All at once it was as if I had been hit on the head by each of the bottles of wine I had drunk that night. My legs turned to water and I had to press my hands on either side of my head to stop it from spinning.

'Where is Matt?' I whispered.

Sarah blinked away tears. 'He's gone home. He called me when he realized you weren't there. Then Danny said he'd seen you outside the Crown with Chris. So I started looking for you. Come on, Kate, it's time to go home.'

'I can't go home,' I said, starting to retch. 'I can't.'

I pushed Chris out of the way just in time to clutch the sides of the toilet seat as I threw up and threw up and threw up.

There was a collective 'ew' from the crowd, which seemed to disperse in an instant, my copious vomiting marking the tawdry ending of the floor show.

I felt Sarah rub my back as my stomach clenched and buckled.

'It's going to be okay,' she said, over and over. 'It's going to be okay, Kate.'

But of course it wasn't.

I stayed at Sarah's that night. I heard her on the phone to Matt while I lay awake, staring at the ceiling of her spare bedroom, feeling the duvet lie on me as heavily as if it was made of stone. When I got home the next morning the house was empty. Clearly he couldn't face me. I didn't blame him.

I wrote him a note:

I know she's told you everything. I don't expect you to forgive me — I'm not even sure I can forgive myself.

I'm not excusing what I did, but maybe something had to happen so we could stop making each other so unhappy. I suppose this is it.

I'm sorry.

And then I collected Minnie from the Palmers' house and left for Lyme Regis.

44

I had thought my life would begin again when I'd finally put all my mistakes behind me, as if they had never happened. That with a fresh start and a clean slate and any other cliché you care to use, I would move forwards confidently, with intent and self-awareness. I thought there was no place in my life for error, that making mistakes made you a bad person. But now I think differently, that mistakes are what make us who we are. That the people who can love you despite your mistakes (maybe even because of them) are the people you can trust.

I don't know what I had expected from telling the truth at last — that my family would cast me out in shame? Shave my head and parade me along the Cobb like the French women who slept with German soldiers in the war? In my defence, I had never actually lied. Everyone just assumed, and it seemed easier to let them keep on assuming rather than to confess to my own tawdry behaviour.

Of course my sister was furious, but as she hadn't had much sympathy for me when I was supposedly the victim of a philandering husband, her lack of comforting words now I was revealed as the philanderer was no great surprise. What did surprise me was her insistence that it wasn't too late to do something about it. And Ben's agreement. Neither of them could understand why I was hiding away in Lyme Regis, interfering in their relationship instead of trying to put things right in my own. When my parents and Mrs Curtis joined the chorus of people telling me it was time to face up to my mistakes, I could see I was going to get no rest in Lyme until I did.

More than that, I could see they wanted me to confront my past not as a punishment, but because they cared about me (even Prue), and wanted me to come to terms with what I had done. That moving forwards without accepting my mistakes wasn't worth anything.

I have an overnight bag packed, although I have no idea if I am going to stay the night in London. Or even where I might stay. It's like a reversal of my flight from London, just one month ago, except this time I have borrowed Mum's car instead of taking the train. I want to be sure I can get away quickly if it all goes wrong.

As I drive through the New Forest, I make myself a deal that if it goes as badly as I expect, I am allowed to check myself into the most expensive hotel I can afford. One last hurrah with my redundancy money. I will drown my sorrows with minibar cocktails and a sumptuous bubble bath that uses up all the complimentary toiletries. And if it goes really badly, I might even drown myself for real.

It is time I faced up to the mess I left behind. Dad is right. Things won't have sorted themselves out while I was hiding away in Lyme. It is up to me to sort them out, here and now.

For one moment, I think I might have to stop the car to be sick. I swerve into the outside lane, making the lorry behind beep angrily. Whatever, I think. Your mild annoyance is nothing compared to what will be waiting for me at the end of this motorway. At least the distraction has stopped me feeling nauseous and I carry on driving.

I've often done my best thinking while driving. And my best singing, since there is nowhere better for truly venting your lungs on the high notes with no one to overhear you. But I'm not singing on this journey, and not just because Mum's CD selection is a little too heavy on the Michael Bublé for my tastes. This trip is just for thinking. I do not trust myself to say the right thing unless I have prepared for it. I rehearse conversations over and over out loud, conversations in which I'm faced with fury or sadness or a door shut in my face. I consider what I'll do if there's no one in. How long will I wait, parked outside? Will it make me look desperate? The truth is, I am desperate. Perhaps I shouldn't be ashamed of it. Perhaps it will help to demonstrate how far I am prepared to go to show I'm truly sorry.

By the time I come off the motorway my resolve is wavering, but I press my foot on the accelerator and keep moving. Or at least, I try to. The traffic is slow, and it's raining, which always means half of London forgets how to drive. Everyone seems angry and aggressive — horns blare and pedestrians take alarmingly wild dashes across the road, making me slam on my brakes. The longer I have to wait, sitting in a traffic jam on the Euston Road, watching the windscreen wipers tick-tock in front of me, the more daunting it all seems. To expose myself like this; to take the risk that my apology will be rejected.

I find a parking spot outside the house immediately. This has to be a sign. I unbuckle my seat belt and sit in the silent car for a moment, considering what I will say first. There is a light on, so I know he's home. I realize it is perfectly possible there may be someone else there; a possibility I hadn't planned for in my imaginary conversations.

If it weren't for the fact that it's freezing now the heater's turned off, I could sit out here for ever. But whether it is contrition or fear of hypothermia that makes me open the car door doesn't really matter. What matters is that I cross the road, my hands plunged deep into my pockets as if I might wave them around hysterically like a madwoman otherwise. My chin is tucked into my scarf and the wind blows my hair straight back from my face, as if the elements are conspiring to ensure I cannot hide.

I press on the doorbell and listen. I can hear nothing from inside. I wait for a full minute. I time it on my watch, though it feels longer. It seems almost comical that I have driven here in such furious haste, only for him to be out. I press the doorbell once more, for luck — I need it — and turn to go down the steps to the street.

I'm one step from the bottom when I hear the door open. I turn quickly, before he can shut the door.

'Hello, Kate,' he says, his face registering total shock.

'Hi Chris,' I say, as calmly as I can manage. 'Can I come in?'

★　★　★

It only takes half an hour. No, not that. Oh my God no, do you think I've learned nothing at all while I've been holed up in my home town? Do you think all the time I was staring at the sea I was just contemplating the view and working on my French Lieutenant's Woman impression? Please. I mean, it only takes half an hour for me to apologize to Chris.

I know Sarah thought he was the villain of the piece — the opportunist shagger who always caught me at my lowest — but I was every bit as much to blame. He didn't pour that wine down my throat, I drank it willingly. I wanted to obliterate what I thought had happened between Matt and Sarah, and Chris was just the unwitting conduit for all my misplaced fury. That night I told Sarah to admit it, to own it. Now it's my turn. I can't undo everything I've done, but I can stare it in the face and, although I know it is a small, small thing, I can say sorry.

Once Chris gets over his shock, and realizes I'm not there to either scream at him or make him have drunken sex with me in a bathroom, he reacts pretty well. Which is to say that he sits on the sofa and lets me make my preprepared speech without interruptions. And when I'm finished he says, 'Okay.'

It is more than I deserve. I don't expect anything else. But as I am leaving — I have other calls to make tonight — Chris surprises me by turning my perfunctory kiss on the cheek into a proper hug, squeezing me tightly. There's nothing at all sexual about it. It feels more like the action of a caring friend. How strange.

'You're very brave, Kate,' he says as we pull apart. 'I think you're very brave.'

I thank him, waving goodbye as I head back to my car, but it worries me a little.

Brave is nearly always a euphemism for insane, isn't it? As in, wow, you've had a spectacularly brutal haircut, aren't you *brave*? Paul was really *brave* to climb Kilimanjaro in nothing but a pair of Speedos. Did you hear about the man who fought off two gunmen armed only with a traffic cone? *Brave*. Also, insane.

I can't deny that I feel I may be making an enormous mistake by coming back unannounced. But I've already made so many, what's another one to add to the list? I have had to ask myself difficult questions to be able to do this. Am I apologizing for their sake, or for mine? I would like to present my behaviour as solidly altruistic, that I am making amends to those I have wronged, but that would be a lie. I know this is also for me. I just don't know yet whether it's more for me than it is for them. If I am after absolution at any cost.

I nearly persuaded myself not to come, that Matt is better off without me. But then I remembered his phone calls to my parents, his letter begging me to talk, and I thought that at the very least I owed him that: to talk to him face to face.

Talking to Chris was easy, because there was so little at stake. I don't know if I'll ever see him again, and I don't honestly care. The important thing is that we have parted on good terms, and if I do see him, there is nothing left for either of us to be ashamed of. I can't say I'll be racing back to the Crown to hang out with him and his friends, but if I found myself faced with them, I would be fine.

Talking to Sarah would have been harder, but she is out. Jay, too. I suppose I should have called her mobile first, but I didn't want to give her the chance to say she wouldn't see me. After I've pushed a scrawled note of apology through the letterbox, I stand outside her block of flats, staring up at the dark windows, thinking of the last time I was here. Remembering stumbling out of the front door in the unforgiving morning, nauseous with hangover and remorse, my ridiculous dress covered in a borrowed cardigan. I'd done the walk of shame before, but it was nothing compared to this time. The grief and pain of the memory nearly doubles me over, and I have to sit down on the steps and hold my head in my hands. My breath comes in shudders that shake my ribs. It feels as if I'm struggling to get air into my lungs; the scarf around my neck is too tight and I pull it away from my throat.

I cling to the iron railings that lead up the steps to Sarah and Jay's flat; their cold solidity is anchoring. Clutching onto the hard metal brings me back to the present.

So does an angry old lady who suddenly appears at the entrance to the flats, clad in a dressing gown and wielding a broom.

'Get out of here,' she yells. 'Bloody layabouts. Go on, before I call the police!'

I notice for the first time that the ground near the steps is littered with cigarette butts, and there is a collection of crushed cider cans underneath the nearby hydrangea. Great, now I've been mistaken for a homeless person. The signs for my next apology are not exactly filling me with confidence.

'Don't make me come down there,' warns the woman with the broom, pushing it towards me. I realize she is genuinely afraid of me, so I apologize (I'm getting good at this) and scurry away across the road to my car.

45

Matt is in. Although the living room appears dark I can see a bluish flickering on the wall that tells me he's either watching television or playing on the PlayStation.

The keys to our house are in my handbag, but it feels strangely like I'd be breaking and entering if I used them. Also, I have no idea what I might find. He might not be alone. He'd have every right not to be. Although it would be fairly lame if he was attempting to entertain a new woman by watching television in the dark at nine at night, I can't make any assumptions.

There is movement as soon as I ring the bell. The light flicks on in the hallway and a tall figure approaches, distorted by the frosted glass. I see him stop halfway down the hall and hear him say, 'Fuck,' and then he turns back.

Has he recognised me already? Did Chris warn him I would be on my way over?

But no, he comes back and the door swings open. Matt stands there in pyjama bottoms and the rumpled grey sweatshirt I remember so well, wearing his glasses and holding his wallet open in front of him. He is unshaven and there are dark circles under each eye.

'Hi,' I say.

Matt snaps his wallet shut. He doesn't move to let me in. He doesn't smile.

'Kate? What the fuck? I thought you were the

take-away,' he says, his tone suggesting that a prawn biryani would be a much more welcome sight.

'Sorry,' I say. I guess it's never too early to start apologizing. 'Can I come in?'

Matt casts an anxious glance over his shoulder.

'Are . . . are you alone?' I ask.

Matt looks at me over the top of his glasses, and I finally see a small glint of humour in his eyes.

'I'm hardly dressed for entertaining,' he says. He steps backwards into the hall and holds the door open for me to come in.

Our hall has never been very wide, but it feels as if it might have shrunk in the weeks that I've been away. There's a suitcase near the door, Emirates Airlines tags hanging from the handle, crowding us further, and suddenly Matt feels very close. I have to fight an impulse to turn and grab him, to bury my face in his chest and never let go. I don't have the right any more.

'Where shall I . . . ?' I am suddenly a hesitant stranger in my own home, unsure where I should go.

'Kitchen,' says Matt. 'And Kate, just, look, don't say anything about the mess. If I'd known you were coming it would've been different.'

I steel myself for the worst as I descend the stairs, but it's not all that bad. The lid of the bin is perilously balanced on a tower of takeaway containers, and it looks like every single mug we've ever owned is piled up in the sink. But it's not like he's burned the kitchen to the ground or anything. The mess could be cleared up in no time. It's not irreparable.

'So, um, shall I get us — ' I begin, gesturing at the kettle.

'No,' says Matt firmly. 'You sit down. I'll sort it. I was having a beer. Do you want one?' He looks at me challengingly, as if this is a test.

'Yes, please,' I say quickly, and am rewarded by a look of surprise that flashes across his face.

'Right, beer.'

I can't help looking into the empty fridge as he opens it — there's nothing in it except booze. I turn my head away before Matt catches me, and I take the cold beer from his hand with a wobbly attempt at a smile.

Matt sits down opposite me at the kitchen table. I think of how he always used to sit here on Sunday mornings, his legs sprawled out away from his own chair, his foot nudging me as he read out bits of the paper he thought I'd be interested in. Now he sits stiffly, legs pulled underneath the chair, far away from me. He has both hands on the beer bottle.

'So,' he says, staring down at the table top between us.

'Matt,' I say. He looks up at me. My voice sounds thin and weak. 'I don't even know how to say sorry for what I did.'

Matt laughs scornfully and takes a long pull on his beer bottle. 'You'd better try, Kate. Harder than that. I haven't heard from you in all this time — surely you've had time to come up with something?'

'I haven't even got started,' I say. I take a deep breath. 'Matt, I let you down long before that . . . that thing with Chris. I know you were just trying to help me and . . . and I pushed you away. I shut you out. You deserved better, Matt.'

He just nods, waiting to hear what I have to say next.

'I don't know what happened to me. I just lost perspective on everything after I left Hitz. I can see that now. I think I was scared that if you saw how depressed and low I'd got you'd be horrified. I thought I'd scare you away.'

'Kate,' Matt says. 'I saw it anyway. And it was so much worse that you wouldn't admit it.'

I start to cry now, but I keep talking, hiccuping through the speech I've prepared in the car. 'I got obsessed with trivial things. Things I could take charge of when I'd lost control over everything else. Nothing was working — not finding a job, not having a baby — and so the small things suddenly seemed incredibly important. I just . . . it didn't seem like you understood me at all.'

'Me?' Matt's eyes narrow angrily.

'No,' I say hastily. 'You don't understand. I mean that I got it all wrong. We both knew there were problems, we were just coming at them from different directions.'

Matt frowns.

'And then,' I sob, 'and then . . . Chris.'

'Chris,' repeats Matt slowly.

'Oh Matt, I was drunk and insane and I thought you and Sarah — '

'I know what you thought,' says Matt, his jaw set like stone. 'I just can't believe you thought it.'

Before I can answer the doorbell rings, and I look at Matt in alarm. Who would it be at this hour? Surely Matt won't answer.

But he does. 'Takeaway,' he shrugs. He picks up his wallet from the table and goes upstairs. I even hear laughter as he exchanges a few words with the delivery driver. How can he be so calm in the middle of this?

I twist my hands over and over as I wait for him to come downstairs. I feel like Lady Macbeth trying to wash out that damned spot. It's never going to go. All the apologies in the world can't rid me of it.

Matt puts the blue and white plastic bag on the kitchen table next to his beer, and ignores it. The fragrant smell of curry fills the kitchen. It makes me realize I haven't eaten since breakfast.

'It'll go cold,' I say. I wonder if he will offer to share it with me? That would be a good sign, wouldn't it?

Matt rolls his eyes. 'I know how to work the microwave,' he says. 'Carry on.'

I sniff. 'Matt, I'm sorry for everything. All of it. I've been hateful and spoiled and I've blamed it all on you. And then I slept with Chris and I don't think I'll ever forgive myself for it.'

'I — I — I — I — I,' says Matt, his face as blank as paper.

'Pardon?' I ask.

'Don't you hear yourself?' he says. 'It's all 'I felt this', 'I thought that', 'I did this'. You haven't once even asked me what I think about any of it. The word 'we' hasn't even crossed your lips. This isn't just *your* marriage, you know, it's *ours*. At least, it was.'

'I just . . . I thought,' I stammer.

'But Kate.' Matt sighs. 'Don't you see, you're doing it all again? I've been trying to talk to you for weeks — writing to you, calling your parents — but no, it can only happen on your terms, according to your timetable.'

'That's not true,' I protest. 'I wanted to do it face to face. I thought I owed you that, at least.'

Matt shakes his head sadly. 'It's always all about you, Kate,' he says. 'You haven't asked me a single question. Not even how are you. I don't think you even care. You just wanted to say your piece, and now you've said it I think you should go.'

'I do care!' I say. 'Matt, how could I launch into a load of small talk when we had to address the big question first? Please, you know I care.'

Matt lifts his glasses and rubs at his eyes with the heel of his hand.

'Small talk. Right. Kate, I'm tired. I just got back from Dubai, this is a bad time.'

I bite my lower lip to stop it from wobbling like a child's. I swallow a few times before I speak.

'Can we . . . can we talk again? When you're less tired?'

Matt looks at me through his glasses. The kitchen light reflects brightly on the lenses so I can't really see his eyes.

'I don't know,' he says at last. 'You always talked a lot about compromise, Kate. But you meant that I should compromise. Not you. That can't be how it works this time. What did you think? That you'd just say sorry and it would all be okay?'

'I didn't think that — ' I begin, but Matt holds his hand up to stop me from talking.

'You've taken your time to think; now I need mine.'

I stand up quickly, swinging my handbag over my shoulder and knocking over my empty beer bottle. Matt catches it before it hits the table.

'Reflexes of a ninja,' we both say at once.

Matt smiles at me sadly.

'I should go,' I say.

He just nods. He has a beer bottle in each hand now, which makes hugging him thankfully impossible. I just say a mumbled goodbye and let myself out.

So. That went about as well as I'd expected.

46

I have driven halfway back to Lyme before I remember that I was going to treat myself to a night in a hotel. But that decision feels like it was made by an entirely different person. How could I have thought that Matt's rejection would be softened by a night alone? There will be plenty of nights alone in the future; I don't want another one now.

Last time I ran to Lyme because there was nowhere else to go. It seemed like a place where nothing ever happened, where I could hide away undisturbed. If I'd thought of my family when I left London before, it was as shadowy supporting characters in a drama that was all about me. Now I am surprised to find that I want to see my family because I miss them and want to be with them. They have taken me in at my lowest ebb and proven that, despite all my mistakes, their love is unconditional.

It turns out that showing all your flaws is what allows people to love you completely. But to do that is to take the risk, as I did with Matt, that their love may prove to be conditional after all. How can I blame him for that? While I nagged him about making a mess of my beautiful home, I was making a mess of our marriage. And when I'd pushed it to crisis point, I just ran away and refused to speak to him. Life carried on. Matt's feelings changed.

Who was I to think that I could give lessons in how to be married? I have learned all my own lessons far too late.

When I finally turn the car into the cul-de-sac it is well past two in the morning. Ice on the steep hills down towards Lyme has made me drive slowly, and my body is stiff from sitting in the same position for hours.

Minnie rushes to greet me when I let myself in to the dark bungalow. Before I say hello to her properly, I flick on the hall light. There's a muffled scream and the bathroom door slams, only to be opened again a second later.

'What the fuck are you doing here?' says Prue, peering round the door.

She thinks she is hidden, but I can see from the reflection of the bathroom mirror that she is wearing nothing but a towel, which she must have grabbed from the rail behind her.

'Prue Bailey,' I say, unable to stop myself from laughing. 'You dirty stop-out. Whatever happened to your principles?'

Protectively, she pushes the door closed even further, so that just a slice of her face shows. 'You were meant to be staying in London!'

I drop my overnight bag on the hall floor, and kneel to give Minnie a hug. 'Yeah,' I say.

'That bad?' she asks.

'Worse.'

Prue opens the door a fraction. 'Kitchen, two minutes. Make some tea. I need to put some clothes on.'

'I should say you do.'

She sticks her tongue out at me as she skips

back towards Ben's bedroom.

It is strange to relate but, when she reappears in an old jumper of Ben's, my sister turns out to be a good person to talk to. We sit and talk and eat ginger snap biscuits in the newly white kitchen until the first pale fingers of dawn start to lighten the sky. I think a more sympathetic ear — my mother's, for example — would have made me crumble. Instead, Prue's brisk questioning and complete unwillingness to indulge any of my self-pity acts like a sharp kick up the arse.

'Why are you so sure it's over?' she demands, when I've relayed the entire story to her. 'He let you in the house, didn't he? He listened. You're giving up too easily.'

'Prue, he said he needed time. I have to give him that. And it might just be too late.'

Prue's exasperated sigh ricochets around the kitchen. 'Seriously? Look, I know you have some weird ideas about marriage, but unless I've got it totally wrong, you said you would be with Matt for better or for worse. Remember?'

Minnie looks up from the floor at the raised voices, and I stroke her back with my foot until she drops her head back down.

'Yes, Prue, but not actually against his will, you know? I can't force us back together if he doesn't want it.'

'But what? You think you can just turn up out of the blue, say you're sorry and then it's all hearts and flowers? Marriage is tougher than that, Kate. You have to fight for it if you want it back.'

I do my best not to snap that she, whose wedding is still weeks away, has no idea about marriage. But weirdly she seems to be wiser about it than I am. I take another biscuit and bite it viciously in half.

'So?' she demands while my mouth is full, as if I will turn around and get back in the car this very instant, ready to insist that Matt takes me back.

'I don't know, Prue. I just think it might be broken for good.'

'Don't just lie down and take it,' she says. 'If this was a work thing you wouldn't just say, oh well, it's ruined, I give up, would you?'

'No,' I admit.

'You'd do whatever it took, wouldn't you? You'd find a way to make it happen. So what's the difference?'

'Jeez, Prue, it's totally different. There's no emotional involvement with work, it's not the same at all.'

'Isn't it? Well, if you're prepared to fight for one but not the other, then I think you've got your priorities the wrong way around.'

'Thanks,' I say, sarcastically, but somehow it must not translate as she takes it sincerely.

'You're welcome,' she says. 'Now stop feeling sorry for yourself and start thinking about what you can do to save this situation.'

We sit quietly for a moment, sipping our tea. I push the biscuits towards her, but she shakes her head. I let her think that I am considering how I will save my marriage. But I am actually thinking of something else.

'Speaking of situations,' I say.

'Not another word,' warns Prue, wagging her index finger at me. 'Not another word, or I am going straight back to bed.'

'To Ben's bed.'

'Shut up.'

'So. What happened to your principles?'

Prue fixes me with her fiercest stare, but I'm not backing down that easily. I've just confronted my husband about the affair that ended our marriage. This is child's play.

She sits stiffly on her chair. 'We are nearly married, actually. What difference does a few weeks make?'

'You tell me,' I say. 'You're the one who always swore she'd stay pure. So, how was it?'

There is a long pause during which Prue cannot meet my eyes.

'Amazing,' she says at last. 'Completely amazing.'

'Really? First time?'

She puts down her mug on the kitchen table and looks at the floor. Then she looks back up at me with a rare expression on her face. Doubt.

'God, no, Kate, it was absolutely awful. Terrible.' She shakes her head and buries her face in her hands. She mutters something indistinct, and I have to ask her to repeat it.

'I said,' she lifts her head, 'what if I'm making a terrible mistake?'

'Prue,' I say, glad to be the one offering advice for a change, 'it's just sex. It's not like the movies. It's nearly always awful the first time.'

'This . . . ' she drops her voice and looks

furtively around the room, as if Minnie might be taking notes. 'This wasn't the first time. We did it before. Last week. And it was awful then, too.'

'Twice? Twice ever and you think it's not worth getting married?'

Prue pulls her legs up onto the chair and wraps her arms around her knees. 'I . . . I thought it was going to be something really special. I thought it would have been worth waiting for.'

Her lower lip trembles and I see she is close to tears.

'Um, so, was it Ben's first . . . were you Ben's — '

'Of course!' she snaps. 'I mean, I don't know. But I think so.'

'Oh Prue.' I am trying not to laugh. I may have some regrets about having put it about in my youth, but at least I haven't spent years dreaming of losing my virginity as some beautiful and spiritual experience that can only disappoint. 'It just takes practice. Honestly. The more you, er, do it, the better it gets.'

'You should know,' mutters Prue. Her mouth twists into a smile. 'Slapper.'

'Harsh.'

'Harsh,' agrees Prue. 'Sorry. I didn't mean it. You're not a slapper.'

'Not all the time, anyway,' I say.

47

Because the universe would not dare fail to give my sister what she wants, the morning of New Year's Eve dawns with a light dusting of snow, like icing sugar on the roofs of Lyme. The winter has been unseasonably warm and wet, but this one day is crisp and clear; a low, pale sun made the hoar frost glitter on the trees as I walked Minnie first thing, and the sky is a cloudless blue. It is the perfect day for my sister's perfect wedding.

I have been perfectly dreading it.

Not because of Prue. Of course I want her to have the day she dreamed of and, thanks to her ferocious planning, that is exactly what she will have. The staff of the Alexandra told us they had never met such an organized bride. Prue preened with delight at the compliment, while a fleeting glimpse of a look exchanged between the manager and deputy manager told me that by 'organized' they meant 'terrifying'. The Ball-Basher Bailey baton has been passed on.

No, I am dreading the wedding for entirely selfish reasons. Today I will have to confront my extended family and friends for the first time since I split up with Matt. I know how it is at weddings. Somehow the usual rules of politeness are loosened — probably by champagne, let's be honest — and everyone my mother's age and up will feel it's quite acceptable to ask deeply personal questions. Where is your husband? Are you getting a divorce? Why couldn't you make it work? What are you going to do with the rest of your life?

And I'm not entirely sure of the answers.

I am hopeful about the future. I have to be. Now everything has fallen apart, it is time to start putting a new life back together. A different one. I've already spent my first Christmas as a single woman, and it wasn't that bad. I went with Eddy and his girls to Mrs Curtis's Christmas morning swim; we huddled on the shore with a thermos of tea and a hip flask of whisky as she and her hardy friends emerged from the waves. We all wished each other merry Christmas, exchanging damp hugs and toasting the festive season with our plastic mugs. Grace and Charlotte gave Minnie a squeaky dinosaur toy, and Minnie, with some assistance from me, gave them a packet of princess stickers each. Mum, Dad, Prue and I spent what is bound to be our last Christmas as a family of four, and it didn't feel stifling or strange, it felt comforting.

It wasn't what I was used to, but that was fine. I can't erase my past. It's done. But I can build on it all over again, like the Undercliff, regenerating itself after a landslip. It will be different; not better, not worse.

And I've made peace with my home town. I can't imagine myself living here for ever, but it is more than just a place to run away to. I have friends here, family, people I can rely on. Perhaps more importantly, people who know they can rely on me.

In any case I can't stay here because the bungalow is sold. The estate agent called to tell us that the sour-faced woman will be taking it, despite the fact that Ben does not come as part of the deal. His call, while welcome, was unnecessary, as Mrs Curtis had already bustled over at the crack of dawn, a damp towel still tucked under her arm, to pass on the gossip she'd heard at the beach. It seems the woman's son is nothing of the kind; he's actually her much younger husband. The thrill of this news was not shared by Ben, who had been dragged out of bed to answer the door, but the cul-de-sac is agog with expectation.

For all that renovating the house was my idea, the quick sale does render me imminently homeless, which is why I have started putting feelers out about work back in London. It's time to go back. But first, it is time for Prue's wedding.

Over at Mum and Dad's it is complete chaos. Packing crates fill the kitchen, and there are damp clothes hanging off every radiator in the house, making the air thick with the smell of wet wool. The kitchen table is piled high with bottles of suncream and travel guides. Mum is a blur of action, shuttling piles of clothes from one room to another, while still in her dressing gown.

'Anything I can do?' I ask. It's only an hour till we're due at the hotel, and Mum's hair is still wet from the shower.

'No, love. I know it looks like a mess, but I know where everything is, and it will only confuse things. You can go upstairs and talk to your sister while she has her hair done. It's probably best if you're out of the way while I pack.'

'Where's Dad?'

Mum rolls her eyes. 'Prue's cut down his father-of-the-bride speech a bit. Well, a lot. By at least half. I think he's having a sulk somewhere. Leaving me with all this! Honestly.'

But despite her annoyance, there's an air of hardly suppressed excitement about my mother. And it's not just because she's about to see her daughter become a bride. As soon as Prue is married, Mum and Dad are off to South America for six months, maybe longer. With Dad's pension kicking in this year, they agreed that Prue and Ben could buy them out of Baileys' with their share of Granny Gilbert's bungalow money. Now the newlyweds will have free rein to maximize opportunities for growth in the south west region without stepping on the parental toes. And as a side benefit, they can live in the parental home rent-free.

And I thought nothing ever changed in Lyme. It's a new start for all of us.

As I climb the stairs to the bedroom I can hear Prue telling the hairdresser exactly how she wants the flowers arranged in her hair. I push open the door to see my sister looking astonishingly beautiful. A slim column of filigreed lace is draped over a simple white shift that drops to the floor. The lace rises up to my sister's throat and extends down to her fingers. Her fine blonde hair has been looped and plaited into a chignon, into which the browbeaten hairdresser tucks star-like white flowers and ivy leaves. Prue looks delicate, virginal and more like a princess than any of the pictures on Eddy's girls' stickers.

'So,' I say, leaning on the doorframe. 'You still decided to wear white, then?'

Prue looks up. 'If you say *anything* — '

'Prue, just joking. You look beautiful. Really.'

I move to kiss her cheek but she pushes me away, complaining that I'll ruin her make-up. As I sit down on the bed to watch the finishing touches to her hair, my phone buzzes in my handbag.

Prue's head whips round. 'Is it Matt?'

I sigh. 'Prue. Give it up. It's not going to be Matt.'

'But you gave him your new number, right?' She regards herself in the mirror, turning her head from side to side. The hairdresser hovers anxiously, awaiting further instructions.

I did. Weeks ago. And I got back a terse 'thanks.' Since then, nothing. At Prue's continued urging I have sent him more texts since then. And three emails. Plus a long handwritten letter. Next she will be encouraging me to use a carrier pigeon just to ensure I have tried every possible method of contacting my former husband. But still no reply. I can't blame him. At least now he knows he can contact me when he is ready. If he is ready.

'Anyway, it's the caterers,' I say, looking at the lit-up screen. 'They say do you want the champagne to keep going until everyone sits down for the meal, or do you want to put a limit

396

on the number of bottles?'

'I've told them this already!' says Prue. 'Twice! Give me the phone.' She crooks her fingers to demand I pass it over.

I hold it out of her reach. 'You're not allowed to get stressed on your wedding day, Prue, it's the law — that's why they've got my number instead of yours. I'll sort it. Just tell me what you want. Remember I used to do this for a living, okay?'

She glowers, unsure whether she can trust me to live up to her exacting standards. Finally her face relaxes a fraction. 'I suppose you need the practice if you're going back to work. Non-stop champagne is what I said, and non-stop champagne is what I want.'

I convey this to the caterers as politely as possible, and manage to avert a canapé misunderstanding without my sister even being aware of it. By the time I get off the phone, Prue's hair is finished and the hairdresser has gone downstairs to start on Mum. Prue has decreed my own hair can do without professional assistance, since I am not a bridesmaid, but merely the sister of the bride, so apparently no one will be looking at me.

'Prue,' I say, as she fiddles with a strand of ivy that's coming loose from her chignon. She looks up.

'What?'

'Prue, I really am sorry for everything. For interfering with Ben. He's a good man. I know you're both going to be very happy together.'

'Of course we are,' says Prue briskly, applying

a final blast of hairspray to hold the ivy in place. 'And let's stop going on about that stupid foster husband business.'

She turns to face me, hands on her knees, and looks at me with infinite patience and, dare I say it, a little bit of pity.

'Kate. You were mental, you weren't thinking straight and you made a lot of bad decisions. I get that. Everyone gets it. So you're forgiven. But if you ever, ever try to shove your nose into my business again, know that I will fucking kill you. Okay?'

'Okay,' I agree. It is her wedding day, after all.

Prue gets up and smooths the delicate lace down over her hips. 'And you're going to be happy too, Kate,' she says, her expression softening. 'I know you don't think so right now, but you will. It's a New Year, and a new start for all of us. You'll see.'

In her white dress with her blonde hair, Prue appears like a storybook angel, come down from on high to offer me a blessing. I decide to believe her.

48

If you think this story is going to end with me hijacking my sister's wedding to deliver a nicely summarizing speech about what I learned about my own marriage, you are very much mistaken. Firstly because I've always thought that seems massively inappropriate when it happens in Hollywood movies — someone else's wedding is not about *you*, you crazy narcissist — and secondly because there is no way Prue would let me anywhere near the microphone at her nuptials. Dad's pre-approved speech opened with a hint of resentment that you would only notice if you were a member of the family, but by the time he got to the end he was wiping tears from his eyes about his baby girl and so were the rest of us.

The hotel staff have excelled themselves under Prue's watchful eye, and now that the meal is over, they are busy pushing back tables to create space for a dance floor. There is a small buffet set up for people who will be joining the evening party, and although it has been laid out for only a few minutes, Mrs Curtis is already stationed next to it, surreptitiously transferring pork pies into her handbag.

The DJ taps his microphone to tell us all that it will soon be time for the bride and groom's first dance, and I pick up my handbag from underneath the top table, ready to get to the front of the crowd. I have done my sisterly duty in entertaining aged aunts, tolerating mildly racist jokes from uncles who should know better, and answering as blandly as possible all questions about my relationship status. Even better, I've done it all without getting mind-blowingly drunk, since there's been so much to do that it's been like a work event instead of a party.

When the music starts — 'It Had to Be You' — Prue and Ben take to the dance floor with Dad trailing them closely, his newly purchased video camera clutched in his hand. I wish Jay or Danny was here to see how seriously Dad frames every shot, going for avant-garde angles whenever possible. Mum appears next to me, nudging my elbow.

'Francis Ford Coppola over there.'

'Aw, he's loving it,' I say.

'I'll be lucky to get my hands on that camera once when we get to South America,' says Mum.

I lean into her and she puts her arm around my waist. 'I'm going to miss you,' I say.

Mum kisses the top of my head as we watch my sister and her husband move around the dance floor, accompanied by the paparazzi flash of a hundred camera phones.

'I'll miss you too, love,' she says. 'But you'll be back in London. Living your life. It's not like you were going to stay here for ever.'

'I know,' I say. I try not to feel like a baby bird being pushed out of the nest before it's quite ready.

Dad suddenly appears in front of us, pushing

the camera in our faces, until Mum persuades him to put it away and dance with her instead. The floor fills with couples, including Mrs Curtis clutching tightly onto Ben's terrified-looking best man.

No one notices me slip away.

I squeeze past the cluster of smokers gathered at the back of the hotel, making an excuse about having to sort out the fireworks. It almost makes me miss smoking, the way it gives you a bit of time out for yourself without anyone thinking you're being weird or antisocial.

I'm heading for a bench out on the far lawn. In daylight it offers a sweeping view across Lyme Bay, but even on this starlit winter's night it's possible to make out the curl of the Cobb, its back hunched against the sea, as if it is protecting the town. The bench is hidden from the hotel behind the thick waxy leaves of a rhododendron bush, so I know I will be out of sight. I can take some time to be alone for a moment, away from the endless questions. What next, Kate? What are you going to do with the rest of your life? And, worse, the sympathetic looks from those who aren't brave enough to ask.

I hear someone stumbling in the bushes behind me, and I stay very still. I expect it's just a drunken wedding guest — no doubt some bloke who's decided an alfresco pee is more manageable than negotiating the carpeted corridors of the hotel in search of the Gents. There's a muffled exclamation as someone walks into a branch, then suddenly I am rocked forwards when a figure lurches out of the undergrowth, knocking into the bench.

'Fuck's sake,' says Matt.

Matt?

I spin around on the bench in disbelief.

'I mean, Kate, I've been looking for you,' says Matt, pulling leaves out of his hair. 'Oh shit, this is going all wrong already. Shall I just begin again?'

'What . . . what are you doing here?' I ask.

'Your sister asked me,' says Matt, straightening his suit jacket and coming to sit on the bench next to me. I stare at him as if he's an alien who has just stepped out of a spaceship.

'Prue?'

His mouth twists into an awkward smile. 'Yes, Prue, unless you've got some other sister getting married this weekend?'

'But she never said. I wasn't expecting — '

Matt takes my cold hand in both of his. I feel like he is holding my heart right there, beating between his warm palms. As if he could cradle it or crush it, whichever he chooses.

'Remind me again why you're sitting outside on the coldest night of the year?' he asks.

'I just . . . I just wanted to be by myself for a little while,' I say.

He raises an eyebrow and lifts a corner of his mouth. 'Should I go then?'

'No!' I put my free hand on top of his. 'Matt, don't go. Please don't go.'

'Steady on,' he says, laughing. 'Do you think I've come all this way to be put off that easily?'

I shake my head, not sure if I trust myself to speak. It's time to let Matt say his piece. I've said mine already, weeks ago.

Matt doesn't speak either. He just looks at me, like he's reading my face, as if he's forgotten it and has to remind himself who I am all over again. He is half hidden in shadow, the moonlight catches just the side of his jaw, and the hair that flops over his forehead into his eyes. I have to stop myself from pushing it back like I used to.

'So,' he says. It is not exactly the declaration of love and devotion that I was hoping for, but it's a start.

There is a nervous fluttering in my chest; I have to breathe through my nose because I'm afraid that otherwise I might start gasping embarrassingly, begging Matt to say what it is he has to say. He wouldn't have come all this way to ask me for a divorce, would he? Not at my sister's wedding.

'Why . . . why did you come, Matt?' I ask at last, unable to stop myself.

He drops his eyes down to the bench, where our hands are still joined.

'I don't even know, Kate,' he says, forcing out an unconvincing laugh. He pulls his hands away from mine and runs his fingers through his hair, pushing it off his face. 'I wasn't going to. I thought I didn't want to see you again.'

I nod, my lips pressed tightly together.

Matt sighs heavily. 'You always seemed to want something else — something different to what you have. You didn't know how to be grateful for what we had. I felt like I just disappointed you all the time,' he says. 'As though what we had wasn't enough for you.'

I start to say, no, you didn't disappoint me, I disappointed myself, but he lifts his head and silences me with a look from under his dark brows.

'I kept thinking about how angry you were with me all the time. About how I couldn't make you happy. And, God, the truth is I'm not even sure if *you* can make you happy, Kate.'

I say nothing, it's not my turn. And I don't know how to answer.

Matt reaches for my hand again. 'And then I thought, Why am I thinking about Kate all the time if it's really finished?'

'So you think — ' He puts a finger on my lips and holds it there. It feels strangely more intimate than if he'd kissed me.

'I don't know what I think. Seriously, I don't. I just got in the car and drove down here, thinking of what I was going to say, and now I'm here I'm as clueless as when I started. I just wanted to see you. I miss your face.'

I feel my throat close up and my eyes burn.

'I miss your face too,' I whisper.

Matt moves along the bench. I can feel the warmth of his body next to me. He's so close now that it would be strange to look at one another. Instead, we both look out towards the sea, as if we hope that someone is going to rise up out of the waves and tell us what we should do.

'Have I fucked it up for ever?' I say. My shoulders are tight and hunched up around my ears, ready to hear the wrong answer.

'I don't know,' says Matt. He puts his arm around me, and I allow myself to lean against him. It's the closest we have been for months. My eyelids sink shut as I let myself feel the luxury of having him here, even if it's just for now.

Matt rests his cheek on the top of my head. I can feel his breath against my hair, or is it the wind?

'Kate.' He sighs. 'I can put this all behind us, but can you?'

I think for a moment, my eyes drawn upwards beyond the Cobb.

'No,' I say truthfully. 'No, I can't.'

Matt pulls away from me, leaning backwards to look at me. His eyebrows are drawn close together and his eyes glitter darkly in the moonlight.

'Then what the fuck have you been doing emailing me all the time? Begging me for another chance?'

He turns his head away and pulls his coat around him, wrapping his arms across his chest.

'Matt,' I plead, reaching for him. 'No, you don't understand. I mean, I do want to try again, but I can't pretend all of this didn't happen. Or, don't you see? It will just happen again. Not . . . not Chris, but something . . . the distance. The not talking.'

He looks back at me over his shoulder, his expression forbidding. But he is listening.

'I did a stupid, terrible thing,' I continue, putting my hands in my pockets and hunching down into my coat. 'And then I tried to run away

405

from it. Matt, the worst of those things was the running away. I want to face up to what I did. We can't go back to how we were before. We can only make it work by starting where we are. With all our mistakes.'

Matt turns to face me.

'My mistakes,' I say. Hot tears hover on my eyelashes.

He lets out a short, angry laugh. 'You can't take all the blame. I admit, I thought you should for a while. It made me feel better to think it was all your fault.'

'It *was* my fault,' I say.

'It was,' admits Matt. 'But it was mine, too. I gave up on you. I couldn't reach you and I just stopped trying.'

'Matt,' I say. 'I slept with someone else. It *was* my fault.'

Matt shakes his head.

'If you face your fuck-ups, I can face mine, too,' he says. 'I should have helped you, made you talk about things. Not said you were crazy for being upset about not getting pregnant. I dismissed it all and left you to deal with it on your own.'

I stare at him in surprise. I'd never thought there might be an apology from him. I thought what I'd done had somehow wiped out any mistakes he'd made — my own error big enough to negate any of his.

He takes my chin in his hand, turning my face towards him. The moment stretches out between us, the only sound the waves far below us on the shore.

'Yeah,' I say, trying out a smile. 'Come to think of it, it probably was all your fault, Matt.'

'I guess this is what they mean by for better or worse,' he says, pinching my chin playfully. 'I'm better and you're the worst.'

'Do you think you can stand to try it all over again?' I ask. 'Really?'

'I reckon I'll take my chances,' he says. My eyes rake over his face, the laughter lines at the corners of his navy eyes, his dark hair black in the moonlight. 'You may be the worst, Mrs Martell, but you're the only wife I've got, and I'd like to keep it that way.'

He leans in towards me until our lips touch; his fingers are entwined in my hair, drawing me towards him. I don't remember when I last kissed my husband like this. I don't plan to forget again.

It already feels like I've come home.

Other titles published by
The House of Ulverscroft:

UNSUITABLE MEN

Pippa Wright

After eleven years of coupled-up domesticity, Rory Carmichael is single for the first time in her adult life. Her reliable boyfriend, Martin, wasn't the most exciting man in the world, but when she discovers he's not actually dependable Mr Right after all, but a cheater, she's forced to consider that everything she knows about relationships might be wrong. Now, striving to reinvigorate her love life — and her lacklustre career — her mission is to date as many unsuitable men as possible. Toyboys. Sugar daddies. Fauxmosexuals. Maybe the bad boys she's never dated can show her what she's been missing in life. But if Mr Right can turn out to be so wrong, maybe one of her Mr Wrongs will turn out to be just right.

THE GUEST LIST

Melissa Hill

When funny, kind and gorgeous Shane proposes, Cara is over the moon. Excitement, however, quickly turns to apprehension when it seems that everyone has a fixed idea of the perfect wedding and offers to 'help' with the planning. With tussles over the ceremony and the size of the guest list, sibling rivalry and insistent in-laws-to-be, Cara can see the vision she has of her big day being ripped to shreds. So she and Shane determine to make a stand and do things *their* way. But when they announce their plans for a beach wedding on a beautiful Caribbean island, there is uproar. Threats are made, family secrets are revealed, and things turn decidedly stormy. Will Cara and Shane manage to overcome all the obstacles? Or will their dream wedding turn into a nightmare?